Watch That River

by Gary Schaffer

PublishAmerica
Baltimore

First printing

All characters appearing in this work are fictitious. Any resemblance to real persons, living or dead, is purely coincidental.

ISBN: 1-4241-3554-0
PUBLISHED BY PUBLISHAMERICA, LLLP
www.publishamerica.com
Baltimore

Printed in the United States of America

For my family,
and everyone who treats animals with respect.

Acknowledgments

During the last thirty years my immediate family has packed up and moved nine times to eight different states. My wife Diane, daughter Noelle and son Tony were forced to start over with each move. But they never gave up on me and I will always be grateful for sacrifices they had to make.

I would like to thank my mother who found time to read to me while I was growing up. She ingrained the importance of family in my life. I hope every family has such a person to look to with respect as my mother provides for us.

The Humane Society of the United States constantly works to improve the way animals we live with are treated. Unfortunately cruelties such as dogfighting still go on. I want to thank everyone who is working to end this type of sadistic behavior.

Chapter One
Face to Face With Evil

A young boy decided that it was time to start for home after an afternoon of ice fishing. He knelt on the ice and looked with pride at the fish lying beside him. His catch would provide a couple of nice meals for his family. The fishing spot that he and his dad had found two months earlier again had proved to be excellent.

It was early spring, but winter did not want to relinquish its hold on Northwestern Wisconsin. The day had turned cold and a light snow shower began to fall. The trees that bordered the ice helped to block the wind, and if you weren't familiar with the area you would never know that a river snaked through the trees. Three deep water ponds branched off from the river and were separated by peninsulas of forest and meadows that extended into the hills on each side of the river. His mother, who lived by the river all her life, told him that the ponds were formed to help the Fox River handle the water from the spring rains and melting snow.

The boy finished picking up his ice fishing equipment and smiled to himself as he placed the fish in his pail. The size of one of the fish would give him some bragging rights at home, and he knew his dad would say that he wished he had come with. He started to walk across the ice toward the river, but it was getting late and following the river the entire way home would make him late for evening chores. So he decided to cut across a wooded peninsula to the river. It was a good plan, and the short-cut would save him a half-hour or more.

As he walked through the woods he heard the sound of dogs barking in the distance. He came to a clearing and found that the barking was coming from an old shed positioned in the middle of a meadow. His curiosity got the best of him and he decided to investigate. When he approached the shed the barking stopped and the boy knew the dogs inside must have sensed him.

The building was a large rectangular structure and looked as if it had been recently remodeled. A driveway to the building came out of the trees from the west, and the snow had been plowed to make the road travelable. No vehicles were parked in the driveway, so he saw no harm in looking inside to make sure the dogs were all right.

All the windows had shutters on, but he found one that was unhooked and was able to pull himself up to look inside. There were ten to fifteen dogs inside the building. The dogs were either tied with heavy chains to posts, or locked inside pens. These dogs were not normal acting farm dogs or pets. They were all good sized, muscular dogs of various breeds. The chained dogs saw the boy watching and tried to get to the window. They bared their teeth, and let out growls that sent chills down the spine of the boy. The collars dug into the necks of the dogs as they savagely pulled against the chains, trying to break free.

As the boy scanned the building he noticed that the dogs locked in pens had numerous cuts through out their body, and some looked as if they were starving. This bothered the boy and he wanted to help. He lowered himself to the ground and walked along the building to see if there was a way to get inside. A large sliding wood door at one end of the building was locked, but he found a regular entrance door located at the opposite end ajar. He was able to pull the door open enough so that he could get his arm in and unhook the door. He set his ice fishing pail next to the outside wall, and slowly pushed the door open. He took a few steps inside, and a dog chained to the nearest post made a dash at him with teeth showing. The momentum of the savage lunge caused the dog to swing in the air when it reached the end of the chain, but this only seemed to make the dog more defiant and determined to get at the boy.

There was enough space between the chained dog and the first pen for the boy to get by safely. The dog in the first pen watched the boy approach and rushed towards him jumping against the gate. Startled, the boy quickly backed away and the chained dog grabbed the boys pant leg. The boy turned to face his attacker and fell backwards onto the floor. The dog clenched onto the boy's pant leg, and started to back up, pulling the boy across the floor. He desperately kicked at the dog with his free leg, and managed to escape from the dog's hold when his pants ripped apart. The dog had the piece of pant leg clenched in his teeth and continued to pull against the chain trying to get at the boy. The boy sat on the floor trying to catch his breath and was getting ready to sprint for the door when he noticed that two of the dogs locked in center pens had not gotten up. When he looked closer he realized that these two dogs were severely injured.

He stood up and cautiously walked toward the pens where the two dogs were lying. As he approached, both dogs lifted their heads and began to growl. Fresh cuts covered the dogs' faces and upper bodies. One of the dogs tried to stand, but fell back to the floor, and the boy noticed that his back leg was injured.

The boy knew that whatever was going on here was not right. When he got home he would tell his parents, and he knew they would take care of this ugly situation. However, he couldn't leave the two dogs that were severely injured without trying to help. Cautiously he walked to the pens and untied the ropes that held the gates shut. He slowly opened the gate to the first pen and stepped inside. The intensity of the warning growl from the dog increased as she lies on the floor in pain, and the boy realized he had to be careful. The dog was a longhaired mixed breed. The cuts on her face and upper body were long and deep, and part of the dog's ear was torn apart. The dog slowly rose to her feet and lowered her head, but never took her eyes off the boy. The dog's stare became more pronounced when the boy noticed that she had one gray eye and one blue eye. The boy whispered to the dog, trying to convince her that he meant no harm, and only wanted to help.

"Easy girl, let me see what I can do to help."

The dog sensed the sincerity of the boy, and slowly lay back down. As the boy stepped closer he glanced at the dog in the next pen, and saw that a gash in the dog's upper thigh had reopened and blood was running onto the shed's floor.

He decided that this dog needed immediate attention, and opened the gate to the pen where he was being held. As he stepped inside the pen he scanned the building for something that could be used to wrap around the wound to stop the bleeding. In the far corner of the building, next to the sliding wood door he saw an old shirt hanging on a nail. He cautiously walked toward the door, taking every precaution to avoid being seized by one of the chained dogs.

As he took the shirt off the nail he heard the sound of a vehicle approaching. He ran to the sliding door and peered through a crack. A blue pickup and a white car were coming up the driveway. The boy thought he had better leave quickly. As he ran along the wall past the two pens he had opened, he saw that the two dogs were gone. Some how they had managed to gather enough strength and escape through the door that the boy had come in. When he stepped out the door he heard the vehicles come to a stop, and the car doors open.

"Look over there, them two dogs have gotten out," the passenger in the blue truck said.

"They won't get far in the shape they're in, I'll get the shotgun. One of you idiots must have left the gates open," replied the driver of the white car.

Without hesitation the boy picked up his pail and started to run up the hill toward the river.

"Look up there," one of the men yelled.

"We better get that kid so we can talk to him," the guy in the white car said.

"Do you think he let the dogs out?" the driver of the blue truck asked.

"Hell, I don't know, but we better find out, and then decide what we're going to do. You two get the kid and I'll shoot the dogs."

The boy looked over his shoulder and saw the two men running across the field after him. When the boy reached the top of the hill, he threw his bucket behind one of the trees, so it wouldn't slow him down, and ran down the hill to the edge of the river. The river was open at this point, so he ran along the bank towards a spot that he knew was frozen over and would allow him to get across and into the woods on the far side.

The boy looked back up the hill and saw that one of the men had already reached the peak and was starting to run down the hill after him. He ran along the bank, and could tell by the sound the man's feet made as they crushed against the frozen earth that he was gaining on him. The man was getting so close that the boy could hear his heavy breathing.

The boy reached the crossing area and without hesitation jumped from the bank to the ice. The sudden impact caused the ice to break and the boy disappeared into the cold water. He came to the surface, and was able to get his arms on top of the ice. As he struggled to pull himself out of the river he looked up and saw the man who was chasing him standing on the bank watching. The man stood on the edge of the bank and looked down at the boy. Their eyes met, and the man smiled.

The boy rested for a few seconds, clinging to the ice. He then pulled all his energy together, and managed to lift himself halfway out of the water, but the pressure he made against the ice caused it to break, and the boy went under the water. The current grabbed and forced him down river under the ice. He tried to break free, but slowly his energy gave way and his thoughts turned to home. He knew his parents were waiting for him so that he could help with chores and evening milking. They would have to do the chores without him tonight.

The wind was becoming more intense, and made a rushing sound as it blew through the trees standing along the riverbank. The snow was starting to fall at a heavy rate, and it wouldn't be long before everything would be covered in white.

The man on the bank watched the boy go under the icy water and continued to smile. When the boy disappeared from view, the man turned and started to walk away.

The other man arrived, and walked to the edge of the bank. He looked down at where the boy had broken through the ice.

"Did he get out? What do we do now?" he asked.

"Nothing we can do. He must have got out before we got here. Can't really tell which way he went with the way this snow is coming down. There's no way in hell we'll be able to find him in this blizzard anyways, we might as well let him go."

The second man then turned from the riverbank and followed the other man up the hill. The second man glanced back at the river, but the first man walked on looking straight ahead.

"He did it to himself. He got what he deserved. It's not our problem," the first man said under his breath.

"What did you say?"

"Nothing, I was just wondering if the boss got those two dogs. Let's get back before we get lost in this blizzard."

Chapter Two
Don't Let Them Sense That You're Afraid

"Don't let the screen door slam," my mother said as I ran out of the house.

I was already down the front porch steps as the door slammed shut before my mother finished her request. I sprinted across the yard with my dog Blackie running beside me.

It was 1957 and this was our second year living at a place that my dad was renting from a local farmer. The house was a hundred yards from the Fox River, and was surrounded by large oak trees with a row of evergreens on the north side that helped block the wind in the winter months.

There was an old, faded red barn on the property that stood between the house and river. It had a nice high wall on one end, and I spent many hours tossing a rubber ball against that wall and catching it with my mitt as it bounced off the wooden planks. In my mind I was the Hank Aaron of Northwestern Wisconsin. The Milwaukee Braves were the best and Hank Aaron and the rest of the team were heroes to both boys and men in rural Wisconsin.

Between the barn and the house was the water pump. I made countless trips carrying pails of water from the pump to the house. North of the water pump was a shed filled with tools and other items that people seemed to put away never to use again. About fifty feet from the shed was the outhouse.

Using the outhouse at night was an adventure. The path to it was dark, and the oak that it sat beneath would create all kinds of strange noises and shadows as it swayed with the night winds. If nature called and I had to take that journey into the shadows, I probably set speed records in all three categories of: getting there, going there and returning from there.

Directly north of the outhouse was a large pigpen. My dad enjoyed raising pigs, but he didn't like to maintain fences. Therefore, a lot of time was spent chasing pigs that escaped through breaks in the fence, and getting them back into the pen.

The house was a typical two-story farmhouse. It had a root cellar off to the side that was used to store canned foods, and provided a place for shelter from storms. A screened porch extended across the front of the house, and from the porch you entered a large kitchen.

There were two bedrooms downstairs and two bedrooms up stairs. The up stairs would get pretty cold in the winter, so my brother and sister had to sleep downstairs. However, being the eldest, I was allowed to stay in my bedroom through the cold winter months. It was my room.

This rented farm had become my domain, and I knew every inch of it. The buildings and the physical setting will be imprinted in my mind forever. The events that happened to me while I lived there set a mold for me to grow into, and will always affect my outlook on life.

"Shorty, check the pigs before you go," Mom said to me as I sprinted towards the shed.

How my dad ever came up with that nickname I'll never know, but it stuck.

Check the pigs! Check the pigs! Check the pigs!

I didn't mind feeding the pigs, they had to eat, but checking the pigs meant to see if they had gotten out, and if they had, Mom and I would have to get them back into the pen. This usually became very time consuming, and reduced the time we both had planned for doing something more enjoyable.

Mom was deceptively quick, and she could throw a mean rock. She never swore, but I think the rocks she would pick-up and throw was her way of saying, *you son of bitches or no good bastards get back where you belong*. I always saw her grin when a rock bounced off the side of one of the run away pigs.

Blackie and I made a quick trip around the pen looking for broken sections in the fence or escaped pigs. To my delight everything was where it was suppose to be. I ran back into the yard and met my mother who was on her way to the pump to get some water.

"The pigs are all in," I boasted.

"You're getting to be a good fence builder, Shorty," she said.

I smiled at the compliment. "Thanks, Mom." The repairs that I had made to the fence in the last couple of days did seem to be keeping the pigs where they belonged.

"Good luck fishing, and try to be home by dark."

"I will," I said and took off on a run to the shed to get a shovel and coffee can.

I then went behind the barn and dug some dirt to expose the angleworms that were living in the rich black soil. Fat, juicy angleworms were good bait to entice the fish. I put the angleworms in the coffee can and covered them with dirt. With Blackie trotting beside me, I put the shovel back in the shed and placed the can of worms in a pail that I also used to carry spare fishing equipment. Then I grabbed my cane pole and picked up the pail, and headed for the river.

Blackie was a medium sized dog, about forty pounds with a short, shiny coat. She was all black except for a white tip on the end of her tail. Dad had brought her home as a pup two years ago. When I asked him what type of breed he thought she was, he told me that she was just a mixed up mutt.

"She's more than likely got a little bit of every thing in her. You know a little of this and a little of that mixed together over the years," he said.

He thought that was a major reason for her being so mellow. She didn't have to live up to the expectations placed on purebreds. When I was home, Blackie was continuously by my side. In the winter my mother allowed her to sleep in bed with me. I couldn't ask for a better companion to share adventures with or tell secrets to.

It took about ten minutes to get to the area of the river where I usually fished. The fishing spot was located in a bend of the river that had bushes growing out of the water next to the bank. The bank was dry and the grass was soft, if fishing was slow, it was still a nice place to lie back and let the sun shine down on you. I usually caught a lot of rock bass between those bushes and the bank, but the fish were not being cooperative on this day. The bobber rested on the surface, and only moved when a breeze pushed it along.

As I was lying on the soft grass to plan my next move, I saw a shy-poke fly over. With its neck tucked in, I thought it resembled a prehistoric flying dinosaur. I watched as it glided past and flew up river. "Maybe the shy-poke knows a better spot," I said to Blackie, who was dozing off on the bank beside me. I stood up, pulled my line in, collected my gear, and me and Blackie started to walk up river.

About a hundred yards from where I was fishing the river widened and became shallow. We used this area of the river to cool off on hot summer days. I took my shoes off, rolled up my pants and waded across. Blackie was right beside me.

Fox River curved through the rolling hills and woods that were common to this part of Wisconsin. On past explorations I had followed the river for about three miles to the north. It was early afternoon, and I had plenty of time before supper, so off we went in search of a better fishing spot.

A half mile up river from the swimming hole there's a bridge that allows a county dirt road to pass over. The bridge is next to a driveway that goes to our neighbors, the Raycart's. Across the road from the Raycarts' farm, Sam Raycart lived in an old hunting cabin. Sam is a brother of Mr. Raycart and I didn't know what he did for a living, he didn't farm, but he always had money for beer. I thought he was a pretty nice guy. He always was quick with a smile and would offer me a ride when he saw me walking along the road.

Getting past the Raycart farm was an adventure in itself. They had these three dogs that would charge out, growling and showing their teeth, whenever they saw me going past. They had never hurt me, but they definitely made me aware that the farm was their territory, and no trespassers were allowed. Making new friends was definitely not part of their intentions. They never attacked Blackie, but Blackie knew the farm was their domain, and it was not in her best interest to challenge that. However, deep down I knew that it was only a matter of time before they caught me and ripped me apart. I was convinced that this was inevitable, so the best action was to avoid them as often as possible. Why give them the opportunity to make minced meat out of me?

Then there was the lady who sat in the porch swing and would not call the dogs off. Instead, she just stared straight ahead and continued to swing back and forth. She paid no attention to what was going on, and at no time did I ever see her turn to look. I thought she either couldn't hear or just didn't care if her dogs ripped me to shreds.

My dad and grandpa would always tell me, "*Just don't let them sense that you're afraid and they'll leave you alone.*" I didn't buy into that theory and decided that finding ways to sneak around them was a safer and more reasonable solution. Therefore, I would quietly follow the river using the bank on the opposite side from their farm and go under the bridge, or I would sneak along the road past their driveway by using the ditch for cover and pray they didn't notice me, or were off killing someone else.

On this particular day we got by without any problems by staying on the side of the river across from their farm. I crouched down and made my way along the riverbank to the bridge, climbed the bank, and crossed the road. Safely on the other side of the road I crawled under the barbed wire fence and walked down to the riverbank.

"We made it," I whispered to Blackie. I swear she smiled in agreement. Then we continued to walk up river in our search of a better spot to fish.

Time was not a major concern and we walked along the bank enjoying the warm June day. We came to a bend in the river that was about twenty feet wide and very deep. There was a tree lying across the river and I decided this looked like a good spot to try my luck. I made my way down the bank, sat on the fallen tree, and put my line in the water. I didn't have my line out long when the bobber went down. No nibbles or messing around, the bobber went down deep and fast. I pulled the line up and felt the weight of something significant on the other end. Then out of the river I pulled the biggest black bass that I had ever seen. I had the fish about two feet above the surface, and was swinging it to shore when it shook free of the hook and fell back into the river. That big fish wiggling on the end of my line, and reflecting off the water in the sunlight was a beautiful sight.

When I look back at growing up in Northwestern Wisconsin, I wish I had taken more advantage of exploring the environment I had around me. However, work usually got in the way and you forget to appreciate, or took for granted the wonders that were within your grasp.

After my battle with the black bass, I continued to try and catch it (or maybe a close relative). I stayed in the area and moved back-and-forth from the fallen tree to the bank. I thought it was only a matter of time before that big fish struck again, but nothing happened. Time has a way of slipping by when you're trying to complete a task, and before I knew it the sun was starting to go down. Grandpa told me once that right before sunset was a good time to catch fish, because that was a natural feeding time. I didn't know if that was true or not, but felt it was worth a shot. I tried for a few more minutes, but no luck, and now the sun was setting.

"Blackie, we better head for home. Mom will be worried."

I gathered my gear and started to walk home. The moon was full and it was going to be a bright June night, so Blackie and I took our time. The moon was setting high in the sky when we reached the Raycarts. I used some rocks in the river as stepping stones to get to the bank opposite their farm. They were done with milking and the cows had been turned out to pasture for the night, so I figured the dogs were hanging out by the house. We scooted by without incident.

We followed a cattle path along the side of the hill that snaked through the trees and brush. A short distance from the road I stopped for a breather, and looked up-river at the bridge. The moon reflecting off the water below the bridge was a beautiful sight. I was enjoying the view, when suddenly something passed below the bridge that blocked the reflection of the moon off the water. It sent a chill down my spine. Was it my imagination or maybe I had just blinked? I searched the bank, but saw nothing. I called for Blackie; she was sniffing around in the brush, and came out onto the path about ten feet in front of me. She waited for me to get to her, and then we continued on our way.

You ever get that feeling that someone is watching you, but you don't see them? All of a sudden that feeling took hold of me. I'm certain that Blackie had a similar feeling, because she stopped her exploration of the surrounding bushes and was walking close beside me. We were about a hundred feet from the shallow area in the river when I thought I heard something on the path behind me. I sheepishly glanced over my shoulder and thought I saw something or someone on the same path not too far behind us. Was my mind playing tricks on me? I decided not to wait around to find out.

I took off on a run and Blackie was right by my side. My imagination was switched into high gear and so was I. I ran as fast as my legs could carry me and when we reached the shallow area of the river I didn't slow down a lick as we crossed. We ran through the water and I looked ahead and saw our yard light flickering in the distance.

We were in the middle of the swamp not far from the river, and I stopped to catch my breath. Blackie stopped about ten feet in front of me. She looked at me and then looked behind me, and I knew she wanted to get going. Then I heard something run through the part of the river that we had just crossed. I took off and never looked back. I held the pole in one hand and the pail was swinging from the other as I dodged through the swamp grass. At any time I expected to be tackled from behind. The glow from the yard light was becoming more intense. I was close to being home, when suddenly I stumbled and fell. As I hurried to get to my feet I heard a hissing sound, and there he was at eye level. A snake was coiled around a stalk of swamp grass. It was not poisonous I'm sure, but it had its head pointed towards me with its tongue out and was not pleased with me for intruding. Blackie was not concerned with the snake; her eyes told me to quit screwing around and get moving. Whatever was chasing us was gaining ground. I could feel the hairs stand up on the back of my neck as I heard our pursuer running through the swamp.

I scrambled to my feet and ran like the wind. When I got to the barbwire fence, I threw the pole and pail over and rolled underneath. I sprang to my feet and glanced back into the swamp and saw shadows. Goose bumps were forming on my arms as me and Blackie sprinted for the house. I left the pole and pail on the ground where they landed; whatever was chasing me was welcome to it. When I got to the pump, the yard light brought a feeling of relief, but I felt I was still in danger of being caught. I didn't slow down as I passed under the yard light, and when I got to the house I leaped from the ground to the top step. As I pulled the screen door open I looked back at the yard light and thought I saw something watching me from the shadows. I quickly got inside the porch and let the screen door slam shut behind me. My beautiful family was sitting at the table when I entered the kitchen. Immediately my mother realized something was wrong and met me before I reached the table.

"What happened?" Mom asked.

"Something was chasing me," I said as I was trying to catch my breath.

"It probably was one of those damn Raycart dogs," Dad said.

Mom walked into the porch and looked through the screen door. She hooked the screen door shut, and then returned to the table. She placed a plate in front of me, and wearily smiled as she looked toward the screen door again. She then looked at my dad, and used that silent language she was so good with to communicate a request.

"I better go out and check on the pigs to make sure those dogs aren't stirring them up," Dad said.

Dad was outside for about a half-hour, and when he came back in he reported that everything was okay.

After supper I went upstairs to my room. I pulled the curtains back to look over the swamp, and could see the Fox River in the background. I searched and searched the skyline, but didn't see anything out of the ordinary. I was certain that something or someone had chased us. It was not my imagination. Maybe Dad was right, it was one of the Raycarts' dogs, but I never heard any barking. I lay down on my bed and stared at the ceiling trying to make sense of it all. What if whatever it was had caught us? I got out of bed, walked to the window, and pulled the curtains aside. The full moon provided good light, but I couldn't see anything other than shadows. Then the same feeling came over me that I had when I was on the side of the hill walking back—something or someone was watching me. I quickly pulled the curtains closed. There was something out there, and I was totally convinced that it wasn't my imagination. I lay back down on the bed for a moment and remembered that Blackie was still outside. I jumped to my feet and ran down stairs; Mom was in the kitchen.

"What's wrong?" Mom asked.

"Where's Blackie, is she..." Before I could finish my question I saw Blackie lying on a blanket next to the front porch door.

Mom came over and stood by my side. "She was scratching at the screen door, so I let her come inside. She probably sensed that you were nervous and wanted to be near you."

That made perfect sense to me, Blackie was my dog. I walked to the screen door and looked in the direction of the pump.

Mom put her hand on my shoulder. "You better get to bed; you've had an exciting day." She leaned over and kissed me on the cheek.

I knelt down and patted Blackie on the head and started to walk toward the stairs. I turned to look outside once more and saw that my mother was scanning the yard. She turned and shrugged her shoulders. "Whatever it was, Shorty, it's gone; now you get to bed."

When nature called that night, I used the pan under the bed. There was no way I was going outside and take that walk in the shadows to the outhouse. No matter what Mom or Dad thought, I was fully convinced that whatever followed me across the river was still out there.

The next morning was Friday, and my dad had already left for work. When I got downstairs Mom was ironing clothes, and a bowl of cornflakes was waiting for me on the kitchen table.

"How did you sleep?" she asked.

"Okay, I guess."

"What do you think you saw last night?"

"I don't know," I said. "But it sure spooked me."

"I know it did, it even spooked Blackie. We haven't seen cougars around these parts for years, but this morning when your dad was getting ready for work, he told me that he remembered once when he was a kid that a cougar had been shot over by Mirror Lake. He checked the pigs again this morning, and said they seemed fine. Whatever kind of animal it was must have been just passing through, and thought it would have some fun chasing you through the swamp."

"Maybe you're right, and I hope that whatever it was had fun, but I sure didn't," I said.

"From now on, you be home before dark."

"Okay, but I don't think you have to worry about that."

Mom grinned at my response. "When you finish your cornflakes, bring in a pail of water before you start chores."

While I was pumping water, I remembered that I had thrown my pole and bucket over the fence, so I walked over to retrieve my equipment. I found the pole standing against the fence and the pail was sitting on the ground next to it with all the contents neatly placed inside. My first thought was that Mom must have picked everything up this morning, or Dad did it before he left for work. I looked over the swamp towards the river. One thing I knew for certain, no cougar had stood that pole along side the fence. If my parents hadn't done it, then it must have been a person chasing me last night.

I put the bucket and pole back into the shed and returned to the house with the pail of water. Blackie never left my side, and she found a cool place to lie in the shade when we reached the house.

"Mom, did you find my pole and bucket this morning?"

She was busy dressing my younger brother. "No, I haven't been outside yet."

"Okay, it must have been Dad," I said, trying to reassure myself.

I walked into the porch and noticed that Blackie's blanket was still on the floor. "Mom, are you going to let Blackie stay in again tonight?"

"We'll see," Mom said. "Now you better get going on those chores, they're not going to get done by themselves."

I hung around the house that day, fed the pigs, collected the eggs, helped Mom weed the garden, and played with my brother and sister. Dad got home late that night, and I was already in bed. The next morning at breakfast I asked him if he had picked up my bucket and pole.

"No, why?" he asked.

"No reason, just wondering is all."

As I finished breakfast, I tried to recall the previous night's events. Maybe in the excitement I did pick up the fishing equipment, or maybe that's how it landed when I tossed it over the fence.

Mom broke my concentration. "Some things that happen are hard to explain, and some never are explained," she said.

She was right about that. To this day I can't explain how she always seemed to know what I was thinking.

Chapter Three
At Times Life Is Not Fair

That weekend I stayed away from the river. If Dad was right and a cougar or some other strange animal had chased me through the swamp, I saw no problem with giving him a few days to move on. Saturday morning I went with Dad to his brother's farm, Uncle Joe, and helped pick rocks. I could never figure out where all the rocks came from, you clean a field one-year and the next year there are just as many to be picked. You know how you rate things on a scale from one to ten, with ten being the best and one the worse. I feel picking rocks deserves a minus rating.

The day consisted of collecting the rocks from the field and throwing them on a wagon, then taking the wagon and unloading the rocks onto a big pile—the "rock pile." The rock pile increased in size every year, so the rocks didn't find their way back from the pile to the field. Where do they keep coming from I would ask?

"I think they come from China," Dad would always say, and then bend over and pick-up another rock.

After we spent what felt like an eternity picking rocks, I stayed and helped Uncle Joe with the milking. I fed the calves, dumped the milk, and curried the cows while Uncle Joe milked.

After milking we let the cows out of the barn into the pasture, and then retired to the house. Uncle Joe was a bachelors, bachelor. We would sit in the kitchen and watch his new television. He liked the war shows, and so did I. He always had cookies, and if the box didn't go empty, there was no limit on how many I could have.

Uncle Joe never drank beer when he was home, but when he was out-and-about he would at times drink a few too many beers. At times the beer brought out a form of belligerence that unfortunately was directed at some people. The bar closest to his house, Mirror Lake Tavern, had blackballed him because of a run in he had with the owner. One night I over heard Dad and Mom talking after someone had called to let my dad know that Joe was heading into trouble because of his choice of conversation with some people in the bar. While Dad was getting ready to leave to get Uncle Joe, he told my mother that Joe wasn't like that before he went into the Army and off to Europe in World War II. Mom agreed, she said the beer brought demons out that he picked up over seas, doing what he was sent over there to do. Uncle Joe never talked about the war much, and I never asked many questions. I didn't feel like it was the right thing to do.

One evening while watching a war show on television, he laughed out loud during a scene where a soldier who had just been shot was begging the medics to get him patched up so he could return to the front. I asked him what was so funny. He must have thought I deserved an honest explanation. He told me that it reminded him of a time in France when he and a buddy were walking down a road trying to hook up with their unit that they had been separated from. A truck loaded with U.S. soldiers stopped and told them to hop in. They were more than happy to accept the invitation and climbed in the back. Uncle Joe noticed that the soldiers looked fresh, and found out that they had just arrived in Europe. He asked where they were headed and an energetic, clean shaven, young private told Uncle Joe that they were replacements and were going to join the fight at the front. Uncle Joe said he looked at his buddy and his buddy looked at him, and they jumped out of the truck. As the truck drove away they waved goodbye to the recruits, and wished them luck. One of the young soldiers responded to their well wishes by hollering back that he would see them in Berlin. I remember how Uncle Joe looked at me and laughed a soft laugh as he leaned back in his chair and smiled while looking up at the ceiling. "I wonder if any of them made it to Berlin," he said.

He was very good to me and I enjoyed being around him. He had a large, orange colored, long-haired chow mix called "Red," which was his pride and joy. The name may not have been too original, but it fit. He treated that dog like it was his son. He always made time to play with the dog, and spoke to him as if Red understood every word. Red lived in the house and ate what Uncle Joe ate. Nothing was too good for that dog and Red provided excellent companionship for Uncle Joe. I can still picture him getting on his hands and knees and wrestling with that dog. "*Come on, you red-haired, black-tongue devil, let's see what you got.*" The dog understood the challenge and would jump at Uncle Joe, and they would roll around on the floor until Uncle Joe was too tired to continue. Then Uncle Joe would lie on his back, and the big red dog would walk over and give him a big lick across the face. Uncle Joe would laugh, and the red dog would find a cool spot to take a nap.

I trusted Uncle Joe, and was not afraid to ask him anything, because he treated me more as a peer than a kid full of annoying questions.

"Uncle Joe, I think someone followed me home from Fox River Thursday night on my way back from fishing."

"Was it dark?"

"Yes it was."

"The dark can play awful tricks on a person. You start to imagine all sorts of things, and that can help make shadows come to life," he said.

"Dad thinks it was a cougar."

"Your dad is probably right. It could have been one of the Raycart dogs or a cougar."

"Why do the Raycarts have those mean dogs, anyway?" I asked.

He smiled and said, "Don't let them sense that you're afraid and they won't bother you."

I rolled my eyes at the all too familiar statement. How many times did I have to hear that adult declaration?

"Do you really believe that's true?" I asked.

"Dogs, like all animals can sense things that humans can't. I believe they can sense fear, but probably more important, they can sense if someone is a threat. It's hard for any person to block out fear. But being afraid doesn't mean that you're also a threat, and I think dogs have the ability to make that distinction."

"I don't know. When those dogs are running after me I know that I'm not threatening them, but I don't think I'd ever dare take a chance on waiting for them to figure that out. They sure seem mean to me. When you go to the Raycarts, do those dogs attack you?"

He thought for a while and said, "You know, I haven't been to the Raycarts since Joan lost her last child. I don't know where they got these dogs. The only dog I remember them having was a small spaniel, and it was about as mean as a chipmunk."

"What happened to their child?" I asked.

"*If I remember right it was the spring of fifty-one, yup, about five or six years ago.*

Time goes by too fast. You would have been about six and wouldn't remember, or better yet, were probably not even told about it. Your old enough now, so I don't see any harm in letting you know what I know. The Raycarts' son drowned in the Fox River. They found him about a mile up from the bridge in a deep bend of the river under the ice. He was about the age you are now. It was early spring and the boy must have fallen into the river or broke through the ice. Joan and Hank looked for him that night, but couldn't find him. They called the neighbors and we all went searching for him. Sam and his buddy Toad found him the next morning. The boy must have slipped into the water while returning from ice fishing, or broke thru the ice some where up stream, and got caught underneath and couldn't get out. It was a hell of a deal."

"That's sad."

"Sure was, especially when you add that Joan loss another child at birth two years earlier, it was the same year that their six year old son died from polio. The drowning affected Joan in such away that she has built a mental barrier that shuts everyone out. When you see her in town with Hank, she just sits in the truck and stares into space. She was about forty when it happened and these past five years she has only dug a deeper hole to let her mind rest in."

Uncle Joe sat quietly for a while and then continued, "Maybe the dogs aren't mean...Maybe they're protecting Joan."

Uncle Joe reflected for a moment on his last statement and said, "Yes, maybe that's it, the dogs are warning you to be careful, because they're protecting Joan."

"You know, I don't see her all the time when I walk by. But when I do see her, she's either sitting in a swing on the porch, or sitting in a chair by the riverbank. But she never gets up to call the dogs back. Did you know her very well?"

"She's a couple years older than me. I remember when we did thrashing at their place she would always be so perky. She made dinner for the men, and helped in the fields. She could pitch those oat bundles into the wagon with the best of men, and her son was a go-getter too. The last time I was there before his drowning was in August of 1950 for thrashing. Your dad was there. The boy was helping in the fields by driving the tractor while his parents loaded the wagon. He...What am I saying, his name was John. She was very good with John, and didn't pamper him at all. I wouldn't have blamed her a bit for keeping a tight rein on him. Hell, she had just buried her two other children. That damn polio was a curse: You know I should go over and visit, but people say it's no use. Hank talks a bit, but he was always very quiet. Like you said you only see Joan sitting on the porch swing or down by the river, or you don't see her at all. Damn shame, life isn't fair at all some times."

Before I could ask another question we saw car lights coming up the driveway, Dad was returning. While I was helping Uncle Joe with chores my dad went to Mirror Lake Tavern to play cards.

"Let's go, Shorty," Dad said.

"If you two get bored tomorrow you can come over and pick some more rocks. It's about time we teach Shorty how to cultivate. I think he'd sit on that Ford tractor pretty good," Uncle Joe said.

Dad smiled. "I think you're right, he's as ready as he'll ever be."

Dad and Uncle Joe talked for a few minutes, and then we left for home. It was a five-mile trip, and my dad was in a very good mood. Mom considered his visits to Mirror Lake Tavern a source of unfavorable temptations. However, Dad considered it a venue for the working class to discuss and provide solutions for solving world problems.

Dad parked the car and we went inside. Mom was busy placing bread dough into pans for baking, and shot Dad a stern look.

"Well did you and your cronies come up with a plan that will benefit all mankind?"

"Not quite yet, Maddie, it takes time. Sometimes I think we might have put too much of a burden on our shoulders, but I think we're making progress," Dad said with a grin.

"I know it makes me sleep better knowing that we have placed the fate of the world in the hands of such conscientious men," Mom sarcastically replied and then turned her attention to me. "Shorty, you better get to bed, bible school starts tomorrow, but make sure Blackie has water before you go upstairs."

As I walked to the pump, I looked into the darkness of the swamp. Shadows were everywhere, but none seemed to be moving. I filled the dish and returned to the house as fast as possible. With every step I checked over my shoulder to make sure nothing was following me.

Chapter Four
A Great Day

Sunday was church and Mom dealt with all obstacles put in the way by weather, man, or sickness so we could attend. Dad would drop us off at the church entrance and then drive over to Mirror Lake Tavern. He and three of his friends would meet at the tavern and play smear while we attended morning services.

The small white church sat next to a grove of pine trees and had a graveyard in back. There was no bell in the steeple, but you were welcomed by the sound of organ music, and the fragrance from local flowers that decorated the inside. Some members attended regularly and some required a special event, or what my mother called a gentle coaxing.

The Preacher, Pastor Wilcox, was young and had only been our pastor since February. Mom said he seemed like a very nice person, and was doing well. He had a big job, because he was also the pastor of a church in Middleton, which was ten miles away.

After Sunday services Mom helped with the younger grades bible study. I was in a class with eleven to fourteen year olds, which was taught by Mrs. Wright. We were learning the significance of the Ten Commandments, and she was very patient with us. Bible school lasted an hour and then Mom, my brother and sister and I would walk the half-mile to Mirror Lake.

"How did your class go?" Mom asked.

"Fine, I like Mrs. Wright."

"That's good," she said. "I can't figure out how she can be so nice, and those two boys of hers are such hellions."

Her statement caught my attention. "What do you mean?"

"It's just a shame that's all. Alice is so nice, but those two boys of hers are always in trouble, and they never go to church."

Mom was right. Bruce and Dale Wright did always seem to be the talk of the adults when the conversation got around to people not exactly living the proper life.

"What about Dad? He doesn't go to church very much," I asked

"That's true, but your dad would give the shirt off his back to a person in need, and his family always comes first. As for not going to church on a regular basis, I don't think that makes a person good or bad. They're a lot of people who will get into heaven who have never set foot in church, and there are some people who go to church every week who will be turned away, because they go for the wrong reasons."

"Then why do..."

Mom cut me off before I could finish my question. "Because it never hurts to get a little extra help at times, and you can use the opportunity to put in a good word or two for those who don't attend on a more regular basis. And don't roll your eyes at me, you might trip."

I was walking in front, and my mother's comment about me rolling my eyes took me by surprise. I wondered how she knew I was rolling my eyes. I looked over my shoulder at her and she smiled.

"Mothers can just sense those things," she said.

When we entered Mirror Lake Tavern, Dad was sitting at the end of the bar playing cards. Tommy Frost was Dad's partner and they were playing against Sam Raycart and a local farmer, Leroy Johnson. Tommy was the owners' son, and had just finished his enlistment in the army. His parents, Ruth and Roy Frost bought the bar last spring, and had developed a good business. Tommy helped his parents run the bar, and he and my dad had become close friends. As a matter-of-fact my mother thought they got along too well at times, because Tommy was young, carefree, and prone to play rather than work. Mom said that Tommy was a good guy, but could be a distraction, because he made my dad think about his younger years. When Tommy saw us, he immediately went to the cooler and gave us each a bottle of pop.

"On the house," he said.

Mom politely thanked him, and then we sat at a table by the juke-box. Dad smiled at Mom and he could tell she didn't want to wait around.

"Last game, Maddie, then we'll head home."

The bar had fifteen to twenty bar stools and eight tables were placed strategically across the floor. A bumper pool table sat in front of the juke-box and a shuffleboard table extended along one wall. Two people, Bruce and Dale Wright, were playing shuffleboard, and they were already in a party mood. Sam's friend Toad was watching the Wright boys play.

Bruce saw me and looked at my mother. "Say, Maddie, is it okay if Shorty plays shuffleboard, so that we can have teams and don't have to waste time walking back and forth?"

Hesitantly Mom agreed. "I guess there's no harm, but just one game, because we got to get going."

"Come on, Shorty, let's flip for partners. Toad, get over here and play," Bruce said.

"What we playing for?" Toad asked.

"Let's play for a beer," Dale said. Dale caught my mother's concerned glance and responded quickly, "Easy, Maddie, Shorty will play for a pop and I'll back him."

Dale and Bruce decided that they would be on opposing teams, and flipped a coin to match-up partners. I ended up being Dale's partner, and would be playing against Toad. Toad and I walked to one end of the table, and Bruce and Dale went to the other end. Dale slapped me on the back as he walked past.

"Come on, partner, let's show these two birds how this game is played," Dale said.

I had been down to Mirror Lake quite a few times with my dad. While he played cards, I practiced on the shuffleboard table, and was getting pretty good.

Toad was a grumpy guy, who never had much to say. He and Sam were in and out of the bars in the area on a very regular basis. Toad would get so drunk that when he talked it was difficult to understand what he was saying. However, it was Sunday morning, and he was still in a relative sober state.

Dale and Bruce, like most brothers were very competitive, but it was easy to see that they liked each other a lot. They were fun to watch as they joked around and tried to distract each other. Toad on the other hand was as serious as a heart attack. Winning the game meant a free beer, and that was important to Toad.

Shuffleboard had become a very popular game in the area, and all the bars had one. Each bar had a shuffleboard team, and area bar leagues, and tournaments were routine, especially during the winter months.

Each team has four pucks, and the object is to have at least one of your pucks farther down the table than your opponents. Players slide the puck down the playing surface and if the puck stops between the first and second line it's worth one point; between the second and third line is two points; over the third line is three points. If the puck stops at the very end of the table and part of it is hanging over the edge it's worth four points. At the end of each round the player with the puck farthest down the table is the winner of the round. That player totals the points of all his pucks that are ahead of any of his opponent's pucks and then adds the total to the team score. The team to reach fifteen first is the winner.

It turned out to be a very good game. Dad had finished playing cards and was sitting by Mom watching. I had beaten Toad most of the time during the game and both Dale and Bruce were ribbing him about it. The score was twelve to eleven in favor of Toad and Bruce, and the pucks were at our end. It was Toads turn to shoot first.

"Come on, Shorty, you got Toad's number today. Just win the turn like you have all day, and I'll put my brother in his place," Dale said.

Bruce playfully pushed Dale aside and said, "Toad, just don't let Shorty score four on you, and I'll make this kid brother of mine eat his words."

Toad slid his first puck down the board and it stopped in the three-point segment. Then I shot and knocked his puck off the board, but in so doing my puck also went off the board.

"Good shot," Tommy said. "Too bad it didn't stay on."

Toad shot again and this time his puck stopped in the two-point section. I looked at Dale, and he winked at me.

"Don't rely on me to tell you what to do, Shorty, you're holding your own."

I shot and lagged it by Toad's puck and it came to a stop in the three-point section of the table.

"You little twerp," Toad said.

He then shot and knocked my puck off the table. It was a very good shot because when he knocked my puck off, his puck glanced off and slid in front of his other puck. He now had a puck in the three point section, and his other puck blocked it so that I couldn't hit it straight on. I shot the next puck and it stopped between the two of his pucks, and off to the left. I thought it was setting in a position where I could use my last puck to bump it over and knock Toad's lead puck off the board.

Toad looked at me and said, "I see what you're planning, but it ain't gonna work."

He shot his puck so that it stopped in back of my puck.

"Good shot, looks like we got the game sewed up," Bruce said.

"Easier than shootin' deer out of season. That beer is going to taste mighty good," Toad bragged.

I had only one chance, and that was to try and lag my last puck up the outside of the table and hoped it stopped in front of Toad's. There was about two inches of board left between Toad's lead puck and the end of the table.

"Shorty, do what you want, but I'd just give it hell and see what happens," Dale said.

He meant for me to slide my last puck with as much force as possible, so that when it collided with the other pucks the resulting collisions might cause the front puck to get knocked off. However, I went with my original plan and slid the puck carefully up the side of the table. The puck slowed as it slid up the table past Toad's puck and stopped just before the end of the table.

Dale jumped in the air and slapped his brother on the back. "What a shot, you got a damn hanger. That's four points! That's four points! We win!"

Bruce shook his head and smiled. "That was a hell of a shot, Shorty. Next time you're on my team."

Toad was ticked off to say the least. He reached in his pocket and tossed a quarter onto the top of the shuffleboard table. "Here you go, you lucky little twerp."

Tommy started to laugh. "I don't think it's luck, Toad. I watch him practice, and you know what they say, practice makes perfect."

Mom was even smiling, and my brother and sister were laughing and singing, "Shorty won, Shorty won."

Dad walked to my side, reached over and tousled my hair.

"Let's hit the road and go home for dinner."

Dale and Bruce were also leaving. "Thanks for letting him play, Maddie," Dale said.

"You're welcome, thanks for allowing him to play," Mom sincerely replied.

Dad looked at Bruce and Dale. "You guys stay out of trouble and have a good day."

"Tell your mother hi for me," Mom said.

"Sure will, Maddie, maybe next time you can have her walk down with you," Dale said, and out the door and to their truck they went.

Toad walked across the floor to the bar, sat beside Sam and ordered another beer. Dad waved goodbye to Tommy, and we left.

"That was fun. I don't think Dale and Bruce are bad guys at all," I said.

Dad looked at Mom and smiled. "They get in trouble once in a while, but they have never seriously hurt anyone that I know of. They just have to learn that it's alright to back down from a fight once in a while. It's getting so that now wherever they go people want to test them."

"Maybe they aren't so bad. I never really talked to them before, they seemed nice enough today. Sometimes we are guilty of judging others too quickly, and can end up with our foot in our mouth. Besides, they can't be as bad as people say, just look at their mother, she's such a sweetheart," Mom said.

"I agree, kind of reminds me of the way some people react to the group I meet up with at Mirror Lake, and the discussions we have," Dad said.

Mom looked at Dad, closed her eyes, and slowly shook her head back forth.

It was one o'clock when we drove into our driveway. Mom had saved some bread dough from the previous night's baking, and fried it up for dinner. I don't know if it was the fried bread or the sweet addition of syrup, but it was one of my favorite meals. After dinner I asked Mom if it was okay if I went fishing. Both she and Dad said to go ahead, but were quick to remind me to be careful.

It was turning out to be a very good day. I dug some worms and walked to the river. I looked at the area of the swamp that I had run through in fear a couple nights earlier. The peaceful setting caused me to reconsider what may have taken place. Maybe it was a cougar or some other animal that had chased us, or it might have been just following us. Or maybe it was nothing, but the shadows mixed in with an overactive imagination.

When I reached my fishing spot, I threw the line out and sprawled out comfortably on the bank. Blackie was lying on her back next to me with all four legs in the air, rolling back and forth in the grass. My fellow river dweller the shy-poke was back, and I watched as it glided in for a landing. I closed my eyes and was starting to drift off when I heard foot steps on the grass behind me. I quickly sat up and turned around, it was my dad. Dad seldom came down to the river, and I wondered what prompted him to take the walk today.

"How ya doing?"

"Not so good, I haven't had a single bite."

"That's not a good day, unless you're the fish."

He then bent down, picked up my cane pole and tossed it into the water.

Needless to say this maneuver surprised me, and I looked at him like he was nuts.

"Sometimes you have to wake 'em up," he said.

He was by no means a fisherman, so I didn't consider his statement the least bit credible. However, as I was watched my pole float on the water, the bobber suddenly went down. Dad ran and found a long stick and managed to extend it out and pull the pole in. At the end of the line was a nice size black bass. I had never caught a black bass in this area of the river before.

He smiled, and I smiled. "What you think?" he said.

"I think that's pretty unbelievable, maybe we should try it again to see if we can hook some more for supper."

"You can keep fishing if you want, but I'm going to go back and see if I can get the Braves on the radio."

"That sounds like a good idea to me, should I bring the fish? It's only one, but we could clean it and put it in the icebox."

"You're right, it's only one, and we could let it go to grow some more."

"It's pretty good size already, but it would be nice to let it grow some," I said.

I took the fish off the hook and placed it in the water. We watched the bass flap its tail back and forth a couple of times and then disappear beneath the surface.

"I wonder if that could have been the black bass that got off my line about four miles up river a couple of nights back?"

"If it was, then it must be living a charmed life to stay out of the frying pan after being caught twice," Dad said.

On the way back to the house we disturbed a killdeer and it ran along the ground in front of us pretending to have a broken wing.

"Those killdeer always pull that trick. Don't they Dad?"

"Yes they do, but they're doing what they can to protect the nest and their young," he said.

As we walked along I wondered if Dad had come down to the river for that same reason. Was he checking on me because of what happened a couple of nights back?

When we got to the house, Dad turned the radio on and tried to find the Braves game. He patiently adjusted the dial until the static cleared and we could hear the game. We sat back and listened intently to the broadcaster's play-by-play descriptions. Warren Spaghn was pitching a masterpiece and hammering Hank Arron hit a home run into the center field seats. You could hear the crowd cheer, and we clapped our hands as if we had been watching from behind home plate. The Braves won and the commentators were already talking pennant winners, and it was only June.

After supper, Uncle Joe came to visit. We walked to the pens to check on the pigs and saw Blackie running around in the field next to the swamp. She dashed across the field and ran into the swamp. "Must have picked up the trail of a rabbit," Dad said.

Uncle Joe asked if I would like to help with haying. He was going to hire Alfred Jest to do the baling. Ronnie, who was Dad and Joe's younger brother, and only four years older than me, would load. Uncle Joe and I would unload.

"What time should I be there?" I asked.

"Anytime after ten would be fine."

Uncle Joe visited with Dad and Mom for a while, and before leaving he let me know that Ronnie would pick me up in the morning.

As soon as Uncle Joe left I walked around calling for Blackie. It was starting to get dark, and usually by this time she was waiting at the front porch to be let in for the night. I filled her dish with water and put some scraps Mom gave me in her other bowl. I called for her again and waited, but she didn't come.

Mom stepped out the screen door onto the porch steps. "What's wrong?"

"I can't find Blackie," I said.

Dad had followed Mom out and addressed my concern. "She's probably off chasing that rabbit and lost track of time. You know how that can happen. She'll most likely be waiting for you when you get out of bed in the morning."

"Your dad's right. Come in now, it's time for bed. You'll need your rest if you're going to work for Uncle Joe tomorrow."

Since my incident on the Fox River I had developed a nightly ritual. Before getting in bed I would go to my bedroom window, and scan the area of the swamp between the river and our house. Tonight I searched through the shadows with extra care, hoping to see Blackie returning home, but there was nothing except the usual shadows. That night before going to sleep I tried to reassure myself that Dad was right, and Blackie would be home in the morning. Then a black cloud spoiled my hopes. What if whatever had chased me through the swamp had caught Blackie?

Chapter Five
A Conversation in the Garden

When I came downstairs Monday morning, Dad and Mom were sitting at the kitchen table having coffee. Dad was on night shift for the next two weeks, so he didn't leave for work until two in the afternoon, and returned home around one in the morning.

I immediately went outside to check for Blackie, but she wasn't home. After chores I walked to the river and back calling out for her, but there was no response. My spirits were beginning to sink lower with each unanswered call. When I walked into the house for breakfast Mom and Dad were playing cribbage.

"Mom, have you seen Blackie?" I asked.

"No, Shorty, I haven't."

"That dog won't be gone long. She ain't dumb. She knows what a good thing she's got going. She'll be back," Dad said. He was trying his best to raise my spirits.

Ronnie arrived at nine-thirty. He had just received his drivers' license, and that only added to his teenage arrogance. He was wearing a white tee-shirt and his hair was slicked back, so that a neatly combed duck tail decorated the back of his head.

"Ronnie, you look like you're ready to go to a dance instead of spending the day tossing hay bales around," Mom said.

"You're right, Maddie. I didn't know Joe hired some girls to help hay this year, or have you talked some into coming out to visit?" Dad asked Ronnie.

"Maybe," Ronnie replied. "Come on, Shorty, we better hit the road."

"You watch that foot," Dad said. "I know you think you're hell on wheels, but if the county boys catch you they'll yank your license and you'll be back to pedaling a bike on dates."

"I will," Ronnie said.

Dad was right; Ronnie did think he was hell on wheels. When we got to a corner, Ronnie pushed the gas pedal to the floor and the rear end would slide around throwing gravel into the ditch. He laughed, and I laughed.

"Don't tell your dad or Joe," he said.

"I won't."

However, deep down both of us knew that they more than likely were aware of his cornering tactics. We arrived at Uncle Joe's just as Alfred Jest was pulling into the driveway. My grandpa and grandma had also arrived. Grandpa would help with the haying, and Grandma would make lunch for everyone.

Alfred Jest was a large, heavy set man that always seemed happy. He owned a farm a couple of miles from Uncle Joe and did custom baling for area farmers. Not many farmers had hay bailers yet, so Alfred was in high demand. He liked his work and enjoyed being with people. Ronnie rode on a wagon that was pulled behind the bailer, and stacked the bales on the wagon as they came up the chute from the bailer. Grandpa would drive out and bring the loaded hay wagons in, and Uncle Joe and I would unload. It was hot work, but each person handled their part and all went well.

When we went in for lunch, Uncle Joe asked if Blackie had come home.

"No, not yet," I said and a concerned look must have swept over my face.

"Don't worry; she probably hooked up with some local male. She'll be back in a day or two," Grandpa said.

Grandma didn't like the off color reference and thought it was not suited for a child's ear. "Hush, Morgan, watch your language," she said.

"Oops, sorry about that, Shorty," Grandpa said as he gave me a wink.

"I thought I saw a dog that looked like yours down by the Sycamore schoolhouse," Alfred said. "If I see it again I'll bring her home for ya."

"Thanks. That would be great."

Sycamore school was a country schoolhouse located two miles from where I lived, and about one mile from the Fox River Bridge. If Blackie wasn't home tonight, I was already planning on walking to the school tomorrow morning to see if I could find her. The first day of haying went very well, and I was dog-tired at the end of the day. That night I slept like a baby.

When I woke on Thursday morning it was raining, so there would be no haying today. Blackie had now been gone for four days. I fed the pigs, did my other chores, and then walked to the river and back. When I returned to the house for breakfast Dad detected my concern.

"Any sign of her?"

"No, nothing," I replied.

"I got about four hours before I have to go to work. Let's take a drive, and see if any of the neighbors have seen her," Dad said.

"Mr. Jest said he saw a dog that looked like Blackie by Sycamore. Do you think someone else might have seen her?" I asked.

"We won't know until we ask." Dad replied, and then turned towards Mom. "Maddie, me and Shorty are going to check with the neighbors to see if anyone has spotted his mutt."

Mom smiled. "I think that's an excellent idea."

Hopeful anticipation was running through my mine, and I was out the door waiting by the car before Dad finished his last sip of coffee.

"Hold your horses, Shorty, I'm coming."

Our first stop was at Frank and Mabel Wilson's farm, which was just up the road from our house. They were outside working in the garden and walked over to meet us when we drove in. Dad asked if they had seen Blackie and they both replied that they hadn't.

Their daughter Elizabeth was home from nursing school. She would always smile and say, "Hi, good lookin'," which caused my face to turn beet red. While Dad was talking to Frank and Mabel, Elizabeth walked to my side of the car, reached in the window and ran her hands through my hair.

"Hi, good lookin'."

I could feel the red inching up my neck.

"Hi," I stuttered.

"I hope you find your dog. I'm driving into Middleton this afternoon, and I'll be sure to watch for her. If I see her I'll bring her home to you."

"Thanks," I said.

As we drove out their driveway, Dad looked over at me.

"You know something; I think Beth has got her eyes on you."

"What for?" I asked.

Dad laughed at my innocent question and it didn't take long for me to realize what he was suggesting. Ronnie and his friends called Elizabeth the "fox" of Fox River. I already had an overworked imagination, and now Dad had managed to stoke the furnace.

"Oh," I said, trying to act unconcerned, but knew I was probably blushing.

A half mile down the road from the Wilsons' was the Raycart farm.

"Let's check with Hank," Dad said.

Immediately I recalled what Uncle Joe had told me about Mrs. Raycart and how she had blocked the rest of the world out since they had buried her son, John. When we approached their driveway the three dogs were waiting for us. They stood at the end of the driveway and came tearing towards the car when Dad turned in. We stopped in front of the house and saw Mrs. Raycart sitting on the porch swing. Dad had his window down and was about to say something when he saw the dogs approaching. He quickly rolled the window up and looked at me.

"Shorty, you get out and ask Joan where Hank is."

I looked at him, looked at Mrs. Raycart, looked at the dogs, and then looked back at Dad.

He started to laugh.

"I'm with you, Shorty. There's no way I'm getting out either. You know I don't think Joan even knows we're here, but those dogs sure do."

I just nodded my head in agreement, and gave a sigh of relief because I didn't have to get out of the car. Then the "don't let them sense that you're afraid" declaration that Dad used on me came to mind. I was about to suggest to him some of his own advice when we saw Mr. Raycart walking out of the milk house. Dad started to drive toward the milk house, and I decided not to challenge him with his own advice.

As we drove ahead I turned to look at Mrs. Raycart. She continued to glide back and forth, staring straight ahead. Except for the motion of the swing she never moved, and I seriously doubted that she was even aware that we had driven in.

Mrs. Raycart was still a very handsome lady. She had on a sleeveless blouse and was wearing an ankle length skirt. Her arms were tanned to a golden brown and you could easily see the lines of muscle that flowed down each arm from her shoulders. If it wasn't for the blank stare, she had the appearance of any normal hard working farmer's wife.

I watched as one of the dogs returned to the house and sat on the ground in front of the porch steps. The other two followed our car to the milk house. Their barking had stopped and was replaced with deep growls that were more intense than any I had ever heard. They were definitely warning us to be careful.

Hank walked toward the car as Dad drove up. He was over six feet tall and thick through the shoulders. His dark black hair topped off a muscular frame and he reminded me more of a lumberjack than a farmer.

Dad opened the car door and started to get out. My first thought was that he was making a big mistake and was giving those dogs an opportunity to attack. However, Mr. Raycart quietly calmed the dogs and they stopped growling and walked back to the house.

"Hi, Hank, we're looking for my son's dog, Blackie, and wondered if you might have seen her," Dad said.

Hank bent down and looked in the car at me and smiled. "I haven't seen her, Mike. If she had showed up here, I'm sure Joan would have brought her in. That's how she got the other three. Two were strays she found along the river and Wrench she brought on three years ago."

"Wrench is a strange name, why'd she pick that?" Dad asked.

"Oh no, I named him, Joan doesn't talk anymore. I don't think she has any need for it," he said, looking in the direction of the porch. After a silent pause he continued.

"Toad found him lying in our ditch all tore up. The dog must have got in a fight with something that got the best of him. Toad wanted to finish the job and was going to hit him in the skull with a wrench. But just as he was coming down with the wrench, Joan scooped the dog up and walked away leaving Toad cussing to the wind. Joan carried Wrench to the house and she worked her vet skills on him. In a few weeks, Wrench was as good as new, and now like the other two he sticks close to Joan."

The way he presented the story left little doubt that he was proud of his wife. Hank then turned toward the milk house. "I left the water running in the cow tank; better go and shut it off."

Dad walked with Hank into the barn and I turned to look at the house. The porch swing was swaying back and forth but Mrs. Raycart was no longer on it. I looked around and saw her walking toward the river with her three dogs close behind. When she reached the riverbank she sat on a chair that was next to an old table. She sat motionless and seemed to be staring at the river. The three dogs positioned themselves so that they formed a protective circle around their master and then quietly lay down.

It wasn't long before Dad and Hank came out of the barn. Dad shook Hank's hand and said, "Thanks a lot."

"What's the boy's name?"

"Oh sorry about that, we call him Shorty. He's suppose to be helping my brother Joe hay today, but the rain has put that off, so we thought we'd use the time to look for his dog.

"Alfred is going to come and do my baling when he finishes up at your brothers."

"To bad you guys couldn't work something out to help each other," Dad said.

"Yup, that would be a good deal, but I don't like to leave Joan alone for too long."

"I understand, let us know if you need a hand. Shorty is getting to be a pretty good worker, and I'm sure he'll have some time on his hands when Joe finishes."

"I might do that," Hank said. He looked at me and waved. "Take care, Shorty, hope you find your dog. If we spot her we'll bring her over."

I think I said thanks, but in reality I was questioning why my dad had just volunteered me to work for them. I'm sure Dad was aware of the stories going around about how strange Mrs. Raycart was. Many people believed she had power over the dogs, and could direct them with her mind to do whatever she wished. As Dad backed the car around to leave, I looked at Mrs. Raycart sitting by the river. Hank saw that I was watching her and smiled.

"That's one of Joan's favorite spots," he said.

When we crossed the Fox River Bridge, I looked down at Mrs. Raycart. While I was watching she raised her head and looked directly at me. For an instant our eyes met, and I became uncomfortable and turned my head away. I was convinced she knew I had been watching her.

As we drove to the next neighbor, I wondered if any of the stories I heard about Mrs. Raycart were true. Could she really control the dogs with her mind? Did she have some kind of unnatural powers?

"Shorty...Shorty..." I was concentrating so much on what I had heard about Mrs. Raycart that I didn't realize Dad was trying to get my attention. "What are you day dreaming about?"

"I was just thinking about Mrs. Raycart. How she never talks, and how those dogs are always around her, like they're waiting on her. Uncle Joe said the dogs might be protecting her. People say she can control them, so that they do whatever she wants. What do you think?"

"From what Hank told us, Joan saved those dogs' lives, so I think Joe has a legitimate point. As for what people are saying, most of it's just talk. Things have happened that people can't explain, and so some make up stories that satisfy their needs. The stories spread, and details are added, and before you know it you got vampires living in the attic. All I know is that Hank and Joan have had a very hard road, and they sure as hell have had more bumps along the way than ninety-nine percent of the people around here couldn't even imagine having. I doubt very strongly that I could have withstood what they have been forced to live with. They have each decided to handle it in their own way, but still need each other. Hank is a working fool; he always had a passion for the farm. Joan had that same passion, they loved farming, and they were a team. They still are a team; did you see how neat the place looked, how well kept? Joan has withdrawn into herself, and I know there are a lot of stories being spread about her. She has withdrawn from people too, and ever since what happened in the church on the day of her son's funeral most people have withdrawn from her and Hank. I think most have done it because they feel Hank and Joan need to be left alone, but a lot have done it because they have built a fear up about Joan. Fear is a natural result of people not being able to understand something."

I was about to ask what happened at the funeral, but we were turning into Jason Abners driveway. His place was located on a hill just before the Sycamore school house. His house was in disrepair and a couple of old sheds and a barn stood equally neglected. Jason didn't farm, but he worked as a hired hand for Harold Strum. Dad parked in front of the house, got out of the car and walked to the front steps. As he started to climb the porch steps, the barn door opened. Jason came out of the barn and began to walk toward the house. Jason was in his late sixties and had a reputation for being less than friendly. As he approached I heard barking coming from the barn.

"Hi, Jason," Dad said as Jason walked toward the car.

Jason was tall and slender. He had on a pair of bib overalls, but no shirt underneath. He walked with the gait of a much younger man and as he approached you immediately got the sense that he didn't have much time for visitors.

Instead of returning Dad's greeting, he pointedly asked, "What ya need?"

Dad described Blackie and asked Jason if he had seen her around his place in the past couple of days. Jason was quick to respond.

"Nope, haven't seen no stray dog around here. Is the dog a chicken killer or deer chaser?"

"No, she's just a mutt who makes a good companion for Shorty. She's been gone for four days now and she's not a runner. We thought someone might have spotted her and took her in, and is waiting for the owner to come around."

Jason then looked at me. "If she was a chicken killer someone has probably put a bullet in her head. I sure as hell haven't seen her." Jason noticed that Dad was looking towards the barn. "Only dogs I got are a couple of coon dogs."

"If you happen to see her, let me know or give us a call."

"If she's been gone for over four days she's probably dead and laying in some ditch," Jason said.

"Hope not," Dad said as he got into the car. Before Dad turned the car around Jason was walking back to the barn.

"That Jason is a weird, mean old bastard. I trust him about as far as I can throw him. It's hard to believe he's Joan's dad."

"You mean Mrs. Raycart?"

"Yes, one and the same. It's hard to believe that Joan made it to adulthood with that man as her pa. Joan is about ten years older than me and I never knew her very well growing up, but I remember Joe telling of what happened the day she turned sixteen. Old Jason came right into the school and took her out. He told the principle she didn't need any more damn schooling, and to get the hell out of his way. He took her and left."

"Did she want to leave?"

"I seriously doubt it. About a year later she met Hank, and a year after that Hank took her away as his wife." Dad then looked at me. "And yes, Shorty, I believe she wanted to leave that time."

Dad then looked down the road. "We got time for one more stop, and then we better get home so I can get ready for work."

The next stop was Harold Strums. He was the richest farmer in the area. He had all the new equipment to go along with a very nice farm. When we pulled into his driveway, Harold was sitting in the porch. When he saw us come up the drive he came out of the porch and walked down the steps to meet us. He was a heavy, stout man, who always seemed to have a cigar fit sternly between his lips. He was always smiling, but you got the impression that it was a fake smile, one that was put on as a show. He liked to make the first move and definitely wanted to be in charge of the situation, no matter what it was. He walked up to the car as Dad came to a stop. Dad got out and without hesitating Harold threw out his hand to shake Dad's.

"How you doing, Mike, and how is that good lookin wife of yours"?

"Doing just fine, Harold, how about yourself?"

"You know me, Mike, everything is smooth as butter on this end. No worries except to keep those two boys of mine in line. They always want to buy more land and more cattle. Guess they're kind of taking after the old man."

"Sounds like it," Dad said.

"As a matter of fact they took the truck into St Paul today to sell some cattle at the stockyards, and then were going to stop at an auction on the way back to see if they can pick up some young stock for a good price."

"Stuck you with night milking then," Dad said.

"No...No...Margaret will milk the cows and Jason will be over to help with the chores," Harold said emphatically.

"Hey, Margaret," he called out in a loud voice, "bring these boys a cool drink."

"No thanks, I have to get back home and get ready for work."

"How's the factory life treating you, Mike?"

"Okay," Dad said. "It's a pretty good place to work. A little drive, but that's not bad since we all take turns driving."

"I know there are a lot of people working there who couldn't make it farming."

"I don't know about that, but there are quite a few who still farm a little on the side."

"I think you got to do one or the other, hell they can sell me the land if they can't make it. If you know anybody who may be interested in selling, have them give me a call. I'll give 'em a fair price. What about your brother Joe, does he want to sell?

"No, I don't think so, Harold, he's pretty happy with what he's got."

"Well if he ever wants to get out, let me know."

I could tell Dad was getting somewhat annoyed with the conversation, and Mr. Strums arrogance. "Joe is doing what he likes and selling is the last thing on his mind."

"Maybe, but his farm is too small. One or two bad years and I'll probably be buying it from the bank."

Then he remembered that it had been a few minutes since he summoned his wife to bring drinks. "Margaret, what's taking you so long, these boys are getting thirsty?"

"No, don't bother, we're fine," Dad insisted, but it was too late Mrs. Strum was walking across the yard carrying a tray with a pitcher of lemonade and glasses. Mrs. Strum was a small woman, but you could tell she did more than her share of the work. Her face had wrinkles from the weather mixed in with age and the pressures of hard work. She stepped up to my dad and handed him a glass. Dad accepted the glass with a smile, and she poured it full of lemonade.

"Thanks, Margaret, but you shouldn't have," Dad said.

"Nonsense," said Harold, "Margaret has always got something cool for us, don't ya?"

"Yes I do," Mrs. Strum replied. She then walked around the car to my window. "Hi, Shorty, how you doing?"

"Fine," I said. The way she presented herself brought a smile to my face, I felt good about taking the glass of lemonade.

"Please tell your mom hi for me, and I'll see her at church Sunday."

"I will, and thanks for the lemonade."

"What you two out driving around for? Are you selling something?" Harold asked.

"No, we're looking for Shorty's dog, Blackie. She's been gone for over four days now and we're checking to see if any of the neighbors might have seen her."

"Not me, Margaret, have you seen a dog running loose?"

Harold didn't give his wife the opportunity to answer. "No, she hasn't seen any stray around either. If we see it we'll give you a call. Did you check with Jason?"

"Yeah, we just stopped by his place," Dad said.

"I don't believe it helps much to have a dog. All they do is cause more work and cost more money. I was thinking about getting a good cow dog once, but Margaret has got these cows pretty well trained, so a dog would just get in the way."

"Well, thanks anyway. We better get home," Dad said. He finished his lemonade and gave the glass to Mrs. Strum. "Thanks again, Margaret, and you have a good day."

"You're welcome, Mike, tell Maddie I said hi. Shorty, I hope you find your dog, I'll watch for her."

I finished my glass and handed it to Mrs. Strum, and thanked her again. She automatically gave a smile that complimented her sincerity.

Mr. Strum had turned and was walking back to the house. "Margaret," he commanded, "you go down and start chores, I'm going to check on some things in the office."

Margaret didn't answer. She followed her husband's instructions and placed the tray on a picnic table in the yard, and silently walked toward the barn.

As we drove home, Jason's remark about Blackie laying dead in some ditch entered my mind and I found myself checking the ditches.

"Don't let that bastard Jason put thoughts in your head," Dad said.

When we returned home we had a bite to eat and Dad left for work. Mom was weeding the garden, so I went out to help. She loved to work in the garden; she wore a straw hat for shade from the sun and always went barefoot. She said the soil felt good between her toes. She assigned me a row to work on, and we worked in silence for about a half-hour.

"Shorty, what's wrong?" she asked.

"Nothin'," I said.

"I know better than that, now how about a penny for your thoughts? If it's about Blackie, I'm sure she'll be home soon."

"I sure hope so. I miss that mutt."

"I know you do and I miss her too. Now what else is on your mind?"

"I was just thinking about something Dad said in the car this afternoon."

"What was it about? Maybe I can help."

"It was about Mrs. Raycart. What did she do in church on the day of her son's funeral?" The question brought a solemn look to my mother and she got off her knees and sat on the ground.

"I'm ashamed of myself for not going over and visiting Joan."

"I don't think she visits much," I said.

"I know, but I should have tried."

I could tell by the look on Mom's face that she was going to go into a silent mode, so I asked again, "Mom, what happened at the church?"

"Shorty, you sure like to ask a lot of questions and that's a good thing most of the time. I think you're old enough to start forming your own opinions, and this is as good a time as any to let you know what I know; besides, I think it will help both of us."

Mom was right, we both benefitted from the conversation in the garden. It was not only directed to enlighten me, but was also a means to help Mom start to come to grips with thoughts that had been troubling her. It helped in her never-ending search to find a way to make sense out of such a tragic event. She took a deep breath and let out a sigh.

"It was a day too remember, that's for sure. It split the members of our church and some are just now finally starting to get back together."

I stopped weeding and sat down on the ground next to my mother and listened.

"It was a very sad day. Our pastor at the time was Pastor Brown and the church was full. The coffin was in front of the congregation and it was still open for the viewing before the funeral service. Joan and Hank had just been ushered in and were sitting in the front row.

"Pastor Brown stepped to the front and stood beside the altar, and gave his opening address to the congregation: 'I know that this is a tragic accident and we all are asking ourselves why God could let such a thing happen. We can all be assured that however tragic, it is God's will that John be with him now in heaven.' He then motioned to the pallbearers to come forward and close the coffin. At that moment Joan stood and looked directly at Pastor Brown and said, 'It was not God's will and it was no accident.'

"The church became very silent and everyone was watching Joan. She looked at her son lying in the coffin and then turned and walked into the aisle. As she walked past, the look of sorrow on her face was replaced by an expressionless stare. It was as if all the tears she had shed and the meaning they held were left with her last child.

"Hank stood beside his wife and followed. When they reached the end of the aisle and exited the church the coffin lid closed before the pallbearers reached it.

"Neither Pastor Brown, nor anyone in the congregation knew what to do or say. Pastor Brown then collected himself as best he good and told the congregation, 'Let's take John home.' He then motioned to the pallbearers and they secured the latches on the coffin, gently picked it up and followed Pastor Brown to the grave site.

"Most of us followed, but some remained in the church, because they felt they had just witnessed an unholy act.

"When we walked outside, Joan and Hank were standing by the grave site. The coffin was lowered into the grave and the pastor began the burial sermon. Before he completed it, Joan with Hank by her side, walked to their truck and drove away. She hasn't spoken a word since that day."

"What do you think happened?" I asked.

"I don't know, Shorty. I just don't know, but it shook the foundations of our church. To this day Mabel Wilson, Joan's closest neighbor, feels that Joan and Hank are unholy and God took their kids because they would be better off with him in heaven than in the hands of Hank and Joan."

"Do you think Mrs. Wilson is right?"

Mom put her hands on her lap and looked down on the ground and then back up at me. "No, Shorty, I don't think Mrs. Wilson is right. As a matter of fact I think that she and the others who feel that way are wrong and need to come forward and say as much, or the rumors and untruths about Joan will continue to grow and no good can come of it."

"What rumors?"

"You know most of them, Shorty."

She was right I did know most of the rumors, but for some reason I needed her to tell me.

"Mom, those dogs they stay right beside her. Uncle Joe says they are protecting her and Dad agrees. What are they protecting her from? It's like she can talk to them without speaking. Do you think she has power over the dogs and other things like people say?"

"I don't know, Shorty, I really don't know. Even if she has developed a way to communicate to her dogs without speaking, that doesn't make her evil."

"Did the dogs get protective and mean when her son died?"

"That's where the rumors started, Shorty."

"Why? What do you mean? Weren't they always like that?"

"No, Shorty. When John was alive they only had one dog and it was just a small spaniel that they used to help with the cows. About a week after John's funeral, Pastor Brown and three members from the Ladies Aid drove out to see Joan. They said when they arrived; two very vicious dogs greeted them. The dogs wouldn't let them out of the car and Joan just sat on the porch swing ignoring what was going on. Hank must have been in the fields. The pastor and the ladies gave up and left. Not long after rumors started that evil dogs had come to Joan out of no where and she controlled them with her mind."

"Mr. Raycart told us the dogs were strays, where do you think they came from?" I asked.

"I don't know, Shorty, but I do know that Joan is not evil, and I hope you don't believe that she is. She has been through a very unfair life and it's not right that she should have to endure so much pain. I can't blame her for shutting us all out, we may deserve it. I have to go visit Joan and Hank. I don't know if it will help them, but it will help me."

She paused for a moment, brushed her hands together and said, "But I do know one thing for certain."

"What?" I asked, expecting more details and words of wisdom from the heart.

"I know that these weeds aren't going to jump out of the ground by themselves, so we better get back to work."

Mom left to make supper around five and I continued to weed. When she came back to let me know it was time to eat, she looked over her garden and smiled.

"Now doesn't that look as pretty as any picture?" she said.

That night before bed I performed my nightly scan of the river and found it looked as peaceful as the garden we had weeded that afternoon. I had a difficult time falling to sleep because questions continued to pop in and out of my mind concerning Mrs. Raycart. Where did her dogs come from? Does she have unnatural powers? What if they are evil powers? Did she really believe that her sons' drowning wasn't an accident? What about her son?

I closed my eyes and tried to force my mind to produce a vision of her son. I saw the coffin sitting below the church altar but as I tried to focus on the boy lying inside, the lid closed and the coffin slipped away into the depths of my unconscious. Everything turned gray for a moment and then pictures in the shape of puzzle pieces began to flash through my brain. I saw the dogs chasing something, saw Jason Abner laughing at me, saw Toad hitting something with a wrench, and I saw Blackie lying in a ditch. The fragmented visions floated in every direction and suddenly something began to take shape in the center. I saw the porch swing on one side and the chair by the river on the other, but they were both empty. Then Mrs. Raycart came into focus and she was staring directly at me. I tried to look away but couldn't. She began to speak to me. I could see her so clearly, but couldn't make out what she was saying. Then she lifted her hand and pointed behind her. I looked to where she pointed and saw the river. In an instant I was in the water. I couldn't get my breath.

I sprung straight up in bed.

I looked around my room in the darkness and saw the light from the moon shinning through the curtains. It was sure some dream, but I wasn't frightened. I felt somewhat exhausted, and as I lay back in bed I made the determination that Mrs. Raycart was trying to tell me something. The stare in the dream was the same as the one I encountered when she looked up at me from her chair by the river. I didn't feel she intended to do me any harm. It was more as if she was trying to look inside of me. She was searching for something or trying to tell me something.

Maybe she was trying to tell me where Blackie was, or what had happened to her.

Chapter Six
The Storm

The next morning I awoke to the sound of rain bouncing off my bedroom window. Mom as usual was in the kitchen.

"Good morning, Shorty, how would you like pancakes for breakfast?"

"Sounds good to me," I said.

I looked all over for signs of Blackie and again found nothing. I was beginning to accept that she might not come back. While doing chores I thought about the visits we had with our neighbors. I thought about the dream I had last night and wondered if it was possible for Mrs. Raycart to sense where Blackie was. I believed that my mother even felt it was possible for Mrs. Raycart to have some kind of power that allowed her to communicate with her dogs. Maybe her dogs knew where Blackie was and could relay that information to Mrs. Raycart. Even if that was possible, Mrs. Raycart couldn't tell me, because she doesn't speak.

What about Jason Abner, Alfred Jest said he saw a dog that looked like Blackie by Sycamore school and Jason's farm is close to the school. Plus there were dogs in his barn and he was quick to counter when my dad looked at the barn that they were just his coon dogs. Was he hiding something? Maybe he had Blackie tied up in his barn. By the end of chores I had convinced myself that Blackie was at old man Jason's. If Blackie wasn't there, I had a strong feeling that Jason knew where she was.

When I finished chores the rain had turned to a light mist. When I returned to the house, Mom was busy frying pancakes. As I watched her I thought about our conversation in the garden. I think my mother had some kind of power herself, because as she turned to bring a plate of pancakes to the table she asked, "So what did you think about our little talk in the garden?"

"I think you're right, Mrs. Raycart isn't evil, but I still think she has some kind of power. But what about her dogs, where did they come from, and why did they show up right after her son drowned? Do you think she can talk to her dogs?"

"I don't know, but I'm not ruling it out. As for where the dogs came from I haven't the faintest idea, but I definitely don't believe the devil placed them on her door step."

"What you talking about the devil for, has Mabel Wilson got you worked up again, Maddie?" It was Dad.

"No, she has not, and what are you doing up so early?"

"I have to take a pee and want to let you know to wake me at nine, because we're going into work a little early today to take advantage of some overtime."

"Okay," Mom said. Then she asked Dad as he walked past, "Do you know where Joan got her dogs?"

"Nope, don't know. We found out yesterday that the third dog named Wrench; she took from Toad, because he was going to kill it and Joan nursed him back to health. I think the other two came from the devil himself," Dad said, and winked at me as he walked by.

"Get out of here," Mom said, and then threw the dish towel she had hanging over her shoulder at him. Dad laughed and walked outside.

Just then the phone rang and Mom answered it. "Shorty, it's for you."

It was Uncle Joe. He called to let me know that he wasn't going to cut any hay today. The weather report was calling for the rain to continue, and there was a good chance it would hang around for a few days. He didn't want to cut a bunch of hay just to have it lay in rain water. Instead he was going to grind feed and wait to see what tomorrow brought. I told him that it sounded like a good plan to me, and I would be ready to go tomorrow.

I relayed Uncle Joe's decision to Dad when he came back to the house.

"Thanks, Shorty. I'm sorry we won't be able to go looking for Blackie today."

"That's okay," I said.

Both Mom and Dad detected the concern in my voice. "Don't give up on that black mutt, she'll be back," Dad said.

"Your dad's right, Shorty, don't give up."

"I won't."

However, I think each of us was beginning to have some doubt. Dad went back to bed, Mom started to wash clothes, and I picked up my mitt and went outside to throw the ball against the barn. As I played catch with the red wall, I couldn't get my mind off the idea that Blackie was at Jason Abner's place. I had to find out.

The weatherman might have been wrong, because the sun had broken through the clouds and it was turning into a beautiful summer day. Dad left for work at half past nine, and Mom was taking advantage of the unpredicted sunshine by hanging clothes on the line to dry.

At noon Mom prepared a plate of peanut butter sandwiches and a gallon of grape nectar. Grape nectar was always a welcome treat on a warm summer day. I poured myself a second glass and interrupted Mom as she walked through the kitchen with a basket of clothes.

"Looks like the rain has stopped, think it would be okay if I went to the river?"

"It's okay with me, but don't forget to be home by supper. Are you going fishing?"

"No, just thought I'd do some lookin' around."

"I understand, and it looks like it might be a beautiful day for looking around."

Mom was right it was turning out to be a beautiful day. As I walked along the riverbank, I found myself being more aware of the surrounding terrain. I watched for movement in the brush and marsh grass. Was I being more aware because I was hoping to see Blackie or to be prepared to run in case I came upon a cougar or something else hiding in the brush?

When I came to the shallow area that we use to cross the river, I carefully scanned the area for signs of movement. I decided that Mom and Dad were more than likely right. Whatever followed me that night was no longer around. It was just passing through.

I took my shoes off and crossed the river. When I reached the other side, instead of continuing to follow the river I hiked up the hill. At the top of the hill I crawled under a barbed wire fence into a pasture. Cows were scattered throughout the pasture feasting on the fresh June grass. They looked at me in a disinterested way as I walked between them to the dirt road located on the far side of the pasture. I crossed the road and climbed a hill that was covered with trees and brush. I made my way through the brush to the top of the hill and crouched behind a large stand of lilac bushes. I was well hidden, but had a clear view of Jason Abners place.

I didn't see anyone and concluded that Jason was either inside or not at home. After what seemed a significant amount of time, I decided it was safe to move in for a closer look. Moving from bush to bush, I made my way down the hill. At the bottom of the hill there was a gully that looped around to the back of Jason's barn. I ran from the brush to the gully and used it as a path to get in back of the barn without being detected. I crouched low and followed the gully until I reached a position that put me directly behind the barn. I cautiously crawled up the bank of the gully and found that I had a clear view of the back of the barn.

I was just getting ready to run to the barn, when I heard a car entering Jason's driveway. A car door slammed, and I heard Jason's front screen door open and close. I couldn't see who had driven in because the barn was between the house and my hiding spot.

By this time the adrenaline was pumping through my system. I was Davy Crockett and the Green Hornet rolled into one. I wanted to see who had driven in, so I slid down the bank and followed the gully to a point that allowed me to see the house. The car was a neat looking new black Thunderbird convertible. Who did Jason know that owned a car like that?

Two men had gotten out of the car and were standing next to Jason. One of the men was as big as Jason, but I didn't recognize him. The other person stood with his back to me and wasn't participating in the conversation. I was to far away to hear what was being said, but the big man seemed angry. He threw up his arms and started to walk to the barn. Jason and the other man followed close behind.

I slid down the bank and followed the gully to my former position behind the barn. I crawled to the top of the bank to get a better look, and the back barn doors opened. Jason stepped out and I quickly slid down the bank and hid beneath an overhang of brush. I heard the men approaching and my heart started to beat a mile a minute. My first thought was to make a run for it, but it was too late, they were standing on the edge of the bank directly above the overhang where I was hiding.

"It can't be far," Jason said.

"You better find it, and finish it off," the large man said.

"I don't know why, it sure as hell can't talk, but if that's what you want, I'll get the gun," Jason said.

"Yes that's what I want and I want it done now. If it lives, there might be questions about how it got chewed up. We got a good thing going, and we have a chance to make some big bucks. The boss wants to move the training site again."

"Where to?" Jason asked.

"We'll talk about that after you take care of this business, but I think the boss wants to use the old site. How in the hell did you let it get away in the first place?" the big man asked.

They turned and walked back to the barn and I couldn't make out any more of their conversation. I stayed in my hiding position for a few more minutes and then slowly crawled out to look over the bank. They were out of sight, but had left the barn doors open. I had no doubt that one, if not all three, were coming back, and more than likely it was going to be sooner rather than later. I knew I had to leave or risk being caught.

I slid down the bank and followed the same route back to the top of the hill. When I reached the top I ducked beneath a bush and looked back at the house. Jason was coming down the steps and he was carrying a shotgun. I didn't know what he was intending to shoot, but I wasn't going to wait around to find out. I decided to head for the river, because there was more cover, and the banks along the river provided good places to hide.

I ran to the bottom of the hill and was only a few yards from the fence that bordered the river when I heard a clinking noise coming from some nearby brush. I listened for a moment, and then detected a whimpering sound also coming from the brush. I cautiously moved closer and spread the brush apart. The whimpering sound was Blackie, and she had a wire wrapped around her tail with a bunch of tin cans tied to the wire. I crawled in and began to untangle the wire, and saw that it had started to eat through her tail. I reached down to pet her head and instinctively drew my hand back when I saw she had a cut over one eye and another cut in her shoulder. She must have gotten into a fight with a badger or something. I was afraid to take the wire completely off her tail because I thought I could cause more damage. I found a weak point in the wire about six inches from the tail and bent the wire back and forth until it snapped. I let the wire and the cans lay and crawled out of the brush. Blackie followed me; she had stopped her whimpering and was doing her best to fight off the pain to show that she was glad to see me.

"I have to get you back home so Mom can look at this."

Blackie then looked up the hill.

"What is it, girl?" I turned to look and saw Jason standing at the top of the hill. My heart fell into my stomach. I was certain he saw me, and decided I had no other option but to run.

"Let's go, Blackie. We gotta get home."

I started to run for the fence. I took about five steps when I heard the shotgun blast and I fell to the ground. Sweat ran down my forehead into my eyes. I rolled onto my side, checking to see if I had been shot. Other than being frightened beyond all imagination, I was not hit. Then my thoughts switched to Blackie, was she shot? I called her name and she came running to my side. I pushed off the ground and looked up the hill and saw Jason looking directly at us. As I watched, not knowing what to do next, Jason lowered the shotgun to his side and disappeared into the brush.

In all the excitement I didn't notice that storm clouds had moved in. I heard the rumble of thunder and could see flashes of lightning getting close. I jumped to my feet and ran towards the fence hoping to out run the oncoming storm. As I ran along I looked over my shoulder up the hill, but didn't see any sign of Jason.

What did it all mean? I was sure Jason saw us. What did he shoot at? Was it a warning shot for me? I could feel tears starting to form in my eyes. The relief from making it through the days events and having Blackie back was bringing out deep emotions.

"Come on, Blackie, let's go home."

As we neared the fence the storm caught us. The thunder echoed, the lightning flashed, and the rain started to come down in buckets. The sky had turned black and in no time I was soaked to the skin. I continued to run along the fence until I saw the Fox River Bridge. I started to climb across the fence, so I could get to the bridge for cover. As I crossed the top of the fence my trousers caught on the barbed wire and I gave a quick jerk to break free. My trousers ripped leaving a piece hanging from the wire and I tumbled to the ground. I hit the ground on my side and rolled to the edge of the river bank. The severity of the storm was increasing and I knew my mother would be worried. I got to my feet and started to sprint for the bridge. As I ran up the bank I stepped into a hole and twisted my ankle. The pain instantly caused me to sit on the bank.

"Not going to be able to run anymore," I told Blackie.

The storm was getting worse. The trees were bending in the wind and the rain was being blown side ways. The river was rising and the momentum of the water as it sped past, crashing against whatever was in its path made its own thunder. I limped to the bridge and found a place underneath, where I was safe from the water and the storm. My ankle was starting to throb and I decided to sit the storm out until it was safe to continue home. I looked up and down river, but only saw sheets of rain. Then it started to hail, and I heard a sound riding the wind.

"Ooown...Ooown..." the eerie sound made as it echoed through the storm.

The sound was coming from the direction of the Raycarts' farm. I moved closer to the side of the bridge that faced the Raycart farm to see if I could identify what the sound was. Whoever or whatever was making the sound was definitely getting closer.

Blackie sat by my side, she had no intentions of leaving. I looked up river to determine if it was safe to leave before whatever was making the sound joined us. As I peered though the curtain of rain I saw a figure making its way in the water along the bank towards the bridge. The rain and hail made it impossible to tell who it was, but it wouldn't be long before whomever it was reached the bridge. Had Jason followed us through the storm?

I turned to face the direction the sound was coming from. It was getting closer, so I decided to take my chances with the storm. There was no logical reason to share this spot with whoever or whatever was coming from either direction. There was no Green Hornet left in me, I wanted to be home. I looked at the figure getting closer to the bridge and turned and ran into a tree. At least I thought it was a tree, it was solid enough, and then the tree grabbed me around the shoulders.

"What in the hell are you doing here, Shorty?" I looked up; it was Hank Raycart.

He was the sound in the wind. He was calling for his wife Joan. With little or no effort he lifted me from the ground and gently set me off to the side.

His voice quieted and he said, "Joan, you alright?"

He then walked down the bank and along the edge toward the approaching figure. The figure came into view, and I saw that it was his wife Joan. Hank took her hand and pulled her from the water. She was drenched from the storm, but the expression on her face looked the same as when I saw her sitting on the porch swing. Then from the river her three dogs sprang to the bank.

I was as scared to the bones as I was wet to the bones, but all I could do was stand there and look. The dogs stood in silence next to Mrs. Raycart and stared at me. I was scared and the dogs knew I was scared, but they didn't move. For some reason I thought of Dad's theory that they wouldn't bother me if I showed them that I wasn't afraid. There was no way I could play such a part, and was preparing to fall to the ground and play dead if they attacked.

However, they had more important responsibilities to adhere to, and they stood like sentinels around Mrs. Raycart.

"Joan, you have got to quit wandering off like this. You had me scared out of my wits when I came in from chores and realized you were out in this storm."

Then Hank remembered I was present, and turned to look at me. "Are you okay, Shorty?"

I nodded yes, because my voice was not working very well at the moment.

"What's wrong with your dog, she looks pretty banged up?" Mr. Raycart asked.

"I found her in some brush in back of Jason Abner's, all tangled with wire. I think she got in a fight with a badger or something."

Hank started to walk up the bank towards me, but quick as a cat, Mrs. Raycart walked around Hank and stood facing me. She looked at me, and suddenly put out her arms. I closed my eyes, waiting for her to grab me, and feed me to her dogs. No she wouldn't do that, she's not evil. Mom is always right. Mrs. Raycart is not evil, I said over and over to myself in silence.

However, it wasn't me she was reaching for. Instead she stooped down, gathered Blackie in her arms, and walked into the rain with her dogs following close behind.

Hank looked at me and said; "well, I guess we're leaving now. At least the hail has quit. Come on up to the house and get dried off. I think Joan is going to look your dog over and then I'll take you home. Your folks are probably pretty worried by now."

I started to follow Hank, but could hardly walk, because of the pain from the injured ankle.

"Looks like you're a little banged up too."

Hank reached down, grabbed me around the waist, swung me over his shoulder, and into the rain we went, following his wife to the farm.

Mrs. Raycart never slowed her pace as she walked along the river bank with Blackie cradled in her arms. She walked by the chair where I saw her sitting when Dad and I were looking for Blackie and across the yard to the porch. Her three dogs walked calmly beside her. When she reached the porch, the dogs stopped, and watched her as she opened the screen door and went inside. They must have determined she was safe, and crawled under the porch to get out of the rain. It was as if their mission was complete, but they remained on guard.

She walked through the porch and while holding Blackie with one arm she opened the kitchen door and walked inside. Mr. Raycart put me down by the porch steps, walked up the steps and opened the door. He then turned and saw that I was somewhat hesitant to follow.

"Come on, Shorty, I know there are lots of stories going around about Joan, but she doesn't eat children, or feed them to her dogs."

I hobbled up the steps and into the porch. There was a light in the porch and my eyes fixed upon Mrs. Raycart's porch swing. I started to squat down to sit on the floor.

"No, come in the kitchen, and let's see how bad that ankle is," Mr. Raycart said.

I limped into the kitchen and found it similar to ours. There was a wood stove, an ice box and cupboards along the wall on each side of the kitchen sink. Mrs. Raycart had placed Blackie on the kitchen table. She was stroking her along the neck and it must have had a calming affect because Blackie looked pretty content. I watched Mrs. Raycart as she ran her hands softly over Blackie, checking each scar with the tip of her fingers. Hank walked over and bent down to look at Blackie's condition, and gave a nod to his wife. Mrs. Raycart was soaking wet and it was hard to tell, but I thought I saw a tear form under her eye and run down her cheek. Hank took his big hand and wiped her cheek; Mrs. Raycart turned her head and stared at him. Then suddenly she turned and walked by me as if I wasn't even there, and went out the kitchen door. I heard the screen door slam and turned to Mr. Raycart.

"Is she all right?" I asked.

"Yes, Shorty, she's fine; she's going to get some medicine to fix your dog up."

He then looked at Blackie and checked the tail. "She's going to lose that tail. Hope infection don't set in. Where did you say you found her?"

"In a bush behind Jason Abner's place," I said. "I don't know how she got so tangled up in that wire."

"Blackie may not have done the tangling," Hank said.

"What do you mean?"

Before he could reply his wife walked into the kitchen. She was carrying a jar with some kind of salve in it and set it on the table next to Blackie. Then she went to the cupboard, opened the drawer, and pulled out a knife. My eyes must have gotten as big as butternuts, because Hank started to laugh.

"Hang tight, Shorty, it'll be fine. Joan knows more about fixing up animals than Doc Spriggs, especially when it comes to dogs."

Mrs. Raycart walked to the kitchen table and placed a hand over the eyes of Blackie. Blackie laid her head on the table and looked as if she was going to sleep. Mrs. Raycart dipped her fingers into the salve and gently applied it to each of Blackie's wounds. She then wiped the salve that was left on her fingers onto her dress and began to unwind the wire from Blackie's tail. Blackie suddenly raised her head in pain, but Mrs. Raycart took her left hand and stroked Blackie's neck, and she slowly laid her head back on the table. Mrs. Raycart looked closely at the wound and saw that the tail was just about eaten through. She then took the knife and cut the tail completely off. Blackie didn't even move. She washed the tip of what remained of Blackie's tail and gently spread salve over it. Blackie stood on her four legs and wagged what was left of her tail. The white tip was gone.

Mrs. Raycart lifted Blackie from the table and gently placed her on the floor. Then she cleaned the table and walked out the kitchen door. I heard the creaking of the porch swing and looked at Blackie and then at Mr. Raycart.

"Your dog will be fine. Now let's take a look at that ankle."

I sat on a chair by the kitchen table and Hank knelt on the floor and carefully removed my shoe and sock. The ankle had swelled significantly. He took hold of my foot with his large hands and gently rotated it. He watched me for any indication of pain and said, "I don't think it's broke, but it's sprained pretty good. I better get you home."

It was six thirty and I was sure that Mr. Raycart needed to do the night milking. "I think I can make it home," I told him.

"You probably could, but your ma is more than likely worried sick by now with the storm and all, and you still gone."

Of course he was right; my mother would be very worried.

"Your mother can put that ankle in some hot water and take care of it. We better go."

He handed me my shoe and sock, and then went into the pantry and brought out a pair of crutches. They were set a little short for me, so he extended them to the proper length.

"Try these," he said as he handed me the crutches.

"They'll make it easier to get around."

He opened the kitchen door for me. I walked through and was facing Mrs. Raycart who was sitting on the swing. Her eyes seemed to be focused on something in the distance, and she never so much as blinked as I hobbled by her toward the porch steps. Hank brought a towel from the kitchen and wiped the rain off his wife's arms and neck. He then placed the towel in her lap and leaned forward and kissed her on the cheek.

"Joan, I'm going to take Shorty home. I'll be right back. You better go in and get some dry clothes on or you'll catch a good cold."

I turned to face Mrs. Raycart when I reached the porch steps and said, "Thanks."

She didn't give any indication that she heard me, and continued to glide back and forth while staring blankly in my direction. Then the silence was broken when the dogs came out from under the porch and started to bark and growl. I immediately turned to face the screen door and decided it was better to let Hank go out first. However, it wasn't me the dogs were barking at, but a car pulling off the road into the driveway.

"It's Sam," Hank said. "I bet he's half shined up by now. Come on, Shorty, let's go."

Hank walked onto the porch steps and held the screen door open for me. I used the crutches for support and took a step forward. Just as I was getting ready to take another step I felt Mrs. Raycart's wet dress brush against my side. Quick as a cat and just as quiet Mrs. Raycart was standing beside me. Her quick movement startled me. Before I could turn to look she extended her arm and placed her hand so that she was holding my jaw between her thumb and fore finger. In the same continuous motion she turned my face so that I was looking directly at her. I slowly looked up and met her piercing stare. Her face was so close that I could see my reflection in her green eyes. It was as if I was looking into a deep pool of water, there was no ripples in her eyes, just a calm steady stare. I felt like she was trying to read my mind and I was frightened out of my wits. I glanced away, hoping that Hank saw what was happening, so he could come and rescue me. Hank was walking toward the oncoming car and the dogs were busy showing their displeasure at the visitors. Hank turned to see if I was following and saw my desperate situation.

Mrs. Raycart continued to stare at me for what seemed like an eternity, and then with a firm voice said, "Watch that river."

I tried to shake my head yes, and I think I muttered that I would, but in all honesty I was petrified. Mrs. Raycart continued to stare directly into my eyes for a few seconds, and then as suddenly as she had grabbed me, she let me go. I watched her walk back to the porch swing and when she sat down her unearthly stare was directed toward the river. I pulled myself together as best I could, and walked down the steps and saw Hank watching his wife. The unexpected incident had brought an expression of surprise to his face and a small smile formed.

We both regained some composure when the car slammed on its brakes and came to a stop beside Hank. It was Sam and his buddy Toad, and as Hank predicted, they were both half in the bag.

"What you two up to?" Hank asked.

"Oh, nothing," Sam said.

"We're on the way to Mirror Lake and I'm pretty close to empty, so was wondering if I could get some gas."

Then he looked over at me and saw Blackie.

"Did one of Joan's dogs kick off and she got a replacement already?" Sam asked.

"Can't you count," Hank said as he pointed to the dogs by the car.

"This is Shorty's dog and I'm going to give them a lift home. You can go down and get some gas."

Toad hit Sam on the arm and stared at Sam and then at the dogs. Sam looked at Toad and nodded his head to signify that he knew what Toad wanted.

"Hank, will you keep the dogs by you so that it's safe for us to get out?" Sam asked.

"Okay, but hurry up, I got to get Shorty home and get back for milking."

Toad then said the wrong thing. "We wouldn't need you to watch the dogs if you'd put them down. They're no good for a damn thing, except protecting that weird woman of yours. Hell, they don't even run deer or hunt coons."

Hank quickly dropped his arms and walked to the passenger side of the car. Sam realized that Toad had said the wrong thing and was quick to interject something before his brother pulled Toad through the window.

"Hank, don't bother with old Toad, he's drunk and don't know what he's saying." Sam said.

Hank stopped and gave Toad a threatening look. Toad's eyes filled with fear and he became very silent. Hank shook his head in disgust and walked away.

"Wait here, Shorty, I'll get the truck out," Hank said.

Hank walked to his truck and Sam drove to the machine shed where the gas tank was located. Hank brought the truck to the front of the porch, got out and stood beside me. The dogs never stopped growling, and were now positioned in front of the porch. Sam filled his car with gas and waved to Hank as he passed by. Hank responded to his brother with a nod.

"Let's go," Hank said and helped me into the truck.

As we drove out I watched the dogs return to their post under the porch.

Mrs. Raycart continued to slowly swing back and forth. We turned onto the road towards home and Hank turned to me.

"Shorty, that was the first time I've heard Joan say a word in over five years."

"Five years is a long time," I said.

"You don't know how long, Shorty…You don't know how long."

We both sat quietly the rest of the way. When Hank turned into our driveway I saw my mother looking out the porch screen door, and she ran to meet us as we drove in. Hank stopped the truck and walked around to open the door for me. I used the crutches for support as I stepped to the ground and Blackie jumped to the ground beside me.

"What happened?" Mom asked.

"Shorty had a little accident while looking for his dog. His ankle is pretty swelled up, but I don't think it's broke," Mr. Raycart said.

Mom saw Blackie wagging what was left of her tail and smiled. "There definitely is a story here. Hank, do you have time for a cup of coffee?"

"No thanks. I better get home and get milking done."

He walked to his truck and as he opened the door he looked at my mother and asked, "Say, Mike said Shorty might be available to help me out during haying. Do you think that would be possible?"

"I don't see why not," Mom replied.

I felt a little more at ease with the idea now myself.

"We'll see," Hank said.

"Don't forget the crutches," Mom said.

"No, that's alright, we have no use for them."

Mom waved and thanked Hank again as he drove out the driveway.

Then she turned to me and gave me that look. That glad to see you, but you have some explaining to do look.

"I've been worried sick, come on in, and let's see what we can do with that ankle."

We went inside and Mom heated some water and poured it into a bucket. She placed the bucket in front of me and I gently tried to put my foot into the hot water. It took quite a few times of dipping my foot in and out of the water before I got used to the temperature. Mom pulled up a chair and sat next to me.

"I knew you were going to search for Blackie. Now tell me where did you find her?"

I told her the entire story, except for the part of spying on old man Jason and the episode with the shotgun. When I finished, Mom sighed, and put her hands on my head and ruffled my hair.

"Your home and Blackie is back, and someday I'll get the rest of the story."

After supper I went directly to bed. When Mom came to tuck me in she brought a glass of water and a couple aspirins.

"Here take these, they'll help reduce the pain and let you sleep easier."

She then sat on the side of my bed and took my temperature.

"How's the ankle feeling?"

"It hurts some, but feels a lot better than it did."

She brushed my hair back and gave me a kiss on the forehead.

As she closed the door she said, "Sleep tight and don't let the bed bugs bite."

We didn't have bed bugs, but that was one of my mother's favorite sayings after she tucked you in and turned off the lights.

"Mom, how can a person go for five years without talking? That seems impossible."

The question was enough to prompt my mother to come back in and sit on the bed beside me.

"Before the accident, both Joan and Hank were considered by everyone to be hard working, good, decent people. Like I told you since their son's death people have left them alone, but stories have surfaced about them. You're familiar with some of the stories. One thing I do know is that no one knows how they would react if the same things happened to them. If anyone says they do, I think most of them would be grasping for straws. For whatever reason, Joan has decided not to speak. How long that may continue I have no idea, but one thing we know for certain is that Joan not being able to speak didn't stop her and Hank from helping you and Blackie out today."

"You're sure right about that."

"Now you try and get some sleep. I've got to go over and thank them tomorrow. Mike can drive me over before he goes to work, or I can walk. I'll bake them a pie or something."

As I lay in bed the realization that Mrs. Raycart spoke to me kept me awake. What did she mean when she said, *watch that river*. I didn't care if she hadn't spoken for twenty years, she was serious. What was Mrs. Raycart doing out in the river, in the rain? I recalled Mr. Raycart telling his wife that she had to quit wandering off like that. So it must not have been the first time. What about Jason, what was he hunting for? Did he see me?

I sat up in bed, grabbed the crutches, and walked to the window. I pulled the curtain back and looked over the swamp. Mrs. Raycart was not afraid of the river and Hank said she was always wandering off.

Was it Mrs. Raycart who followed me home that night? She sure had the ability. Was she chasing me or protecting me? When she said *watch that river*, did she really mean to say that she was watching the river.

Chapter Seven
Memories

The rain started to fall again when Hank left Mike and Maddie's. As he turned from their driveway onto the road towards home, uncontrolled tears began to blur his vision. Tears that came not because of pain or sorrow, but tears that are released because there is a possibility of returning to what once was. His wife spoke today, and it was the first time he had heard her voice since John's funeral. Could this mean that she was going to let herself return?

It was a short drive home and Hank didn't brush away the tears. Instead he let them run down his cheeks and with them came the memories.

He and his brother Sam had ended up in this part of Wisconsin as hired men working on farms in the area. Sam was a couple of years older and was more interested in just making it from day to day. Hank, however, saw beauty in the land and felt a sense of accomplishment from working the earth. He saved every penny he could and took out a loan to buy the farm by Fox River.

Then it came to his mind as if it just happened yesterday. He was driving to his new farm, and was approaching the Fox River Bridge, when four Black Angus heifers came out of the ditch and ran across the road in front of him. He slowed down to allow the cattle to pass and saw a girl running behind them in hot pursuit. Hank stopped his car and the girl waved at him as she darted across the road.

"Can you give me a hand? Just stand in the road and don't let them get by you when I bring them back," she said.

That was easy enough. Hank watched as the girl ran along the road and got in front of the escaped cattle. She stopped in front of the cattle and put her hands on her hips. The four Angus stopped and stared at the girl. She then raised her hand and pointed in the direction they had just come.

"Now it's time to quit playing and get back home," she said. Obeying her command, the cattle turned and started to walk back. When they saw Hank they turned and walked across the road into the ditch. The girl smiled at Hank as she calmly followed the cattle.

"Thanks, I think they're ready to go home now."

Hank walked beside her and introduced himself, and asked if he could help. He watched as the cattle found the break in the fence and walked through it. He then helped her fix the fence by holding the barb wire tight as she stapled it back to the post. He remembered her every movement. She was magnetic, they were meant to be together. They both loved to work the land and this love made them inseparable.

They had so many good times. Even during challenging times, when it was a struggle to meet mortgage payments, she never lost her passion for life. This passion pulled them through the hard times, and they established a very nice farm. They made friends with all their neighbors and were always the first to help out when a neighbor came on hard times. Joan brought a spirit of determination and Hank got his energy from that spirit.

Everyone knew that Joan had a hard life growing up, but she wasn't bitter, and she never dwelt on the past or hard times. She had an inner strength that helped her pull through the difficult times, and was able to use that strength to help others see the positive side.

Hank pictured her sitting with him late into the night when they found out that their first son had polio.

"Hank, we have to accept this. Hank Junior will get strong and be able to overcome this curse. We must provide strength for him to pull from. I know we can do it," she said.

Hank could feel her light touch on his shoulder and her gentle kiss on his forehead.

"Everything will be alright," she told him.

Everything did seem to improve. Their other son John was free of polio, and Hank Junior was getting stronger. Hank pictured the birthday parties and the cakes Joan would bake and serve at the table by the river. They were great times and Hank smiled through his tears.

Then his memory spun into that terrible year. They lost their baby girl two days after she was born and six months later Hank Junior died. Not from the polio, but Doctor Thompson said it was from pneumonia. His young body wasn't strong enough to handle both. Hank pictured that day at the hospital. He wasn't able to bring up a picture in his mind of Hank Junior, but he could see Joan. She was sitting on the side of his bed. He watched as Joan released her son's hand and her chin sunk to her chest. Hank remembered helping his wife to her feet and letting her lean on him as they left the room.

Her inner strength had been drained from her that day. She stopped speaking and tried to hide inside herself. Hank remembered the funeral and the burial of their son Hank Junior next to his baby sister, Anne. He could see the coffin being lowered into the earth and saw the new grass that had grown over the grave next to it. Joan was holding onto his arm and he felt her start to collapse. He put his arm around her and supported her through the remainder of the funeral. Hank saw her face flash before him. She had a blank look, and her normal gleaming green eyes became dull. Hank knew that part of her was being buried that day.

The weeks that followed the funeral were fragmented recollections. Joan stopped speaking and Hank could see her sitting on the porch swing or on a chair by the river. He and John would make the meals and he could see their son John carrying a plate to his mother.

"Please eat something, Mom," John would say.

When she didn't respond he could see his son take the fork from the plate and feed his mother. Hank could even make out his son's voice when he brought the plate back into the kitchen.

"Dad, is Mom dying?"

Then Hank remembered the barn door opening and Joan standing there. He and John had just finished with milking and were getting ready to go back to the house. The words she spoke to him will be in his memory for all times.

"I'm so sorry to both of you. I know I've let you down. I miss Hank Junior very much. I thank you so much for letting me work through this. John, you'll no longer have to bring plates to me, but I will always have one for you."

Hank could see her running into the barn and felt her fall into his arms. She was openly crying and the three of them huddled together for some time. It was a moment of rebirth for Joan and her family. Hank pictured the smile and tears on John's face. He had his mother back.

They did make it through and then...and then...

Hank pulled the truck over to the side of the road and stopped. He leaned his head back and pushed his arms against the steering wheel. He realized that

Joan might not make it back this time, and as he sat there staring into the rain a feeling of loss and blame came over him.

As he had done so many times in the past five years, he ran that dreadful day through his mind. He saw John standing in front of him.

"Dad, Mom said it's alright for me to go do some ice fishing. You wanna come along?"

"No thanks, buddy, Peaches is ready to have her calf anytime. I better stick around in case she needs some help. You catch us some supper, and hopefully we'll have a new calf for you to take care of when you get back."

Hank spoke out loud. "Why? Why didn't I go with?"

Then his mind returned to Joan. She spoke today. She will have supper on the table. Maybe having Shorty around will help her work things through.

Hank knew that Joan was becoming more and more distant. He knew that some of his neighbors were becoming afraid of her and that the rumors were growing. When he went into town for groceries, Joan would just sit in the truck. Often he would hear murmurs suggesting that she was possessed and should be put away before her and those dogs hurt someone.

A larger concern for Hank was that she was starting to wander off more frequently. She would always be somewhere along the river, but he couldn't help but always think the worse. He was convinced that Joan wouldn't hurt anyone, and as for the dogs, if no one harmed Joan, there would be no problem with the dogs.

He would never forget that day. It was the first day that Joan had wandered off; it had only been a week since John was buried. He ran up river searching for her and found her kneeling in the melting snow beside the two dogs. The dogs didn't look like they had much life left in them, but when he helped his wife home the dogs managed to follow. Joan nursed them both back to health, and they have been by her side ever since.

The dogs made Hank feel more secure. It wasn't possible for him to be with his wife every minute of the day, but he knew the dogs would always protect her.

He realized that some people thought his wife should be placed in a home. If that ever happened, he didn't know what he would do. Without her, there was no reason for the farm, or anything else. He had to find someway to get her back before something terrible happened.

He put the truck in gear and finished the drive home.

When he walked in the house his wife had the table set and supper on. Hank kissed his wife on the forehead and sat down.

"Joan, I think I'm going to have Shorty come and help with haying this year. He could help you stack the hay. Do you think that would be alright?"

Joan didn't respond, but Hank had become use to the silence. Joan was still with him, and that is what was most important. He could care less what people thought. When he opened the kitchen door to go to the barn he turned and watched his wife clear the table. The table always had three plates set. When she cleared the unused plate from the table she carried it to the sink and looked out the window toward the river. She then scraped the food off and put the dish in the sink.

As Hank walked to the barn he remembered that he had taken the phone out. He would get it reconnected, so he could call in case he decided to ask Shorty to help with haying.

Chapter Eight
A Visit to the Doctor

When I woke the next morning, Blackie was lying at the foot of my bed. She was glad to be home, and crawled up beside me licking my face in appreciation. I swung my legs over the side of the bed and tried to put pressure on the bad ankle, but the pain made me sit back down.

I managed to get dressed and made my way down stairs using the crutches for support. Mom, true to her word, was in the kitchen making pies.

"Sit down, Shorty, and let's have a look at that ankle," she said.

She carefully took my ankle in her hands and moved it in a circle trying her best not to cause too much pain. The swelling had gone down and the skin was taking on a yellowish-black color. However, even with my mother's careful examination, there were tender areas that caused me to flinch and Mom detected each involuntary movement.

"I don't think it's broke," she said.

"Do you think we might have to cut it off?" It was Dad.

Mom told him what happened last night when he returned from work. They agreed to make the decision this morning on whether or not to take me to the doctor.

Dad knelt on the floor beside Mom to get a better look. "What do you think, Maddie?"

"I don't know. Maybe we should take him in, just to be sure."

"I don't think it's broke," I said.

My opinion didn't seem to matter and Mom walked into the kitchen to call Doctor Thompson's office. In the meantime Dad was checking Blackie's condition.

"She sure does look like she got in a fight with something. Maddie said you found her tangled with some wire by Jason Abner's place. I don't trust that old bastard. Shorty, you stay away from his place." He looked at me and didn't wait for a response. "Joan sure did a good job cleaning her up. Your mother's right, we have to go over and thank her."

"Doctor Thompson can see him this morning. Let's take him in," Mom said.

Dad went outside to do my chores and Mom gave me a bowl of cereal. She helped my brother and sister get dressed, and we were ready to go by the time Dad returned. She wrapped a towel around two of the pies and put them in a box.

"We can stop in at the Raycarts' when we come back," Mom said.

Mom was a whirlwind, doing four things at once. She was on a mission and my dad knew it. He picked up the pies and handed me the crutches.

"Let's go kids before the bus leaves without us."

Doctor Thompson's office was in Middleton, which was about ten miles away. We were there by nine and were the only ones in the office. The receptionist was Doctor Thompson's wife, Betty. She was very nice and all the kids loved her because she tried to make the visit with the doctor as comfortable as possible. Plus she always had some kind of candy in her desk drawer to pass out.

"I hear Shorty hurt his ankle. What are the Braves going to do if he's not ready for the World Series?" Mrs. Thompson said.

"That's a good point, Betty. We're counting on Doc to fix him up," Dad said.

Betty gave each of the kids a piece of candy and then opened a door to one of Doctor Thompson's waiting rooms and directed us inside. Mom and I went in and Dad stayed in the waiting room with my brother and sister.

"Shorty, you sit over here and I'll get the doctor," Mrs. Thompson said.

It wasn't long before the doctor walked in. Doctor Thompson had on a long white smock, which buttoned down the front. However, he never took the time to button it and it always took the shape of a cape as he walked around the office. A stethoscope hung from his neck, and was always ready for instant use. He always had glasses, but only wore them when he was reading or looking at something that required some magnification. The rest of the time they were either resting on the top of his head or he was chewing on one of the bows while making a diagnosis. He reminded me of a professor or some famous scientist. He always seemed to be in good humor and never had a problem finding the right words to say.

"Good morning, Maddie. Good morning, Shorty."

He then had me sit on the examination table, and before I could settle into a comfortable position he put a thermometer in my mouth.

"Keep that under your tongue for a few seconds, Shorty." Then he turned to my mother and asked what happened.

Mom told him that I had twisted it yesterday while searching for my dog in a rainstorm. He turned back to me and took the thermometer out of my mouth. He shook it a few times and took the glasses off his forehead, so he could see the results. Then he took my wrist in his hand and read my pulse. He put the stethoscope to his ears and had me breathe in and out as he moved it across my back and chest.

"It all sounds good to me. Now let's check that ankle."

I thought we should have probably done that first. I must have rolled my eyes because when I glanced at my mother she was giving me that stern look. You know the look, where she partially closes one eye and tilts her head slightly to the side. Doctor Thompson pulled up a small stool and sat down in front of me. He slowly took my sock off, and then took my foot in his hand and slowly moved it in a clockwise motion.

"How does that feel, Shorty?"

"Okay," I said.

However, I knew he was going to find a location that wasn't going to be okay, and it didn't take him long. He didn't need to ask how it felt either, because the way I jerked my foot from his grasp gave every indication that it hurt. He then stood up and turned to face my mom.

"I don't think it's broken, but I'd like to take an X-ray to be sure."

Mom shook her head in agreement. He had me get off the examination table and handed me the crutches.

"Follow me, Shorty. We'll get a picture."

We went into an adjoining room and he had me sit on another examination table. He placed a plate under my ankle and swung the X-ray taking device over my ankle. He placed a heavy lead mat over my legs and told me to be still. Then he went behind a screen and pressed a button that generated the X-ray machine. He did this three times, each time placing my ankle in a different position.

"We're done, Shorty. You go back and sit with your mother, I'll be right out."

I went back to the next room and sat quietly beside my mom. We exchanged smiles, but didn't speak. It was as if we were in some sort of sanctuary and I guess in a way we were. My parents put as much trust in Doctor Thompson as they did Pastor Wilcox. Doctor Thompson returned in a short while.

"It's not broken, just a good sprain, but Shorty will have to stay off it for a few days to let it heal. I'll give you some pills to help relieve any pain he may have. Keep the ankle elevated as much as possible and soak it in warm water with Epson salts three times a day. Time is the best healer, and Shorty will know how much to use it as it strengthens. He'll be shedding those crutches before you know it. I didn't know you had a set of crutches, Maddie."

"Oh, we don't. Hank Raycart gave them to Shorty when he brought him home last night," Mom said.

Doctor Thompson then sat at the counter and started to count pills from a bottle as he placed them in a small envelope. When he finished he turned in his stool and handed the envelope to my mother.

"Have Shorty take two of these before he goes to bed." He then took his glasses from the top of his head and started to rap the bows against his teeth. He appeared to be thinking strongly about something. "How's Hank and Joan doing?"

"I haven't seen Joan and only saw Hank for a few minutes last night. He looks fine, but you can tell he's aging faster than normal. We're going to stop by at their place on the way home to thank them for helping Shorty."

Doctor Thompson sat quietly for a few seconds and then he looked at Mom. "Maddie, would you mind if I call you later on today to see how you think Joan is doing?"

"Not at all, but why, is something wrong?"

"No, it's just for my benefit. Both Joan and Hank lost trust in me when Hank Junior died. I went to see them about a year after John's accident and suggested to Hank that he should take Joan into St. Paul for psychological help. I told him I would arrange an appointment with a respected psychologist. I know it's a field of medicine that most around here know little of, but she needs professional help, and care. Hank asked me if I could guarantee that he'd be able to bring her home from such a visit. I had to be honest, and told him that they would want to keep her under their care for treatment and testing until she was well enough to return home, but he would be allowed to schedule visits. Hank wanted no part of that and told me that they would manage. That's the last time I saw either one of them."

Mom detected the concern in Doctor Thompson's voice.

"You don't think Joan could hurt herself?"

"Maddie, I don't know, but I do know that it's not natural for a person to retreat into themselves as Joan has done. I believe that whatever is keeping her silent is building up inside her mind. Someday it's going to come to the surface, and when she relieves whatever is being stored inside, I have no idea what form it will take. And yes, she could hurt herself, or God forbid, someone else."

Mom listened intently and after a short moment responded by quietly saying "oh."

"That's enough of this, now you get this young man home, so he can rest up and enjoy the rest of his summer vacation. Please call me if you have the time." He then opened the door and Mom and I walked out.

The waiting room was beginning to fill. Dad was at a corner table coloring with my brother and sister. He stood when we walked out and Doctor Thompson gave him a short wave.

"He'll be good as new in a few days, Mike."

He then turned to his wife and said. "Who's next, Betty?"

On the ride home, my mother was unusually quiet. It was a little after eleven when we drove into town. Dad saw his younger brother Ronnie at the gas station and pulled his car along side of Ronnie's.

"Maddie, I can still catch the guys for a ride to work. Would it be alright if Ronnie gives you a ride home?"

"That's fine with me, but aren't you tired?" Mom asked.

"I'll be okay. I can catch some sleep on the ride to work." Then he yelled at Ronnie who was sitting on the hood of his car flirting with some girls. "Hey, Ronnie, you got time to give Maddie and the kids a ride home?"

"Sure, no problem."

We all transferred to Ronnie's car. Mom sat in front and the rest of us climbed in back. No fancy turns on this trip. Ronnie watched his speed and took extra care to respect all driving rules. When we reached the road that led to our house Mom stopped Ronnie from turning.

"No, Ronnie, run me up to the Raycarts quick. I want to drop off these pies."

"Okay, Maddie, but what for?" Ronnie asked.

"Hank and Joan helped Shorty out last night and I want to stop by and thank them." Mom felt that Ronnie was being somewhat hesitant. "It won't take long, Ronnie. Is there something wrong?"

Ronnie wasn't very good at hiding his emotions, and it was easy to tell that he was becoming nervous as we approached the Raycarts' farm. He pulled in the driveway and stopped in front of the house. No one was around and Ronnie gave a sigh of relief.

"We might as well go, don't think anyone is home," Ronnie said.

"Wait, I see someone coming up from the river," Mom said.

We all turned to look and saw Hank Raycart leading his wife by the hand, and the dogs were walking close behind. They passed in front of our car and Hank opened the screen door for Joan. She went inside the porch and sat on the swing. In the meantime Mom had gotten out of the car. She gathered the pies in her arm and walked around the car toward the porch. The dogs ignored my mother, but they didn't go under the porch. Instead they stood and started to growl, while staring in the direction of Ronnie's car. Hank watched the dogs and looked closely at Ronnie. He turned to greet my mother, but never completely took his eyes off of Ronnie.

"How's Shorty doing?" Hank asked.

"He's fine. We just got back from Doctor Thompson's. You were right, it's not broken, just a bad sprain, but we wanted to be sure."

"That's good news," Hank said.

"I hope you don't mind us dropping in like this. We sure want to thank you for helping Shorty last night. I have a couple of extra pies and was hoping you would allow me to leave them. I know it isn't much."

"Nonsense, that's very thoughtful, isn't it, Joan?" Mrs. Raycart continued to sit in the swing and sway back and forth. "Please come in."

Mom walked up the steps and went inside. Ronnie was gripping the steering wheel so tight that his fingers were turning white. He stared straight ahead and a bead of sweat formed on his forehead and slowly ran down the side of his face. In a few minutes Mom came back outside and got in the car. Before she even leaned back in her seat Ronnie was backing out the driveway. The dogs followed the car to the road and watched as we drove away.

"What happened, Mom?" I asked.

"I don't think Joan knew I was there. When I touched her arm to thank her, it was cold. She didn't move the entire time I sat by her. It was sad."

She then turned to Ronnie. "Ronnie, what's wrong, what did you do?"

Ronnie looked like he was going to throw-up. When we got to our house, Ronnie came inside and sat at the kitchen table. Mom pulled out a chair and sat next to him. The silence was deafening, and my mother sat quietly waiting for Ronnie to say something.

"Maddie, please believe me, I didn't mean any harm. It was stupid," Ronnie said.

"What happened, Ronnie?" Mom asked.

Ronnie spoke very quietly, almost whispering, as he confessed to my mother. Apparently it had been going on for some time. Teenagers would park by the Fox River Bridge late at night, and then make a game of seeing who could get the closest to the Raycarts' house before the dogs detected their presence. No one had the nerve to walk in the driveway, because they knew the dogs would catch them. So they threw rocks from the road toward the house until the dogs became aware of their presence, and then ran like hell when the dogs started to come.

"Last Tuesday night me and some friends parked by the bridge around one in the morning. We did the usual thing, and walked up the road until we were about twenty feet from the driveway entrance. We threw some rocks toward the house, but no dogs answered our challenge, so we walked back to the car. We were listening to the radio and trying to figure out what to do next. The two guys sitting in the back were joking around and then Ken, who was sitting behind me, became very silent. I swear he turned as white as a ghost, and his eyes were fixed on the back door window that was next to the ditch. We all turned to look, and there was Mrs. Raycart, stooped over and staring at us through the open window. How could she walk up on us like that without being detected?" Ronnie said.

"What happened next?" Mom asked.

"I think I panicked. I started the car and turned on the headlights, and saw the dogs standing on the road in front of us. They were spaced evenly across the road, and I didn't know what to do, so I took off. I think I hit something. I thought I ran over one of the dogs, but all the dogs were there today. What could I have hit?

Ronnie sat quietly for a while replaying the incident in his mind and then looked at Mom.

"I'm so stupid; I didn't mean to hurt anyone. I drove by the next day to check the area, but there were no signs of anything unusual. It was as if nothing happened. Maddie, I'll never be a part of anything like that again. You have my word on it."

"I know you won't, Ronnie. We all do stupid things in our lives that we regret later. Too often we find out that what we have done has hurt other people. We didn't mean to hurt anyone and we wish that we could take that moment back and everything would be forgotten. But we can't. It's done, and life moves on. We have to learn from it and hope our stupid act will make us a better person. I believe you've learned such a lesson."

Mom stood up and walked to the sink. "Ronnie, did you see Hank?" she asked.

"No, I didn't see anyone besides Mrs. Raycart and her dogs, honest."

"No, Ronnie, I mean today, he was watching you the entire time we were there."

"I know," Ronnie said. "I know."

Mom then switched the conversation to something more digestible. She noted that the weather was changing and Ronnie and I would be helping Uncle Joe hay again soon.

"Ronnie, you'll probably have to do twice as much work because Shorty isn't going to be much help because of his ankle."

Ronnie turned his attention to me.

"Joe will most likely have you stand on the hill, so you can give Ma hand signals when she pulls the hay into the barn. Just remember to make sure she's watching you, or she'll pull the hay through the other end of the barn," Ronnie said.

I laughed at Ronnie's comment, but I could see Grandma doing just that. It wasn't at all out of the question, Grandma was a day dreamer. Ronnie thanked my mother again as he was leaving, and we heard the gravel spray as he spun out of the driveway. Mom shook her head as she watched the cloud of dust drift into the woods.

"We'll have to talk about that next time. Now let's get that ankle of yours soaking."

Mom placed a bucket of hot water on the floor in front of me, and I was trying my best to force my foot into the scalding remedy when the phone rang. Mom answered, it was Doctor Thompson.

After a brief exchange of greetings, I heard my mother say. "No nothing unusual, she just doesn't speak. They both looked healthy enough. The house was very neat and the place isn't run down at all."

Mom was silent for a few minutes and when she spoke again the tone of her voice had become more expressive.

"I don't believe they would hurt anyone. As for visiting Hank, I'm sure he'll listen to you, but I won't guarantee that he'll say what you want to hear. I guess it wouldn't hurt to try, especially if you have their best interest in mind."

Not to long after that she politely ended the conversation.

"You're welcome. Please let me know if I can be any help."

After she hung up the phone she came into the living room to see how I was making out. I noticed the look of concern on her face and I asked if something was wrong.

"No, just thinking. Sometimes we think too much, and only make matters worse than what they really are. Joan may have developed a strange way to live out her life, but I'm convinced she or Hank wouldn't deliberately hurt anyone. How's the ankle feeling?"

"Not bad, but I think putting it in the hot water hurts worse than trying to walk on it."

I was trying to make a point, but Mom wasn't listening. The phone conversation with Doctor Thompson had caused her thoughts to be directed elsewhere.

Chapter Nine
Back to Normal

The weather cleared and the next three days I spent at Uncle Joes haying. Ronnie was right; Uncle Joe positioned me so that I could give hand signals to my grandma as she drove the tractor.

Grandpa brought the loaded wagons of hay in from the field and parked them in the middle of a drive located at one end of the barn. Uncle Joe would then pull the hay fork down so it rested on top of the bales. He pushed the tongs of the fork into the bales. Then he stepped out of the way in case one of the bales came loose and fell as it was being pulled up. When he was in a safe position he would wave at me, and I would signal Grandma to start driving the tractor forward. The tractor was connected to a heavy rope, which was strung through a series of pulleys and attached to the hay fork. When Grandma drove the tractor forward the bales would lift off the wagon and when the fork reached the top of the barn it would clasp onto a rail that extended the length of the haymow and ride along the rail until it reached a position where Uncle Joe wanted to drop the hay. He would then signal me, and I would signal Grandma to stop. Then Uncle Joe would give a quick jerk on the rope attached to the fork, which caused the fork tongs to come out of the bales, and the bales would fall to the hay barn floor.

The unloading was going along smoothly, and it looked like we had developed a very efficient operation. The sun continued to shine and Grandma was getting warm. I'm sure there were places that she wanted to be other than sitting on the tractor in the hot sun. On the tenth load of the day, the inevitable happened, Grandma loss focus. Uncle Joe was sticking the fork in the hay and for some reason Grandma thought it was time to drive ahead. She let the tractor clutch out and started to move forward. The bales started to lift off the wagon and Uncle Joe was going up with the hay. He yelled at me, and I yelled at Grandma, but she kept going. I took off toward the tractor as fast as I could get those crutches to move, yelling as I hopped along. Grandma finally noticed me and stopped. She had driven far enough forward so that she could see the wagon being unloaded. A look of desperation came over her face when she saw the predicament she had placed her son in. Uncle Joe was still on top of the hay, but he was now thirty feet off the ground. If Grandma had driven forward five more feet Uncle Joe would have had to make a major decision on whether to jump or ride it out. Either way would have been a precarious choice.

Grandma was a bundle of nerves, and looked to me for advice as I approached the tractor. "Shorty, what do I do now?"

"Just don't move, Grandma, don't move, I'll check with Uncle Joe."

I walked to the hay barn and looked up at Uncle Joe.

"What do we do now?" I asked.

Uncle Joe's hat had come off and he was sitting in the center of the bales with his hair blowing in the breeze. There was no doubt that he was between a rock and a hard place, but he responded to my question by laughing as he waved at his mother, who was frozen in place on the tractor seat.

"Do you think Ma can back up slow and easy and let me down?" he asked.

I looked at him, then looked at my grandma, and shrugged my shoulders. "She's pretty nervous," I said.

"I think you're right about that, I better try and find another way off this perch."

He carefully stood on the bales and raised his arms above his head. His hands were about a foot below a beam that ran below the roof. He started to squat and then rose quickly and jumped for the beam. The pressure of him kicking off from the bales caused three bales to come loose from the fork and fall to the ground, but there he was hanging from the beam, thirty feet in the air. He hung motionless for a short time and then swung his legs up so they wrapped around the beam. He then slowly shimmied along the beam until he reached the side of the barn. The side wall had six inch wide beams, spaced five feet apart that ran horizontally across the wall. He held onto one beam and walked along the lower beam until he came to the corner of the barn. At the corner were two poles that ran vertically from the floor to the roof. These poles had cross members, which he used like a ladder to get to the ground. When he safely reached the bottom he put his back against the wall and slid down until he was sitting on the ground. Beads of sweat dripped from his forehead, and he let out a big sigh of relief. I couldn't help but let out a sigh of relief myself when he reached the floor.

"I'm definitely too old for this kind of stuff. How's Ma doing?"

"I think she's frozen to the steering wheel. She hasn't budged," I said.

"Let's go and see if we can unthaw her."

I don't think my grandma had moved a muscle. Her hands were clasped securely around the steering wheel, one foot had the clutch pressed to the floorboard, and the other foot had the brake pedal depressed as far as it would go. Come hell or high water she wasn't going to let off on either one of them. As we approached she looked at Uncle Joe and shook her head.

"You all right?" she asked.

"I'm fine. How are you?"

"I've been better. Now can I get off of this thing? I need a drink of water."

Not needing any approval, she took the tractor out of gear, stepped to the ground and walked toward the house.

"We never had these kinds of problems with horses," she said as she walked away.

Uncle Joe laughed quietly as he watched his mother walk toward the house.

"Hey, Ma, are you done for the day?"

Grandma turned and extended her arms to the heavens in response to the question. The turn of events had drained her more than the summer heat. She started to speak, but nothing came out. She was going to the house, and yes, she was done for the day.

"Well, Shorty, it's me and you, are you up to it?"

"I can try."

"Can't ask for any more than that. Let's do it."

By the end of the day my ankle was pretty sore from pushing against the clutch, but we got all the hay unloaded. We were sitting on the lawn when Grandma came out of the house carrying a bowl of ice cream.

"Thanks, Shorty, you were sure a trooper today. Let's cool that ankle off from the inside," Grandma said.

Ronnie was lying on the grass and rolled over on his side. "Hey, Ma, me and Joe was wondering if you could arrange to be available this weekend."

"Depends on what for," Grandma asked.

"Well," Ronnie continued, "Middleton has their fair this weekend, and me and Joe figured we could make some extra money by having the kids come out here. We could charge them a quarter each to take your hay barn ride."

"Very funny, I'm just lucky I have a monkey for a son," Grandma said as she looked at Uncle Joe, and smiled.

Joe was lying in the grass wrestling with his dog, Red. They were both having a good time. They were good for each other.

The next three days went much smoother. My ankle improved each day and by the last day of haying I was able to put all my weight on it. The last bale was in the hay barn by one in the afternoon on Saturday, and Uncle Joe was a happy man. It was a good feeling to have that job behind you, knowing that you had a crop in the barn that would help you get your cows through the winter months.

To celebrate Uncle Joe arranged to take me to the Middleton fair that afternoon. He would spend the afternoon at the fair and then return home for milking. My parents were going to meet us there and I could ride home with them.

During the summer months most small towns have fairs. A carnival would roll into town and set up rides, games of chance, and all kinds of food stands. Each town also provided their own food stands and bakery sales as a way for church and school organizations to make some extra money. There were pancake feeds in the morning and steak fries in the afternoon. If a person didn't gain a few extra pounds during fair weekend, it was their own fault.

There were all types of exhibits, each representing a certain part of our rural life. Each exhibit provided blue ribbons for what they considered the best. They had blue ribbons to award for everything from the best choke cherry jam to the most exquisite quilt, or the largest pig. It was a community event that provided a means for people to relax and mingle with their neighbors. It brought farmers and the town people together, and they swapped stories and competed against each other in all types of contest. There were events such as tractor pulls and log cutting contest for the men, and grease pig catching and grease pole climbing for the kids.

We arrived in Middleton at one thirty in the afternoon. The first thing that caught your attention was the Ferris wheel, because it was the tallest ride, and was usually located in the center of the carnival. Uncle Joe gave me five dollars and told me to have a good time. My parents were going to arrive in the afternoon and I was suppose to meet them between four and four thirty at the beer garden.

The beer garden was where most of the adults ended up. The American Legion and the Veterans of Foreign Wars managed the beer garden, and they had large cattle tanks strategically placed under a large tent. The tanks were filled with ice water and the beer was submerged in the tanks to keep it cool. Around the perimeter of the tent a bar was constructed from wood planks. Tickets were purchased from a stand at the side of the garden, which removed the need for having to exchange money at the bar. The bartenders, all wearing their American Legion or Veterans hats would take your ticket and set you up with a bottle of beer.

Uncle Joe headed toward the beer garden, and I headed for the midway. I had five dollars and it was burning a hole in my pocket. I met some friends and together we walked the midway. I bought a foot long hot dog and a coke, took a ride on the tilt-a-whirl, and then tried to win a teddy bear.

There were all types of games of chance, but my favorite game was trying to knock stuffed cats off a wall. The cloth cats were placed side by side on three rows of shelves which were about fifteen feet away from you. You purchased three balls for a quarter and if you knocked off three stuffed cats you won your choice of the various stuffed animals they had hanging around the sides of the tent. It looked easy enough and I thought it would be nice to win a teddy bear for my younger brother and sister.

It took a direct hit in the center of the cat to make it topple off the shelf. I did my best, but the most I could ever manage to knock off was two, so instead of a teddy bear my pockets were full of the second prize rubber spiders and I had strings of beads hanging around my neck. It was going on four and I had a quarter left, but I decided to use it to buy a bottle of pop at the beer garden.

As I approached the beer garden I spotted my parents sitting under a shade tree talking with some friends. Everyone was having a good time.

There was a ruckus going on at one of the picnic tables and whatever it was had drawn a crowd. When I got closer I saw that Bruce Wright was taking on all comers in arm wrestling. He had just defeated a very powerful looking man and was laughing and having a good time. The man stood up and slapped Bruce on the shoulder.

"Here you go," the man said as he handed Bruce a dollar and stepped to the side.

I sat on the ground next to my parents and gave my second prize trinkets to my brother and sister. The way they jumped up and down you would have thought I had given them each a twenty dollar bill. Uncle Joe came over and sat with us.

"Well, Shorty, you want to come home and help with chores, since you're busted?" he asked.

"Might as well," I said.

I said goodbye to my parents, and was getting up to leave when we noticed that the group gathered around the picnic table were becoming more vocal. We walked over to see what was going on and saw that Bruce had apparently met his match. Max Strum was Bruce's competitor, and they were locked in a heck of a duel. The strain of possible defeat was showing on Bruce's face, and Max was close to victory. Bruce's hand was about three inches from the table and defeat. Then out of the blue he gave a yell and slowly began to push Max's arm up. There was no stopping Bruce now. Each wrestler looked as if their veins were going to burst as they strained against the force of the other. Max's hand began to tremble as he desperately tried to overcome Bruce's renewed energy. Then Max's arm gave way, and Bruce slammed Max's hand to the table. Bruce shook his head, and reached out to shake Max's hand.

"I thought you had me, Max."

However, Max didn't want any part of Bruce's offer. He pushed Bruce's arm away and threw a dollar on the table.

"Next time I'll get ya," Max said.

"Maybe, but not today, Max, old buddy. That one wore me out, think I'll take the rest of the evening off and do some recuperation," Bruce said.

A look of disappointment came over Max's face; he had come within three inches of victory only to be denied. He wanted to do something to show the group that he deserved some kind of respect. As he tipped a bottle of beer to his lips he saw an opportunity to gain respect, and at the same time get rid of some pent-up rage. A dog was walking along a fence about twenty feet away. Max watched the dog for a few seconds, and then threw the bottle at the dog. The bottle hit the dog in the back and it took off yelping. A smile formed on Max's face. He had found redemption, and he looked around the group to make sure everyone had witnessed the event.

"What in the hell you do that for, Max?"

It was Uncle Joe, and he said it loud enough so that Max was sure to hear. Max spotted Uncle Joe across the lawn and started to walk toward him at a slow deliberate pace.

"Because I felt like it, you got a problem with that?"

Max was at least six inches taller and seventy-five pounds heavier than Uncle Joe. As Max approached the size difference was very noticeable, but also evident was that Max was becoming more furious with each step. His pace quickened and when he reached Uncle Joe he thrust his arms out so that his hands slammed into Uncle Joe's shoulders and violently shoved him backwards.

"Now, Max, that dog didn't have nothing to do with you losing to Bruce. You simply got beat," Uncle Joe said as he stumbled backwards from the force of the shove.

Whether he meant to or not, I don't know, but Uncle Joe had just rubbed some salt into the wounded pride of Max. Max continued forward and shoved Uncle Joe again. Uncle Joe again stumbled backwards, but still maintained his balance. Max wasn't going to let up and with each shove his anger grew. Then as Max prepared to give Uncle Joe another shove, Uncle Joe put his hands on Max's shoulders. At first I thought he was going to try and push Max off, but instead as Max continued forward, Uncle Joe fell backwards. Max's momentum caused him to start to fall over the top of Uncle Joe. As Max fell forward, Uncle Joe put his right foot into Max's stomach and when Uncle Joe's back hit the ground, he straightened out his right leg and Max when flying over Joe like an out of control tumbler. A loud gasp escaped from Max's lungs when he landed on his back.

It was over in an instant. Uncle Joe quickly sat up and looked over his shoulder at Max. The impact of the landing had knocked the wind out of Max. Dad reached out a hand and helped his brother to his feet.

"Joe, you're getting to old for this circus stuff."

In the meantime Max was regaining his composure, and there was no way he wanted this to be over with. However, by the time he got to his feet, Bruce and Dale Wright were standing between Joe and Max. They blocked Max from continuing and forced him to the side.

"Thanks, boys. I don't have any more tricks. No hard feelings, Max, I just didn't want to take a beating before chore time and leave Shorty to do all the work," Uncle Joe said.

Dad returned to the shade tree where Mom was standing with her hands placed firmly upon her hips. Dad was shaking his head back and forth and smiling from ear to ear, but as he got closer he became well aware that his wife didn't approve.

"You know what? I think I taught Joe that move when we were kids," Dad said.

Mom shook her head in frustration. "I think you guys still act like kids. What would have been the next move you taught him?"

"I think running would have been a good next move," Dad said.

Bruce and Dale had their crowd under control, and they waved to Uncle Joe and me as we walked out of the garden. Max was standing off to the side talking with his brother Martin, and was glaring in our direction as we left.

On the way to do chores I wanted to tell Uncle Joe that I thought he was right for confronting Max for throwing the bottle at that dog, but I didn't say anything. I think he knew.

We had completed milking and were letting the cows out to pasture for the evening when my parents arrived. Apparently after we had left the fair more excitement had surfaced. A person from the city had taken on Bruce and beat him in arm wrestling. They couldn't remember his name, but they thought he was a friend of the Wright and Strum boys. Apparently he was spending money quite freely, and some of the girls were attracted to his unique behavior, which was compounded by the fancy new Thunderbird convertible he was driving.

It was a long day, but it was a fun day. When I went to bed that night, I was asleep before my head hit the pillow.

Chapter Ten
A Cemetery Visit

I awoke late Sunday morning, the previous day activities must have really tired me out. My parents were already up and sitting in the kitchen having coffee when I got downstairs. I sat at the kitchen table still wiping the sleep from my eyes.

"Morning, sleepy bones," Dad said.

"You better put it in gear, and get your chores done, so you can get ready for church," Mom said.

I didn't say anything, but my mother knew by the signals I was putting out that church was not on the top of my list of places to go. I caught her questionable glance and realized that she knew what I was thinking, so I left to do chores before the glance became words.

When I returned to the house Mom was placing the phone receiver back in its cradle.

"Shorty, that was Hank Raycart. He asked if it was alright with us if you could come over and help with haying tomorrow, if the weather holds."

Immediately upon hearing Mom's comment, a hollow feeling entered my stomach. A feeling that comes when you're about to do something new, but you're not yet comfortable with it, because it's new. I thought I had convinced myself that I could handle this job, but there were still so many unknowns that I wasn't sure I could deal with. My parents detected my apprehension and I'm sure they also had some concerns. It was a very quiet breakfast and the drive to church was equally reserved. Dad left us off at the church door, and then proceeded to Mirror Lake Tavern for his own form of spiritual awakening.

Church was a blur. I heard the pastor talking, but I didn't hear his message. My thoughts kept returning to Joan and Hank Raycart. I knew they really helped me out and there wasn't the least bit of evidence that there were any bad or misleading intentions on their part. Why then was I so worried?

While I sat in the pew, next to my mother, my eyes were attracted to the window at the end of the aisle. I could see the graveyard, and I scanned the tombstones trying to focus on the area where I thought the Raycart children were buried. I never thought much about death before. I knew it happened; it was a part of life. But it was something that happened in the distant future and I never had to deal to closely with it, or how it affected people. As I looked at the graves, I wondered how it would affect my parents if I were to suddenly die. I glanced at my mother, who seemed to be listening intently to the pastor's sermon.

I turned my attention back to the graveyard and my mothers head turned to look in the same direction. A smile formed on her face, and she placed her hand over my hand and squeezed. Since Mom's phone conversation with Doctor Thompson, I think she was beginning to have some doubts about me going to work for the Raycarts. I wondered why she didn't tell Doctor Thompson that Mrs. Raycart's arm felt cold to her touch. Maybe she felt it wasn't important, or it wasn't important that the doctor knew. I had the definite impression that Doctor Thompson still wanted Mrs. Raycart to see a psychologist, no matter what Hank thought. After all he is a doctor, and is supposed to know about these things, so why did Mom decide not to give all the information to the doctor?

I knew Hank probably needed help with haying, but that wasn't his only reason for asking me. His wife had spoken to me. I must have brought something to the surface that day in Mrs. Raycart's mind. I sensed it on that night it happened, and I was certain that Hank Raycart also sensed it. All of a sudden my train of thought was disturbed, because people were starting to file out of the church. I had missed the entire service and it didn't seem at all right. It wasn't the first time that I day dreamed through a Sunday sermon, but what bothered me was that I was thinking about important stuff. I was on summer vacation and day dreams in church were supposed to be reserved for fun things like baseball or fishing.

Mom said her hellos and goodbyes, and then we started our walk to Mirror Lake Tavern

"What did you think of the sermon?" Mom asked.

Unfair question, I thought. Mom knew I never paid much attention to any sermon and for me to form an opinion seemed unrealistic. I thought that opinions of this nature were reserved for adults who seemed to enjoy analyzing them, so they could change the opinions of others. I shrugged my shoulders in response to my mother's question, and we continued on our way.

"Do you want to visit the gravesites?" Mom asked.

"I don't know. Do you want to?"

"Yes, I think I would."

We turned around and walked back to the church. The pastor was inside talking with some members of the congregation, so we walked undetected past the church to the graveyard. We walked between the rows of tombstones and stopped when we found the Raycart graves. The graves had not been taken care of. The grass was mowed, but there were no flowers on the plots, as so many of the other gravesites had. Mom saw some wild violets growing along the fence that bordered the graveyard and walked over to pick some. When she returned she placed a handful on the top of each of the three tombstones.

The head stones were nothing special. No fancy angels or shepherds decorated the stones and just a simple verse was etched below each of the children's name.

Called from earth to be with their Loving Father in Heaven. Then below it was etched the date of birth and date of death.

I read the verse and realized that John's age when he died was the same age that I was now. Mom also realized it, and she placed her arm around my shoulder as we walked away.

"Shorty, if you don't want to help Mr. Raycart with haying you don't have to, Dad and I will understand. To tell you the truth I'm somewhat concerned with it myself. I know deep down that it's the right thing to do, and I don't feel you have anything to be afraid of, but it's that unknown of what will happen if Joan comes out of that shell she has put herself in that concerns us all."

"You don't think that she may think I'm John, do you?

Mom stopped. "I don't think so; Shorty, but something in you made her speak that day. It may have opened a door that has been closed for too long. How Joan sees the world when that door is opened is beyond any of our forecast. When I looked into her eyes that day it was like looking into a well that had no bottom. Right now she has withdrawn from this life and part of her is somewhere else. I think Hank feels that she is slipping deeper and deeper into that well, and she may be reaching a point of no return. If something in you can help bring her back, I think it's the right thing to do. I know it's a big load to put on your shoulders, but just be yourself, and I'm sure everything will work out for the best."

"Maddie." It was Pastor Wilcox calling to my mother from the church steps.

He was rapidly approaching and looked like a man on a mission. His arms swung back and forth like a pendulum keeping time with each stride as he walked across the church lawn. We stopped and waited for the wound up pastor's arrival.

"Yes, Pastor, what is it? Is there something wrong?" Mom asked.

"No…No…Nothing is wrong. I was just wondering if I could stop by and see you and Mike one day, that's all."

Mom told the pastor that she would be glad to have him stop by anytime, but warned him not to come with the idea of enticing my dad to become a regular church going member.

"I know you're more than likely working on that, Maddie, and I have complete confidence in your ability," the pastor replied.

The pastor then went on to explain that he was going to visit Mrs. Wilson next week, and since we lived right down the road he thought it would be a good idea to stop in for a visit. Mom told him that my dad was working nights and usually left between noon and one. If he came over around noon, they could have a glass of lemonade and a sandwich before my dad left for work.She told him that I probably wouldn't be home because I was going to be helping Hank Raycart with haying.

That little bit of information changed the preacher's demeanor and he seemed to take a guarded position. He folded his arms across his chest and thought for a moment.

"Shorty is kind of young to be hiring out don't you think?"

"Nonsense, Shorty is a very good worker, and any money that he is given he will definitely have earned," Mom said.

The pastor realizing that he had struck a nerve quickly proceeded to cover his tracks and tried to smooth over a bad choice of words.

"It's just with the condition of Mrs. Raycart, maybe it would be wise to have some other adults around."

The pastor had now brought the spurs out in Mom. She was trying her best to maintain self control and took a deep breath.

"I know Joan is having some problems, but we feel that Shorty will be safe while working for Hank and her. Besides it doesn't seem like many of Hank and Joan's neighbors want to help them out," Mom said.

"Maddie, I don't think it's because they don't want to; I think it's more of a case that they are not being allowed to. Joan and Hank have built a wall between themselves and the rest of our community, and for some reason their neighbors have been turned away. I pray that God will show them a way to remove that wall, or provide us with the means to do it for them."

Mom may have been placed in a position to joust with the pastor on the topic of neighborly intent, but she was going to end the conversation before something was said that she may later regret.

"I hope you're right, Pastor. There are two sides to every wall, and I'm confident God will stand on the right side, but it's some of my neighbors that I worry about. Now we better get going, Mike is waiting for us. We'll be looking forward to you dropping by next week"

She then turned and walked to the road that led to Mirror Lake Tavern and the pastor turned and walked back to Mirror Lake Church. Mom was in deep thought, and her pace quickened so much that my brother and sister had to run to keep up. I think what she whispered as we walked along was meant for her ears only, so I didn't comment.

"Some days I'm tempted to see if Mike has any more room in that congregation of his."

When we arrived at the tavern, I decided not to go in. Instead I walked to the edge of the lake and found some good stones to skip across the calm waters. I was getting into a groove and had the rocks skipping eight to ten times before submerging. It was allowing me to put aside my thoughts from church and relax and enjoy the nice summer day. It wasn't long before my parents were ready to go home. That afternoon I spent most of my time throwing the rubber ball against the barn wall. The Braves had an afternoon game and I listened to it with my dad on the front porch. They lost a close one to the Chicago Cubs. You can't win them all.

After the game I did my chores and we ate supper. After dishes were washed my parents went outside and sat on the front porch steps to talk, and enjoy the nice summer evening. It was going on nine o'clock and the night was peaceful and quiet. There wasn't any wind and the oak trees that formed a perimeter around our house stood motionless in the night air. The chirping of crickets coming from the swamp and the occasional low tone of a bullfrog from the river were at times the only sounds that disturbed the evening silence. It was getting to dark to see the ball coming off the barn wall, so I decided to call it a night. I saw my parents sitting on the porch steps and sat on the bottom step.

"What time do you think Mr. Raycart wants me to be there tomorrow?"

We hadn't talked about it since we got home, but I knew we were all thinking about it. In no way was Mom or Dad going to force the issue. They had both agreed that it should be my decision. I think I grew up some that day. Dad and Mom communicated to each other with their eyes. Dad nodded his head and Mom smiled and said.

"I'll call Hank and let him know that you'll be there, and ask what time," she said.

She went inside to make the call, and was gone for only a few minutes.

"Hank said if possible, he'd like to have you there around ten."

"That shouldn't be a problem," I said.

At nine o'clock I went upstairs to get ready for bed. As I sat on the edge of my bed my thoughts turned to the river, and I walked to the window. It was a bright night. I could easily make out the river banks and my favorite fishing spot. There wasn't any movement at all. The scene resembled a picture in an outdoor life magazine.

As I stood looking at the river, I realized that tomorrow I was going to be working with the lady who may have chased me through the swamp. What was she protecting me from that night? Or was she protecting someone she thought was her son?

Chapter Eleven
It's Just a Job

Daylight came too fast. I jumped out of bed and ran to the window. Wouldn't you know it? It was going to be a beautiful, sunny, summer day. No cancellation because of rain today.

As I did morning chores nervous anticipation began to mount concerning what the day would bring. Blackie followed me as I performed my morning task. Usually she just went where I went, but today was different. She was in a playful mood, and kept bringing this stick and dropping it at my feet. She then would sit next to the stick and wait for me to throw it. I threw the stick as far as I could, each time trying to put it in a location that would require difficulty for her to locate. However, each time she found it without a problem, and was proud as a peacock upon returning it to me. The playing, mixed in with chores, took my mind off my new ten o'clock job. With each toss of the stick I became more relaxed and ready for the day.

Blackie must have sensed that I was nervous, and was doing what she could to relieve some of the tension. It must have worked, because by the end of chores I was feeling good about the coming day. It was just going to be another haying job.

I went in for breakfast and Dad was sitting at the kitchen table. I sat next to him, and Mom set a box of cereal and a pitcher of milk on the table. She then poured her and Dad a cup of coffee, and sat at the table with us. I read the back of the corn flakes box while my parents discussed the weather, and other topics that seemed unimportant, but consumed time.

"Shorty, I'm going to drop you off at Hanks this morning on my way over to see Joe. No sense in you having to walk to a new job on your first day."

"That sounds like a good idea to me," I said.

I meant every word of it, because I couldn't see those dogs allowing me on their property if I showed up all by myself. Mom handed me a paper sack that had a couple of peanut butter sandwiches in it and a pint jar of nectar.

"I know Hank will probably feed you, but just in case, it doesn't hurt to have a little extra along for energy," Mom said.

That was Mom, being Mom, always trying to anticipate a need before it arises. At fifteen minutes before ten, Dad drove me to the Raycarts. I found my morning nervous condition returning and the intensity grew as we got closer. What if the dogs don't like me? What if I screw something up and make Mrs. Raycart mad? Then the biggest fear surfaced. What if while working with Mrs. Raycart, she decides to talk? The last time that happened, I felt she looked right through me into my soul. I think I was starting to hyperventilate, and my heavy breathing was causing me not to think straight.

Dad reached over and put his hand on my shoulder. "Shorty, it's only a job, and you're a very good worker. You just do the best you can for Hank and everything will be just fine. I trust Hank, and you owe him for helping you and Blackie out of a jam."

"You're right, Dad, and I do trust Mr. Raycart, but I'm still a little nervous."

I was getting ready to bring up the "what if scenario" of where Mrs. Raycart starts to talk, but it was too late. We were turning into their driveway. As usual the dogs were there to greet us as we drove in. Alfred Jest was in the front yard and was busy getting his equipment ready for the day. Mr. Raycart was standing next to Alfred and watched us drive in. Dad pulled up along side of where they stood and shut the car off. I followed Dad when he got out and stood next to him. Hank shook Dad's hand, and then he put his hand out to me.

"Thanks for coming, Shorty," he said.

I extended my hand towards his, and thought my hand resembled a baby's hand when wrapped in his. He gripped my hand firmly, and it made me feel good.

"You're welcome," I said.

My mouth was extremely dry and I licked my lips to see if I could bring some moisture to the surface. Alfred's usual welcoming smile was good to see, and he gave me a light slap on the shoulder.

"Hank, this here kid can work with the best of them. You made a good choice to hire him on," Alfred said.

Hank looked somewhat startled when he heard Alfred's comment.

"I'm sorry. I didn't discuss wages with Shorty. It's been so long since we've hired anyone. I don't know what a fair rate is."

Dad noticing that Hank was uncomfortable smiled and said. "Why don't you let him work and then you can settle up with what you both feel is a fair wage."

"That sounds good to me. How about you, Shorty?" Hank asked.

"Sounds good," I said. My mouth was getting dryer.

As Alfred was finishing with his equipment preparation Hank walked with my dad to the car and I was left standing in the open with the three dogs next to me. There was no way I was going to move. They didn't growl, they just maintained their position and watched. Every once in a while one would turn and look at me as if questioning why I was still there.

Dad waved when he reached his car. "Have a good day, Shorty, and remember Mom expects you home by seven to help with chores."

"Don't worry, Mike, I'll be sure he gets home on time. I promise," Hank said.

Hank walked toward me as Dad pulled out of the driveway. The dogs must have been satisfied that I wasn't a threat, because they slowly walked to the house. When they got to the house, each dog seemed to take a predetermined position on the ground in front of the porch. Mrs. Raycart was sitting on the porch swing slowly swinging back and forth while staring straight ahead.

I walked with Hank to the barn and he showed me what I was to do. It was easier to get the hay into the hay barn at Hanks than it was at Uncle Joes. There was no need to pull the hay into the barn via a fork, because the hay barn floor was only three feet off the ground. The tractor pulled the wagon loaded with hay into the hay barn driveway, so that it was next to the hay barn floor. Then the wagon was unhooked from the tractor and left to be unloaded. The bales were thrown from the wagon onto the hay barn floor, and then carried to the back of the hay barn and stacked on the floor. This was continued until you had bales stacked six feet high across the entire hay barn floor. Then an elevator was positioned, so that bales from the wagon could be placed directly on the conveyor. The bales are carried up the elevating conveyor, and fall onto the top of the bales that were previously stacked on the hay barn floor. These bales were then stacked on top of the first tier of bales.

Hank patiently explained the process to me. Hank would be loading hay in the field, and Joan and I would be unloading. In past years Joan would get the wagons unloaded and start stacking by herself, however, she could never stay ahead of the loads being brought in, so they would have to stack bales after night milking, or early the next morning.

"I should be in with the first load in about an hour. Just make yourself at home, and look around the barn and become familiar with the place," Hank said.

He then climbed on the wagon that was being pulled behind Alfred's baler, and I watched as they drove out to the field and started to bale hay. I couldn't see the house from the hay barn and I was becoming very nervous about how my first encounter with Mrs. Raycart would go.

I was standing in the hay barn drive when I caught something out of the corner of my eye walking up from the back of the barn. It was Blackie.

"Blackie, what are you doing here? I think you better get home, or these dogs are going to eat you alive."

I bent over and held her head between my two hands, and playfully shook it back and forth. "Now listen, I'm not kidding around, you got to get home."

She wagged her stub of a tail and tilted her head to one side as if to say, if you're staying, so am I. Blackie had no intention of leaving, so I had to find a place to put her before the dogs got her scent. Some baling twine was hanging on the barn wall and I decided to use it to tie Blackie in the barn so that she would be out of the way. When Hank came in with the first load I would explain the situation to him, and I was certain he would find a safe place for Blackie to stay. I took the twine off the wall, turned around and discovered that I wasn't alone anymore. Directly across the hay barn drive stood Mrs. Raycart and her three dogs. They must be able to walk as silent as cats, because I hadn't heard a sound.

I stood as still as a rock and started to chew on my lower lip. Mrs. Raycart stood in front of me like a statue, then slowly turned her head and looked from her dogs to Blackie. I tried to speak, but nothing came out. Then she started to walk towards me. As she approached I thought about making a run for it, but her three dogs had already formed a semi circle around Blackie and me. All avenues of escape or retreat had been eliminated.

Mrs. Raycart walked by me as if I was nothing more than part of the barn wall. She walked around the corner, and I heard the door open to the milk house. Her dogs remained behind, standing at their post. Blackie didn't seem to be uneasy about the situation at all and calmly sat on the floor beside me.

There was no doubt that I was nervous enough for both of us, and when I saw Mrs. Raycart return, I almost bit through my lower lip. She was carrying a pan of water and set it on the ground next to Blackie. Blackie immediately accepted the invitation and began to drink.

Her dogs had not moved while she was gone, and needless to say, I remained glued to the same spot. Mrs. Raycart watched Blackie enjoy the water for a moment, and then she stood up straight and walked to the far end of the hay barn driveway. She moved quietly across the ground and her silent steps seemed to match the unexpressive look on her face. She wore a light jacket and took it off as she walked along. When she reached the end of the hay barn drive she hung the jacket on a nail and then sat on the hay barn floor. I watched her every step. I know I was staring, but I couldn't make myself look away.

Mrs. Raycart apparently was where she wanted to be, but what about me. What was I suppose to do? I turned my head to look at the dogs and saw that they were staring at me. I got the impression that they were waiting for something. They continued to watch me and must have determined that everything was all right, or sensed that I was not a threat. One by one they left their position, and walked over to lie down by their master. As the dogs walked across the drive the one that resembled a wolf turned and looked directly at me. It had long gray hair, and her shoulders were wide and muscle bound. As we looked at each other, I saw that she had one blue eye and one grey eye. I continued to watch the dogs to determine if it was safe for me to move. It was probably only for a few minutes, but it seemed like hours, until I heard the sound of a tractor. Hank was bringing in the first load of hay.

I was never so glad to hear the sound of oncoming work as I was on that day. Hank drove the wagon into the drive and stopped. He unhitched the wagon from the tractor, and saw his wife sitting on the floor.

"Joan, it looks like you're ready to go," he said.

He then noticed Blackie sitting by my side, and smiled. "Looks like your buddy didn't want to be left home today."

While Hank was talking, his wife had climbed on the wagon and was starting to throw the bales off. Hank saw that I was intently watching her toss the bales to the hay barn floor.

"Shorty, I don't know if she realizes that you are even here, but don't worry, she won't harm you. I think the work is good for her and there was a time when she made work fun for me. If you could stack the bales at the back of the barn it'll be a great help."

I finally found my voice and told Hank that I would be all right. As Hank drove away I walked over and picked up a bale and carried it to the end of the barn. As I made my trips back and forth across the barn floor, I continued to watch Mrs. Raycart. I was beginning to paint an everlasting portrait of her in my mind.

She was tall and slender. She had on a blue jumper like dress that came down about six inches below her knees. She had long dishwater blonde hair that bounced around in the air as she tossed the bales from the wagon. The muscles in her arms flexed as she picked up the bales. The impression her legs left against the skirt as she moved across the wagon showed that she was in very good physical condition. She moved with ease and had an athletic quality in her step. Her neck was long and added to the graceful movement that her body made as she worked. I admired the fluid motion she made as she tossed the bales from the wagon.

Her face was hard to explain, but to this day I can close my eyes and trace each facial line. Her cheeks were high and there was a hollow area that followed from her cheek to her chin. Her lips were narrow and were always held tight together. She had narrow eyebrows that matched the color of her hair. Lines of worry and age crossed her brow, and crow's feet came off the corner of each eye. Her eyes were a dark green and never seemed to move, they were always focused straight ahead. When she looked somewhere she always moved her neck, so that her eyes could maintain their straight ahead focus.

She threw the bales off faster than I could get them stacked. When she finished unloading the bales, she jumped from the wagon to the hay barn floor, and without missing a beat she began to pick up the bales and carry them across the floor. She never turned to look at me when we passed each other on the hay barn floor, and I thought Hank might be right. His wife didn't know I was there.

We had the wagon unloaded and the bales stacked before Hank returned with the next load. When we finished unloading she sat by her dogs, and I sat by Blackie. There was one thing for certain; if she kept this pace up all day I was going to be one tired puppy by day's end.

When Hank brought the next load in, I unhooked the loaded wagon, and hooked the empty wagon to the tractor, so he wouldn't have to get off. He saw that his wife was already on the loaded wagon throwing bales off, and he smiled as he watched her.

"Joan doesn't let any grass grow under her feet, but you pace yourself,

Shorty, or I'll be carrying you home tonight."

I smiled at the advice and hurried over to start carrying the bales to the back of the barn. "I will, but your wife doesn't slow down much."

"We'll go in for a bite to eat around one," Hank said as he drove away.

The process continued to go the same way. I stacked the bales as Mrs. Raycart threw them from the wagon, and when the wagon was unloaded she would help stack the bales. As we worked I wanted to say something to her, but never found the nerve. Instead, I talked to Blackie. If Mrs. Raycart heard me, she gave no indication. It was as if she was in her own world and the physical work came naturally, but her eyes were searching for something else. The blank look that came from her eyes gave me the impression that she would continue to do the physical work without slowing, unless she saw something that directed her elsewhere.

At one o'clock Hank drove in with a load, and Alfred was riding with. They unhooked the wagon and Mrs. Raycart immediately got into position to throw bales off. Hank walked to the wagon, took his wife by the hand, and helped her to the ground.

"Let's go in for a bite to eat, Joan," he said.

Alfred playfully grabbed me around the shoulders as we walked to the house.

"You know something, Shorty, if I had two people like you and Joan working for me I could charge double and get done twice as fast. They make a good team. Don't they, Hank?"

"You're right, Alfred, they are something too watch," Hank said.

I got the feeling that Hank wished there was more. Was he worried that his wife might be drifting farther away and reaching a point of no return? When we entered the kitchen Hank directed me to take a seat between him and Alfred, and then he pulled out a chair for his wife, and she quietly sat down. There were five table settings. The chair between Hank and Joan was left vacant.

Alfred was a person who was happy with the world and he liked to spread that joy of life to others. You couldn't help but smile when you were around him, but when he looked at the vacant table setting his lower lip began to quiver. He looked at the empty setting, and then looked at Mrs. Raycart, and a tear found its way from the corner of his eye and rolled over his puffy red cheeks. He brushed his hand over his eye and looked at Hank.

"I'm sorry, Hank; I guess I'll never be able to get used to this."

Hank walked behind Alfred and put his hand on his friend's shoulder. "I know, Alfred. You're a true friend. These last five years if you wouldn't have helped me out with the crops, we would never have made it. I think most everyone else has written us off."

"That's baloney. People forget how you and Joan were always available to help out the neighbors with threshing and the like. Look at Shorty. His ma and dad have trust in you. I think you should let me ask around. I bet I could get you more help than you realize. There's some that are just, are just..." He couldn't find the words that he wanted, but it was easy to tell that he was truly upset.

"I know, Alfred, but if Joan gets too many people around it really upsets her. I can't take a chance on something like that happening again."

"I understand. Now let's get some food in here, so we can get Shorty primed up enough so he can keep up with Joan this afternoon."

Mr. Raycart brought out a plate stacked high with ham sandwiches, and took a bowl of potato salad out of the icebox and sat it on the table. He prepared a plate for his wife, and set it on the table in front of her. He then picked up a fork full of potato salad and put it to her lips. She took a small bite, and then he placed the fork in her hand, and she slowly began to eat.

"Shorty, you want milk, or a glass of water?" Mr. Raycart asked.

"Milk would be great."

During dinner Mr. Raycart explained that Alfred would continue to bale hay and let the bales drop in the field while he did the night milking. Hank would pick up what bales he could before dark and finish in the morning. He asked if I could come over early the next morning to help stack the bales, so we were ready for the new day. I told him I could be over around eight when I finished my chores. He was genuinely pleased with that, and probably was thinking I might not come back at all. A feeling of satisfaction came over me, and I felt I was truly needed.

It was easy for me to see that Hank loved his wife very much, and they must have been fun to be around when times were better. Mrs. Raycart would eat for a few seconds, and then stop, and stare out the kitchen window. Each time Hank would reach across the vacant table setting and gently touch her hand, and she would eat some more. The look on Hank's face was sad, but he smiled as he watched his wife. Maybe he was thinking of better times, but the distant stare from his wife's eyes made me realize that there was a chance that neither of them would recapture what they once had. If my being there helped even a tiny fraction, it was worth it.

When we finished eating Alfred and I walked into the porch. Mr. Raycart and Joan cleared the dishes and put them in the sink. I watched as Mrs. Raycart picked up the unused table setting and placed the dishes in the sink. She pushed the chair under the table, and then walked into a bedroom that was adjacent to the kitchen and closed the door. I walked across the yard toward the barn with Alfred.

"Shorty, you be sure to thank your folks for me for letting you come over and help. I'm afraid this might be the last year I'll be working with Hank. Joan is getting worse and I think she's slipping beyond us, and I know Hank feels it. He thinks there's a chance that he may have to let her go, and take her to some institution. If that happens, this place will grow up in weeds. It's a damn shame, but it may be better to get it over with before some of our so called good neighbors have her dragged off. If that happens Hank will kill somebody."

I didn't know how to react to Alfred's predictions. I told him I would be sure to thank my parents for him. He then put me in a headlock and playfully tossed me from side to side.

"Let's stack a few bales until Hank gets back out here," he said.

We worked for about twenty minutes and then Mr. and Mrs. Raycart came back to the barn. The dogs assumed their positions, and Mrs. Raycart climbed on the wagon picking up where she left off.

Blackie had found a nice place in the shade of the barn to lie and seemed content, not at all worried about the dogs, but she never approached them. Once the big white one, which looked like a sled dog just off a long journey, walked over and sniffed at Blackie. He walked around her and then resumed his position by his two companions. It was as if he was letting the pack know that they had nothing to fear.

The afternoon went by fast and Mrs. Raycart didn't reduce her working pace at all. I don't think she looked at me once, but I watched her continuously. It was becoming hypnotic. What was she thinking? Or was she thinking at all?

At five-thirty, Hank brought the last load in before milking. He told me that after we finished unloading he would give me a ride home. I knew that time was a precious commodity, and he had plenty to do this evening before dark. I asked him if it would be alright if I walked home. I told him I had plenty of time, and it would feel good to walk along the river and cool off a little in our swimming hole on the way.

"You have put in a good days work. A dip in the creek sounds like a good idea. I'll see you in the morning and thanks again, Shorty."

We finished unloading the wagon. When I stacked the last bale, I looked around and watched Mrs. Raycart retrieve her jacket from the nail and then walk around the corner out of sight. Her three dogs immediately followed.

I started to walk in the opposite direction, and was a short distance from the barn when I realized that I had forgotten my jar. When I walked back into the barn I saw Mrs. Raycart through a small window in the side of the barn. I walked to the window and watched. I thought she was going down to help Hank with chores, but instead she was walking toward the river and her dogs were faithfully walking beside her. When she reached the bank of the river, she stopped and seemed to be watching the river flow by. Then she quickly turned around and looked directly towards me. It startled me, and I ducked down. Did she sense that I was watching? I cautiously peaked through the window and saw her walking along the bank toward the bridge. I watched her walk under the bridge, and disappear from sight. Right or wrong I made the decision to follow her.

I don't think my intent was to spy on her, but I had worked with her all day and my curiosity was moving me forward. I used the trees on the upper part of the bank for cover and maintained a good distance behind her. When she reached a big bend in the river, that was at least a mile upstream from the bridge, she stopped and placed her jacket on a rock beside the bank. I stopped and sat beside a tree and watched. The large wolf like dog with different colored eyes turned from the group and walked about half way up the side of the hill and stopped. She was looking straight in my direction and was sending me a silent warning. She knew I was there and I was intruding on her master's privacy. I'm not sure if that was her message, but I definitely got the feeling that I shouldn't be there, so I turned and started to leave.

I took a few steps and noticed that Blackie was continuing to watch. I turned around and watched as Mrs. Raycart slowly stepped from the bank into the river. My first thought was that she was just cooling off as I planned to do at my swimming hole. The cool water on her ankles probably felt real good.

She hesitated for a while and then slowly continued to wade into the river. I thought she was going for a swim. However, she didn't raise her hands, or give any indication that she was going to dive into the water. She just continued to move forward and the water got deeper. The river formed an eddy as it passed around her. The water rippled as it came against her body, and swirled, and then became still when it reached her other side. Two of the dogs were lying on the bank watching her, and the large wolf like dog continued to stare in my direction.

The water was now above her waist, and she continued to move forward.

I looked down river hoping to see Hank, but there was no one, and I began to worry. This didn't look good, and I didn't know what to do. I started to descend the hill and walk toward Mrs. Raycart.

Mrs. Raycart continued to walk deeper and deeper into the river. Her arms were tight against her body, and her hands were clutching onto her skirt. She was not attempting to swim. The water was up to her breast and methodically she continued to move forward. Her head didn't turn as she moved forward. It was as if the river was drawing her in.

I began to pick up my pace. My stomach was tying itself into a knot. Each breath I took became deeper the closer I got. The water was now up to her neck, and she kept moving forward. She wasn't going to stop. I ran my hand across my mouth in an attempt to help me think. I was convinced that she was going to drown herself.

When I reached the bank the dog that was watching me from the hillside started to growl. The hair on the back of her neck stood on end; she pulled her lips back and flashed her long teeth. I stopped about twenty feet in front of the dog and looked at Mrs. Raycart. Her head was starting to go underwater, but she didn't take a deep breath to prepare for being submerged. She just continued to move forward, offering no resistance to the river that was swallowing her.

I yelled. "Joan…Joan, stop!"

I ran downstream away from the dog. The water was shallow, so I jumped in and started to wade up stream toward Mrs. Raycart. The other two dogs that were lying on the bank, stood and turned to face me, and started to growl. Then the dog on the hill side started to run toward me.

It was as if everything was moving in slow motion. I stopped and watched as Mrs. Raycart's head disappeared under the water. I could see her hair float to the surface and swirl around in the current and then it was gone. The river flowed on as if nothing had intruded its body.

I started to run up the river. The dog running down the hill jumped from the bank into the water, and started to swim towards me. I crossed the river to the other side and started to climb the bank, but I slipped and fell to my knees. I raised my head and looked up the bank to see the dog with the two different colored eyes standing directly in front of me. She had crossed the river and now was blocking my exit. Her teeth were showing and the growls coming deep from within told me there was no way I was going to be allowed to try and save Mrs. Raycart.

I was confused, terrified, and alone. It was too late to run back and get

Hank. I looked at the area where Mrs. Raycart went under the water and watched the river flow peacefully around the bend as if nothing had happened. How would I explain this? Those dogs loved her, so why didn't they let me try and help her? I sat on the side of the bank, and started to cry. I couldn't hold anything back, I felt useless. Did my being there today cause her to do this?

Then the dogs stopped growling. They calmly turned and walked to the edge of the bank across from where Mrs. Raycart went under the water, and lay down. I looked at the river and saw her hair start to swirl above the surface. She was floating to the top. I was petrified as I watched and was not prepared for this. Then her hair stopped swirling, and Joan's head broke the surface of the water. Her eyes were wide open and she was staring straight ahead. Slowly her body emerged from the water with her hands still holding onto her skirt. As methodically as she had walked in, she now walked out.

It was impossible. She had to have been under the water for over three minutes. I was perplexed and relieved at the same time. I sat and watched as she walked out of the water. You could see the outline of her body through her soaked clothes as she walked over and picked up her jacket from the rock.

She then turned toward me, and stepped back into the river. With that same intense stare she walked across the river towards me. I couldn't move, and watched in silence as she came nearer. Her three dogs walked behind in the shallow water. I felt the water drip from her body onto my legs when she stopped in front of me. She slowly bent her head down towards me and I forced myself to look into her eyes. I saw my reflection in her dark green stare, and her lips slowly started to part.

"You're not John," she said.

The short, matter-of-fact statement didn't sound threatening, but the tone of her voice matched her blank stare. Her words echoed in my brain and they shattered the stillness of the evening. I tried to speak. I took a deep breath, but could only manage a faint whisper.

"I know," I said.

My response was so quiet that I wondered if I had said anything at all. Then the silence was broken by the sound of a rock rolling down the hill on the opposite side of the river. Mrs. Raycart immediately turned her head and looked in the direction the noise had come from. I searched the hillside expecting to see the elusive cougar or some other animal that had chased me through the swamp. The movement of some brush at the top of the hill caught my attention. I jerked my head back when I saw the form of a person making its way through the brush. I focused all of my attention on the figure, but in a few seconds whoever it was disappeared over the hill. I was sure it was a person, but I was unable to make any identification.

My concentration was broken when Mrs. Raycart brushed by me and stepped from the river onto the bank. I sat and watched as she moved along the bank with her dogs diligently walking behind her. All of a sudden the dog with two colored eyes stopped, turned her head and looked at me. She stared for a moment, turned, and broke into a lope to catch up with Mrs. Raycart.

I slowly got to my feet, waded across the river, and walked back to the road. As I left the river I pondered on whether to tell Mr. Raycart that his wife had spoke to me again, or would he be offended that I had followed her? I was trying to consider what was best to do when it came to me that he might already know. That could have been him in the brush.

When I reached the road I decided that I had enough of the river for today and would follow the road home. When I walked past the Raycarts' driveway I saw Mr. Raycart letting the cows into the pasture for the night. The figure I saw on the hill went in a direction that would take him away from the Raycart farm. There was no way Mr. Raycart could get back to the farm so quick. Therefore, I concluded that it was impossible for Mr. Raycart to have been the person in the brush. Who could it have been, and how long was that figure hiding in the brush watching us?

I was deep in thought when the sound of a vehicle approaching broke my concentration. I stepped into the ditch and saw the nice looking Thunderbird I had seen at Jason Abners farm coming down the road. The vehicle started to slow as it approached and came to a stop beside me. Sitting in the passenger side was Max Strum, and the driver was the person who had beaten Bruce Wright in arm wrestling at the fair.

"Driving into the sun makes it hard to see. It's a good thing we saw ya, or we might have hit you, or your dog. You better watch where you're going," Max said.

"I'll make sure I watch," I replied.

"You better, or you'll end up having to find another dog to go wading with you in the river," Max said.

The driver put the car in gear and took off before I had a chance to reply. A cloud of dust trailed behind as the car sped down the road. I stood watching the dust drift through the trees until the car disappeared over the next hill.

"Come on, Blackie, we better get home or Mom will have all our chores done. That Max just likes to talk."

Chapter Twelve
The Bedroom

It was late in the evening when I walked into our driveway. Mom was by the pig pen, and waved when she saw me. She had started to feed the pigs, and they squealed and pushed against each other to try and obtain the best position at the trough. I helped pour the whey into the trough and then walked with my mother to the house. Mom prepared a light supper, which consisted of sandwiches and beans. By the time we finished the sun had set. After dishes were put away we went outside and sat on the porch steps. Mom brought us each a bowl of jell-o to enjoy as an evening treat. It was a warm summer evening and stars illuminated the dark night sky.

"This is the best part of living in the country. Look at those stars, I bet there are millions of them and we can see each one. It's got to be God's work," Mom said.

I leaned back against the porch steps and scanned the night sky in search of the Big Dipper and other constellations, but found that I was having a hard time keeping my eyes open.

Mom noticed that I was starting to nod off and laughed.

"Looks like you worked real hard today. I don't remember you coming back from Uncle Joe's so tired. Tell me how'd it go?"

I sat up straight and began to go through the day's events. I started by telling her how Blackie had followed me, but the dogs never bothered her and Mrs. Raycart brought her water. I told how hard Mrs. Raycart worked, but never spoke. I relayed the dinner event and what Alfred Jest said about Hank thinking his wife was getting worse. I explained why Mr. Raycart asked me to come over early in the morning, and that I told him I would be over after I completed my chores. When I finished I put my elbows on the step in back of me and leaned back.

Mom sat quietly for a moment and then collected the empty bowls and went inside. My brother and sister were running through the lawn chasing after lightning bugs. They sprinted from spot to spot and placed what bugs they were able to catch in a jar. In a few minutes Mom returned and sat on the step beside me.

"What else happened, Shorty? I know young men have secrets that they want to keep to themselves, and I respect that. I know there are times you don't tell the entire story and sometimes that may be a good thing. Especially to a mother who tends to always fear the worse when her children are involved. Like last week when you found Blackie. I know something else happened that day, and one day you may tell me, but don't hold something back so much that it starts to eat at your insides. At times, sharing a concern with a friend helps to take some of the weight off. I'm your friend, Shorty, and I'll always be there for you."

Mom was right. She was my friend and was always there for me. I slid over next to her and told what happened when I followed Mrs. Raycart up river.

"Mom, do you think she was trying to drown herself?"

She put her arm around me, squeezed my shoulders, and surveyed the night sky as if searching for the correct answer.

"No, Shorty, I don't think she was trying to drown herself, but for some reason she's attracted to the river. It took her last child from her, so to her it may be like a church. A place she goes to find answers. Do you feel threatened when you're around her?"

I told her I didn't. As a matter of fact by the end of the day I felt comfortable around her and the dogs. I realized that it was an odd situation and Mrs. Raycart had problems, but I felt good working for them. I rambled on again about how hard Mrs. Raycart worked and Mom listened patiently, digesting every word.

"I think Mrs. Raycart can sense things," I said.

"Like what?" Mom asked.

"I don't know for sure. But she moves around so quietly, and she actually looks towards a sound before it's even made. At times, I think she senses things before the dogs do."

"Maybe her other senses have become keener since she has stopped speaking." Mom paused for a moment. "Maybe we shouldn't let you go back."

"No, I'll be fine," I said and then remembered what Alfred Jest had told me. "Mom, Mr. Jest said that I should be sure to thank you and Dad for letting me help out. He said a lot of people have quit doing that because of something that Mrs. Raycart did."

"I don't know what that could have been, but I do know that Alfred Jest has convinced me that he's a good man. You better get ready for bed; it sounds like you have another hard day of work waiting for you tomorrow."

I went inside, while Mom continued to sit on the porch steps and watch my brother and sister's quest for the elusive lightning bug. She allowed them to run through the grass until their jar resembled a lantern flickering in the night, and then called them inside. She helped them get ready for bed and then walked into the porch and opened the screen door.

"Blackie, come on in, you're probably tired too."

Blackie didn't require a second offer. She was up the steps and in the porch before Mom could blink an eye. I went upstairs to bed and it wasn't long before Mom came in to say good-night.

"Sweet Dreams," she said as she closed my bedroom door. In a few minutes I could hear her voice through the wall as she read a bedtime story to my brother and sister.

My thoughts drifted to the person I saw in the brush, and the more I thought about it the more I doubted that it was Hank. However, I was positive that it wasn't my imagination, because I was convinced that Mrs. Raycart had also seen him. What about Max, how did he know that I was wading in the river? The questions started to fade away. The physical activity of the day had worn me out, and it wasn't long before I was sound asleep.

I awoke with a start and jumped out of bed, got dressed, and ran downstairs. Mom was in the kitchen and had already set a place for me at the table. I thought I had overslept and Mom detected my concern.

"Calm down, it's only six. You're right on schedule. Get your chores done, and I'll make us some pancakes."

I must have had a good night sleep, because I felt refreshed and raring to go. Chores went by fast and the dollar-sized pancakes hit the spot. I finished breakfast, put my plate in the sink, gave my mother a kiss on the cheek, and then started to leave.

"What was that for?" she asked.

"Oh, nothin' much. Just for being such a good friend last night is all."

A smile came to her face and she reminded me to be home by seven for chores. With Blackie by my side I headed for the river. I disturbed a couple of mallards that were enjoying an early morning swim, I watched as their feet skimmed along the water as they took flight. I arrived at the Raycarts a short time before eight o'clock. Mr. Raycart was unloading hay from the wagon, and saw me coming.

"Good Morning, Shorty," he said. "Joan will be here in a few minutes, she's out for her morning stroll. You must have tuckered her out yesterday. She fell asleep on the chair by the river and I had to carry her up to bed. She hasn't done that in quite a while."

He seemed happy about that and didn't mention how wet she must have been, but maybe it wasn't uncommon for her to return from the river soaked to the skin. I said good morning, and started to carry the bales to the back of the hay mow. Hank finished unloading, and then got on the tractor.

"I'll be right back. I got one more load to pull in."

He waved as he drove off. His mood seemed more upbeat today, the air of melancholy that normally surrounded him was not as apparent. It was good to see.

I had just finished putting a bale in place and turned to go for another and there stood Mrs. Raycart with her three dogs. Her quiet unexpected entrance startled me as she stood silently facing me from across the hay barn floor, but there was something different.

Instead of blankly looking past me, she was staring directly at me. I smiled and whispered good morning as she continued to stare. No, she wasn't staring at me, she was watching me. She studied me for what seemed like a significant amount of time, then turned and walked across the barn floor, took her jacket off, and hung it on the nail. The dogs watched, and as soon as her jacket was secure on the nail they assumed their sentinel positions on the floor. Then she resumed the same pattern used yesterday and started to stack the bales, but unlike yesterday, today I felt she was aware of my presence.

Alfred Jest arrived about ten and was very impressed with what had been accomplished.

"Hank, we better get in the field before these two decide to go work for someone else."

"They do make a good pair," Hank said as he nodded his head in agreement.

Hank was actually smiling as he and Alfred drove to the field. Finding his wife soundly asleep by the river and seeing her rest comfortably through the night had caused him to regain some hope for his wife's recovery.

The morning seemed to fly past, and dinner followed the same pattern as yesterday. After dinner I asked Alfred why Mrs. Raycart went into the bedroom and shut the door. The question was unexpected. He tilted his hat back as he took a seat on a bale, and then started to talk without looking at me.

"I'm afraid it's always for the same reason, but how we found out is what helps keep the door closed."

Alfred then delicately recounted what had happened.

"The first fall after John's death, some of the neighbors came over to help with the threshing. There were too many people to fit inside the house, so we placed picnic tables on the lawn. Joan never came out to eat with us. She stayed inside and Hank fed her at the kitchen table. When Mabel Wilson discovered the extra place setting at the table, she made sure everyone became aware of it. It was sad, but most accepted it as a way for Joan to work out her grief."

Alfred paused, reassuring himself that what he was going to say next was correct.

"Why the women had to come that day, I don't know, but I'm sure most were just trying to be helpful. But Mabel Wilson and Francis Beck had no reason to go into the house that day, other than to spy on Joan. They could have helped with the picnic and then went home. We would have finished up the threshing, and that would have been that."

Alfred picked up a stick that was lying on the ground next to him and started to draw circles in the dirt as he continued.

"But for whatever reason, Mabel and Francis went inside the house. When they entered they heard movement in the bedroom and walked over and opened the bedroom door. They saw the clothes that John was wearing when he drowned spread out neatly on the bed. Joan was sitting on a stool in front of the dresser mirror brushing her hair. Mabel and Francis walked to the bed, started to pick the clothes up, and then all hell broke loose. We heard the women scream and we all rushed to the house. The bedroom door was closed, and Mabel and Francis were inside screaming as if Lucifer himself had them cornered."

Alfred looked toward the house to make sure that Hank wasn't on his way out, and then continued.

"Hank was first to get to the house and walked to the door and gently pushed it open. Francis was standing in a corner with her hands over her face, and Mabel was sitting on the floor yelling for Hank to get Joan away from them. Joan had retrieved the clothes from the two ladies and was laying them neatly on the bed. In the meantime, Joan's dogs made it through the group and were standing in the doorway. Their hair was on end, and they were prepared to attack, but Hank took Joan by the hand and led her outside, and the dogs followed. Hank walked Joan to the river and sat her down, and then returned to the house. By the time he returned, Mabel and Francis were preaching to anyone that would listen that Joan was possessed and should be put away."

"The sheriff came out to investigate the next day and found that Joan never touched either of the ladies, but when she grabbed the clothes from their hands she scared the hell out of em. They both swore that Joan had a look of evil come over her and told the sheriff and anyone else that would listen, that they feared for their lives. Each time Mabel and Francis retell the story, the odor of fire and brimstone gets worse."

When he finished he tossed the stick to the side and stood up.

"Shorty, you may think Joan is crazy or sick for doing something like that, but when I'm around Joan I don' feel frightened. It may sound stupid, but I feel she has a reason for what she does, and someday we'll learn what that reason is. What do you think?"

I didn't know what to think, or what to say. So I said, "I think I better get some of these bales stacked, or I'll never be able to stay ahead of her."

Alfred shook his head and laughed. "You're sure as hell right about that."

We stacked a few bales until Hank came out, and then Alfred and Hank returned to the field. Not long after Mrs. Raycart returned, and we finished stacking the bales.

The remainder of the day went along smooth, and I found myself thinking a lot about Alfred's detailed account of what had happened in the bedroom. I didn't know Francis Beck very well, but I knew Mabel Wilson, and she always seemed very pleasant to me. Were their intentions to help or were they trying to find justification to label Mrs. Raycart as a person possessed by something unholy?

I thought about it deeply as I watched Mrs. Raycart work. I definitely didn't feel that she was evil. However, I did agree with Alfred that there had to be a reason for the way she has chosen to react to her son's death, and she's the only person who knows what that reason is.

When we finished unloading the last load, I watched Mrs. Raycart walk to the river, but she didn't look back this time. I walked through the barn to tell Mr. Raycart good night and that I would see him in the morning. He finished connecting a milking machine to one of the cows, and then stepped into the aisle, and shook my hand.

"Thanks, Shorty, see ya in the morning."

As I walked out of the barn I turned and looked to make sure Blackie was following, and saw that Mr. Raycart was walking toward me.

"Shorty, what do you think of Joan?" Hank asked.

"I like her," I said, and walked out to follow the river home.

Chapter Thirteen
Poison

The next few days provided excellent weather for haying. Each morning a warm breeze blew across the windrows, drying the hay, and by early afternoon the temperature reached a point where it didn't take long to build up a good sweat. The sweet odor of fresh cut hay as it lay drying in the fields seemed to make the hard work more pleasant. When Alfred and Hank came in from the fields their shirts were soaked with sweat from working under the hot sun. Alfred wore a large brimmed straw hat to provide shade from the sun, but his face still took on a red fluorescent glow. However, the heat never deterred his jovial mood, and he always had something good to say.

Hank was enjoying the way haying was progressing. He had become more talkative and even joked along with Alfred. It was easy to see that he loved to farm. He and my Uncle Joe were a lot alike in that aspect. Farming was an important part of their being and they worked hard to do right with the land, and treat the animals as an equal part in the success of the farm. It was more than just a way to make a living, it was their life. The success they felt when the crops turned out good or making it through a difficult growing season was the same. The ups and downs of farming revolved around Mother Nature. They accepted that, and it helped to build their confidence, and ability to work the land.

Mrs. Raycart and her three dogs treated Blackie and me as if we were normal fixtures on the place. Joan continued her daily routines, and the dogs never left her side.

One day while I was leaving for the night I asked Hank if the other two dogs had a name. I knew the one was called "Wrench," but what about the others. He told me that Joan called them to her side without the use of names, but he named them for his benefit. He saw no reason why I couldn't try the names out on them to see how they would react.

The large wolf like dog with one grey eye and one blue eye he called "Three Eye." On her walks with Joan she always lagged behind a short distance, and would routinely stop and scan the surrounding area. Hank said it was as if she was making sure to catch sight of anything that was out of the ordinary. To Hank she was Joan's third eye.

The large white dog, he called "Peg." When he followed Joan home his back left thigh was injured so bad that he could hardly walk. Joan attached wooden splints to the leg and the dog hobbled around for over a month like a person with a peg leg. Hank said that when she took the splints off it was as if his leg had never been injured. However, Hank said that if you watch him close you can still see him limp once in a while, but it doesn't slow him down. Of the three, Hank felt that Peg definitely was the fastest.

Hank knew that I heard the story behind the name for Wrench. Hank felt that she was the most dedicated to Joan's well being. When the dogs gather around Joan, Wrench was always the closest to her side. That dog missed death by the swing of an arm, and Hank had little doubt that she would take death head on if it meant protecting Joan.

I thought about the names and on occasion would whisper them in their direction when I got a chance, but I never received any type of acknowledgement. The dogs were Joan's protectors and nothing was going to change that or detour them from that responsibility.

On the third day we started to stack bales on the second level. Hank positioned an elevator so that Joan could place the bales directly from the wagon onto the elevator. The bales would ride up the elevator and drop on top of the bales that we had already stacked. Joan unloaded at a steady pace, and I did all I could to keep the area below where the elevator dropped the bales clear. I tried to stack as many as possible, but most of my time was spent tossing bales to the side in order to make room for the bales that were falling from the elevator.

I arrived earlier than usual on the fourth day. Hank was in the field, and Joan was on her river walk. I climbed the ladder that was mounted on the side of the barn wall to the second tier of bales. The mound of bales was increasing in size, so I thought I'd use the extra time to try and catch up some. I had just started to stack the bales when I heard a car door slam. I made my way to the hay barn wall and peered through a crack between the planks. I saw a cloud of dust by the side of the road, whoever it was had already disappeared in the distance. I didn't give it any thought and went back to work. A short time later Hank came into the yard with a load of hay and saw me in the hay-mow, and waved.

"You got up early today, everything okay?" Hank asked.

I told him everything was fine and that I had finished my chores early, and just wanted to see if I could get caught up before Joan started to unload. He placed the wagon next to the conveyor and started to drive back to the field.

"Don't wear yourself out before noon. It's going to be a hot one today," he said.

As I heard Hank drive away, the conveyor started. I walked to the edge of the bales, looked over the side, and saw Joan placing bales on the conveyor with her normal fluid like motion. I said good morning, but as usual there was no response. However, when I glanced at the dogs, I saw that Three Eye was looking up at me.

"At least you know I'm here, don't you girl."

I grabbed a bale and started to carry it back, and then the bales stopped coming, and the dogs started to bark. I threw the bale to the side and ran to the edge to see what was going on. Joan was walking towards the road and her dogs were running ahead of her. When I looked in the direction they were going I saw Blackie standing in the ditch by the road. What had she done to make the dogs so mad?

I quickly climbed down the ladder and sprinted toward the road. The dogs had surrounded Blackie and were forcing her away from a sack that was lying in the ditch. The dogs stood between Blackie and the sack, and were now watching Joan. I slowed to a fast walk and watched Joan walk to her dogs. Three Eye was watching me and took a few steps towards me as I got nearer, but then returned her attention to Joan.

I stopped when I saw Joan stoop down beside the sack. One corner of the sack was torn open and she placed her finger inside. She then touched the finger to her lips and stood up. She immediately turned and walked toward Blackie who was now lying in the ditch. Blackie looked puzzled as she watched Joan approach. The dogs stopped barking and watched as Joan knelt on the ground beside Blackie.

She gently positioned her hands over Blackie's muzzle so that she could use her fingers to pry Blackie's mouth open. Then without hesitating she put her fingers inside Blackie's mouth and moved them around. All of a sudden Blackie started to throw up. I had seen Blackie do this quite often in the past after eating grass, and was not too concerned. I stepped toward the bag, but Peg and Three Eye were having nothing of that. Blackie was now standing on all fours, but her belly was heaving in and out as she tried to force herself to continue to throw up. Joan seemed to be studying Blackie's every movement. Quickly she stood, wiped her hands on her skirt, and in one swift movement bent over and picked Blackie off the ground. She stood cradling Blackie gently in her arms for a few seconds and then walked towards the house.

Wrench and Three Eye walked beside her. Peg stayed by the bag as if to be guarding it. When Joan reached the house she laid Blackie gently on the ground beside the porch steps and went inside. She returned momentarily and was carrying a bottle that had some kind of dark colored liquid in it. She knelt on the ground beside Blackie, and forced the liquid into Blackie's mouth. Blackie immediately began to vomit. When the episode was complete, Blackie lay on her side, but her stomach continued to expand and retract rapidly with each breath. Blackie's look of puzzlement had turned to a look of pain.

Joan stroked the sides of Blackie's stomach and used her fingers to open Blackie's eyelids wider. She then bent forward so that she was able to look directly into Blackie's eyes, and after a few seconds, began to rub a spot behind Blackie's ears. She then released Blackie's eyelids, but continued to gently rub the area behind Blackie's ears. The dogs and I stood watching as Joan slowly massaged the area on Blackie's head, and it wasn't long before Blackie fell asleep.

In the meantime Alfred had arrived and Hank was back from the field with another load of hay. They both came to the house and stood beside me watching Joan. As Blackie lie sleeping Joan got to her feet and stared in the direction of Peg. Hank followed his wife's stare and immediately walked toward Peg. When he reached Peg he saw the sack lying in the ditch, and turned to look at his wife. Hank then picked the sack off the ground and threw it in a barrel that was setting in the yard. He then walked to the machine shed and returned with a can of gasoline. He poured the gas over the sack and set it on fire. He stared at the flames for a few seconds, and then put the gas can back in the shed. He returned to the house, sat on the porch steps, and watched his wife.

While Hank was disposing of the sack and its contents, Joan had gone inside. She brought a blanket out, and placed it over Blackie. She then knelt on the ground and opened Blackies eyelids. She stared into her eyes for a few seconds and then let the eyelids close. She then brushed her hand over Blackies head, stood up, turned, and walked to the river. I stood silently and watched as she and her three dogs walked along the bank. It wasn't long before they walked under the bridge, and were out of sight.

"What happened?" I asked.

"I think your dog ate some poisoned meat," Hank said.

"Poison, I don't understand. Why? How could it get there?"

Hank was now standing like a statue looking down at Blackie. The expression on Hank's face was blank, almost lifeless.

"It wasn't meant for your dog, Shorty. I think it's getting time for me and Joan to move on."

"Will Blackie be alright? Is Joan going to come back and take care of her?" I asked.

"I think she's done all that can be done right now. Blackie needs to rest," Hank said.

This was beyond my comprehension. I was at a total loss. Everything had been going so nicely and now something like this had to happen.

Alfred was standing quietly next to me, and then suddenly he broke into a chorus of cuss words. Words not being enough to console his anger, he took his straw hat, threw it on the ground, and then kicked it into the driveway. He walked over and picked it up only to throw it down again.

"Someone has got to pay for this. The sneaky coward bastard who did this can burn in hell. If that dog dies, whoever done it should die. If I find out who it was, I'll kill the bastard myself. They have poisoned more than a dog here."

Alfred was out of control. He continued to pace back and forth, cussing to the world.

"I gotta go back to work or I'm going to be a basket case. Come on, Hank; let's get your hay in while the weather holds. Shorty, you do what you feel you have to, but as for me I got to work. Joan and nature are more capable to handle this than any of us, and if there is a God in heaven, I hope he strikes the bastard down who did it," Alfred said.

Alfred and Hank returned to the field. I knelt beside Blackie and brushed my hand across her forehead, and watched the blanket move back and forth with each troublesome breath.

Alfred was right; there was nothing we could do. So I walked to the barn, climbed the ladder, moved the bales away, and then went down and finished unloading the wagon. Work supplied a way to escape, but it didn't provide a means to cope with the situation. I wasn't able to unload the wagons and stack the bales, so I let the bales fall into a large pile in the hay mow. The noon meal was very somber; each of us had our own feelings to deal with. Joan hadn't returned from her walk and Blackie hadn't moved, but the blanket that covered her continued to go up and down with each breath.

When we finished eating I stepped into the porch and saw Joan walking toward the house from the river. She was soaked from head to toe, and I was certain I knew where she had been. She walked to the porch steps and without so much as a pause in her movement lifted Blackie off the ground. With the dog cradled in her arms she turned and walked toward the river. When she reached the river bank, she gently placed Blackie on the ground, and adjusted the blanket over her. Her three dogs watched intently. When Joan sat in her chair, the dogs lay on the bank, and continued to watch as Joan stared into the river that was flowing past.

The afternoon went by and the mound of bales continued to get larger. It would take a good amount of time to separate the hay bales and stack them properly. Periodically I would stop working and look at Joan setting by the river. Most of the time she seemed to sit motionless, but every once in a while she would stand and walk over and kneel beside Blackie. Each time she would stroke Blackie's head while she stared into Blackie's eyes. I felt that Blackie was in good hands.

When Hank brought the last load in before milking, he went to the house, and then came out to the barn. He helped me unload and I started to climb the ladder, but he stopped me. He walked over and put his hand on my shoulder.

"Shorty, don't worry about those bales, I'll shut Alfred off for a day and we'll stack the hay. I called your ma and explained the situation the best I could. I told her I thought it was best to keep Blackie here with us tonight. You go home now, and we'll see what tomorrow brings."

I shook my head in agreement and looked toward the river at Joan. Hank nodded at me.

"I think your dog would like it if you said good-night," he said.

Three Eye met me half way, and walked beside me to where Blackie was lying. I knelt on the bank and padded her on the head.

"You'll be alright, girl. Joan will take care of ya."

She didn't open her eyes and her breathing continued to be heavy. I stood up and walked over so that I stood facing Joan.

"Thanks, Joan, I gotta go home and do chores. I'll see you in the morning. It wasn't your fault."

I didn't pick up any indication that she heard me; she seemed to be searching for something in the river. I watched the river for a moment and then looked toward the barn and saw Hank watching. I gave a half wave and started to follow the river home. Three Eye followed beside me for a short distance and then turned and walked back to be with Joan.

Mom was waiting on the porch steps, and walked to the pump to meet me when I walked into the yard. She put her arm around my shoulders and we walked to the house. It was a quiet night. My brother and sister even sensed that something wasn't right, and were unusually quiet.

When Mom came to tuck me in that night, she brought with her that natural ability to provide comfort. She sat quietly on the edge of my bed, brushed the hair away from my forehead, and gave me a soothing kiss on the cheek.

"Mom, I should never have let Blackie come over there. The other dogs knew that there was poison in that sack, but they just couldn't get there in time to stop Blackie. Now I got a sick dog and I'll never be able to get those bales stacked so Hank has room for all his hay."

"Don't beat yourself up, Shorty. None of this was your fault. Some people can say and do the cruelest things for no logical reason. But I have no doubt that Blackie belongs by your side. You treat her very well and in return she gives you unconditional love. Too many of us humans have lost that natural response; too often we want more. Now you try and get some sleep."

"Alfred says that Blackie might die."

"I'll be sure to include her in my prayers tonight, and you do the same. Don't forget, Blackie has Joan on her side." She smiled, and closed the door.

The thought of God and Joan working together brought a smile to my face. As usual Mom provided a way to see the sunny side of things; maybe it was her unconditional love working some magic.

Chapter Fourteen
Help Thy Neighbor

When I awoke the next morning I had a hard time getting out of bed. My first thought was that yesterday was just a bad dream, and none of it really happened. But that wish soon faded and my thoughts turned to Blackie. For some reason while doing chores, the worse scenario kept creeping into my mind. I pictured Blackie lying under the blanket, but the blanket didn't move.

I finished chores as fast as possible and returned to the house for breakfast. Mom already had the table set and was frying bread dough and bacon.

"Thought I'd try and perk you up some this morning with one of your favorites."

During breakfast I continued to recall the events of yesterday, but the black cloud of Blackie being dead kept invading my thoughts. I finished eating as fast as I could and started for the door.

"Don't forget you nectar."

I walked back to get the jar and Mom shared some of her morning thoughts with me.

"Hank hasn't called, so that must mean Blackie is doing better," Mom said.

"I sure hope you're right."

I walked the road that morning checking the ditches for sacks. If I had walked the road yesterday I may have spotted the sack before Blackie got to it. Then I remembered the car door I heard slam yesterday morning. Whoever had been there must have left the sack while I was in the barn.

Three Eye was standing at the end of the driveway and she walked beside me to the front porch. Joan was sitting in her swing, but I couldn't see Blackie anywhere. I slowly walked up the steps and opened the screen door. I was relieved when I saw Blackie lying in front of the swing. I knelt on the floor to pet her and although she didn't acknowledge my presence I felt that her breathing was more relaxed. It definitely was a ray of sunshine. I eagerly stood to greet Joan.

"Good Morning, Joan. Blackie seems better."

As usual there was no response, so I turned to open the screen door. As I pushed the screen door open, I felt Joan's hand on my shoulder. I slowly turned around and met her stare. Then she reached down, grabbed my hand, and pulled me into the kitchen. I started to pull back, but she tightened her grip and pulled me across the floor. We were going towards her son's bedroom and even though I was resisting, I couldn't stop my forward motion. She stopped in front of the door and took hold of the knob with her left hand and pushed the door open.

Her body blocked my view of the room. I didn't know what to expect, but I was expecting the worse. I had visions of seeing her son's spirit sitting on the bed, so I shut my eyes tight as she pulled me into the room. I stopped when I felt my leg come against the side of the bed and then she released my hand. My arm dropped to my side as if a weight had been attached to it. Then I heard the door close and felt her standing next to me.

I didn't know what to do, but slowly I forced my eyes open and looked around the room. It wasn't much different from my bedroom. A blue ribbon hanging from the top of the dresser mirror caught my attention. I couldn't read what the ribbon was for, but my eyes fixed on it, and I wasn't planning to look anywhere else.

Then Joan took my left hand and pulled it down, but there was no way I was going to look. I had no idea what it felt like, but I was sure I was about to have a heart attack. My mouth became very dry and my hands were starting to sweat. Then Joan placed my hand on top of some clothing that was lying on the bed, and I swear my heart stopped.

Joan knelt on the floor next to the bed, but she didn't let go of my hand. Instead, she pulled so hard that I was forced to kneel beside her. She then took my hand and started to slide it over the piece of clothing while I continued to look at the blue ribbon. I couldn't make out what the ribbon was for, but for now it allowed me to evade whatever Joan was trying to show me.

Joan slowly guided my hand along the piece of clothing until I felt a tear in the cloth. I reluctantly lowered my head to look, and saw a boy's pair of blue bib overalls neatly spread out on the bed in front of me. One leg was torn from the cuff to the knee and a piece of the pant leg was ripped off. I turned to look at Joan, hoping to find some reason for all of this.

Joan continued to guide my hand over the pant leg, but her eyes were not watching me, instead they were focused on the bib overalls. Then suddenly she stood up and pulled me to my feet. She released my hand and walked to a stool that was setting in front of the dresser mirror and sat down. I watched her in the mirror as she picked up a brush and began to run it through her hair. I stood there frozen in time and watched. I could see my reflection in the mirror, and Joan turned her head so she was looking directly at my reflection. I turned cold and returned my focus to the blue ribbon, trying desperately to avoid looking at her in the mirror. I strained to make out what it said and then it came to me. It wasn't an actual blue ribbon for winning a prize. It was one you purchased for a gift and had a personal message printed on it in white lettering. I took a cautious step toward the mirror so that I could read what the ribbon said.

It read; *First Place awarded to Joan Raycart for being the World's Best Mom.*

Part of me wanted to go over and give Joan a hug, the other part of me wanted to make a dash for the door. I returned my gaze to Joan and watched as she methodically pulled the brush through her hair. She wasn't looking at my reflection, but seemed to be staring into the reflection of her own eyes. I got the impression that she no longer knew that I was in the room, or that she no longer needed me to be in the room. I walked to the door, pushed it open, stepped into the kitchen, and silently closed the door behind me.

I walked into the porch, knelt down to pet Blackie, and then went outside. Hank was pulling in a load of hay. He stopped, climbed off the tractor, and waited for me.

"I think Blackie is going to pull through. I doubt if Joan will be able to help today. I think she's going to spend the day caring for Blackie. Just do the best you can to clear the bales from the end of the conveyor, and if it gets too backed up we'll throw them on the ground and I'll pick them up later, or we'll quit baling for a day so we can catch up."

"Hank," I said.

It caught both of us by surprise: I had never called him by his first name before. It pleased him and a smile formed across his face.

"Yes, Shorty, what is it?"

I looked at him and to this day I have never made a more sincere comment.

"We gotta help Joan. It's not right for her to have to live her life as if it doesn't matter."

"You are helping, Shorty. I know it isn't fair to put this on the shoulders of a young man, but you have brought something to the surface in her. She needs a window that'll give her a chance to break free. Since you've been here, I've seen a change in Joan. I hope you can find time to stop by once in a while after haying is done just to say hi."

"I sure will," I told him and started to walk toward the barn.

Before I reached the ladder I heard the screen door shut. Joan had Blackie in her arms and was carrying her toward the river. When she reached the table she put Blackie on the ground and sat on a chair facing the river. I smiled to myself and climbed the ladder to the haymow. I knew one thing for sure; Blackie was in good hands.

Hank was placing the bales on the conveyor from the wagon and I was clearing the bales as they dropped from the conveyor. He stopped when he heard the dogs barking, and we saw them running toward the driveway. We both looked up the driveway and after a few minutes saw Ronnie's car turn in. Ronnie drove to the barn and parked off to the side.

The dogs surrounded the car and no one was going to be allowed out. The back window started to roll down and I saw Uncle Joe sitting in the back seat. He rolled the window part way down so the dogs had no chance of jumping through, and then waved at Hank.

"Hank, you got a minute? I don't think I want to get out unless you say it's alright."

Hank walked over to the car to quiet the dogs, and the car doors opened. Ronnie had a car full, and one-by-one the passengers exited. Uncle Joe, Dad and Grandpa were in the back and out from the front passenger door stepped my mother. Ronnie was the last to get out and it was easy to tell that he was quite nervous. The dogs followed the group as they made their way to the barn. Hank stopped and waved for me to come down.

"Shorty, it looks like we got company. What you think?" Hank said.

I was at a loss and didn't know what to think. And my mother, she was wearing overalls, and her hair was tied up in a ponytail with a red handkerchief. She saw me looking at her and stepped to the front.

"What's wrong? You don't think I have to wear a dress every day, do you? Since Joan is helping with Blackie we asked Hank if it would be all right for us to help you get caught up, and he has graciously allowed us to do just that. Now let's get to work, so Hank can get this haying behind him," Mom said.

Dad and Joe hopped on the empty wagon that Hank was getting ready to take out to the field to pick up another load. As they drove off Mom and Grandpa climbed onto the wagon, and started to unload. Ronnie had already climbed the ladder; I think he felt safer because he was out of the dogs reach. When the wagon was unloaded Mom climbed the ladder to the top of the stacked bales, and Grandpa found a nice bale to sit on, so he could rest until the next load came in.

When Mom reached the top of the ladder she was grinning from ear to ear. There was no doubt that she felt good about this. As a matter-of-fact there was a spirit of camaraderie in the group, and it was easy to tell that each one was happy with what they were doing. Mom held her own, and only fell a couple of times when her foot slipped between the bales, but each time she fell it only seemed to make her more determined.

Alfred arrived at his usual time and riding on the tractor with him was his wife, Martha. She was a female replication of her husband. She had the same rosy cheeks and was always quick with a smile. Alfred was surprised, but outwardly pleased to see all the help.

"I brought the boss with to do some mowing and raking, so Hank doesn't have to stay up so late, or get up so early to do it," Alfred said.

Uncle Joe stayed in the field stacking the hay on the wagon behind the baler and Dad came in to help stack the bales in the barn. Hank drove back and forth from the field bringing in the loads, and helped unload until it was time to go for another load.

Ronnie, Dad, Mom and I were hay stacking fools, and by noon we were half way caught up. At noon Ronnie and Mom drove to our house, and returned with a basket full of sandwiches. Alfred and Martha came in for lunch and everyone found a bale, or spot on the empty wagon to eat. Hank went to the house and brought out a bowl of potato salad. Mom watched as he dished up a plate, and then carried it to his wife. Mom started to walk toward the river, but Dad intercepted her and put his arm around her shoulders.

"Maddie, why don't you wait till later? Let her be for now, and let's finish helping Shorty out," Dad said.

"You're right," Mom said, and went over and started to climb the ladder to the haymow.

I started to follow Mom, but for some reason thought about my brother and sister, and asked where they were.

Dad was quick to respond.

"They'll be fine: We put 'em in the kitchen closet and left them a box of corn flakes."

"Mike, someday, someone is going to put you away for the way you talk. Grandma is watching them, and I imagine by now they're full to the brim with cookie dough," Mom said.

Ronnie was doing the work of two men. It was as if he had set a goal and he wasn't going to stop until that goal was met. Dad had taken the day off from work and together we all worked through the day like a well-oiled machine. At five, Uncle Joe rode in with Hank and took Ronnie's car, so he could go home for milking. While Hank did his milking, Dad went to the field to work with Alfred, so there would be no bales left lying in the field for Hank to pick up in the morning. When Dad brought another load in, Ronnie helped Grandpa unload.

Throughout the day Mom periodically stopped to catch her breath and would use the time to watch Joan. At approximately six in the evening Mom walked to the haymow edge and looked in the direction of the river. I walked to her side and saw Joan walking along the bank toward the bridge with her dogs.

"Where's she going?" Mom asked.

"She's going to her place. The place I told you about," I said.

Mom continued to work for about an hour, and Ronnie noticed that she was starting to look a little fatigued.

"Maddie, you look bushed, why don't you sit down and take a break. Me and Shorty will have this caught up in a few minutes."

At first I thought Mom was going to comment on Ronnie's insinuation that she was tired, but she agreed with him and climbed down the ladder. Hank was finishing with the milking and Alfred, Dad and Martha were coming back in with the last load for the day. Mom saw that Joan hadn't returned yet, so she walked to the river and knelt on the bank beside Blackie.

The next thing that happened probably put the first gray hairs on my mother's head. While she was bending over petting Blackie, Joan's three dogs came rushing up the bank. Mom heard them coming. She quickly turned, and fell on her butt as the dogs surrounded her. It was a sight to see, Mom sitting on the bank with the three dogs walking slowly around her, growling. They were definitely letting my mother know that she wasn't supposed to be there.

Mom sat motionless and only turned her head to watch the dogs. Then Three Eye turned to look at the bridge and Joan came into view. I think Hank was right; Joan could communicate with her dogs without speaking, even if she was out of their sight. Three Eye stopped growling and lay on the bank. Soon after the other two dogs must have received the same message, and assumed a similar position, but they made sure there was room for Joan to walk through.

Mom stood up and brushed herself off, trying not to show that she was having some difficulty collecting her wits. Joan walked past my mother and immediately knelt beside Blackie. Mom then knelt on the other side of Blackie. Mom watched as Joan gently stroked Blackie, and after a few moments Joan took my mothers hand, and placed it over Blackie's heart. Mom looked at Joan and then looked toward us and smiled. Joan then let go of my mother's hand and gently picked Blackie off the ground and carried her to the house. The dogs followed and Mom watched them walk away while she continued to kneel on the bank. When Joan reached the porch, she managed to cradle Blackie with one arm and open the screen door. When she got inside the porch she lowered Blackie to the floor, and then sat on the porch swing.

Mom returned to the barn, and watched as Joan glided back and forth on the swing. I think in that short encounter a bond was formed between Joan and my mother. No one said a word, the scene that had just unfolded expressed more than any words could ever attempt to.

While Mom joined us at the hay barn, Uncle Joe pulled into the driveway. Hank came up from the barn just as Ronnie was climbing down from stacking the last bales. Ronnie nodded in satisfaction as he reached the ground, because all the bales were properly stacked, and he had achieved his goal. Uncle Joe and Hank reached the group at the same time, and it was very apparent that Hank was at a loss for words. He was struggling with trying to find something appropriate to say. My mother sensed his predicament and came to the rescue. She reached her hand out to Hank.

"Thanks again for all you have done to help Blackie, it's the second time you and Joan have come to her aid. Alfred says that if we have one more day like today we can finish up. So if you don't mind, we'd like to come back tomorrow," Mom said.

Hank gently shook my mother's hand. He then walked to each person and shook their hand, and earnestly expressed to each his gratitude. Ronnie was standing by the ladder, and looked up nervously as Hank approached. Without hesitating, Hank extended his hand to Ronnie. Ronnie smiled, accepted the invitation, and put his hand in Hanks.

"Ronnie, you're a good man. I can see where Shorty gets his work attitude, and I want to thank you very much," Hank said.

Ronnie was embarrassed, but proud. He had healed some wounds that day. We all climbed into Ronnie's car and left for home. Ronnie helped me with chores and when we returned to the house, everyone was sitting in the porch enjoying a cool beer or glass of root beer nectar. Grandma came in from the kitchen and passed a plate of cookies around.

"Cookies and beer, you can't beat it," Uncle Joe said.

"You're right, this root beer is pretty tasty, Joe," Grandma replied as she sat down.

Joe picked up his mother's subtle message, and was quick to reply.

"Of course that's what I meant, Ma. How did your day go?"

"My day went great and the kids behaved better than any I ever had. How did the day go for you all, did you get much accomplished?"

Everyone looked at each other and Dad responded to his mother's question, "I think it went real good, don't you, Maddie?"

My mother thought for a minute, and then answered, "Today provided me with as much inspiration as any church sermon I have ever heard, and it made me feel just as good, if not better inside."

A silent confirmation rose from the group in nods and smiles of agreement.

What a difference a day makes. This morning my mind was full of dreadful expectations, but tonight those thoughts had been replaced with encouraging feelings of hope.

Chapter Fifteen
Haying Is Done

Grandma and Grandpa stayed over that night, so Grandma could watch my brother and sister again the next day. The next morning after chores; Mom, Grandpa and I rode to the Raycarts with Dad. Friday was pay day, so Dad would leave around noon for work. We arrived at the Raycarts at nine thirty, Ronnie and Uncle Joe drove in right behind us. The dogs met us at the end of the driveway, but were not in their normal threatening mode; instead they stood quietly and watched as we drove by. After we drove past they looked up the road, and then quietly returned to the house where Joan was sitting on the porch swing.

Mom pointed to the porch as we drove by. "Look, I see Blackie."

Dad stopped the car and sure enough there was Blackie looking out the screen. I ran to the porch and opened the screen door. Blackie was standing on all fours, but when I opened the door she lay back down. I think she wanted to show me that she was getting better. A familiar gleam had returned to her eyes, but seeing her resting on the floor reminded me that she still needed more time to recuperate. Mom had followed, and was standing behind me on the porch steps.

"I believe that dog has cheated death again. Shorty, do you think Joan would mind if I come in?"

I looked at Joan and then looked at her three guardians standing in front of the porch.

"They don't seem to mind, so I'm pretty sure Joan won't mind."

Mom entered the porch and walked over to Joan, and put out her hand.

"Joan, we're in your debt again for helping us, thank you very much."

Mom's arm was outstretched, and she was desperately looking for some kind of acceptance, or acknowledgement, but nothing happened. Joan continued to glide slowly back and forth while staring straight-ahead towards the river. Mom lowered her arm and turned to leave. A look of disappointment shadowed her face, but then she looked at Blackie and smiled.

"Shorty, let's go to work. Joan has done her part, now it's time for us to do ours."

I followed my mother outside and left Blackie resting comfortably on the porch floor. As I stepped from the porch I turned toward Joan and said thanks, but there was no response. I walked beside my mother, and she turned to look at Joan. The dogs had walked about fifteen feet from the house and were watching us leave, but Joan continued to stare at the river.

"Maybe Joan can't find a way to let us know what she's feeling deep inside, so her dogs are trying to show us some of what Joan wants to bring out," Mom said.

I didn't reply to my mother's out of the ordinary comment, because I thought she was using some off the wall thought pattern she called abstract thinking. I know that each of us would have liked nothing better than for Joan to have taken my mother's hand, or given some sort of response that showed she knew we were there.

Alfred had arrived and everyone was standing by the barn. As we approached Hank detected our somber state and walked across the drive to meet us.

"I know it's hard. You long for her to say something, or at least give you some kind of sign that she knows you're there, and when nothing happens it makes you feel as though you've failed. I believe she knows that we're trying to help, but at times I get a notion that she's afraid to let me know," Hank said.

The day went very well and by eight that night we had finished. Joan had returned from her nightly walk and was sitting in her chair by the river. Blackie was on the rug by her side, and Joan's dogs had taken their guardian positions on the bank.

We were getting ready to leave, but Hank asked us to wait a minute while he got something from the house. While Hank went inside Mom walked to the river. I watched her stoop down to pet Blackie; she then walked to the front of Joan and knelt on the ground. She looked up at Joan and placed her hands on top of Joan's hands. With her hands resting on top of Joan's, she stood up from her kneeling position. She then removed her hands and as she walked away reached out and placed her hand gently on Joan's shoulder to say goodbye.

As Mom walked up the hill, Hank came out of the house with his arms full of gunny sacks. The sacks were filled with garden vegetables and frozen meats, which he handed to Mom, Grandpa, Uncle Joe and Martha. Then he gave an envelope to Ronnie and me.

"I know this isn't nearly enough and I may never be able to settle up proper."

Mom was quick to respond to Hank's act of gratitude.

"Hank we're glad you allowed us to help, and God knows we may be the ones who won't be able to settle up proper."

When Ronnie opened the envelope and found a twenty dollar bill inside, he stepped forward and put his hand out to give the envelope back.

"Hank, I can't take this. I don't deserve it," Ronnie said.

"You earned it, so in my book that means you deserve it, and it would make me feel good if you took it," Hank replied.

"Hell, he's just like his dad, so he'll more than likely have it spent in a week chasing girls. Ain't that right, Dad?" Uncle Joe said.

Grandpa was worn out from the last two days of unaccustomed physical work, but he thought for a minute and replied matter-of-factly to his son's inquiry.

"Joe's got a point, but don't forget, if I didn't chase the girls neither of you would be here." Then he hesitated and added, "Don't any of you tell Rose I said that."

The remark by Uncle Joe and response by my grandpa brought laughter to the group. A task that required hard work had been completed and was closing in a manner that strengthened the spirit and resolve that is always present among family and friends. As we drove out of the Raycart's driveway I had a feeling of satisfaction from our accomplishment, but at the same time felt a tinge of sadness, because haying was done.

Grandpa was sound asleep in the back seat by the time Ronnie turned into our driveway. We left him sleeping in the car while we went inside. Grandma was waiting on the porch steps and saw her husband sleeping like a baby in the back seat.

"What did you do to poor Morgan? He's dead to the world and smiling like a fox in a chicken coop."

Uncle Joe took the opportunity. "I think he's probably dreaming about how he used to chase you around when you were younger, Ma."

Grandma replied without so much as batting an eyelash.

"What makes you think he did the chasing? But I guess you're right, two days ago I was younger."

After everyone left I sat at the kitchen table and took the envelope Hank had given me from my shirt pocket. *Thanks Shorty* was written on the outside and inside there were five ten dollar bills.

Fifty dollars was a lot of money for a week's work and I showed the money to Mom.

"Do you think I should give some of it back?"

Mom pulled a chair away from the kitchen table and sat down next me.

"No, I don't. It's a lot of money, but like Hank told Ronnie, you earned it."

She stirred her coffee and stared at the spoon going around the cup. By the serious expression on her face I knew that whatever she was concentrating on was very important. I must have counted my money for the hundredth time when she finally put the spoon on the saucer.

"I've been thinking all day about what Hank told us this morning...how at times he feels that Joan is afraid to let him know she realizes he means well."

"Yes, I remember that," I said.

"Shorty, that day when you saw Joan go in the river, when she came over to you, was she crying?"

"Mom, I'll never forget the way she looked at me. It was as if she was looking inside of me, and believe me, there were no tears, only river water. Why?"

"Because tonight when I went down to say goodbye to Joan, I could feel her hands tremble, but they weren't moving. She was soaked, so she must have been in the river, but I also didn't see any tears. But I got this feeling that she had been crying."

Did she look at you, I mean stare at you."

No, she didn't, I didn't even see her blink. Her eyes were wide open, but there wasn't any indication that she was aware of anything around her. Shorty, for some reason she has looked at you, it may be because you're about the same age her son was when he died. I don't know. Maybe Doctor Thompson is right, and a psychiatrist is the answer. I wish I knew."

"But Hank feels that if he lets the doctor take her to a psychiatrist, they might lock her up or something and he wouldn't be able to take her home again."

Mom thought for a while, and then stood up and placed her cup and saucer in the sink.

"You're right, if Joan was taken from Hank it's hard telling how it would affect him."

Mom must have determined that it was time to change the conversation.

"It'll be dark soon you better see to the pigs."

I had forgotten all about the pigs and chores, but I found some reserve energy and started for the door. Before I reached the door, Mom asked, "What are you going to do with all that money?"

"You know, if it's alright with you and Dad, I'd like to buy one of those fishing rods that I saw in the Montgomery Wards catalog and put the rest away."

"I don't see why not, it's your money. You earned it," Mom said.

By the time I finished chores the sun had disappeared over the horizon and a warm night breeze made its way through the swamp. Chores had taken what energy I had left and my body was ready to fall asleep standing up. I went upstairs to get ready for bed, walked to the window, pulled the curtain back and raised the window to let the night breeze in. I looked toward the river and sat on the bed. While I was taking off my shoes a vision made its way through my fatigue and registered in my brain. I returned to the window and saw what I was afraid I had seen. On the bank of the river I saw something or someone walking. I watched for a few moments, and saw that it was heading directly towards our house. I let the curtains go and ran downstairs.

"Mom, something is coming up from the river through the swamp. I saw it from my bedroom window."

Mom came out of her chair as if she had been sitting on a spring and ran into the porch. She peered out the screen door, looking in the direction of the swamp.

"Are you sure? I don't see anything."

We both stared into the night, and then out of the shadows by the shed a dog, or wolf slowly came into view. We looked at each other and Mom raised her hand and checked to make sure that the screen door was hooked. The animal stopped, looked in our direction, and then started to walk towards the pump.

"What we gonna do?" I whispered.

Mom put her finger to her lips indicating for me to be quiet. She then took me by the hand and pulled me off to the side, away from the door. When we stepped back Mom turned off the porch light, but we were still able to see the entire yard and the silhouette of the animal standing in the shadows. Whatever it was didn't move for a couple of minutes, but then it turned its head and looked back towards the shed.

We stood in the darkness of the porch, and from the shadows of the shed the form of a person stepped out and walked towards the pump. Mom motioned me to follow her to the kitchen. She slowly opened the kitchen door, and took me by the arm so that I was in front of her. As Mom gently pushed me, I glanced out the screen door and saw that the person had already walked past the pump, and was about twenty feet from the house. Mom turned to look, and suddenly put her hand over her mouth.

"Well I'll be," she whispered.

Immediately we both recognized who our visitor was. It was Joan Raycart with her dogs, and she was carrying Blackie. We walked to the screen door and Mom unhooked the door and stepped outside.

"Shorty, you stay here," Mom directed as she cautiously walked down the steps.

"Hi, Joan," Mom said.

All three dogs were now standing between Mrs. Raycart and my mother. They made low warning growls, and Mom took a step back and stood still. Joan stood motionless, holding Blackie and staring straight ahead. The lower part of her dress was wet and muddy from walking through the swamp. If she carried Blackie all the way from their place to ours she had to be exhausted, but she wasn't breathing heavy or showing any signs of fatigue.

Mom turned to look at me. "I don't know what to do. Shorty, you better try and call Hank. His number is two shorts and a long."

While my mother spoke to me, Joan turned and started to walk back towards the pump.

"Mom, Mrs. Raycart is leaving."

Without hesitating Mom started to walk after Joan, but the dogs didn't like that. They hadn't moved and now their growls became more intense. Mom stopped abruptly and watched Joan walk away. Mom's posture stiffened as she held her arms tight to her side, and I could see her hands opening and closing in nervous repetition.

When Joan reached the pump she stopped and then turned and began to walk back towards the house. She walked to where she had been standing before and stopped. She stood there for a moment then turned and walked back to the pump. She continued to pace back and forth in this same manner and gave no indication that she would ever stop. It was as if Mrs. Raycart was a guard walking her post, but instead of a rifle she was carrying a forty pound black dog.

Mom was at a loss for what to do; every time she tried to make a move towards Joan the dogs became more defiant.

"Shorty, I think Joan is lost. She's never been here before, and she's not familiar with the surroundings. We have to get Hank. Try calling him."

I ran to the phone and tried calling, but there was no answer, so I returned to the screen door.

"No answer, Mom, he's probably out looking for her. What should we do?"

Mom was shaking her head back and forth in desperation.

"I don't know, but she can't keep this up, she just can't. I got to get to her."

Mom took a step forward and the white hair on the back of Peg's shoulders stood up straight. Mom took another step, and the dog lunged at her and came to the ground about two feet in front of my mother with his teeth showing. Mom quickly stepped back and I opened the screen door.

"You get back inside and close that door right now," Mom ordered.

Three Eye walked past Peg and looked towards the end of our driveway. After a few moments we saw car lights coming down the road and the car turned into our driveway. It was Hank. He pulled into the yard and stopped by the pump. As soon as he got out of the truck he immediately walked to his wife and put his arms around her shoulders

"Joan, Joan, it's all right, I'm here. You're safe."

Joan stopped her pacing and Hank tried to take Blackie from her arms, but she wouldn't let go. Hank looked at my mother.

"Maddie, are you okay? The dogs didn't hurt you, did they?"

"No, I'm fine, may have aged a bit, but I'm fine. What happened?" Mom asked.

"When everyone left tonight I went to sit by Joan at the river. She was still wet so I went to the house to get a blanket for her, but when I got back she was gone. I thought she went up river. She always goes up river. I went to get her and bring her home, but I couldn't find her and then it dawned on me that Blackie was also gone. An hour had already passed by the time I got back to the farm. I found Joan's tracks in the mud heading down river and figured the only place she could be heading with Blackie would be over here. I shouldn't have left her sitting out there by herself. She can move away so quietly, but she has never gone down river before. I shouldn't have left her alone."

"You can't watch her all the time, Hank," Mom said.

"I know, and I don't, because the dogs do, but she always goes up river, it's like her second home."

While Hank and my mother were talking, I stepped outside. I walked down the porch steps leaving the screen door close behind me. The dogs had stopped their growling and were now lying on the ground, seemingly content with the situation. I stopped when I reached the bottom of the steps, because Joan was walking towards me.

Joan stopped in front of me, knelt down, laid Blackie on the ground and quickly stood up. She stood motionless, as if frozen in time. We all stood motionless; the only movement was the leaves on the trees from the night breeze passing through. We all watched Joan, and waited for a miracle to happen.

Then as quickly as the silence had set in, all hell broke loose. The dogs sprang to their feet and went tearing towards the pump. They ran past the pump into the darkness apparently chasing something, but it sounded more like they were attacking something.

I looked into the darkness where the dogs had disappeared, and Joan grabbed my hand. She pulled me to the ground and placed my hand on Blackies head, and then let go. Before I had time to react, she stood up, and started to walk towards the pump with Hank and Mom walking beside her. We could hear the dogs barking in the distance, and then all of a sudden it became silent. All that could be heard from the swamp was the sound of crickets and the night breeze rustling the swamp grass.

Then just as quickly as they had left, the dogs returned from the shadows. They ran to the pump and silently positioned themselves around Joan, but each of them were looking in the direction of the swamp. We were all looking in the direction of the swamp. Hank walked to the fence and we could hear him step through the barbwire. In a few minutes he returned and walked up to his wife and placed each of his hands on her shoulders.

"What was it Joan?"

Joan resembled a statue that was set in a position always meant to stare into the darkness. If she heard Hanks question you couldn't tell it by looking at her, and slowly she started to walk into the darkness. Hank ran after her and gently took her arm, and led her back into the light.

"I think I better get Joan home. Whatever was out there, the dogs have scared it so bad that it's probably in the next county by now. Shorty, I think the reason Joan came over was to bring Blackie back to you. She must feel that

Blackie has got her health back, and needs her buddy. Maddie, are you and the kids going to be okay?"

Mom was still giving all her attention to the swamp, and the question startled her.

"Oh, yes, yes...we'll be fine, but what about Joan? She walked the entire way through the swamp carrying that dog; she has to be close to exhaustion."

Hank had not let go of his wife's hand. He escorted her to the truck, opened the door, and helped her in. Once in the truck Joan sat up straight and looked as if she was in a trance. Hank opened the tailgate and the dogs immediately jumped on the bed of the truck. Then Hank walked to the driver's door and opened it, but before he stepped in he looked at us, and a serious look came across his face.

"I had so much hope. I really thought she was coming back. I may have to let her go before she hurts herself. She's not coming back, is she, Maddie?"

"Hank, I don't know. I know it has to be hard on you, but don't give up. That day by the river when she took my hand and put it on Blackies heart, I felt as if she was trying to tell me not to give up, no matter how bad it seems."

"I think I know what you mean," Hank said.

He climbed in the truck and smiled at me.

"Shorty, don't you be a stranger now. If it's all right with your folks I might call to ask you for some help once in a while."

"That'd be fine with me, and thanks for the money."

"Believe me you earned it," Hank said as he backed his truck around.

We watched him drive up the road and it wasn't long before his lights disappeared from view. We walked to the house and found Blackie waiting for us by the steps. She was able to climb the steps on her own, and Mom made a soft place for her to lie down in the porch. Before we went into the kitchen Mom made sure the porch screen door was locked, and then she carefully scanned the area of the swamp that Joan had walked through.

"I'll unhook it when your dad gets home," she said.

"What do you think those dogs were chasing?" I asked.

"I don't know, maybe that animal that chased you through the swamp was following Joan tonight."

"Why didn't it chase her, like it did me?"

"I imagine it's because of her dogs. I don't think they have any fear, and I would feel sorry for anyone or anything who tried to harm Joan."

"Were you afraid tonight Mom?"

"Yes I was. When that white one jumped at me, I thought I was going to have a cow."

"You know if you don't show your fear they'll leave you alone," I said.

"Now where have you heard that? Besides these aren't regular dogs," Mom said.

"I've been telling you that all along, and I still believe Mrs. Raycart somehow talks to them."

"Everything sure does seem to revolve around Joan as far as those dogs are concerned."

"Do you still like Mrs. Raycart? She was a little scary tonight?"

"It was an interesting night, that's for sure. Your statement that if you don't show your fear they'll leave you alone, may have some merit too."

I didn't understand what my mother was trying to say, but before I could ask her what she meant, she tried to make it clearer for me.

"What I think I'm trying to say is that Joan may have found that the best way to hide her fear is not to speak, because then people will leave her alone. And if they leave her alone, then there's no way that she can be responsible for any more sorrow."

"Oh," I said.

I still didn't completely understand, but I knew that today my mother had spent a lot of time reflecting on Joan's condition and was trying to figure out what would be the best way to help.

The conversation made me forget about the episode of the dogs chasing after some animal in the swamp. However, Mom didn't forget. When I started to climb the stairs for bed I saw her looking out the screen door towards the swamp.

"You go to bed, I'm going to stay up and read for a while."

The first thing I did when I entered my room was to go to the window and search the swamp. I carefully looked over the swamp and paused for a brief time whenever I came across a suspicious looking shadow, but I didn't see anything out of the ordinary. Hank was more than likely correct, whatever kind of animal was in the swamp tonight, those dogs probably scared it so bad that it's still running.

The pillow felt very comfortable and I was close to dozing off when a thought surfaced. If the thing that followed Joan through the swamp was the same thing that chased me, then it was no animal, because an animal can't stand a fishing pole neatly against a fence. It had to have been a person, but it wasn't Joan or Hank.

My thoughts caused me to go to the window for one last look, and I saw that the lights were still on down stairs. Whatever was out there had my mother concerned, and she wasn't going to go to bed until her husband returned home from work.

Chapter Sixteen
Summer Days

Saturday morning while I was doing chores, Dad walked through the swamp to the river and back. When he returned Mom was preparing breakfast. She poured him a cup of coffee and then sat at the table.

"Did you see anything? Mom asked.

"No I didn't, only the local residents and they seemed to be going about their daily routine with no problem. I think Hank was right; whatever was out there last night is long gone. I know one thing for sure. Joan has got to be in very good shape, and as sure footed as the animals that live out there. I'm ready for a nap from just walking through it a couple of times, and I wasn't carrying a sick dog. Hell, I tripped and fell twice. And it was day light."

Mom gave a muffled laugh. "You're right, whatever kind of animal it was is more than likely long gone. I probably made a mountain out of a mole hill. You didn't hurt anything when you fell did you?"

"No, but I swallowed my tooth pick, and when I was getting to my feet after the second fall I saw two woodchucks and a ground squirrel laughing at me. It hurt my feelings some, but give me a break I don't live out there."

Dad always seemed to come up with some sort of humorous antidote that took the edge off a serious situation. More often than not it allowed people to relax and try to find the brighter side. I think it was a family trait, because everyone in his immediate family used the same tactic.

Mom laughed.

"I bet you were a sight, and probably are the talk of the entire swamp. But when those dogs charged into the swamp last night, they were attending to serious business."

"Those dogs mean business every day, Maddie. Maybe they guided Joan through the swamp." Dad paused for a moment.

"Shorty, you got your chores done? We got a date at Joe's to get you started on your cultivating career."

When we left for Uncle Joes, Mom was outside hanging clothes.

"Try to keep some of the corn in the ground. See you at supper," she said.

I made a few mistakes in my initial days of cultivating, but all-in-all I caught on fairly fast. The remainder of June and July flew by. I worked a lot of days at Uncle Joe's, but Hank never called. However, I stopped to say hello whenever I went by their place.

The dogs no longer considered us a possible threat, so they didn't find it necessary to chase us or issue warning growls when we visited. It sure made life a lot easier and one night I experienced something that made me feel the dogs weren't just tolerating us, but may have actually accepted us. Joan was sitting by the river and I walked to the bank and sat on the ground next to her.

"Sure is a pretty day, isn't it, Joan?"

As usual there was no response. However, while I was sitting there, old Three Eye stood up and walked over and lay down beside me. I cautiously extended my arm and placed my hand on top of her head, and then slowly moved my hand along the top of her fur down to her shoulders and back. She was lying with her head resting on the ground and didn't move her head, but instead raised her eyes to look at me. I smiled at her, and she lowered her eyes to smile back. I sat on the bank for a few moments gently stroking the top of Three Eyes body when Joan stood up. It was time for Joan's nightly ritual and I watched her walk to the bridge. When she reached the bridge she stopped, and turned so that she was facing me. Three Eye immediately stood and ran to Joan, obeying her silent command. I then walked to the barn to say hi to Hank.

Hank was letting the last of the cows out for the night and smiled when he saw me.

"Hi, Shorty, catch anything today?"

I showed him the six rock bass that I had caught.

"That'll make a good meal, good job. In a couple of weeks I'm going to try and get some more hay in, can you help?"

In two weeks most of the farmers would be in the middle of oat thrashing.

Hank didn't raise oats anymore because harvest required lots of help, and the last time he did it the incident with Joan and Mrs. Wilson occurred. To eliminate a chance for a similar episode he stopped planting oats and used the acres to grow hay and corn, which he harvested by hiring a person such as Alfred Jest. Hank bought the oats needed for making cattle feed at the mill, and the extra hay that he raised he sold to farmers who ran short in the winter months.

"I know you'll be busy with threshing at that time, but if you get a break let me know. I have arranged for Alfred to come over around the tenth."

"I'll be glad to help, you can count on me. There's so many people at thrashing, so they won't miss me anyway."

Hank walked into the barnyard and looked up river. He was chewing on a long piece of hay and thinking of days gone by.

"Thanks, Shorty, I know thrashing is a fun time, everyone getting together and all. And you can't beat the cow tanks full of cold pop."

There was a touch of melancholy in the tone of his voice that was probably brought on because he missed those days of hard work and neighbor helping neighbor. It had been taken away from him, it didn't seem right, so many things taken away.

"It's getting late, I better get home. Come on, Blackie." I stopped half way across the barnyard and yelled, "Besides, me and Joan are a hay stacking machine."

"Yes you are. Tell your folks hi."

He waved to me as I headed down river, and he started to walk up river.

As we walked along an emotion of pride swelled up from deep inside. I had made a commitment that day. Not because I had to, but because I felt needed. Thrashing was fun and all the free pop and games were abundant after a day's work, but this was more important, and it made me feel good about myself. It was a nice walk home and we were there well before dark. Ever since the night Joan brought Blackie home, I was always home from the river before dark.

Mom remained busy with her garden, the chickens, the kids, the berry picking, the canning and every thing else that made Mom be Mom. Most of what my mother did we took for granted, but when I look back and reminisce about my younger years it's very difficult to figure out how she made time to do it all. There was no bible school after the middle of June, so Dad had to cut his card games short at Mirror Lake Tavern. However, every other Sunday after church Dad and Mom made a point to visit the Raycarts. Mom would speak to Joan, and even though the one-sided conversations ended with both ladies sitting in silence, Mom never believed that her visit was a vane attempt to capture something that was unobtainable. When it was time to leave, my mother would take Joan's hands and offer her a parting vow that always included an attached wish.

"Joan, we'll see you in a few days, but if there's anything that you may need me for sooner, don't forget that we live just down river."

While Mom sat in the porch visiting with Joan, Dad would visit with Hank, and I'd get stuck watching my brother and sister, so they wouldn't get to dirty, or fall into the river. And the dogs just watched. We never stayed long, but it was easy to see that Hank enjoyed the visit, and actually looked forward to us coming.

During the drive home from one Sunday visit Mom told me that she and Dad were afraid Joan was withdrawing more. I didn't ask why, because I probably didn't want to believe it, but Mom explained their reasoning.

"Hank told Dad that at times he now has to spoon feed Joan for the entire meal, and she's wandering away more often, and going farther up river."

How could a lady who could work with the best of them and was able to carry a forty-pound dog through the rough terrain of a swamp not be able to feed herself? It didn't make sense to me. I didn't want to accept it, so I put it out of my mind.

Summer, like most summers, was going by way too fast and before we knew it the hot dog days of August were upon us. On one of those hot August afternoons I had taken advantage of the cool shade while fishing and time slipped away, so I decided to walk the road home in order to make-up some time. I was walking past Sam Raycart's driveway as he was pulling onto the road and he stopped beside me.

"Can I give you and your dog a lift?" Sam asked.

It was getting late, so we accepted his offer, and Blackie and I got in the back seat. The car was a mess; empty beer bottles scattered on the floor and the air reeked of cigarette smoke. Toad was riding in the front and was as drunk as a hoot owl.

"Did you catch any good sized ones today?" Sam asked.

"A few, but most were suckers, so I let 'em go," I said.

The statement perked the attention of Toad, who looked to be on the verge of passing out.

"You should just throw them bastards up on the bank for the varmints."

He continued to mumble on, but his speech was so slurred that I couldn't make out what he was saying. He had a bottle of beer in one hand and took a long swig until it was empty then tossed it out the window into the ditch. He took another bottle out of a bag that was on the seat beside him, and then turned so that he was looking at me and Blackie.

"How'd your dog get them scars?" Toad asked

"I don't know, I think she got in a scrap with a badger or something."

"I see the crazy bitch's dogs don't bother you anymore. What ya do, kick their ass so they're afraid of ya? They need a good ass kicking. I should have finished the one off when I had the chance," Toad said.

Sam burst out laughing.

"You sure won't be the one to give them a licking, you're afraid to even get out of the car when they're around."

Sam was feeling no pain either, but he wasn't quite as drunk as Toad. Toad turned and faced the front. Sam's comment annoyed Toad.

"You should talk, ya member when you lost us all that money? I told ya that weird-eyed dog was a good fighter, but no, you had to kiss up to Jewel and bet on the Rott. Five hundred bucks threw down the drain, and they didn't even give you the dead Rott."

Sam glanced in the rear view mirror at me and then turned his attention to Toad.

"Shut up, Toad, you're so full of baloney."

"Okay, okay, but that dog must still be pissed at you for bettin' against her, because it won't let you out of the car either." Toad then started to nod his head up and down.

"You gotta fess up; we do better when we bet on the ones that come from the slim man. He can make them bastards...he can make them bastards, bastards..."

Toads thought patterns were anything but coherent, but after he took another drink from his bottle he managed to end the sentence.

"Yup, he can make them bastards meaner than ten badgers."

As Toad was finishing his remarks, Sam stopped at the end of our driveway.

"I'm going to let you out here, we'll see you around," Sam said.

"Thanks for the lift."

As I walked away from the car, Sam reprimanded Toad.

"Toad, you talk too much."

Toad countered by waving his arm at Sam, indicating that he could care less what Sam thought.

"Let's go to Mirror Lake and I'll beat you out of a couple of beers with the dice box."

"Fat chance, old Toad, open me up a beer, or I'll make you walk."

I watched as they drove away. I tried to make some sense out of what Toad was trying to say, but he was as drunk as a skunk and I doubted he even knew what he was saying.

Grandma and Grandpa came over that evening to visit. After supper Grandpa took a small jar from his overall front pocket and handed it to me.

"Here's something I picked up at Johnny's bate shop in Sun Set, and thought you might like to give 'em a try."

The jar contained three different sized fishing lures called dare devils.

"Maddie said you have a new fishing rod coming from Montgomery Wards. Thought maybe you could give these a try when you get it. The guys at Johnny's say they bring in the big bass."

"Thanks, Grandpa, I'll sure give 'em a try."

The next Saturday afternoon the rod and reel came in the mail, and it didn't take me long to read through the instructions, and have it ready to go. Dad saw that I was more than somewhat eager to try it out.

"I'd like to see you use it myself. Let's go down to the river and put it to the test. Maddie, you want to come with?" Dad said.

"Sure."

We all walked to the river and I immediately started to practice casting. There definitely was a learning curve and on more than one occasion an errant cast caused my hook to get snagged in some brush, or lily pads, and once I even hooked my mother's skirt.

"Don't throw me in...Don't throw me in..." she jokingly pleaded.

"Looks like it's going to take away from your day dreaming time," Dad said.

I then showed him how I could attach a bobber and throw the line out the same as with a cane pole, but to locations that a cane pole wouldn't allow me to reach. Dad shook his head to confirm that he understood what I was doing.

"I see, you've narrowed the field. You're not going to wait for the fish to swim to you, you're gonna bring the attraction of a free lunch to them," Dad said.

I was aware that my dad knew about rod and reels, because most of his friends used them and he may have been pretending to know less than what he really did. Never-the-less, a feeling of self importance came over me, because I was able to illustrate to my dad something that he had no first hand knowledge of. In my mind Dad was my student and I was instructing him on the proper way to use a rod and reel. My casting accuracy improved with each toss and I caught three nice bass that afternoon, and successfully coached my dad through a few throws with the rod.

"Maddie, I might get one of these. It makes fishing a little less boring."

"I think that's a very good idea, and if you remember what you learned here today, I see no reason why you couldn't catch a few."

On Sunday I practiced casting most of the afternoon, and by the end of the day I was fairly confident in my ability.

"It's all in the wrist," I told everyone at supper.

"That big black bass won't get away this time," Dad said.

"You're right about that, and if Uncle Joe or Mr. Raycart don't need me tomorrow I'd like to go back to that spot, and give it a try."

"I don't see any problem with that, do you, Maddie?" Dad asked.

"As long as you get chores done and are back before dark, it's fine with me."

The next day I hustled through chores, devoured breakfast, and Blackie and I left for the river. We were on a mission to catch that infamous black bass. Blackie had mostly recovered from the poisoning episode and was able to stay beside me as we walked along the river. When we reached the Raycarts, Joan was sitting in the porch and Hank was working on the side of the house. I waved and said hello to Joan as I walked around the corner to show Hank my new fishing rod. .

"Hi, Shorty, going fishing I see," Hank said.

I told him that I was and then showed him my new fishing rod. He was genuinely impressed and took the time to stop what he was doing to carefully look it over. I saw that he had just finished replacing a couple of window panes and thought maybe a partridge or some other bird had mistakenly flown into the closed window, and broke the glass.

"What happened, did a bird fly into it?" I asked.

"No, I'm afraid it wasn't a bird, more of just a misunderstanding I guess. If it's not to late, stop in on your way back and show us what you caught with that new rod."

"I will," I said. "I bought it from Montgomery Wards with the money you gave me for haying."

My added comment brought a smile to Hanks face, but it only lasted a moment. It was apparent that the job at hand was occupying his mind, so I turned and walked to the river. When I reached the bridge I looked back at the house and saw Hank picking the broken glass off the ground and putting it in a pail. He saw me watching and responded with a sweeping wave.

"Good luck," he said.

I later found out that the window panes were broken by someone throwing rocks from the road late at night while Hank and Joan were sleeping. The sound of the truck approaching and the broken glass had awoken both the dogs and Hank. However, they weren't able to catch a glimpse of the intruders, because whoever threw the rocks was riding in the back of a pick up truck. That way they didn't have to stop, but only had to slow down as they passed by.

It was no longer a teenage game to arouse the dogs, but a deliberate attempt to cause harm and promote feelings of ill will against the Raycarts. Rumors about Joan were continuing to grow and as the rumors increased so did the fear and false interpretations of Joan's condition. Some people were beginning to talk more openly about Joan being evil. They were saying that it wasn't safe to have her or her dogs in the area, because there was no telling what she or the dogs would do next. Unfortunately with this growing fear came an increase in verbal and physical hostility toward the Raycarts. To many they were no longer neighbors who were trying to make the most out of what life had dealt them, but instead were labeled as a threat to the community, and must be dealt with as such.

Chapter Seventeen
An Embarrassing Accident

I walked under the bridge and followed the river bank up stream. It was a beautiful day, but the morning sun had already made it unusually warm. When I reached the bend in the river, I sat on the edge of the bank, took my shoes off, and put my feet in the water. The cool water was soothing and I remembered my mother telling me that she thought Joan might be using this bend in the river as a place to meditate. I agreed with her and then later consulted the dictionary to see exactly what, mediate, was all about. It was a good word to describe why Mrs. Raycart probably came here. It was her temple, a private sanctuary that was well hidden by the trees and steep banks. It was a place where she, or anyone else for that matter, could use the comfort of the natural surroundings and the quiet solitude to focus, and think things through, or not think about anything at all.

However, I felt it was not a place for fishing, so I put my shoes in my pail and continued to walk up river along the bank. About one mile further up river I came to the spot where I hooked the large black bass. I walked out on a tree that had fallen across the river and started to cast into the pool of dark water. I wasn't having any luck with my angleworms, so I decided to try the dare devils that Grandpa had given me. I attached one of the lures to the end of the line and cast it into a deep hole that was close to the far bank, and started to reel it in. The red and white lure glimmered beneath the surface as it twirled through the water. Suddenly from out of no where a large bass began to follow my lure, but when the lure broke the surface the fish quickly retreated into the deep water. That was my bass, he was still here, and I had just about tricked him into thinking that my new lure was a meal fit for such a large fish. I cast toward the same area a few more times hoping that the large bass would take the bait, but nothing happened. I was beginning to get frustrated, because I wasn't quite able to cast the lure into the same location, so I looked around for a better vantage point to continue my pursuit. A large rock protruded out of the water about five feet from the bank and I just knew it was the exact location I needed to get to. If I was on that rock there would be no problem in casting my lure to the same location that originally had brought the large bass out of hiding. I set my pail on the tree trunk, put the jar that contained the lures in my back pocket, and walked the fallen tree to the bank. Holding the rod in one hand I took a few steps backwards, and then made a running jump from the bank to the rock. The distance was no problem, but when I landed on the wet rock I was unable to maintain my balance and fell backward. As soon as my rear end hit the rock I felt the pain from the broken jar as the glass ripped into my butt. I sat stunned for a moment and then slowly stood. I gently placed my hand on the back of my pants and found that it was wet, but it wasn't from the river water.

As I was examining the blood that was soaking through my trousers I heard a car, and saw a red sedan stop at the top of the hill. I couldn't make out who it was because the trees blocked my view, but after a few minutes the car doors slammed shut and the passengers started to walk from the car to the river bank. It was Tommy Frost and Elizabeth Wilson.

Tommy waved when he saw me. "Well I'll be, it's Shorty. How you doing, buddy?"

Tommy was holding Elizabeth's hand as they walked down the bank. I guess they had also been looking for a spot to be alone, but I don't think it was for meditation.

"What's wrong, good lookin'?" Elizabeth said.

She saw that I wasn't in the best of condition and began to pull Tommy down the bank.

"Come on, Tommy, I think he's hurt."

While they were climbing down the bank I realized that I had dropped my new rod, and got on my hands and knees to see if I could retrieve it. The water was deep and I couldn't see any sign of it. Tommy immediately jumped to the rock when he reached the edge of the bank and helped me up.

"You're bleeding pretty good, Shorty. How's your leg, anything broke?"

"I don't think so, I had a jar in my back pocket and it must of broke when I fell."

I began to feel somewhat light headed when I looked at the water and saw it turning red from the blood running down my leg. Elizabeth didn't hesitate to take charge of the situation.

"Bring him over to the bank, Tommy."

Tommy held onto me as I leaned out to reach for Elizabeth's hand, and together they managed to get me to the bank.

"Hey, good lookin', you have to take your pants down, so I can see how bad that cut is."

"What, no way," I said, and I meant it.

There was no way I was going to take my pants down in front of the fox from Fox River.

"You're bleeding pretty bad, Shorty. Beth is close to being a full fledged nurse and she knows what she's doing. She hasta look at it, so she can get the bleeding stopped."

I knew Tommy was right, but Elizabeth didn't look like any nurse I had ever seen. She had a swimming suit on under a pair of shorts and she reminded me more of one of those ladies who carried a sign around the boxing ring to announce the number of the next round than a person from the medical profession.

"Can't you look and tell Elizabeth what you see?" I pleaded.

"Okay, buddy, but let's look at this quick before you lose more blood than your body can tolerate," Tommy said.

I unbuckled my belt and slowly dropped my pants.

"Shorty, you have to pull down your underwear so we can get a better look," Tommy said.

Elizabeth stepped next to me and placed her hand on my shoulder.

"Shorty, I'm going to help you take your underwear down so I can prevent any more pieces of glass from entering the wound," she said. She was trying to make it sound as professional as possible, but I was totally embarrassed.

This was becoming far too much for me to bare both physically and mentally. I thought I'd be better off if they just threw me in the river, because I didn't think I was going to live through the embarrassment anyway. As Elizabeth began to pull my underwear down a page from the Montgomery Ward Catalog popped into my mind, and I saw all the ladies advertising braziers staring at my bare butt. Then I felt her fingers press against my rear end.

"Shorty, the first thing we have to do is stop this bleeding, and then we'll get you somewhere to clean the wound. Tommy get my blouse, it's in the front seat."

Elizabeth's blouse tied around my rear end, this couldn't be happening. It was that damn black bass's fault. Elizabeth continued to put pressure on the wound while she waited for Tommy to return with the blouse. Tommy ran down the hill and handed the blouse to Elizabeth.

"Shorty, I'm going to wrap this around your leg and tie it as tight as possible, so we can stop the bleeding," Elizabeth said.

"Can't Tommy do that?" I asked.

Elizabeth giggled as if she was trying to catch her breath before responding to my plea.

"Shorty, we have to stop the bleeding and get you to a doctor. You're going to need some stitches and the wound has to be checked for glass and cleaned properly. I know this is the last place you want to be right now, but can't you see how bad a cut you have," Elizabeth said.

I slowly turned to look at the cut. Elizabeth's hands were red and the blood was flowing through her fingers. I started to feel faint and then the lights went out.

When I regained consciousness I was lying across the lap of someone, and I could feel a hand pressing firmly against my butt. Please don't let this be who I think it is, but my wish didn't come true. I was in the back seat of Tommy's car and Elizabeth was holding my butt. Then all of a sudden she bent over and I could feel her upper body on my back.

"Sorry, good lookin', but we're going by my house and my mother hasn't quite made up her mind about Tommy yet. How you feeling?"

"Where we going? Did you bring my pants? Where's Blackie? Do you have a blanket?" I asked.

"Relax, Shorty, Blackie's up front with me, and we'll be at your house in about five minutes; besides, you're in good hands," Tommy said.

"Well thank you for the compliment, Mr. Frost," Elizabeth said.

"You're quite welcome, Miss Wilson. She'll make a good nurse, don't you think, Shorty?"

I was in no position to discuss a person's career path, because a more pressing issue weighed heavily on my mind. How was I going to stop this from getting out to my friends? Would Elizabeth and Tommy sign a pledge of secrecy?

"I think the bleeding has stopped. I should be getting my pants back on," I said.

"In a minute, Shorty, we're just about at your house," Tommy said.

Mom had seen the car coming in the driveway and was standing on the porch steps waiting.

"Hi, Tommy, what are you doing in these parts?" Mom asked.

"Maddie, we got a situation. Shorty fell and cut himself, and Beth thinks we should take him in for some stitching."

Mom was down the steps on a run and opened the back door to see the situation first-hand. I don't know if she smiled or not when she saw her half naked son lying across the lap of her neighbor's daughter, but it must have been a sight.

"Hi, Elizabeth, how bad is it?"

"I think he'll be fine, but he's going to need some stitches. Do you have something that we can wrap around Shorty before we take him inside for a better look?

Mom ran to the front yard and took a towel off the clothes line. When she returned to the car she wrapped the towel around me as I lifted myself off Elizabeth's lap. I felt a little weak in the knees, but I shrugged off any helping hand as I walked to the house. Mom respected my quest to regain some dignity, but once inside she immediately escorted me to the bedroom and had me lay on the bed. She brought in a pan of water and then unwrapped Elizabeth's blouse from my rear end and started to clean the cut.

"Don't want you getting lock jaw," Mom said.

As Mom was cleaning the cut, Elizabeth explained what happened.

"Shorty, you're making this a summer to remember," Mom said as I lay there with my bare butt sticking up in the air. "Elizabeth, do you think we should put some iodine on before we put a bandage on, or will the doctor take care of that?"

"I think that's a good idea, it would reduce the chance of infection. The doctor will clean it out again, but you can't ever be too clean," Elizabeth said.

As soon as Mom applied the iodine the burning sensation began. In my book the stinging sensation that accompanies iodine couldn't be any worse than the piercing pain that must accompany people who have to walk through the gates of hell.

"Here, let me try to cool it off. I know it must be stinging. I can't believe Shorty is handling it so well," Elizabeth said.

"No, I'm fine; it's going away; it don't hurt at all," I said.

Mom was a firm believer in applying iodine as a way to reduce the chance of infection and she was also aware of the stinging sensation that it caused. To counteract this, and make the process more bearable she would blow across the cut to cool it off after the iodine was applied. However, as great a tool this had proven to be in the past, cuts on the finger or arm in no way could be compared to the location of my current laceration.

I had little doubt that I would never recover from this episode, and if the word got out I'd probably be mentally scarred for life. Then I felt a cool breeze come across my rear end and satanic visions appeared before me. A rustling sound brought me back to earth and I strained to get my head around, to see Elizabeth using a magazine to fan my cut. The fanning took some of the sting away, but I was just as grateful for the method used.

While Mom and Elizabeth attended to my cut, Tommy called Doctor Thompson. We were to meet him at his office. Elizabeth used the sink to wash the blood off her hands and Mom put Elizabeth's blood soaked blouse in a dishpan filled with cold water.

"I don't know, Elizabeth, the blood has set in, your blouse may be ruined," Mom said.

"Don't worry about it, Maddie, it's only a blouse," Elizabeth replied.

Mom had me put on an oversized pair of shorts and brought a pillow for me to sit on as we drove to Doctor Thompson's office. My brother and sister sat in front between Elizabeth and Tommy, and I sat in the back with Mom. My mother hadn't seen Elizabeth much and most of the trip they spent catching up on current events. Mom was impressed that Elizabeth was finishing nursing school in the fall and complimented Elizabeth on her choice of profession. I dozed on and off during the trip, but from what I heard Mom seemed to be pretty impressed with Elizabeth, and Elizabeth had the same opinion of my mother. When we entered Doctor Thompson's office his wife led us directly into the examination room.

"The doctor will be with you in a minute. Shorty, we're going to have to start charging you room and board," she said laughingly as she closed the door.

Mom and Elizabeth came into the examination room with me, and Tommy stayed in the waiting room with my brother and sister. We were only in the room for a couple of minutes when Doctor Thompson came in.

"Good afternoon ladies. Shorty, I see you're back again. You realize that you're supposed to catch the fish and not the other way around. Come on over here and let's have a look."

Doctor Thompson had me take off my shorts and lie face down on the examination table.

"You ladies did a fine job cleaning the wound; I don't see any glass, good job. The cut's pretty deep; he must have bled quite a bit."

"Thank God Elizabeth was there, she had the bleeding stopped by the time they got Shorty home," Mom said.

"Elizabeth, I understand you're going to get your nursing degree in the fall. You going to try and get a job in one of the local hospitals, or are you off to Minneapolis, St. Paul?" Doctor Thompson asked.

"I hope to fine something around here, so I can live in the area."

"I can put a word in for you, if you'd like."

"I would really appreciate that, Doctor."

"Not a problem, I'll be more than happy to do what I can. Shorty, we're going to have to put a few stitches in, and you're going to have a nice scar to show your grandchildren. We'll give you a shot to numb the area and then we'll sew it up."

The doctor went into the next room and returned with the needle and the procaine. He lowered his glasses to fill the needle with the anesthetic, and then pushed the glasses back onto the top of his head.

"Elizabeth, would you like to administer the shot?"

"I wouldn't mind if Shorty doesn't mind," Elizabeth replied.

They both turned to look at me, as if waiting for my approval.

"Why not?" I said.

I could see my mother leaning against one of the cabinets; she was biting on her lower lip and had positioned her right hand so that the thumb was under her chin and the forefinger rested between her lips. She was trying not to laugh, but at the same time showed pity for the predicament I was in. Elizabeth took the needle from the doctor and he placed his finger where he wanted the shot to go.

"You're one brave kid, Shorty," Elizabeth said.

The tone of her voice seemed somewhat shaky and led me to believe that she hadn't done this before. I didn't really want to be the first one, but it was too late. I closed my eyes and clenched my jaw shut as tight as it would go. I have to admit she did a good job. I wanted to tell the doctor that it was less painful then the shots he had given me in the past, but decided it was in my best interest to remain silent, because he had the sewing yet to do.

"Good job, that should do the trick. We'll let it set for a few minutes and then do the stitching. Here, Elizabeth, pull that stool up so you can get a better look," Doctor Thompson said.

Everyone sitting patiently waiting for the numbing process to take hold reminded me of a section in our science book we had gone through last spring. The section had illustrations of scientist observing rats during various experiments. A comparable situation was taking place in Doctor Thompson's office, and I was the rat. The only thing missing was a cage around the examining table, so I couldn't run away.

"Looks like we're going to have to put in about ten stitches, Shorty," the doctor said.

He lowered his glasses from the top of his head, threaded the needle, and went to work.

"Let me know if you feel anything, Shorty."

"I will."

Elizabeth was watching intently as the doctor made a couple of stitches and then stopped.

"Here, Elizabeth, you finish up and I'll watch. I know it's something you probably won't be called upon to do as a nurse, but it doesn't hurt to have first hand experience just in case."

Elizabeth looked at me, and I must have rolled my eyes, because a big smile spread across her face.

"Shorty, is it alright with you?" Elizabeth asked.

"Sure it's okay," I said. What else could a caged rat say?

Elizabeth finished the sewing job and helped the doctor apply the bandage. When the doctor was satisfied that everything was properly taken care of he tapped me on the shoulder.

"There you go, Shorty, you're all back together again," the doctor said.

I was off the table and had my pants pulled up before any more experimentation could be thought of.

"Maddie, bring him back next Tuesday and I think we'll be able to take the stitches out. In the meantime keep it clean and change the bandage and dressing daily. Elizabeth, thanks for the help and good luck in the fall."

Mom and Elizabeth both thanked Doctor Thompson, but before we reached the door the doctor had another question for my mother.

"Say, Maddie, how is Joan and Hank doing?"

Mom replied in a political fashion. She didn't want to lose the doctor's vote of confidence; but at the same time she didn't want to open the door for further questions.

"They're doing fine, like all of us they have their good days and bad days. Joan still is quiet, but she's very gentle, and she definitely is physically fit.

Shorty found that out when he helped them with haying," Mom said.

"That's good to hear. How did the haying go, Shorty?"

"Great, Mrs. Raycart works harder than most men I've worked with."

The doctor smiled at my comment and escorted us into the waiting room. Tommy was sitting outside on the lawn with my brother and sister, and came to meet us when we stepped outside.

"How'd it go?" Tommy asked.

"Just fine, Shorty is one brave young man," Elizabeth said.

Everyone on the ride home was satisfied that we had all done what was needed, but Mom looked for a way to further express her gratitude.

"Elizabeth, Tommy, I want to thank you both again. Shorty was sure fortunate you two came along. With the way Shorty must have been bleeding, there's no telling what could have happened. I'm going to make sure your parents know what fine kids they have," Mom said

Elizabeth and Tommy smiled at my mother's compliment, but when they exchanged glances a look of concern was evident. Elizabeth put her arm over the front seat and turned to face my mother.

"Maddie, I don't know how to ask this, but we'd appreciate it very much if you wouldn't let my mother or dad know that you seen us two together today. Mom doesn't care very much for Tommy, because of the bar and his somewhat tarnished reputation, plus he's five years older than me. I plan to tell them soon, and think it would go over better if it came from me."

Mom didn't hesitate. "I promise we won't tell a soul, other than Mike of course, but I think we need a favor in return."

"Thanks, Maddie, now what do you need from us?" Elizabeth asked.

"Well, I think Shorty would appreciate it very much if you didn't tell other people what happened today until he's thirty or older."

That Mom, she always found a way. I was nodding my head in agreement with her request with such vigor that the seat shook. Tommy laughed and glanced at my mother over his shoulder.

"I can identify with that, be assured my lips are sealed, how about you, Beth?

"Shorty, you have my word on it. You were a trooper through this and I know it was embarrassing for you, but what about me? I got to see the good lookin' kid from Fox River half naked. I'd be the envy of all my classmates at school."

I didn't have to worry about my cut starting to bleed; most of the blood in my body had rushed to my head. Elizabeth's pledge affected my mother differently and she began to laugh.

"I'll never forget the look on your face when Doctor Thompson handed Elizabeth that needle," Mom said.

"Doctor Thompson was very nice to me today. He's concerned about Hank and Joan Raycart, isn't he?" Elizabeth asked.

"I'm sure he has the best of intentions and he is a doctor, but I'm not convinced that he knows what's best for Joan or Hank," Mom replied.

"I don't know either Joan or Hank very well and that's a shame, because I live just down the road from them. I feel it's best for me to stay out of all the gossip, because I don't know what's true and what's not true," Elizabeth said.

"Elizabeth, more people should take that approach. I think too many people around here form judgments based on all the rumors and gossip that is floating around," Mom said.

"I hope you all get it settled at the meeting," Elizabeth said.

"Oh, what meeting is that?" Mom asked.

Elizabeth gave a questionable look towards Tommy, and then turned to face my mother.

"Maddie, I hope the reason you haven't heard about the meeting is because they haven't called you yet. My mother and Francis Beck have set up a meeting for the twenty-seventh of August at the Mirror Lake church about Joan and Hank. I thought they called everyone. I love my mother dearly, but once she gets something in her head that she believes is right, it's near to impossible to divert her from that course. Mom, Francis, and some of the others believe that if Hank cannot help Joan, they must step in. I'll make sure to ask if they forgot to call you."

"No...No...I'm sure they'll call. Has Joan done anything lately to bring this on?"

"You probably know that my mother has always been somewhat concerned that...well you know about the rumors. They have always been aware of Joan sometimes walking the river, but last week when my parents were driving home, they crossed the Fox River Bridge around ten and saw Joan placing lighted lanterns in the trees. That just added more fuel to the fire and now Mom has picked up the cross and is leading a crusade. I think like Doctor Thompson, my mother has the best of intentions, and I hope you all can come to some kind of common ground at this meeting."

"I hope so too, Elizabeth," Mom said.

When we reached our house, Tommy pulled the car close to the front steps and stopped. Mom opened the back door and placed her hand on the back of Tommy's shoulder.

"I think you two make a very nice couple," then she looked to Elizabeth, "and this here one needs someone to settle him down a little. Thank you both very much, I'll have Mike give you some money for takin' us over, Tommy."

"Don't worry about it, Maddie, I'm glad we were able to help," Tommy said.

When they drove out I saw Elizabeth slide over, so she was sitting close to Tommy.

"Come on in, you *good lookin' kid* of Fox River. I got to start supper and it's going to take you longer to do chores, because you have to be extra careful. No jumping over fences or other acrobatics, okay?" Mom said.

"Don't worry, I'll take it slow. Do you plan on going to that meeting Elizabeth was talking about?"

"Yes I do, like Elizabeth said, it may be a way for us all to reach some common ground on this matter, and truly help Hank and Joan."

Chapter Eighteen
Finding the Rod and Reel

Dad got home from work a short time after we had returned from the doctor's office. After talking with Mom for a few minutes he came out to help me with chores. It was not unusual for him to come out and help, but I could tell by the grin on his face that there were ulterior motives in the wind.

"How ya feeling? I can't remember ever being hurt in such a place, does it hurt when you laugh?" Dad asked.

"I don't know, I haven't been laughing too much," I replied, knowing that I had to choose my responses carefully during this conversation, because I just knew he was looking for a way to bait me.

"Seriously, Shorty, you take it easy and let me do the heavy stuff. Maddie says you lost quite a bit of blood today, and we don't want you to over do it. Besides you gotta rest up so you can heal fast."

"Thanks, Dad, I plan on taking it slow and easy."

"That's good; maybe you'll be able to take that other job offer your mom just got a call about."

I thought Hank must have called and asked my mother if I would be available to help him with his last crop of hay.

"Yes, I think I'll take it. Hank says it'll only be for a couple of days, and I'm sure Uncle Joe will understand. I'm sure I'll be all healed up by then."

"No, the call your mother took is for a job at Hillside. I guess it'll only be for a couple of days and it won't interfere with any haying or thrashing jobs.

Ronnie can give you a ride up and I'll pick you up when I come home from work."

"What kind of job is it?"

"They want you to help out with the Esrun Pull. Maddie says the pay sounds pretty good, and they'll even supply breakfast and dinner. She told them that she'd talk to you about it and get back with them tomorrow morning. It's getting close to going back to school, and the extra money would come in handy," Dad said.

"I guess if Mom thinks it's okay, it's all right with me. What's an Esrun Pull anyway?"

"It involves the Hillside College. Next week they start preparing for fall finals and they never can get enough volunteers for the pull, so they've been paying kids that are off on summer vacation to help out. It fulfills a need for the college and at the same time provides some spending money for kids in the area. You know the college gets a job done and at the same time receives positive public relations. Makes quite a bit of sense when you think about it, It's a win, win situation, and as long as the pull goes well everyone is a happy camper. Well, you think about it and let your mother know what you decide. You don't have to if you don't want to. Now we better get washed up for supper."

It was seven o'clock when we finished supper. Mom was washing dishes, Dad was drying and I was sitting at the kitchen table.

"Mom, about this Esrun Pull, how much did they say they'd pay and what do I have to do?"

Dad was quick to interrupt. "You remember, Maddie. They said Shorty would be perfect for the job because of his work ethic, and his ability to remain calm in a difficult situation."

"Yes, he can remain calm in a difficult situation, but I'm—I'm not sure what..." Mom started to say.

"Is it okay if I tell him?" Dad asked.

"Sure, go ahead, sounds like you want to anyway, and I'm interested to see what Shorty thinks and what I think," Mom said.

"Well, Shorty, the Esrun Pull is a dethreading exercise that the nursing students have to become proficient at before they can graduate. All you have to do is bend over and let each nurse pull out one stitch," Dad said.

I didn't know if I was going to laugh or throw a plate at my dad. Mom made the choice for me and took a pan full of dishwater and poured it over his head.

"Esrun Pull, get it, Shorty, nurse spelled backwards," Mom said.

"Your father should go on stage...The first one out of town..."

Dad was laughing hysterically as he wiped the dishwater from his face. It turned into something contagious and soon we were all laughing for no apparent reason.

"With all the excitement I forgot to ask if you caught that big black bass with your new rod?" Dad said.

"Oh heck, I forgot I dropped the rod and reel in the river and couldn't reach it. We should go and get it now," I said.

"What do you say we get a good night's sleep and tomorrow when I get home from work we'll go and get it out of the river," Dad said.

"I think your dad is right. You look pretty beat, and sleep is the best thing for you right now," Mom said.

Reluctantly I gave in and it wasn't long before I was fast asleep. When I woke the next morning, I was lying on the downstairs couch. Mom said I had lain down to read a comic book, but never got past the first page. Instead of waking me to go up stairs they felt it was more reasonable to let me be.

I had slept for over ten hours and you would have thought that would be more than enough. However, during the day I even took a couple of naps. Mom reminded me that I had lost quite a bit of blood, and said that my body needed some extra rest in order to replenish itself. By the time Dad got home from work I was ready to go and retrieve my rod and reel from the Fox River. We finished chores and instead of eating supper Mom packed some sandwiches so we would have more daylight available for our search

I directed Dad through the field that Tommy had taken the previous day. The field was adjacent to Sam Raycart's place; however you couldn't see his home very well because of a stand of evergreens that formed a boundary between his place and the field. Dad parked in the same location that Tommy had parked, and we walked to a point where we could see the river. I pointed out the infamous rock to my parents, as they walked down the hill. Mom thought that it wouldn't be a good idea for me to try and descend the steep grade, so I remained on top of the hill with my brother and sister.

I watched as my dad lay on the rock, put his hands on each side of his face to shade out the evening glare and looked into the water. He then found a long stick lying on the bank and used it to scrape along the bottom of the river, but wasn't able to locate the rod. He tossed the stick into the river and watched it float down stream. Dad saw that we were watching and jumped from the rock to the bank.

"It's not here; the current must have taken it down stream. We're gonna walk down and see if it got caught up in some brush. We'll be back in a few minutes. You kids go ahead and have a sandwich," Dad said.

As I watched my parents start to walk down river some movement in the brush on the opposite side of the river caught my eye. The hillside was thickly covered with trees and brush and the leaves made it almost impossible to see through. I scoured the hillside and saw a dark mass in the middle of a thicket of brush that was standing below two river birch trees. I stared at the thicket trying to make out what it was hiding and after a few moments a sensation came over me that whatever was in the thicket, was staring at me. I quickly looked down at the river intending to call out a warning to my parents, but they were already out of sight. I turned my attention back to the thicket, but whatever was there was now gone. I looked up the hill behind the thicket and saw a figure walking between the birch trees, and I watched as it disappeared into the brush. Whatever had been hiding in that thicket was watching us.

"Was that a bear?" my sister asked.

My sister and brother noticed that something had caught my attention and were standing beside me. My sister must have also caught a glimpse of something moving on the hillside.

"Oh no, there aren't any bears around here, it must have been a deer or something," I said.

They both continued to look into the hillside covered with green and then my brother disappointed because he hadn't seen anything walked to the car.

"I didn't see anything. Can we have a sandwich now?" my brother asked.

I followed my brother and we sat on the hood of the car and ate our sandwiches. The hill we were parked on allowed us an excellent view of the river valley. The blue of the river winding through the green tree covered hills was a very peaceful setting, and in the distance you could see the ponds branching off from the river. I hadn't been far enough up river to reach those ponds, but I planned on doing it before winter set in. I pointed out the blue ponds to my brother and sister.

"I bet there are fish in those ponds that could swallow you in one gulp," I said.

"What's that?" my brother said, pointing toward the ponds.

He was thrilled because he had seen something that neither I nor our sister had noticed. I followed the direction that he was pointing and saw a cloud of brown dust filtering through the trees. A dirt road snaked through the valley and a car or truck was creating the dust. We watched the cloud of dust trail behind the vehicle. It wasn't long before the vehicle was out of sight and the dust disappeared into the air as it floated toward the ponds.

We continued to scan the valley and I'm certain that both my brother and sister hoped to catch a glimpse of something before anyone else noticed. We were watching a hawk riding the air currents above the ponds when we heard voices and it wasn't long before Mom and Dad came into sight.

"No luck, Shorty. Looks like it's gone," Mom said.

"There were a lot of spots we couldn't get to because of the underbrush, so we could have missed it. It's starting to turn dark and the shadows are making it hard to see into the water, so we might as well call it a night," Dad said.

When we were all in the car and starting to leave Dad took the palm of his hand and slapped it against his forehead.

"I know what happened to that fishing rod," Dad said.

"What happened?" Mom asked.

"That damn black bass got it and drug it under one of the banks, pretty smart fish."

"Shorty, told us that the fish in those ponds are so big they could swallow me in one gulp, is that true, Mama? My sister asked.

"I think your dad and Shorty are two of a kind. There's a better word for it, but for now we'll label them both as story tellers," Mom said.

When Dad started to drive onto the main road from the field he suddenly applied the brakes, because a car was approaching at a high rate of speed. The car roared past and the driver honked his horn and waved. It was the black Thunderbird.

"That man likes to drive like a bat out of hell," Dad said.

"Who is it?" Mom asked.

"It's a person from the cities, they call Jewel. You know the one who beat Bruce in arm wrestling at the fair. I see him around on the weekends mostly and he's been chumming with the Strum boys. He drives that flashy Thunderbird and flirts with the local girls quite a bit. He made a play for Elizabeth last week and I thought old Tommy was going to take a poke at him. I think Tommy is getting pretty serious about Elizabeth."

"He could do a lot worse. I think Elizabeth would be good for him," Mom said.

"Hell I thought she was waiting for Shorty," Dad said.

I was trying to remember where I had heard the name Jewel before when my dad's comment drifted into my mind.

"Ha, ha, very funny," I said.

"Mike, let's drive over to the Raycarts. We haven't been there in a while and I'd like to stop and say hello since we're so close," Mom said.

What Elizabeth's mother had said she saw Joan doing late at night was bothering my mother and she was concerned for Joan's welfare. She needed to find out if there were any significant changes in Joan's behavior that would warrant a secret community meeting.

"Good idea, Maddie," Dad said.

The sun was beginning to set when we arrived at the Raycarts, but the heat that was generated during the day was going to make the night very warm. The dogs met us at the end of the driveway and escorted us into the yard. The warning growls and threatening looks that we experienced in the past had been replaced by a more vigilant behavior. The dogs watched us closely as we exited the car, and when they determined everything was safe they returned to their positions by the porch. Joan was sitting in the porch swing and Hank was sitting on the steps. Hank immediately stood up and walked over to greet us as we drove in.

"We were out trying to find Shorty's new fishing rod, and thought since we were in the neighborhood we'd stop in to say hi," Dad said.

Dad went on to explain that I had dropped my new fishing rod when I slipped on the rock. However, my dad also believed that if you're the one telling the story you have the right or obligation to make the story as amusing as possible for the listener. So in Dad's account the reason for me getting cut was not because of an avoidable accident, but was because I tried to turn the river red when that big bass out-smarted me. For a moment I thought he was going to bring up the role that Elizabeth played in the ordeal, but that was safely tucked away, for now. Hank shook his head and smiled as Dad told the story.

"One thing for certain, Shorty is one-hundred-percent boy and he's becoming a part of this river. There's no doubt about it," Hank said.

Mom closely monitored Dad's version of what had happened and then walked to the porch. She reached to open the screen door and all three dogs began to growl. When Mom turned to look at the dogs the screen door opened and Joan walked out. Without hesitating Joan walked past my mother and when she reached the bottom of the steps she stopped and stared in the direction of the bridge. Hank immediately walked to his wife's side.

"What's wrong, Joan? What do you see?

In the meantime the dogs had gathered around Joan and were also looking toward the bridge. Their growls became more intense and their body language gave every indication that they were ready to spring into action at any given moment. However, they maintained their on guard positions beside Joan, and every few seconds would glance at their master, as if waiting to be told what to do. Joan continued to stare in the direction of the bridge and after a few minutes she started to walk toward the river. The dogs immediately began to walk beside her, but now their growls had taken on more of a guttural sound. The hair on the back of Three Eye and Peg was standing straight up. Hank walked to the side of the porch to get a lantern that was hanging on a post, and started to follow his wife.

"Do you mind if we walk with Hank?" Mom asked.

"Maddie, it's okay with me, but I'd like Shorty to come with too, if you don't mind."

Mom didn't answer, and a look of uncertainty came over her face as she turned to face her husband. She was asking for his advice without speaking.

"Hank, those dogs have caught the scent of something. Have you seen any signs of wolves, cougars or something different in the area?" Dad asked.

"No, I haven't and it's too early for our normal nighttime visitors."

"Maddie, I'll stay with the kids, you and Shorty go with Hank. I don't feel too good about this, but I know it's something you need to do. Hank, it won't upset Joan, will it?" Dad asked.

"No, she's fine. The dogs will protect her."

Mrs. Raycart had already reached the bank of the river and was starting to walk toward the bridge. Hank lit the lantern and we began to follow his wife, who was now going under the bridge. Joan walked under the bridge and the dogs followed close behind, making growls that sounded more eerie as they echoed off the riverbanks. Mom and I walked behind Hank using the light from the lantern to avoid tripping or stepping into potholes that were scattered along the bank. Hank would stop for a brief moment every once in a while, and use the light from the lantern to scan the banks of the river. Joan didn't stumble or alter her slow steady pace as she walked over the uneven terrain, and she never looked at the ground. It was as if the placement of each step was being mysteriously guided, and she continued to walk where her stare led her.

As we followed Joan along the bank I realized that it wouldn't be long before we reached the bend of the river that Joan had went to meditate. The growling of the dogs never stopped. I was convinced that they knew something or someone was out there. When Joan and her dogs reached the shallow area of the river that preceded the bend, Three Eye walked around Joan and Joan stepped into the river. Three Eye continued to walk along the bank and the other two dogs followed Joan into the water. Peg walked through the water to the far bank and Wrench remained by Joan's side.

Hank stopped and we all watched as his wife walked forward in the water. Mom grabbed my hand and held on tight. We exchanged glances and I think each of us thought that Joan was going to continue to walk into the water until she was submerged, but then Joan stopped.

She stood motionless as the current brushed against her legs, and stared across the bend of the river into the darkness of the hillside. Then all of a sudden she thrust her arms upward and let out a scream that would have scared the devil himself. Without hesitating Three Eye and Peg charged into the darkness in pursuit of God knows what, but Wrench remained by Joan's side.

"What's happening?" Mom said.

Hank remained standing in the same spot, so Mom walked around him, and pulled me along behind. When she reached a point on the bank that was adjacent to Joan she let go of my hand and stepped into the water. She cautiously felt her way along the rock covered river bottom, and stopped when she was directly behind Joan and Wrench. Mom then began to reach out with her arms in an attempt to comfort Joan, but lowered them to her side when she saw Joan lower her arms.

Everyone remained standing still for a short moment, and then Joan walked to the far bank and sat on its edge. Wrench followed Joan and leaped from the water to the bank and lay down beside her. Wrench had stopped growling, and seemed to be satisfied with what had just happened. Mom looked at me and then began to walk to where Joan was sitting. When she was a few steps from the edge of the bank she suddenly stopped and stared straight ahead.

"Shorty, come over here," Mom said quietly.

I stepped into the river and crossed to where my mother was standing. She took my hand and nodded in the direction of the bank. I followed her gaze and there lying on the bank in back of where Joan was sitting was my rod and reel.

Mom shook her head in disbelief and then climbed onto the bank on her hands and knees. She started to reach for the pole, but Joan reached out and put her hand around my mother's wrist. Mom calmly pulled her arm back and then turned around and sat beside Joan on the bank.

"Shorty, why don't you see if Joan will let you take it?"

I took a deep breath, climbed the bank, walked to where the rod was laying and bent down and picked it up. Joan didn't even turn to watch, but instead was staring at the water as it ran over her legs.

The rod wasn't damaged and the reel had the line wound tightly around it with the lure securely attached. There wasn't any evidence that the rod had even been in the river, as a matter of fact it looked like it had just been taken out of a storage shed. Was it possible for the rod to be swept down river and deposited on this bank without being damaged? The bank was a good three feet above the water line. There was no way it could have washed up on the bank. It had to have been placed there. I tried to convince myself that it was just a matter of luck, and then I remembered my cane pole standing neatly against the fence. Whoever chased me through the swamp that night was still wandering the river. It must be the same person my sister and I saw watching us from the hillside this afternoon.

I searched through the trees on the far bank and wondered if the dog's were chasing the person responsible, and noticed that Mom had taken her left hand and placed it on top of Joan's right hand. A calm silence surrounded the river and Mom was using the peaceful setting to try and console Joan. On the other side of the river Hank had not moved from where he had stopped, and was now sitting on the bank. The lantern was sitting by his side and the light revealed a worried man. He was watching the river and the expression of sadness seemed to make the light go dim.

Then from across the river came sounds of the dogs running through the brush. They were both now on the same side of the river and didn't stop running until they were on the bank where Joan was sitting. As soon as the dogs arrived Joan stood and started to wade across the river, with Three Eye and Peg following.

Mom turned and looked at me. "I guess it's time to go, Shorty."

Mom and I began to walk across, but Wrench stayed behind. Hank stood when he saw us coming and reached out to take Joan's hand. Mom looked at me and we both realized that Hank had been crying.

When the bridge came into view we saw the light from a lantern coming towards us. The light swayed from side to side as it approached and Hank stopped and waited to see who it was. It was my dad; he had my sister sitting on his shoulders and was carrying my brother. When we met each other, Dad spoke quieter than I was accustomed to.

"Nice night. Hope you don't mind, Hank, I found another lantern. The kids were getting restless, so thought we'd walk to meet you and get rid of some of that extra energy."

Hank had regained his composure, but was not going to let go of his wife's hand.

"Good idea, Mike. I bet those kids have more energy than both of us put together."

When we reached the house, Hank led Joan to the porch steps.

"I better get Joan to bed. I'm glad you found your rod and reel, Shorty. If it's still okay with your folks I'll probably be calling next week to see if you can help me put up some hay."

Dad quickly turned to look at me, and a look of amazement crossed his face when he saw I was carrying the rod and reel. Then he looked back at Hank.

"I see no problem, how about you, Maddie?" Dad asked.

Mom was thinking about something else and the question seemed to awaken her from whatever she was concentrating so deeply on.

"No...No...I don't see a problem with it," Mom said.

We didn't pay much attention to a car that was approaching on the main road, but Hank watched it closely until it was out of sight. When we drove out of the yard I looked toward the river and out from the shadows of the bridge I saw Wrench returning. She must have stayed behind to make sure everything was secure.

As soon as Dad turned onto the road home he looked at my mother, and asked, "What was that scream all about, and where did you find the fishing rod?"

"Joan was the one who screamed and I don't mind telling you it sent shivers down my spine. I don't know why she screamed, but when she did, two of those dogs took off into the woods just like they did that night at our house when Joan brought Blackie home. I don't know what they were chasing, but I'm convinced there's something out there, and I think Joan and those dogs know what it is," Mom said.

"I hear what you're saying, that scream made me and the kids jump. What about the rod, where in the river did you find it? It's hard to believe it floated all the way down without getting snagged on something. Hell...that's two miles."

"It wasn't in the river. It was lying on the bank. Joan stopped me from touching it, but she let Shorty pick it up. I think she knew it was his. Shorty, did you show your new fishing rod to Joan?" Mom asked.

"She might have seen it the day I showed it to Hank, I can't remember."

"Did the river beat it up pretty bad, Shorty?" Dad asked.

"No, it looks good, real good."

"It must have been carried down river with the current and washed up on the bank, or else Joan found it and put it on the bank. She definitely knew it was yours. I can understand why Hank wanted you to come with. Joan has some kind of connection with you, Shorty," Mom said.

"What's your feelings about Joan now, Maddie? I know that meeting coming up is bothering you. Do you think Mabel and that battle ax Francis have a legitimate concern?" Dad asked.

"I don't know...I just don't know. When I was sitting by her tonight I felt a sense of calmness from her. I still don't feel the least bit threatened by her or Hank. When she screamed I think there was a reason for it, and whatever is prowling around in those woods was the cause. And that cause may be a major part of why Joan has separated herself from all of us."

Mom was looking out the window, searching for answers in the dark.

"One thing that concerned me tonight was Hank: I think he may be losing hope for him and Joan to return to any sense of normalcy. As for Mabel and Francis, well...It's going to be interesting to hear what they have to say, or better yet to hear what they want," Mom said.

"What makes you feel that Hank is giving up?" Dad asked.

"I don't know if it's giving up as much as giving in. Tonight when we reached the place where Joan screamed, Hank never went any further. He just sat down and cried."

Dad drove into our yard and parked the car. When he turned off the ignition he turned to me.

"Shorty, this place where Joan goes to be alone, is it the first big bend in the river up from the bridge?"

"Yup, that's the place," I said.

"Why do you ask that, Mike?" Mom said.

"Because, if I'm not mistaken that sounds like the spot in the river where they found John's body trapped beneath the ice."

Chapter Nineteen
The List

The bobber went down fast and I pulled as hard as I could. Whatever was on the other end was stronger and it started to pull me into the water. I couldn't let go of my fishing rod. I had just got it back. Then the line gave a quick jerk that I wasn't prepared for, and before I knew it I was under the water. I let go of my rod and started to swim for the surface when something grabbed my leg. I tried to break free and looked down to kick at whatever was holding onto my leg. It was a boy about the same age as me, and he was motioning me to follow him. I told him I couldn't follow because I had to do chores.

"Shorty...Shorty...Wake up...You're having a bad dream." I opened my eyes and saw my mother sitting on the edge of my bed. "You must have been having a nightmare, you okay?"

I sat up and rubbed the sleep from my eyes.

"Yes. I'm fine, had a weird dream is all," I said.

Mom brushed the hair from my forehead and in the same motion used the tip of her fingers to see if I was running a fever.

"Do you still want to work for Hank? More things seem to be going on than when you went to work for him in June. With all that's happened this summer we would completely understand if you didn't want to work for him," Mom said.

"No, Mom, I want to work for Hank. I like him and I think I really help him. Or do you and Dad not want me to?"

"I agree with you, Shorty. You do help Hank, probably more than you even realize. You have provided a shoulder for him to lean his hopes on, and he may be right in feeling that you can help to bring Joan around."

She paused to reflect on what she was going to say next and to reinforce her reasons for saying it.

"But there's also one thing that we all have to be very conscious of and be prepared for. Joan may never get well, and there's the possibility that she may get worse or is getting worse. Can you accept that?"

"I think so, but if she has the power to communicate with her dogs, she's gotta have the power to get well. Don't you think?"

"You're definitely right; there's a bond between her and those dogs. It's beyond anything that I've ever experienced in my life. We have to continue to pray for both Joan and Hank, and help them out as much as we can."

Mom stood up and started to walk to the door.

"Mom, what do you think those dogs were chasing in the woods?"

"I don't know. Dad still believes it's some kind of animal that's not normally found around here. He may be right. It's a puzzle that's for sure. Now get some sleep. Tomorrow is a new day."

The next week I made a trip to Doctor Thompson to have my stitches removed and there was no comparison to the day that the stitches were put in. We were in and out in no time flat and there wasn't the usual conversation concerning how the Raycarts were doing. Doctor Thompson didn't mention them once, and he seemed to be in an unusual hurry to get the stitches removed so that he could move on to his next patient. Although his bed side manner seemed different, it was fine with me. I had more than enough baggage to carry the rest of my life concerning that scar.

In the last week of August Hank called and asked if I was available to help put up some hay. We had finished with Uncle Joe's thrashing and the trashing crew had moved to the next farm. As much as I'd have liked to go with Uncle Joe to help his neighbor thrash, I didn't hesitate to tell Hank that I'd be there. Uncle Joe understood completely and praised me for keeping my word.

"People could learn a lot from you, Shorty," he told me.

During the last week of August the temperatures reached the upper nineties, and the high humidity added to the discomfort of the heat wave. Blackie looked forward to our morning walks to the Raycarts because she was able to walk the river and cool off. I got the impression that Joan's three dogs were even glad to see us. They didn't run to meet us wagging their tails as we arrived, but they didn't growl or make any signs that we were unwelcome. Dad suggested that in their eyes, Blackie and I had become a member of their pack.

The barn was still full of hay from the June haying season, so Hank was going to store the hay baled in August in a pole shed he had built next to the barn. Alfred Jest again did the baling and was his old jovial self. Needless to say the heat took its toll on the large man and sweat poured from his face. *"I believe I sweat worse than a pig,"* was one of his favorite afternoon sayings. He had attached a large umbrella to the seat of the tractor and it provided some shade, but he still had to wipe his brow constantly to keep the sweat from running into his eyes.

Hank would bring the loaded wagons in, Joan would unload, and I would stack. I didn't have as far to carry the bales this time, so we were usually done unloading before Hank arrived with the next load. Joan was the normal relentless worker and the heat didn't slow her down at all. Hank tied a large rimmed straw hat on her head to provide some shade from the hot sun and she looked as normal as any farmer's wife. We worked together as if we had been doing it for years.

Instead of eating dinner in the house, Hank brought ham sandwiches and potato chips to the table by the river. There was usually a breeze and the large oaks provided welcomed shade.

"Hank, you're gonna have a hard time gettin' me out of this chair and back on that hot tractor," Alfred said, but after a couple of sandwiches and a cool drink he was up and ready to go.

He looked at the pole shed and saw that we had all the hay stacked.

"I don't think we're going to get ahead of Joan and Shorty this time," Alfred said.

"I think you're right, Alfred, they're pretty amazing," Hank said, smiling in agreement. "You want a cold pop to drink on the way back out?"

"Sure, what you got?" Alfred asked.

"Come on over and pick what you want," Hank said as he motioned us to follow.

We followed Hank to the tank that was kept full of cool water for the cattle and in the bottom numerous bottles of pop were also being kept cool.

Alfred reached in and brought out a root beer. "This will hit the spot," he said.

"Shorty, go ahead and grab one," Hank said.

I reached into the cool water and brought out a bottle of Nestles orange pop. Alfred laughed as he watched.

"Harold Strum, don't provide a better variety for the thrashing crews at his place," he said.

"Thanks," I said to Hank as he reached in to grab a bottle.

"It isn't much, but you help yourself whenever you want," Hank said as he opened the bottle of pop and poured it into a glass.

We watched as he carried it to his wife and put the glass to her lips. After a few seconds she took the glass from his hands and slowly sipped the pop.

"I'll be dammed, haven't seen pop in this cow tank since, well since...the last year we thrashed here and John was alive. I think it's a good sign," Alfred said to me as he walked to his tractor.

The afternoon got very hot and each time Hank brought a load in he would remind me, "Don't forget there's pop in the cow tank, you help yourself."

Needless to say by the fourth and final day I had a path worn between the cow tank and the pole shed. On the afternoon of the fourth day I was returning from the cow tank and saw Joan sitting on a bale of hay staring in my direction. At first I didn't pay much attention, but as I walked closer I felt that she was watching me.

She was leaning forward with her forearms resting on her knees and the fingers of her hands were locked together. Even though she was leaning forward, her head was tilted back so that she gave the appearance that she was watching me as I approached. I couldn't see her eyes because the brim of the straw hat blocked my view. My first thought was that the heat might be starting to affect her, so I returned to the cow tank to get another bottle of pop. I opened both bottles and returned to the pole shed and sat on a bale of hay about ten feet away from Joan. After I sat down I looked at Joan and saw that she had turned her head and was looking in my direction.

"It sure is hot. Would you like a drink of pop? I have orange or grape."

There was no response, but she continued to look in my direction. The straw hat shaded her face, but I could now see her eyes and felt that she was definitely watching me. I watched a bead of perspiration form on her brow and follow the curve of her cheek and fall to her dress. I realized then that we were staring at each other, and I began to feel uncomfortable.

"I'll give you the orange, it's really good."

I slowly stood up, took a deep breath for courage and walked toward her. The dogs got up from their position in the shade and went to her side, but her eyes never veered from me as I walked closer. I stopped in front of her and started to hand her the bottle of orange pop and remembered that Hank always gave the pop to her in a glass.

"I'm sorry, I'll go get a glass and be right back."

I turned and started to walk to the house to get a glass.

"Do you know John?"

I stopped dead in my tracks at the sound of her voice. It was like I had been struck by lightning; my legs felt weak, and I was afraid to turn around, but there was nothing else I could do. Slowly I turned to face her; she was still sitting on the bale and hadn't moved.

"No, I don't. They call me Shorty, and I...I...I live down river and I'm just...I'm just helping you and Hank with the haying."

I didn't know what to do next. I was having a difficult time maintaining any kind of eye contact and tried to switch my focus to the dogs standing by her side. Even though I wasn't looking at her, I knew that she was continuing to watch me. I nervously stood still expecting her to say something else, but at the same time hoping she wouldn't. She sat there in the hot sun with the straw hat for shade and I struggled to find something appropriate to say, but only managed to bring forth an awkward whisper that allowed me to retreat.

"I'll be right back; I have to get a glass."

I slowly turned and walked away. As I walked to the house I looked over my shoulder and saw that she was continuing to watch me. When I entered the kitchen I found myself trembling as I took a glass from the cupboard. Joan had spoken to me again. Should I get Hank or call my mother? I was confusing my self, but finally decided that the best thing to do was to sit with Joan and wait for Hank to bring in the next load.

Joan never took her eyes off me as I walked across the yard toward her, and her dogs remained by her side, watching my every move. I poured the orange pop into the glass and held it out in an offering position, but her hands remained clenched together as she watched me.

"It's cold and tastes real good. Please try some," I said.

She didn't respond, so I reached out and touched her hand, and immediately Three Eye stepped closer. I placed the glass next to her hand, but nothing happened. I looked directly at her eyes and found that she was staring into mine. Then I felt her hand on the glass and I slowly released it to her. I smiled as she took the glass. I know it will be rare indeed to ever experience an act that will provide such a profound feeling. I then sat in my usual resting spot.

"Won't be long and Hank will be in with another load. We better rest up," I said.

I watched her as she watched me, and after a few seconds she raised the glass and took a sip. She lowered the glass and the silence was broken by the sound of Hank driving up.

"Sorry I'm a little late, but we had a minor breakdown. Alfred got it fixed and he has only one more round to make and we'll be done. I'll pick up the bales after milking. I'll help you stack these, and then..."

Hank became aware that something was different and he stopped in mid sentence. He looked at his wife and then he looked at me. Hank saw that Joan had a glass of pop and he smiled.

"Shorty, I see you got Joan a pop?"

"Yes, sir, and...and...she spoke to me."

Hank was walking towards his wife. "What did she say?"

I found it difficult to speak. "She asked if I knew John."

Hank looked at me and then walked up to his wife. He took the glass from her hand and then he gently placed each of his hands on his wife's shoulders.

"Joan, Shorty here never met John, but they're a lot alike. I'm sure they'd have been best of friends."

This was getting to be too much for me. I needed a place to run to or something to do before the emotions unfolding got the best of me, so I started to unload the hay bales from the wagon. I had only tossed a few bales to the ground when I heard a faint whisper from Joan.

"When is John coming home?" she said.

These were the first words that Hank had heard his wife speak directly to him since their son's funeral. The emotional impact had to be overwhelming, and this man, who was built like a tree, began to weep uncontrollably. But he found the strength to answer his wife's question.

"John's in another home now, baby. But you're still home with me, and together we can make it."

Hank put his arms around his wife and pulled her close, but after a few seconds he slowly took his arms from around her and helped her sit down. Hank had been holding his wife, but she hadn't returned the embrace. He smiled through teary eyes at his wife sitting in the sun, and walked to the wagon.

"Let me help you, Shorty." He paused and looked at his wife. "For a moment I thought she was back, but damn she did speak to me, didn't she?"

"Yes she did." I didn't know what else to say.

Hank began to carry the bales back to the shed and I continued to unload them from the wagon. One of the bales broke apart when it hit the ground and

I jumped off the wagon to retie the twine. As I was putting the bale back together I heard the wagon creak and turned to see Joan climbing onto the wagon bed. She grabbed a bale and threw it to the ground and I watched to see if there was any change in her expression, but nothing had changed. In her eyes the events of the day apparently were lost, and unlike her husband, the moisture on her face was caused by working in the hot sun.

Hank smiled as he watched his wife. "Looks like one of our jobs has been taken."

Not long after, Alfred pulled his tractor and baler in from the field.

"Hank, you got about forty bales on the ground. I'm gonna go home and find a cool spot. Shorty, as usual it's been a pleasure working with you. Be sure to tell your folks hi for me," Alfred said.

"I will," I said.

"Thanks for everything, Alfred. When you figure up what I owe bring it by and I'll settle."

"Will do, Hank, be sure to let me know if you need anything else."

By the time we finished stacking the rest of the hay it was time for night milking.

"You want to have a pop to drink on the way home? Hank asked.

"You bet," I said.

I walked with Hank to the cow tank and he pulled out two bottles of pop. He handed me a bottle and looked at his wife who was now sitting in the chair by the river.

"Well, Shorty, another job well done. If it's okay with you I'll drive over to your place tomorrow and settle up. I'd like to talk to your parents about something. Will they be home?"

"Yeah that's fine. I'm sure they'll be home, especially if they know you're coming."

"Thanks, I'll call before I come over. Now you better head for home."

Blackie was lying on the bank with the other dogs and as soon as I called her name she came running, wagging what was left of her tail. We started down river and I turned to wave to Hank, but he was watching his wife walking toward the bridge. He stood watching his wife until she walked out of sight and then he went into the barn. I imagine he went through that same procedure every night.

I took my time walking home and waded in the river whenever possible to take advantage of the cool water. Mom was putting a tablecloth on the picnic table when I walked into our yard.

"Hi, Shorty, it's still pretty hot in the house, thought we'd eat supper out here. How'd your day go?"

"We finished up," I said.

Dad got home from work while I was finishing chores and we all enjoyed the picnic supper. After the supper dishes were put away Mom and Dad came back outside and sat at the picnic table.

"If the mosquitoes weren't so bad, I think I'd get a blanket and sleep out here tonight," Dad said.

"It's going to be a hot one, that's for sure. Don't the Braves play tonight?" Mom asked.

Dad winked at me. "Now I know the Braves are going to win the pennant, because they even got Maddie interested."

"What do you mean? I've always been a fan. Just because I don't jump around like some lunatic when Henry Aaron hits a home run or want to fire the manager because they lost two in a row, doesn't make me any less of a fan than you two guys."

"You're absolutely right, Maddie. I don't know what I was thinking."

Dad then gave my mother "the nod" while giving a side ways glance in my direction. The nod/glance was a silent cue that Dad often used to direct my mother's attention to a particular individual, so she could find out what was bothering that person. Mom did have a way about her that allowed people to share what was bothering them. Dad called it interrogating techniques, but my mother felt that she was just a good listener.

"Shorty, you were awful quiet tonight; don't you think the Braves are going to win the pennant?" Mom asked.

"What do you mean? Of course I think they're going to win the pennant and I think they're going to win the World Series too. I was just thinking about something else is all."

"School starts Monday, you worried about school?" Mom asked.

"No, I'm kind of looking forward to it."

"Shorty, what happened at the Raycarts' today? I'm going to that meeting tomorrow night and if there's anything I should know I would appreciate it very much if you told us."

"Joan spoke to me today," I said.

"What did she say?" Mom asked.

"She asked if I knew John."

Mom looked at my dad and leaned forward and put her elbows on the picnic table; she then put her hands together in a manner that allowed her chin to rest on her two thumbs. It was as if she was praying, but needed additional support. She stared at the table for a few seconds and then raised her eyes so that she was looking at me.

"Then what happened?" she asked.

This was my cue and I shared in detail everything that had happened. It felt good to relay what had happened, and I couldn't help but wonder what Hank wanted to talk to my parents about. A feeling of uncertainty had taken control of my thoughts, and that feeling had only grown in intensity since I left the Raycarts. I could still picture how Hank lowered his head and walked into the barn after he had watched his wife walk out of sight under the bridge. It was as if they were going in two separate ways.

When I finished both Mom and Dad remained silent for a few seconds and then Mom spoke.

"Hank didn't say what time he'd call, did he?" Mom asked.

"No he didn't."

What if he changes his mind? Mom asked.

"If Hank doesn't call by ten, we'll call him or drive over to their place," Dad said.

Mom shook her head in agreement.

"That's a good idea," she said.

The Braves game was already in the fourth inning when Dad finally got them tuned in, and even though they loss the game, it was a nice way to spend a hot summer evening.

"Can't win 'em all," Mom said.

"I think they should fire the manager," Dad said.

Mom started to say something, but decided it was better to let it rest, and just shook her head from side to side and went inside.

I didn't have any strange dreams that night and slept as sound as a rock. It seemed as if I had just put my head on the pillow when I was awakened by a couple of cardinals making all kinds of racket outside my window. The female cardinal was positioned on a higher branch and definitely was leading the conversation. The male must have done something to tick her off and his bright red feathers glistening in the morning sun couldn't even soothe her. He probably accused her of not knowing anything about baseball.

When I went downstairs Mom was scrubbing the kitchen floor. Whenever company was expected to drop in, my mother cleaned the house in preparation for the visit. When Mom was in a cleaning frenzy both Dad and I made sure to stay out of her way. So we took our time doing chores that morning and waited for the dust to settle before going back to the house. When we finished chores we made sure our clothes were brushed cleaned and left our shoes in the porch so as not to track in any dirt, and thus avoid being scolded.

"What time is the big meeting?" Dad asked.

"Eight o'clock," Mom said.

"How'd you find out anyway?" Dad asked.

"Last Sunday after church I was visiting with Margaret Strum and I asked her if she was going to the meeting next Saturday. Now that Harold's an elder he stays after to count the collection money and meet with the board, and Margaret waits for him in the car. Anyways, she told me that she was going, and I told her it was going to be a busy day because I planned on picking chokecherries that day. She then told me she was just glad it was going to be at night when it was a little cooler."

Mom then stopped and sat at the kitchen table and started to thumb through a catalog.

"Wait a minute how'd that tell you that the meeting was going to start at eight?" Dad asked.

"It didn't, but when Margaret saw Harold coming she cut the conversation short and said to me, '*You know chokecherries taste bitter direct from the tree but they make sweet jam. I bet you'll have a lot of them changed from bitter to sweet by eight.*' Then she smiled and winked at me as Harold opened the car door."

"Maddie, you're lucky Margaret bailed you out. You could have been in big trouble with the lord, scheming that way," Dad said.

"That Margaret is so sweet," Mom said.

"She sure is and a heck of a farmer too, but I can't believe they trust Harold with counting the money," Dad said.

Then the phone rang and Mom picked up the receiver and said "hello." The conversation didn't last long. Mom said "good morning, Hank" and listened for a few seconds and said "that'll be fine; we'll see you in a few minutes."

Mom was starting to say something else but Hank must have hung up, so she put the receiver back on the hook and sat down.

"Hank doesn't talk long does he?" Dad said.

"No he doesn't and he doesn't beat around the bush either. He asked if he could drive over now and talk to us before he lost his nerve. Shorty, do you have any idea why he's coming over?"

"Nope, he just said that he wanted to talk to you and Dad about something."

"Whatever it is, it must be damn important. I can't picture Hank losing his nerve about anything," Dad said.

Mom cleaned off the table one more time and then stood by the kitchen sink and looked out the window.

"I know I shouldn't be, but I'm nervous about this," she said. "Looks like dishes will have to wait, I see a truck heading this way. It must be Hank."

In a few minutes Hank drove in and my parents walked out to meet him. Hank stopped the truck and immediately opened the door and got out, but Joan continued to sit motionless on the passenger side.

"Good Morning," he said, as he walked to the back of the truck and lifted out a wash tub. "Me and Shorty couldn't drink all this, so I thought maybe the kids would like some. I'll set it over here in the shade."

The tub had ten bottles of pop splashing around in the cool water and Hank carried the tub over to the yard and placed it at the base of a big oak.

"You didn't have to do that, Hank, but thanks," Mom said.

My brother and sister seized the moment and didn't hesitate to ask if they could have one.

"Oh, I don't see why not," Mom said, "but first, what do you say to Mr. Raycart?"

They thanked Hank and before the bottles had a chance to settle to the bottom they each had one in their hand. The gleeful thank you's brought a smile to Hank's face and he turned to look at Joan.

"You're very welcome." He started to search through his pockets. "I forgot the opener."

"We'll get one, Hank. Shorty, go in the house and get a church key," Dad said and then he caught the stern look from Mom. "I mean the bottle opener. Sorry, I always seem to forget that you're not supposed to need a key for a church."

"Why don't you and Joan come inside and we'll visit," Mom said.

"Joan usually seems more comfortable sitting in the truck when we go places. She hasn't been in another person's house for some time, but I feel that she trusts you. I'd like Shorty to be in on this too if you don't mind," Hank said.

Hank then opened the truck door and took his wife by the hand. Joan clasped her hand around Hank's fingers and followed him up the porch steps. I looked at my mother and saw that she was also watching the same thing and she smiled at me. Joan followed not because she was being led, but because when they joined hands they were linked as one, and where one went the other was going to go.

We all went into the kitchen and Hank helped his wife sit in a chair at the kitchen table. Blackie managed to slip in with the rest of us and found a spot on the floor next to Joan.

"Hank, would you and Joan like something to drink and a cookie or something?" Mom asked.

"No thanks, Maddie, I don't want to take up much of your time. I've never been good with words and always relied on Joan to guide me through difficult conversations."

A smile that really wasn't a smile formed on his face as he continued.

"But things have changed, so please bear with me."

Mom and Dad didn't say anything; Mom just nodded her head in understanding.

"First off, here's what I owe Shorty."

He took out an envelope from his pocket, handed it to me, and reached across the table and shook my hand and smiled.

"Thanks, Hank," I said.

"I'm sure Shorty told you what happened yesterday, about Joan speaking and all. Well, I've given it a lot of thought and to be very honest with you I'm feeling like I'm losing control. I trust you both and you deserve some explanations," Hank said.

While Hank was reaching in his shirt pocket I looked at Joan and saw that she was staring in the direction of the cupboard. On the cupboard was a family picture that was taken at the Middleton Fair this summer. Dad was holding my sister, Mom was holding my brother and I was standing between them. I couldn't tell if Joan was staring at the picture or just staring in that direction.

Hank brought a piece of paper out of his pocket and placed it on the table in front of him. He studied what was written on the paper for a few moments, and then turned his attention to everyone seated at the table.

"I wrote some things down last night to help me get through this," he said.

He then placed his large hands on each side of the paper as if to make sure it couldn't be swept away and took a deep breath. Slowly and steadily he started to speak and occasionally would look at his wife and then return his focus to the paper.

"After John's funeral when Joan stopped speaking I thought she just needed time. Doctor Thompson said I needed to take her to a psychiatrist, but he didn't know how long she'd have to be gone or if she'd ever come back.

When he told me I could only visit, I told him no.

Joan wouldn't hurt anybody. She found them dogs and I know she wanders up and down the river, but she wouldn't hurt no one and those dogs love her.

It's been five years and when she spoke to Shorty I thought it was my chance to bring her back. Shorty brings something to the surface in her.

I thought things were getting better and when she spoke to me yesterday I was certain of it.

But even though things seem better, they maybe aren't.

More and more of my neighbors are becoming afraid of us and the night visits are getting worse. Someday I'm afraid someone is going to get hurt.

Joan still takes her normal walks up the river, but now once a week she hangs lanterns in trees on the north side of the bridge. It worries me.

The dogs and Joan are sensing things along the river, and a couple of night's back I thought I saw someone watching Joan when I was walking up river to make sure she was alright.

Three times in the last two weeks Joan has left the house at night and I didn't wake up. That's never happened before. I always wake up.

Maybe Doctor Thompson is right and I should take her in to see a psychiatrist. She spoke to me yesterday, so there's still a chance, but at the same time I feel her slipping further away."

Hank then refolded the paper and put it back in his shirt pocket. He looked at his wife and then turned to look in the direction that she was staring. When he saw the picture, he also thought his wife was looking at it and walked over to get a closer look.

"Do you mind?" Hank asked.

"No...not at all," Mom said.

Hank then brought the picture over and set it on the table in front of his wife.

"Look at this, Joan. Pretty happy bunch, don't you think?"

Joan didn't react and continued to stare in the direction of the cupboard. Hank set the picture back on the cupboard and returned to his chair.

"What I came to ask from you is..."

Hank never asked for much from anyone in his life and this was very unfamiliar ground for him. The large man was very nervous. Although he had silently rehearsed what he wanted to ask, he still was searching for the proper way to ask what he thought was such a large favor.

"What can we do, Hank?" Mom asked.

"I remember one night Shorty came in the barn and said to me that we've got to help Joan. I could tell he meant every word of it." He paused for a moment and looked at me and smiled. "Maybe I've waited too long for Joan to come out of this on her own, so if it's alright with you, I'd like for Maddie to call Doctor Thompson and see if he'd come out and see me."

"If that's what you want, Hank, I can call him right now," Mom said.

"No, Monday or Tuesday would be fine; if he comes out I'd appreciate it if you could be there. I want to ask him if the psychiatrist could visit with Joan on the farm. I'll pay for the visit and all the time it takes. I've spoken with Harold Strum and he'll buy my cows. I feel deep down inside that if I take Joan away from the farm to Saint Paul she may never return. What do you think?"

"I think it's an excellent idea, what do you think, Mike?" Mom asked.

Dad was listening intently, but he wasn't as eager as my mother to jump right in.

"I think it's a good plan, but I don't think you should sell your cows until you find out what the cost is. Because I know one thing for sure, if you sell something to Harold for one hundred dollars one day, it'll cost you one hundred and fifty to buy it back the next."

Mom looked from Dad to Hank.

"I agree with Mike, and I'm sure Doctor Thompson and whoever the psychiatrist is, will gladly accept payment at a later date," Mom said.

Hank thought for a few seconds and then he slid his chair back and put his hands down firmly on his knees and stood up.

"I feel good about it, but Mike is right. There's no sense in us selling off more than we have to, but I want you to know that whatever it costs, if it helps Joan it's worth it."

"How about I talk to Doctor Thompson on Monday?" Mom said.

"I think that's fine and any day he can visit is good with us," Hank said.

"Now we've taken up enough of your time; it felt good to talk to someone about it. Thanks for listening."

"You're more than welcome," Mom said.

Hank reached down and touched Joan's hand and she immediately held onto his. We walked with them to their truck and Mom waved as they drove out.

"It's going to be another hot one, let's have one of those bottles of pop," Dad said.

Mom and Dad sat at the picnic table and I sprawled out on the grass.

"I sure hope this turns out for the best, I really think it's a good idea," Mom said.

"I do too, but old Doc Thompson hasn't bought into it yet and he can be a strange duck at times," Dad said.

"Why wouldn't he, he told us that day at his office that he wanted to help Hank and Joan?" Mom said.

"It's probably nothing, but I always get the impression from Doc that he likes new ideas, if they're his new ideas."

"Hank has really done some soul searching to make up his list; do you think he's afraid Joan is going to get hurt?" Mom asked.

"No, I don't think that's it. I think he's more concerned with what might happen if he catches one of those night visitors as he calls them. I can just imagine what kind of damage he could do if he got those big hands of his on one of 'em," Dad said.

Mom had her back leaning against the picnic table and her legs stretched out in front of her.

"I hope they touch on those night visitors at the meeting tonight."

"Wouldn't surprise me none if some of them are at the meeting," Dad said.

"I hope you're wrong about that." Then Mom stood up and stretched. "Say, let's take the kids to Mirror Lake for a swim this afternoon."

"Wait a minute; I thought you told the Lord you were going to pick chokecherries this afternoon. Maddie…Maddie…Maddie…I'm afraid you're going to lose some points with the Almighty."

"That's all right; I can win them back and probably pick up some bonus points by drowning a husband who always picks on a poor defenseless woman."

"Defenseless as a she wolf. Isn't that right, Shorty?"

A lesson I learned growing up was that at times it's more prudent not to answer a question even if you know the answer. This was one of those times.

Chapter Twenty
The Meeting

It was a few minutes to eight when we pulled into the church driveway. All the parking places were taken, so Dad stopped the car in front of the church entrance.

"Looks like you're gonna have a full house. I'll take the kids over to my mom's and then wait for you at Mirror Lake. You sure you don't want me to come in with ya?" Dad asked.

"No, I think it's better this way, but you better prepare yourself to be a good listener when this is over; I may need a good sounding board. Come on, Shorty, let's go visit with our neighbors."

Mom closed the door and leaned forward to look through the car window at her husband.

"Thanks for offering though. I don't imagine it'll take too long. We'll just listen to what they have to say and meet you in a little bit," Mom said.

"Maddie, you just try to control that Hun temper of yours. We don't want to have to pay for any church windows, or have to spend a lot of time mending our neighbor's fences. Do you promise?" Dad asked.

Dad was referring to my mothers temper. When my mother reached her boiling point, she would pace around until she found something to throw that would cause minimal damage. It was her way of relieving built up tension and frustration, and it usually worked. After such an episode, my dad would suggest to her that she was not really a full-blooded German as she claimed, but rather a descendant of Genghis Ghan or some other invading Mongolian. Dad couldn't resist referring to her family tree by saying something like; *"Maddie, I'd bet anything that one of those fierce Mongolians slipped into one of your ancestors hut when they marched through Northern Europe, and some of their attributes have been passed down to you. Look how your eyes get almond shaped, and your throwing accuracy improves when you blow off some steam."*

Mom smiled, because she knew what her husband was implying.

"I promise. I'll be on my best behavior. I really only plan to mostly listen."

Mom was wearing a dress that was reserved for special occasions and she made me wear my church clothes. Mom asked me to come with because she felt I was living proof that Hank and Joan were not dangerous. She assured me that I wouldn't have to speak, but only nod my head if she used me as an example. We walked up the church steps and Mom paused before opening the door.

"I hope we weren't supposed to bring a hot-dish or something to pass around. Oh well, too late now, let's go in."

We opened the doors and stepped into the foyer. The meeting was being held in the church basement and I followed my mother down the stairs. When we reached the bottom of the stairs she stopped, brushed her hair back with her hands, straightened her dress, and slowly rotated her head while holding her eyes tightly closed. I was already somewhat nervous, but that intensified as I watched her get ready to make her entrance. I realized that this was no normal meeting we were going to attend, and Mom's intentions were maybe to mostly listen, but she was preparing for battle. She smiled at me, and then slowly pushed the basement door open.

People were starting to take their seats in the folding chairs that were neatly placed in rows across the basement floor, and everyone turned to look at us as we walked in.

Mom noticed the questioning glances and was quick to respond.

"I'm sorry if we're late, but these summer days just fly by so quickly. I hope we didn't miss anything important."

While she spoke we made our way to two vacant chairs in the third row from the back.

Mrs. Wilson was standing in front and was quick to take up the challenge.

"Oh no, Maddie, we were just going to start. I'm sure glad you could make it. Is Mike coming?"

"No, he's watching the kids. If there's a follow up meeting he said he'd like to attend."

"I doubt if that'll be needed, and I don't think that this meeting will take very long," Mrs. Wilson replied.

I could sense the tension in the air; it was as if battle lines had been drawn in preparation for the opponent's next move. Sitting behind Mrs. Wilson was Pastor Wilcox, Harold Strum, Francis Beck, Sheriff Mead and Doctor Thompson. I was surprised to see Doctor Thompson and Sheriff Mead, because they weren't neighbors or members of our church. We sat next to Margaret Strum, and she leaned over and whispered to Mom.

"How was the chokecherry picking?"

"I'm afraid we didn't go. It was very hot, so we decided to take the kids swimming instead," Mom said.

"I think that was a better choice, don't you, Shorty?" Mrs. Strum said.

I smiled and shook my head in agreement and hoped that would be the last time I'd need to do that tonight. The church basement was packed. There were more people at this meeting than normally attended church service on Sunday. Most of our neighbors were present, and everyone was wearing their Sunday best. We knew all of them by name; however, as in any community we knew some better than others.

After everyone was seated, Mrs. Wilson addressed the group.

"I want to thank everyone for coming; before we start Pastor Wilcox would like to say a short prayer."

Pastor Wilcox stood up and looked around.

"I'm very pleased that we can offer our little church as a place for neighbors to assemble for discussion. I know there are people present who are not members of our church and I want to take the opportunity to welcome you all. Please bow your heads. Lord please lead this group of neighbors to work together in the same way that they do during thrashing time, so that they can come to a favorable understanding that will benefit our community and receive your blessing. Amen."

The sound of silent whispered "Amens" echoed through the church basement and Mrs. Wilson resumed her position in front.

"We are here to discuss Hank and Joan Raycart. As you know we live right down the road from them, and everyone here is aware of the tragedies that have happened to them. It's been over five years since they buried their son John and each passing day they not only continue to separate themselves from us, but they have become unstable. Some of us feel that it has reached a point where one day they are going to hurt themselves, or God forbid one of us or our children."

She paused and looked around the group. Once she felt satisfied that she had everyone's attention, she continued.

"I asked Doctor Thompson and Sheriff Mead to attend so that they can share with us what medical and legal courses of actions are available."

She turned to recognize them both, then turned back to face the assembly.

"One of my major worries is that one of those killer dogs is going to harm a passer by. An adult wouldn't have much of a chance and a child could be killed."

She paused and extended her arms and opened her hands so that her palms faced upward.

"I have many more concerns, but first I feel it would be only right to ask if anyone here has concerns they would like to share with us."

Francis Beck immediately stood up.

"There's something evil going on at that farm. We tried to help her once, and sounds came from her that were not...well they were just not normal. And she walks the river at all hours of the night, and now she's placing lanterns in the trees. It's like she's worshipping something, but whatever it is, it isn't God, and something has to be done."

There was a cutting edge in the sound of her voice that comes from a person demanding retribution for a wrong that they feel has been done to them. When she finished she looked at Pastor Wilson, who seemed uneasy, but smiled nervously back at Mrs. Beck, as she sat down. Mrs. Beck's short speech caused a murmur to go through the crowd, and one-on-one conversations began to take place. I glanced at my mother and saw that she was starting to stand, but Alfonse Peterson was already on his feet.

"Are these dogs with her when she's walking the river at night? Where did they come from in the first place, and if they're so damn dangerous why can't we just have them destroyed?" Alfonse said.

The milk hauler, Jacob Matthews, replied from a sitting position.

"The dogs don't bother me none when I go in to get the milk. They usually are up by the house or down by the river with Joan. They were probably strays Joan found in the woods. We know how people leave their dogs off when they get tired of 'em, or don't take care of them and let 'em run. I've shot a few myself when I caught them chasing deer. If I were to see Joan's dogs chasing deer I wouldn't hesitate to shoot 'em, but from what I see Joan has control of them pretty good."

"Thank you, Jake," I heard Mom whisper.

Jacob's comment brought Francis Beck to her feet and she wasn't going to wait for permission to speak.

"That's another thing that's not right. She can control those dogs without speaking, and I'm telling you it's not natural. I don't care what anyone here says it's not natural what goes on at that farm, and it's getting worse."

The majority of the crowd seemed to agree or was starting to agree with Mrs. Beck. Lamar Smith a large farmer, who some said was in competition with Harold Strum to see who could own the most land stood up.

"It seems that the issue here is Joan Raycart. Why don't old Harold just buy them out?"

Harold Strum couldn't allow his name to be mentioned and not comment.

"It's interesting that you bring that up Lamar, because I'm currently in the process of dealing on buying Hanks cattle. When he sells the cows he won't be able to make it, and the farm will be up for sale soon. You can take that to the bank, and I'm ready to buy him out lock, stock and barrel, right now."

Harold then gave Mr. Smith *a take that grin* and sat back down.

Mrs. Wilson walked to the center.

"We all agree that something needs to be done. We feel threatened and we can't set by and simply wait for something bad to happen before we act. I would like to now ask Doctor Thompson to say a few words."

"I don't feel threatened." It was my mother.

She was standing and facing Mrs. Wilson and clutching onto a hymnal so tightly that her fingers were turning white. I looked at Mom, closed my eyes, and made a quick prayer. *"Please don't let her throw that book at Mrs. Wilson."*

"As you know we live down river from Hank and Joan. This summer my son Shorty here has worked for Hank with no problems. As a matter a fact on two separate occasions this summer they have helped us out. Once when Shorty sprained his ankle bad and another time Joan saved our dog Blackie who ate some poisoned meat that was thrown in the ditch in front of Hank and Joan's house. Just yesterday they were at our house, and Hank brought bottles of pop for the kids. We have visited with them at their house, and not once have I felt threatened by Joan or Hank."

Mom sat down and I knew she wanted to say more, but was taking a discretionary route. Heads that turned to watch my mother speak now turned back toward Mrs. Wilson. After a short period of silence, Mrs. Wilson responded.

"Maddie, you and Mike have only lived here for a few years and are just renting, so you can move on whenever you want. Most everyone else in this room has lived in the area for most of their life and have had farms passed down from previous generations. I for one feel threatened and the majority of the people I speak with feel the same way. Now let's please listen to what Doctor Thompson has to say about this dilemma we find ourselves in."

Doctor Thompson was dressed in a three-piece suit and he looked more like a politician than a member of the medical profession. He put his glasses on and walked up and stood beside Mrs. Wilson.

"Thank you, Mabel, for inviting me."

Mrs. Wilson smiled at the acknowledgement and returned to her chair. Doctor Thompson slowly turned his head and scanned the entire audience.

"I know everyone in this room and have had the opportunity to deliver your babies and treat you for all sorts of ailments. I hope you all feel that I've always had your best interest at heart."

Most in the audience were nodding their heads in agreement. Doctor Thompson definitely held their trust.

"This case has intrigued me from the first time I visited with Hank and Joan. I have done a substantial amount of reading on the subject, and have corresponded with people in the medical field who are experts in such cases."

He was holding a magazine in one hand and while looking at the audience he raised his arm so that everyone could see the magazine. Everyone automatically looked at the magazine and waited for the doctor to explain the symbolism.

"The medical field of psychiatric care and doctors of psychiatry are the only means to solve and or control Joan Raycart's problem. It's my opinion that she must receive this care or future developments could be tragic."

The audience was very silent and then Jacob Matthews raised his hand.

"Yes, Jake, what is it?" Doctor Thompson asked.

"You're using a lot of big words here, Doc. Have you ever talked with Hank about this psychiatric stuff and what are you saying could happen if Joan don't get this care?" Jake asked.

"Very good questions, Jake, and I'll do my best to explain."

He was treating the people in the room like students. They had questions and because of his knowledge and background most in the room felt he had the correct answers. Doctor Thompson sensing he was gaining complete control of the audience continued.

"First of all, I did speak to Hank about taking Joan to see a psychiatrist, but he refused. As a matter of fact right now I'm not ruling out that Hank might also need similar treatment. As for Joan, she definitely needs to be under psychiatric care. She may have already reached a point of no return, and I feel the need for continuous monitoring is not out of the question. I feel that in her mind she has allowed those three dogs to be substitutes for her dead children."

A simultaneous gasp came from the audience. I looked at my mother and saw that her mouth had dropped open and it was easy to see that she was having a hard time holding her self back.

Doctor Thompson let his last comment linger for a moment and then continued.

"To answer Jake's last question of what could happen. The more I read on the subject and look into similar cases; it's not at all out of the question that Joan could become violent. No one fully understands how the mind works, and no one can forecast what will happen. However, documented cases recorded in medical journals state that a person who seems docile and disconnected one day can abruptly change and perform acts of violence without any warning on themselves, their families, or on people who they come in contact with. This medical evidence cannot be ignored."

Then he dropped the bombshell.

"It is my professional opinion that Joan Raycart should be committed to psychiatric care for her safety and the safety of those around her."

"Wait a minute."

It was Mom and she meant business. She didn't wait for any acknowledgement or permission to speak; she didn't need any.

"I don't know why, but for whatever reason, you're intentionally instituting fear in these people. And as you stated, you're not a psychologist, and just because you've read a few books on the subject doesn't make you one, nor does it give you the right to make a diagnosis on something you have no training in. Would you be against having a psychologist come out to visit with Hank and Joan on their farm, and get a true professional opinion?"

As quickly as my Mom had stood up, she sat back down and waited for the doctor to respond. Doctor Thompson's body language indicated that he didn't take kindly to my mother's accusations or her unforeseen interruption. He was rolling the magazine in his hands and had turned so that he was directly facing my mother.

"Maddie, I know you want what's best for Joan, and I'm sure we all do. However, I firmly feel that psychiatric treatment is essential in this matter and no I don't feel it should be done on the farm. It must be done in a controlled setting. I'm sorry you disagree, but believe me I have researched this as professionally as possible."

"I'm sorry too." Mom was on her feet again.

"I'm sorry that this meeting is being held in a church basement, because there's no compassion here. I'm sorry that no one has addressed how to stop the people in our community from driving by Hank and Joan's place and throwing rocks at their house. And I will be most sorry if Shorty and I are the only people in this room who feel that this meeting has taken on the form of a witch-hunt. I'm afraid to ask how you propose to carry out this commitment process, or has the tar and rail method been reinstated in Wisconsin?"

Mom quietly sat down. She was emotionally spent. I was sure most of the people in the room truly liked my mother and I was equally certain that they respected Doctor Thompson's opinions. However, my mother's last comments had hit some nerves and separate debates started throughout the room. Mrs. Wilson walked forward and held her arms up as a gesture for silence.

"Maddie, I can't believe you suggest that we're on a witch-hunt, as Doctor Thompson said we want only what is best for Hank and Joan Raycart. With God as my witness that's the only purpose of this meeting. I know it's difficult for some, but I agree with Doctor Thompson, and I have asked Sheriff Mead to look into the commitment process."

Mrs. Wilson had not expected anyone to question Doctor Thompson's professional opinion, but she was determined to have the meeting proceed. I don't know if any shades of doubt had invaded her crusade, but my mother's rebuttal had definitely placed a fly in her ointment. However, not to allow her agenda to be side-tracked, Mrs. Wilson quickly returned to her seat and Sheriff Mead walked to the front of the audience. He didn't bother with any formal introduction or greetings, but instead immediately addressed what Mrs. Wilson had asked him to check in to.

"Concerning this commitment thing, from what I've looked into it takes a member of the immediate family to file for the process, and then it goes through the courts. The only way this initial step can be bypassed is if the person to be committed has done something that directly causes harm to others, or the family members are found incompetent."

"Mead, are you calling me incompetent?"

Everyone was startled by the sudden question that came from the back of the room, and the entire audience turned to see who had made it.

Standing in the entrance to the church basement with the door resting against his right shoulder was old man Jason Abner. He had been standing outside the basement door listening and apparently Sheriff Mead's comment had prompted him to enter. He definitely looked out of place, but his appearance only emphasized that he was someone you approached with care, if you approached him at all. He was wearing a pair of bib overalls, with no shirt on underneath and his long bare arms hung at his side. He had a pair of old leather boots on that blended in very well with the muscle tone and skin color of his long lanky frame. He turned his head to see if anyone was standing along the back wall and in so doing revealed a scar that ran from below his left ear, down his neck and out to the top of his shoulder. The long straggly gray hair that fell from his head partially concealed the scar, but it was too wide to ever be completely hidden. A two to three day growth of gray whiskers covered his long face and made him look old, but his piercing green eyes that glittered in the basement light made you overlook the gray. As I looked at him I could see the resemblance of some of his physical characteristics with Joan Raycart. It was hard to believe that this formidable man was Joan's father.

He stepped into the room and let the basement door close behind him. The sound of the door closing emphasized the silence that had come over all in attendance. After taking a few steps forward he stopped and slowly looked over the audience as if he was studying each of them on an individual basis. Sheriff Mead slowly walked down the center aisle toward Jason.

"Yes, sometimes you can be incompetent, Jason. What you doing down here anyways?"

"I heard there was a meeting that had something to do with me and I wanted to see what it was all about," Jason said.

"The meeting is just about over with, Jason, and it didn't have anything to do with you, so you might as well be on your way," the sheriff said.

"You don't have to lie to me Sheriff, I'm not a voter. I heard everything, and it sounded like the meeting was about my kid, so I guess if it's about my kid, it's about me."

"Jason, you don't care about your kid. You never have. I know it, and I think we all know it. I think the best thing you can do right now is leave, so these people can finish their meeting."

It was apparent that Sheriff Mead and Abner Jason had past encounters. The sheriff continued to approach Jason not taking his eyes off him and stopped when he was about ten feet away. Jason on the other hand, calmly looked around the room again as if he was making a person by person survey to see how they reacted to the Sheriff's statement. When he finished his scan of the audience he turned to face the sheriff, and spoke in a voice that was loud enough for everyone to hear.

"Frank, you don't know what I care about or don't care about, and most of the people in this room don't know a damn thing about me. You're right I don't belong here, so I'm going to leave, but I want everyone here to know one thing."

The Sheriff was becoming more uncomfortable with Jason and was quick to respond.

"And what might that be, Jason?"

"If anyone hurts my kid and I find out who it is, they'll answer to me and that goes for the rock throwers too," Jason said.

Jason turned and started to walk toward the door.

"That sounds pretty much like a threat, Jason, and that's not a good idea," the sheriff said.

When Jason reached the door, he turned back to face the sheriff.

"You're right, Frank, it did sound like that, so I guess it was. I'll be seeing ya around."

As the words were being absorbed by all present, Jason pulled the door open. He didn't turn to look at the group, but everyone saw him pick up a shotgun that he had left leaning against the outside wall. The door closed behind him, but everyone sat quietly and continued to watch the basement door. We could hear each step as Jason climbed the basement stairs. The sound of the church entrance door opening and then closing again brought a sigh of relief from some. Most of the people in the room were visibly shaken by Jason Abners visit, but none more than Mrs. Wilson. The sheriff had walked back to the front of the room, but Mrs. Wilson didn't seem to be paying any attention. She remained seated, but was now resting her head in both hands and was staring at the floor. I don't think she ever dreamed something like this was going to happen.

"I think Jason was hitting the sauce early tonight. I'll be sure to keep a close watch on him. Now back to our discussion about committing Joan Raycart for psychiatric care. I have told you all that I know about the issue; the next step depends on what Doctor Thompson finds out from lawyers in Madison who deal with such matters."

The sheriff then took his seat. His fast paced closing statement had given Mrs. Wilson some time to gather her thoughts and she stood to address the group.

"I know this is difficult and Jason's outburst has only added kindling to the fire. But I feel if we don't do something, and something does happen, well it would be hard for all of us to live with. I support Doctor Thompson and feel we must get Joan professional help. If it can't be done voluntarily, then we must find other means."

Mrs. Wilson was looking directly at my mother when she finished speaking, and Mom stood so that she was directly facing her neighbor.

"I don't agree with this and I think a huge mistake is being made because fear of the unknown is clouding your judgment. If you take Joan Raycart off that farm and put her in an asylum for what Doctor Thompson calls continuous monitoring, instead of a chance for her to recover, I feel there's a better chance that she'll wilt away in seclusion and Hank will die or disappear. But you will have removed the fear and each year the memory of Hank and Joan will fade, and eventually it'll be as if they never existed at all, and everyone will be happy."

Mom remained standing for a few seconds and then started to make her way to the center aisle.

"Come on, Shorty, we gotta go, your father will be wondering what's taking us so long."

A cool night breeze met us when we exited the church. The basement was warm and stuffy, but the breeze gave some immediate relief. It was a clear night and Mom looked at the sky.

"It's a beautiful night for a walk, don't you think?" she asked.

I knew that my mother was disappointed. She truly believed that Hank's plan would be welcomed, but Doctor Thompson had shot that out of the water. We weren't far from Mirror Lake Tavern when we walked past a sign that warned people to slow down so that they wouldn't drive into the lake. I picked up some rocks and threw one at the sign.

"Here, Mom, you want to give it a try?"

Mom smiled. "You bet, give me a couple of those."

She then reared back and let one fly. The rock made a clanging sound as it bounced off the tin sign.

"Nice throw, Mom. Dad is right; you do improve in accuracy when you're angry."

She laughed and tossed another rock at the sign and smiled when she heard the rock hit.

"Maybe my aim does improve a little bit, but my eyes don't change shape, do they?"

I walked over close to her side and looked at her face.

"I don't know, Mom, they may be changing some."

She gave me a playful shove. "You're getting more like your father every day, and I don't know if that's a good thing or not."

She tossed a few more rocks and then picked up a good-sized one and put some extra effort into the throw. A loud bang echoed through the night when the rock hit the sign and Mom brushed her hands together to get the dust off while at the same time celebrating her accuracy.

"That's for you Doctor Thompson and how you dazzled everyone tonight with your bull shhh…crap."

You could have knocked me over with a feather. Mom was quick to realize that she had just used what she considered to be profanity, and on more than one occasion had told me that such language was completely uncalled for.

"Don't you dare tell your father I said that, I'd never be able to live it down."

"I won't, I promise."

It was ten thirty when we entered the tavern. Dad was at the end of the bar talking with Tommy and waved for us to come over when he saw us enter. He gave his stool to my mother and Mom took a seat at the bar. Ruth Frost was bartending and came over to see what we wanted.

"Hi, Maddie, what kind of pop can I get you?" Ruth asked.

Mom thought for a second. "Ruth, I think I'll have a whiskey sour."

Dad and Tommy's conversation came to a halt and from the look on their faces you would have thought the Russians had invaded Sun Set and took over the cheese factory. Dad shrugged his shoulders, and then turned his attention to me.

"Shorty, how many windows do we have to pay for?"

"None, Dad, but Mom was great, she held her own."

"I don't doubt that a bit. Maddie, you okay?" Dad asked.

"Yes, I'm fine. We'll talk about it later."

Ruth came over with my mother's drink, a bottle of pop for me, and a beer for Dad.

"This is on old scar face over there. Who is that guy anyway?" Ruth asked.

We looked down the bar and at the other end stood Jason Abner. When Mom took her glass, Jason raised his bottle and gave a short nod. Mom raised her glass, smiled, and returned with a salutatory nod.

"That's Jason Abner, he's one of our neighbors," Mom said.

"You got some mean lookin' neighbors," Ruth replied.

"Ruth, if you think he's a mean looker, you should see the neighbor Tommy's been running around with. Isn't that right, Maddie? Dad said.

Tommy punched my dad on the shoulder and Ruth walked away to serve another customer, but still was able to give her son that motherly inquisitive look.

I watched Jason raise the bottle of beer to his lips and set it on the bar when it was empty. He then picked up a six pack of beer and started to leave. Sam Raycart and Toad were sitting at a table by the jukebox and Toad spoke to Jason as he passed with a voice that was loud enough to be heard over the jukebox music.

"Hey, Slim, are we gonna see you next week, I hear you're gettin' back in the game?"

"We'll see," Jason replied.

Toad was starting to say something else, but Jason had already walked by him and was out the door. I remembered Toad talking about someone named Slim, it was on the day Sam had given me a ride home. Slim, was the one Toad said they should have bet on. So if Jason Abner was Slim, what were they betting on him to do?

Chapter Twenty-One
School Starts

The next day we all went to church, except for Dad of course. Dad tried to talk Mom out of going and I thought his reasoning was pretty sound, but it fell on deaf ears.

"Maddie, you walked into a hornets nest last night and you stirred it up. Don't you think you should maybe let them hornets calm back down some before you rile 'em up again?"

"I'm going to church and that's all we're doing, no more, no less. I have no intentions of riling anyone up for any reason. I'm just going to church."

When we arrived at church Pastor Wilcox was at the front door greeting people as they walked in. As always, he waved to my dad and my dad politely waved back.

"Good morning, Maddie. Good to see you, glad you came," he sincerely said.

While walking down the aisle to our normal pew position, I noticed that there weren't as many people in church as there was at last nights meeting. The sermon was about the eighth and ninth commandments, and how we should continue to help our neighbors and not bear false witness against or be jealous of them. It seemed appropriate and the pastor on more than one occasion mentioned how the neighbors in his congregation helped each other out during harvest and in times of need. He was definitely trying to help mend some fences that may have been damaged the previous night.

As we were leaving everyone exchanged greetings, and the overall atmosphere was polite, but at the same time seemed somewhat cosmetic. Mrs. Wilson even asked me if I was ready to go back to school.

"I can't believe summer is coming to an end already, we'll be picking corn before you know it," Mrs. Wilson said.

When we walked outside, Mom walked over to say good morning to Mrs. Strum. They exchanged pleasantries and after some small talk about the weather and school starting tomorrow I thought the conversation was over.

"Well, guess it's time to go. We'll see you next Sunday, Margaret," Mom said.

"Maddie, before you go, I want to thank you and Shorty for coming last night. After you left there was more discussion on the commitment issue. Jake Matthews and some others brought up that they were concerned that we may be jumping the gun on the issue. Doctor Thompson agreed to let us all know what he finds out before any action is taken, but he's not backing down…and Mabel, Francis and some others are standing firm with him. And they might be in the majority, but there was enough dissention in the air to let them know that they best proceed with caution. If you wouldn't have come and spoke your mind, I'm afraid Joan would have been off the farm within a month. So, I guess what I'm trying to say is that I for one am glad that you took time off from chokecherry picking to join us last night. I know you were really upset, Maddie, but you changed the mind set of some people last night or at least got them to think for themselves, and that's a good thing."

"Thanks for that, Margaret. May I ask you what your feelings on the subject are?"

"You know me, Maddie. I'm not like you. I wish I was, but I'm not. What Harold decides is what I'll decide."

"I understand."

"Maddie, we're all human beings and we do the best that we can. I know what we do isn't always right and it isn't always fair, but we live with it and move on."

"I want this to be fair, Margaret," Mom said.

"Me too. One more thing before I let you go, did you tell Jason Abner about the meeting?"

"No I didn't, as a matter of fact I never met the man before last night. Why do you ask?"

"He works for us off and on and last night was the most I ever heard him talk. He never bothers me and he's a very good worker, but you be careful around him. There was quite a bit of talk about him last night. He scared the begeebers out of a lot of people in that room, especially the older ones. I'm afraid him showing up didn't help your cause any."

"Why's that?"

"Because they say he doesn't make idle threats. Alfonse Peterson, who's about the same age as Jason, relayed a story about him last night and Alfonse isn't one to stretch the truth."

"What did Mr. Peterson say happened?" Mom asked.

"I'm going to tell you, Maddie, because you're getting close to Joan, and now Jason is involved. Alfonse said that the scar on Jason's neck happened when Jason's brother-in-law jumped Jason from behind and stabbed him with a knife one night at deer camp. They had been arguing over how the people in the camp were to divide the venison. If others in the camp wouldn't have tackled Jason's brother-in-law, Alfonse said Jason would probably have been killed. Alfonse said that Jason was bleeding as much as any deer they had shot that day, but Jason stood up, faced his brother-in-law and told him that he was going to bury him."

"Did they send Jason's brother-in-law to jail?" Mom asked.

"No, Jason never filed any charges, but a week later his brother-in-law disappeared, never to be heard from again. Alfonse said Jason just laughed when the law questioned him about it. So please watch your step when you're around him."

"I doubt very much if I'll ever see him again, and he's never been at Hank and Joan's while I've been there. But how did his showing up last night hurt my cause?"

"Because Doctor Thompson picked up on some of the comments made last night. Someone said Jason was crazy as a loon. Then another added that the acorn don't fall far from the tree. Doctor Thompson used what was said to bring out some more psychological facts as he put it."

"Such as what?" Mom asked.

"Doctor Thompson told us that because Jason has proven to be violent, there's a good chance that his daughter has inherited those same traits."

"Now I understand what you mean by hurting my cause. Thanks, Margaret."

"You deserve to know, Maddie, and don't get down on yourself about last night. You injected some common sense into a complicated issue, and if there's one trait people have around here, it's that they rely heavily on common sense when making decisions."

Harold Strum walked up as Mrs. Strum was finishing her message.

"Good morning, Maddie, you look good as ever. Can we give you and the kids a ride down to Mirror Lake?"

"Morning, Harold, but no thanks. It's a good morning for a walk and Shorty has to get use to it since he'll have to walk or bike over two miles every day starting tomorrow."

Mom politely made her exit and we left. The day went by quickly, as most Sundays do when the weather is nice and you can be outside. After supper, Mom told my dad what Mrs. Strum had said about Jason Abner.

"Yup, I'm familiar with that story, and no one knows if Jason did him in or not. There's no doubt that Jason can be a mean bastard, but they say his brother-in-law was just as mean. My dad told us that when Hoot Lucas disappeared, most people felt it was a good thing, so the law didn't spend much time on the investigation. It was like no news was good news. All that's known for sure is that Hoot was never seen or heard from again, and neither Jason or his wife shed a tear. Maddie, if you're going to war, Jason is a person you'd want on your side, but if you're going to a peace conference it would be best not to mention his name. The old timers say he could cut a person's heart out and not blink an eye, because he has no heart."

"I know when he walked into the church basement you could have heard a pin drop. What ever happened to his wife?" Mom asked.

"She died from tuberculosis when Joan was very young. Jason buried her on a hill on his place and they say it's the only spot on his farm that he keeps up."

"Bad events sure have happened in Joan's life, but Jason can't be all bad if he raised Joan on his own."

"Maddie, you always look for that ray of sunshine. True he raised Joan, but it's also true that he wants to be left alone and like my dad says, when a man like Jason Abner wants to be left alone, you leave him alone."

"Like I told Margaret, I never seen or spoke to him before last night and I doubt if I'll ever have reason to associate with him in the future."

Mom then turned her attention to me.

"Shorty, you better get to bed, school starts tomorrow."

I was still thinking about Jason and his brother-in-law and wanted to find out some more, so I asked my dad what I thought was a good leading question.

"Dad, why did they call Jason's brother-in-law Hoot?"

Dad looked somewhat surprised by the question.

"People get nicknames. Look at you, we call you Shorty, but you're not any shorter than any of the other boys your age. But after a while the nickname sticks with you and some people forget what your real name is. I'm surprised you asked, because I remember asking my dad the same thing. He told me they called him Hoot, because you never saw him in the daylight very often, kind of like an old hoot owl, who likes to come out at night to hunt. In Hoot Lucas's case, your grandpa said he liked to come out at night because it was easier to steal under the cover of darkness."

Before I went to bed I made my usual scan over the swamp, and it looked as peaceful and calm as ever. It had been three months since whatever it was followed or chased me through the swamp. I didn't think it was Joan, and I definitely didn't believe it was some cougar or other four legged animal. I was convinced that it had to have been a person. I continued to look out the window trying to figure out what was out there, when I noticed my reflection on the window pane. Maybe that's what it was, a reflection of a person, a spirit.

As I lay in bed I tried to recall what happened that night when I was chased through the swamp. I had a hard time falling asleep because my imagination was taking me to areas I really didn't want to go. What if old man Jason killed his brother-in-law, Hoot Lucas, and buried him somewhere along the river and at night Hoot's spirit roams the river banks. I tried to convince myself that was impossible, because spirits wouldn't make splashing sounds when they cross a river, or at least I didn't think they would. The last thing I remembered before drifting off to sleep was picturing a shadow, and it was watching me from behind a bush on the side hill of the river. When I walked toward the shadow, the sun came through the trees and the shadow disappeared.

I was awakened by the morning sun shinning through my window. I was excited to get up because it was the first day of school. I usually rode my bike to school. I would leave around seven thirty and get to school a little after eight. Sycamore was a one-room schoolhouse for grades one through eight. I don't know why it was called Sycamore, because no sycamore trees grew in the area. Most of the kids arrived by eight and we'd play baseball until classes started. The Milwaukee Braves winning season was a daily topic, and we'd compare Hank Aaron to Mickey Mantle or Warren Spahn to Whitey Ford. We all agreed that Hank and Warren were by far the best.

Twenty-five kids attended the school and our teacher's name was Selma Chance. She was very pleasant and demanded her students treat her and each other with respect. On our first day she made the announcement that this would be the last year Sycamore would be open. Next year buses would take us to schools in Middleton or Sunset depending on where we lived. She told us that it would provide us with a better education and allow us to play a part in a rapidly changing world. We then said the Pledge of Allegiance and began our last year at Sycamore.

The school day finished at three-thirty. I'd usually be home by four thirty or five, depending on how often I stopped along the way. When I biked by Jason Abners place I'd slow down and look up the driveway, but all that could be seen from the road were the top sections of an unpainted farmhouse and barn. If you didn't know better you'd think no one even lived there.

Every day on the way home I made it a point to stop and say hi to Hank. Joan would usually be sitting by the river with her dogs. Hank was always busy doing something, but there was never a day that he didn't take the time to stop and visit with me.

Mom and Dad visited Hank the first Monday after the church meeting. Mom told Hank that Doctor Thompson wasn't in favor of having a psychiatrist visit Joan on the farm, but instead the doctor suggested that Joan be taken to a hospital for monitoring and care. It was like telling Hank that the past five years were wasted and there was no longer any hope for his wife to recover. When Hank received my mother's disheartening message, he sat silently for a while and then calmly put a question to Mom.

"They're going to take her away aren't they, Maddie?"

Mom told me that Hank's question, delivered like a statement, made her blood run cold, but felt it was best to be honest with Hank. She told him that some people wanted to and would continue to try and do so because of their fear of Joan. But she also pointed out that there are many who feel that Joan wouldn't harm anyone and whatever is done should be entirely Hank's decision.

After Hank listened to my mother's response he half-heartedly continued the conversation by stating that it looked like he'd still have to sell some cows, so he had money for a lawyer and not a doctor as he originally had planned. The visit had only lasted a half-hour, and both Mom and Dad agreed that it was necessary, but truly wished they didn't have to be the messenger.

Mom didn't know if what Hank said as he walked them to the car was meant for their ears only, but it absolutely was a rejection of what Doctor Thompson had proposed.

"I've made a decision. I'm not going to let anyone take Joan from this farm," Hank said.

When I stopped to visit on Tuesday of the first week of school, Martin and Max Strum were there with their cattle truck. Joan was sitting by the river and

Wrench was lying beside her, but the other two dogs, Peg and Three Eye were by the truck. I leaned my bike against the yard light pole and walked to the truck. Three Eye turned to look at me for a second and then switched her attention to the barn and started to growl. I started to walk to the barn, but stopped when I saw Hank and the Strum brothers coming out the barn door. Both dogs stood beside me and continued to growl as they watched Martin and Max walk towards their truck.

"Hi, Shorty, how'd school go today?" Hank asked.

"Not bad," I said.

"You're Mike and Maddie's kid aren't ya?" Martin asked.

"Yes I am," I said.

"Does Selma still teach at Sycamore?" Martin asked.

"Yes she does," I replied.

As the Strum boys got closer the growls from the dogs became more intense, and Three Eye stepped in front of me, and Peg remained by my side.

"Looks like those dogs know you pretty good, but I don't think they trust us. Hank, you better let them know that we're here to buy your cows, and not steal 'em," Martin said.

The dogs were making Martin nervous and I wanted to tell him to just show them you're not afraid and they won't bother you, but thought better of it. Max walked around the back of the truck and got in the passenger side, while Martin and Hank stood next to the truck.

"The dogs have become friends with Shorty since he started helping me out this summer, looks like they want to make sure you guys are friendly," Hank said.

Martin opened the truck door and extended his hand towards Hank.

"Hank, you got our offer for the ten head. Give us a call when you want to sell, and we'll come over and pick them up and bring you a check," Martin said.

Hank shook Martin's hand and replied, "I'll let you know if I decide to sell, thanks for coming over. Be sure to tell your parents hello for me."

Martin climbed into the truck and started the engine, but before he put the truck in gear Max leaned across the front seat to make a point to Hank.

"Hank, when we come and get the cows it might be best to tie up your dogs. You know ya have to be careful with them mutts or someone is going to take those growls as threats and shoot 'em or something," Max said.

Hank looked in the truck at Max. "If I sell, I'll be sure the dogs don't bother you, but thanks for the advice just the same."

As the Strum boys drove off, Hank turned to me and smiled.

"Looks like your dogs have taken on another client to protect, doesn't it, Joan?"

I looked over my shoulder and there was Joan. She was standing not more than five feet behind me. I was getting used to her silent entrances, but they still surprised me and caused me to wonder how she could walk so quietly. She seemed to be watching the truck as it pulled out the driveway and crossed the bridge. When the truck disappeared from view, she returned to the river with the three dogs by her side.

"Well, Shorty, if I sell those ten cows it'll mean less work and I'll have more hay to sell this winter. I think the Strum boys feel like it's already a done deal, but we'll have to see about that. I better get to chores. Tell your folks hi."

"I will."

I was starting to leave when I saw Hank pick something up that was leaning against the barn wall. At first I thought it was a shovel or a fork, but it was neither. It was a shotgun.

During supper that evening I told my parents what I saw while visiting Hank and Joan. Mom and Dad weren't at all surprised when I told them that Hank might be selling some cattle to the Strum brothers, but when I mentioned the shotgun, it immediately brought a response from my dad.

"I didn't know Hank even owned a shotgun. I'm afraid he feels like he's being pushed into a corner and that ain't good. You force that big man in to a corner and when he decides to come out all hell is going to break loose. Maddie, have you heard anymore about Mabel's little crusade?"

"No I haven't. I'm not in that loop, but Margaret did say they'd hold another meeting before anything further was done concerning Joan. You don't think Hank has the gun in case they should come with papers to take Joan away, do you?"

"I'm afraid I do. Hank told us yesterday that he wasn't going to let anyone take Joan from the farm, and there's no doubt in my mind that he meant every word of it."

Mom set her fork down.

"There has to be another way…a better way. You're right, Hank feels like he's being backed into a corner and I can't say I blame him for thinking so, but there has to be a better way. Maybe we should have waited and told Hank about the commitment issues after the next meeting. Maybe there won't be a next meeting because Doctor Thompson will find out that they don't have a leg to stand on. But I can't rely on that, I have to do something."

Mom was definitely worked up and having trouble making sense of it all. I watched as she nervously rubbed the thumb of her right hand around the palm of her left. She desperately wanted to find a way to help the Raycarts and the sooner the better.

"Let's wait and see what old Doc Thompson comes up with. If we have to we'll get in the corner with Hank, so that he doesn't end up killing someone," Dad said.

"Yes, I suppose that's a reasonable idea. Let's go over this Sunday for a visit and maybe we can take some of the pressure off," Mom said.

"We can sure do that, at least the visit part," Dad said.

Mom's concerns were now bordering on fear. Those fears you get when you feel something bad is going to happen and you have no control over it. Dad understood his wife's dilemma and was kind of in a corner himself.

"Maddie, I don't know what else we can do."

"I know, but I just got this feeling that something is about to boil over and I can't turn down the heat. Would you mind doing the dishes? I need to take a short walk and do some thinking," Mom said.

Dad realized that it wasn't really a request.

"Sure, Shorty, you wash and I'll dry. That dish water is hard on my hands you know."

While washing dishes I looked out the window and watched my mother walk down the driveway.

"What do you think Mom is thinking about?"

"I don't know, Shorty. But you can bet it's above thinking as we know it. Your mother is searching to find a solution. It's like she can bring everything into view and discard what's unimportant, and concentrate on the things that are important, so that she comes up with a proper solution. She's kind of like a witch."

"Like a what?"

"Not a crooked nose, black hatted witch, but a good witch. Like the one in the Wizard of Oz that helps Dorothy get back to Kansas. You're not going to tell me that you don't believe in witches are you?"

I didn't know how to respond, so I didn't. Dad was now also watching Mom and he had a smile on his face that out did any dancing Munchkin. After a moment he turned his smile toward me.

"I'll take your silence as a I don't know answer. Now let's finish these dishes, so we can listen to the Braves."

Mom returned from her walk in about an hour and she seemed refreshed as she walked up the porch steps. She finished listening to the game with us and was genuinely happy when the Braves won.

"Did you come up with any new ideas while on your stroll? Dad asked.

"Maybe," she said.

Dad looked at me.

"Witches don't talk much when they're contemplating changing the future."

I had had enough. The Braves won the game and my dad was too goofy. It was time for me to read a chapter in my history book and go to bed.

Chapter Twenty-Two
Jason Abner

The next couple of weeks went by quickly. The hot days of August gave way to cool September mornings, and you could feel a touch of fall in the air. Hank didn't sell any of his cows, because he decided against seeking legal advice. He was going to continue to operate the farm because that's what he knew best and it provided a common connection with his wife. Hank firmly believed that the farm provided a window for his wife to return, and if she didn't, it was still the best place for her to be.

Mom and Dad continued to make regular weekend visits to the Raycarts. The visits made all involved feel more comfortable with life, and my mother even got used to the shotgun leaning against the wall next to wherever Hank was sitting.

Joan remained her silent self and continued to walk the river with her dogs and for some reason continued to hang the lanterns in the trees at night. Most everyone who lived in the area was aware of Joan's unusual behavior. Everyone could see the light from the lanterns flickering through the trees when they crossed the bridge at night.

Mom realized this unusual behavior was probably helping to strengthen the commitment argument against Joan, but she also felt that it might be therapeutic for her. Mom believed that hanging the lanterns provided a stimulus for Joan and would allow her to maintain contact with the river through the winter months. Although the river took her last child, it had also become a sanctuary for Joan. Mom felt that Joan's actions illustrated that she was capable of reasoning and acting accordingly. To my mother there was little difference between Joan hanging lanterns in the trees and Francis Beck putting candles in her windows at night. She reasoned that they both did it because it provided them with a sense of inner peace and didn't harm anyone.

School was going along nicely and all the kids enjoyed the atmosphere of studying mixed in with games at recess and lunch. However, when Mrs. Chance dismissed us early one Friday we were all excited to take advantage of a warm September afternoon. The days were getting shorter, but the extra time would allow me to get chores done and still have some time to go fishing. I jumped on my bike and was riding past Jason Abner's driveway when my front tire went flat. I coasted off the road into the ditch and bent down to examine the tire.

"You got a problem?"

The question out of nowhere startled me and I quickly stood up to see who it was. I let go of the bike when I saw Jason Abner walking toward me and it fell to the ground.

"No...No...it's fine, nothing wrong," I stuttered.

"Looks flat to me," Jason said.

He was now standing next to my bike. There was a cool breeze, but he was still only wearing a pair of bib overalls without a shirt underneath. I tried not to, but couldn't help but stare at the scar that traveled down his neck and out to his shoulder blade. Time had allowed the scar to blend in somewhat, but the redness of it and how it protruded from his skin still made it stand out. He looked me up and down and picked the bike off the ground.

"I got some patches. I'll see if I can fix it."

He carried the bike across the road to his driveway and I stood watching. I didn't know what to do. Should I wait for him to come back? Should I start to walk home? Should I follow him? I slowly crossed the road and followed him up the driveway, but I maintained a safe distance behind, so that if anything happened I could run for the trees. However, he never looked back to see if I was following, and he didn't stop until he reached a small shed that set between the house and barn. I stopped and watched as he laid the bike on the ground and went inside the shed. I looked back toward the road, but couldn't see it anymore because the driveway curved and went downhill as it got closer to the buildings. I was about fifty feet from the shed and decided that was a good place to stay. Jason came out of the shed with a wrench in his hand and looked at me standing in the middle of his driveway.

"Here's a wrench, take the damn tire off and I'll see if I can find some patches."

He tossed the wrench on the ground beside the bike and then went back inside the shed. I walked to the bike, loosened the nuts, and took the tire off, but not for one second did my eyes stray from watching the door of the shed. When the door opened I quickly stood and watched Jason step into the sunlight.

"Bring that tire over here and I'll see if the inner tube can be patched."

There was no way I was going to go into that shed. I didn't move, but must have shaken my head to indicate I planned to stay where I was.

"Oh hell," Jason said and he started to walk toward me.

My first thought was to run, but that message never reached my feet, so I stood motionless as if I was glued to the ground. Jason walked up and grabbed the tire from my hand. A lean-to was attached to one end of the shed that had a workbench along the wall and Jason put the tire on the bench. He glanced at me and then went back inside the shed. When he returned he was carrying some tools and a tire pump.

"The light is better out here anyways," he said.

He took the inner tube out of the tire and pumped it up. While he was checking the tube for leaks he spoke to me, but didn't look in my direction.

"You're Maddie's kid aren't ya?"

"Yes."

"We've kind of met before haven't we?"

"Kind of."

"How's your dog?"

"She's fine."

"I heard she got sick and Joan Raycart nursed her back."

"Yes, she did."

"Joan's my kid, but she don't like me much."

"Oh."

I could feel my heart beating against my chest, and I think that was the only part of my body that was moving. Jason found the leaks, drew a circle around each of them on the tube and then let the air out. He smeared glue over the marked areas and applied the patches. As he was setting some bricks on the patches to hold them in place while the glue dried I looked around the lean-to. An old rusty pail setting in the middle of the work bench caught my attention and Jason saw me looking at it.

"You know what that is?"

"It's a pail."

"It's a ice fishing pail. It's used to carry ice fishing gear. I found it this spring. It was setten in some brush next to a tree on the other side of the river."

"Oh."

"You like to fish, don't ya?"

"Yes, I do."

"You're afraid of me aren't ya?"

"Kind of."

"Hell, that's all right. Sometimes I'm afraid of myself."

I didn't know how to reply to such a comment and I don't think he had much more to say. He stared at me for a short moment and then began to remove the bricks from the inner tube. When he was satisfied that the patches were properly dried he filled the tube with air and then checked for additional leaks. No air was found escaping, so he put the tube in the tire and used the hand pump to bring the tire to what he determined was the proper air pressure. He unscrewed the pump from the valve stem and held the tire out to me.

"Here, you put the tire back on and I'll put my stuff away," he said.

I hesitated for a moment, but then walked over and took the tire from his hands. I carried the tire to the bike and knelt down to put it on when I heard a car coming up the driveway. It was the nice looking Thunderbird and Jewel was driving. Jewel slammed on the brakes when he saw Jason coming out of the shed and began to open the car door while the dust was still drifting over the vehicle. He slammed the door shut and started to talk as he walked around the front of his car.

"What's this bull shit that I hear you've quit? You can't quit. We're going to start the training site up next week and you better be there."

"And what if I'm not?" Jason said.

Jewel was now standing in front of Jason and he took his forefinger and pushed it into Jason's chest.

"I don't think you want to go there, Slim."

Jason took his hand and brushed Jewels hand away.

"Guess we'll have to cross that bridge when we come to it, won't we?" Jason said.

Jewel was as tall as Jason and his upper body was larger, but he couldn't match the defiant stare that the old man was returning. Jason didn't like being poked in the chest and his entire body became rigid, but the piercing cold stare from his green eyes made Jewel change his tactics. They stood facing each other for a few seconds and then Jewel took a step backward.

"Listen, Slim, we got a champion in the making and we can make some good money. When I was here in June you told us you'd be ready for the training. We got the old place ready to go, but now you've decided not to fulfill your end of the bargain. If someone would have done that to you, you would have been ready to rip their heart out. What say, you at least come over and look the situation over and I'm sure you'll see we have a winner. There's a small town refereed pit being set up in Hillside next week and we're going to see if the Rott is ready. Frank says he is, and I think with a little more work we'll be able to put him on the circuit and make some big bucks."

Jewel then leaned against the front fender of his car and in so doing noticed me behind the workbench.

"Hey, kid, what you doing here?" Jewel asked.

"He had a flat on his bike and I fixed it for him," Jason said.

"I didn't know you had any Good Samaritan blood in you, Slim. You ain't gettin' soft in your old age are ya?"

"Maybe I am, but not soft enough to be pushed too far, if you get my drift," Jason replied.

"I think we understand each other. If you show up, you're there, but if you don't show, well…then like you said we'll cross that bridge when we come to it."

Jewel then pushed himself away from the car and started to walk to the driver's door.

"Hey, kid, I hear you've made friends with that crazy ladies mean dogs. You better watch them close. You know what they say; you can never tame something that's been wild. Isn't that right,Slim?"

"That's what they say?" Jason said.

"See ya around," Jewel said as he got in his car.

The engine from the Thunderbird roared as Jewel spun it around on the driveway causing the gravel and dust to fly. Jason watched the Thunderbird speed out of sight down the driveway and then turned to face me.

"Looks like you got it back together and it's holding air. You better get home."

I was more than ready to leave, and I started to wheel my bike from the lean-to to the driveway.

"Thanks for fixing my tire," I said.

"Not a problem. By the way, how did you get on the good side of those dogs?"

"I don't know. I think I just showed them that I wasn't afraid."

I couldn't believe I had made such an arrogant statement to a man who probably has killed people.

"I…I mean Joan, I mean Mrs. Raycart has allowed them to be friendly to me."

"I think my kid likes you. She can talk to them dogs you know. She could always talk to them damn dogs and most other critters too. But she don't like me much, so we don't talk."

I was going to tell him that I knew his daughter could talk to the dogs, but he was no longer paying any attention to me. He had already turned and was walking toward his house. As I biked out his driveway, I turned to look back, and saw him sitting on the front steps watching me.

I stopped at the Raycarts on the way home. Joan was sitting by the river, so I rode down to say hello. I laid my bike in the grass and sat on the ground next to her chair. As usual her three dogs were gathered around her, but old Three Eye stood up, walked over and lay down beside me. I waved to Hank who was working on a gate that led to the barnyard, and he waved back.

"You skip out early from school?" he asked.

"No, Mrs. Chance left us out early."

I sat for a while watching the river and then decided to tell Joan something.

"I had a flat tire today and your dad fixed it for me."

Her hands gripped the side of the chair so tight that they turned white. The dogs must have sensed something was about to happen and were now standing on the bank watching her. Her fingers slowly came loose from the chair, and in one continuous motion she was standing and walking toward the river. When she reached the edge of the river she stopped and turned around to face me. She stood still for a few moments and then started to walk toward me. She stopped in front of me and when I looked up I saw that she had turned her head so that she seemed to be watching the river. I looked at the river to see if something was there, and out of the corner of my eye saw her turning her head in my direction. She stood motionless for a short period of time and then bent her neck down so that she was staring directly at me.

"He killed John," she said.

The words came out in a whisper that I could barely hear above the sound of the water running over the rocks. She then quietly turned and walked toward the bridge, but what she had said was still echoing through my mind. The delivery of the silent remark was more piercing than the stare that came from her green eyes. It left me with a hollow feeling. I watched her walk under the bridge and truly wished I had not told her that I seen her dad today.

However, the damage was done, so I wheeled my bike away from the river and started to leave. Hank had finished repairing the gate and met me as I was leaving.

"Why such a sad face, Shorty?" Hank said.

"Don't know, just never can get used to it I guess."

I didn't tell Hank what had just happened. I thought it could only cause more problems and the last thing Hank needed was more problems.

"I know, buddy, but you keep trying and that's important. You probably reach her more than anyone else. I can't tell you how much I appreciate you just stopping by to visit with Joan."

"Thanks, Hank, I better head for home."

"See ya, Shorty. Oh, wait…there's one more thing before you leave. You're Uncle Joe stopped over today. We're going to help each other pick corn this year and we're counting on your help. Joe kind of volunteered you. I hope that's alright with you."

"That'll be fine," I said.

That evening I couldn't get what Joan had whispered to me out of my mind. After chores I walked to the river hoping some fishing would help to erase the memory of what happened. It was about an hour before sunset when Mom, Dad, my brother and sister came down to the river.

"Not going to have many of these evenings left, so thought we'd have a picnic. Kind of a way to welcome in the fall," Mom said.

Mom was right, it was a nice night. October was right around the corner and the days would continue to get shorter and colder.

"Your mother says you're kind of down in the dumps. You want to tell us what's bothering you?" Dad asked.

I told them what happened at Jason Abners while he was repairing my flat tire. Dad wasn't very happy about my visit with Jason Abner and he was quick to emphasis that point.

"I know Jason helped you out today, but you got to promise us that you won't go back there. Not unless I'm with. It doesn't surprise me any that Jewel and him got something brewing. The more I see of Jewel, the more I don't trust him either. He says he buys and sells most anything and that's how he makes his money. Whatever he and Jason were arguing about, you can bet it wasn't about something honest."

That wasn't a difficult promise to make and it definitely was one that I planned on keeping. We enjoyed the picnic lunch and everyone tried a few casts with my fishing rod. We were helping Mom clean up when she looked at me and smiled.

"That was really relaxing and a good way for a person to clear their head. It would be a shame not to take full advantage of such an evening. Might be a good time to let us know what's really bothering you."

I looked to my dad for some assistance, but all I got was a grin while he shrugged his shoulders. It was like my mother had a sixth sense and she wasn't going to leave until she knew what was really troubling me. It was really quite simple. If something bothered me, it bothered her.

"Joan spoke to me again today," I said.

"What did she say that bothers you so?" Mom asked.

"I told Joan that her dad had helped me fix my bike and it really upset her," I said.

"What did she say?" Mom asked.

"She said, *He Killed John.*"

"You mean Joan thinks that Jason killed her son?" Dad asked.

"Maybe I heard her wrong, but it sure sounded like that's what she said."

"My God, she lost her three kids in a little over a year and she feels her dad killed her last child. She isn't living in silence because of grief; she's in silence because she's being tormented. You didn't tell Hank did you?" Mom asked.

"No, there was no way I would tell him. I keep hoping that maybe I heard her wrong."

"There was a complete investigation done by the county and the state and foul play wasn't even mentioned. It was ruled as an unfortunate accident. The boy fell through the ice and got trapped underneath," Dad said.

"It probably was an accident, but something in Joan's mind has triggered her to believe it wasn't. I can't begin to imagine how this is eating her up inside. It's a miracle that she hasn't withered away and died," Mom said.

"I'm going to tell you something, Shorty. I've held it back, because I'm not sure if it's going to happen. I've been corresponding with a psychiatric hospital in Minneapolis and I'm waiting for a final response from one of their leading psychiatrist. He's indicated that he might come out to visit with Joan and Hank. I've told the psychiatrist that Joan has spoken to you and if he comes he'll want to speak to you before seeing Joan. He feels that you, or things that you do, cause Joan to leave a state of mind where she feels safe in order to address whatever you have caused her to think about. This visit isn't a for sure thing yet, so we have to keep it a secret, and go on like we have been. I hope this makes you feel better about what happened today, does it?

Yes it does, but what if the psychiatrist decides not to come?

"Then we'll look for another solution. In the meantime we'll say some extra prayers and continue to show our support for both Hank and Joan."

"It doesn't hurt to cross your fingers either," Dad added.

Dad was a firm believer in all sorts of superstitions and most of them came after the fact. One time we were listening to a Braves game and they were behind by one run going into the ninth inning, but came back to win the game. At the same time my mother was baking a pie. If the same situation came up in a game today, my dad would do everything possible to get my mother to start to bake a pie. In order to cover my bases that night when Mom tucked me in, I crossed my fingers while saying my prayers.

Chapter Twenty-Three
Jason Reflects

Jason watched Shorty bike out his driveway. He felt good about being able to help the kid get his bike fixed and it caused him to reflect on days gone by.

He looked at the big oak standing next to the house and saw a rope hanging from a lower limb. The rope was rotted from the weather, and like most things on his farm was left to waste away because it was no longer a part of his life. He watched what remained of the rope glide back and forth with the afternoon breeze and imagined his daughter swinging on it. She would hold onto the rope until it reached the highest point, and then she'd let go to see how far she could fly threw the air before touching the ground.

He tried to remember those days, but it was so long ago, and it was getting more difficult to bring the memories back. As he watched the rope sway he smiled inside because he was able to bring back flashes of his daughter, and he thought the daughter back then liked him.

He looked at the buildings and saw how run down they had become. He had sold most of his land to Harold Strum and had only twenty acres left. The acreage extended from the farm buildings to the river, and he could see most of it from his front porch. He remembered that his daughter used it to pasture those damn Black Angus. When she ran off and got married he saw no need for them, so he sold the cattle, and let the land grow back to whatever plants were strong enough to outdo the other.

He knew he wasn't a farmer. He was a hunter. He made good money in the early days when there were wolves around to hunt and animals to trap. He laughed to himself, but his kid was a farmer. She liked to take care of the animals and watch seeds turn into plants. He thought she must have taken after her mother. He closed his eyes and tried to work a vision up of his wife, but couldn't. When he thought of her, he thought of the hill between the barn and the river where he had buried her.

He laughed as he looked towards the hill, because that kid might have knelt on her grave when he was sneaking up to the barn.

"That kid thinks I messed with his dog. People sure get attached to them dogs. My kid loved them animals and that's where we're different." Jason was thinking out loud and a feeling of guilt surfaced in his brain. He looked at what remained of an old chicken coop that set between the house and the barn. The roof had fallen in and the rest of the structure looked like it was ready to collapse with the next good wind. He remembered that day when he came out of the house and saw the dog coming out from under the coop floor. He knew it must be taking eggs. He could almost hear himself calling the dog, and when the dog got close enough he shot it dead. He turned and looked at the door to the house and remembered how his daughter charged out when she heard the shot. She claimed the dog only went to the coop to lie under the floor to get out of the hot sun. He could picture her loading the dog in a wheelbarrow and taking it out in the trees to bury.

He looked toward the tree line and then back towards the coop.

"I shouldn't of shot that dog," he said to himself as he stood up and went inside.

Chapter Twenty-Four
The World Series Starts

September quietly slipped into October and farmers were getting ready to pick corn. We already had our first frost and the corn stalks were turning from green to golden brown. Everyone said that it was going to be a good crop. The ears on the stocks had started to turn down and some stocks were leaning in the field giving way to the fall winds and the soft ground. The crop was going to be a little earlier than usual. Most farmers believed they would get the corn picked before the first significant snow.

However, the big news was that the Milwaukee Braves had won the National League Pennant and were going to meet the New York Yankees in the World Series. People who had never paid attention to the game before were now analyzing every word printed or broadcast over the radio and television. They were comparing the teams as if they all had suddenly become baseball experts. Conversations that normally started out talking about the weather or crop conditions, now started out about the Braves. Is Aaron better than Mantle? Can our pitchers match Whitey Ford and the rest of the Yankee pitching staff? It was truly an exciting time.

I continued to stop at the Raycarts on my way back from school. Each day seemed to get cooler, but Joan continued to set by the river. She always was wearing a warm coat and Hank made sure a blanket was draped over her lap. I would still visit with Joan, but I chose my conversation topics with more care. I didn't want to say something that might cause her to get upset, but I didn't want to ignore her either. I talked to her about the Braves, but she didn't give any indication that she heard. The dogs seemed more attentive than she did. Old Three Eye would now lie beside me and allow me to gently stroke her back while I sat with Joan. The dogs had accepted me as a friend, and I think Joan had accepted me too. It's hard to explain, but I felt inside that she was glad I stopped to visit, even though she gave no such indication.

Sometimes while I was sitting next to Joan I would see Hank watching. He always greeted me with a smile and a friendly wave. Hank seemed more at ease lately. The nightly harassment had stopped and people were generally leaving him and Joan alone. This, plus the fact that a good harvest was expected, put him in a position of acceptance. Fate had determined what he and Joan's life was meant to be. He would live with the sorrows of the past and take each day one at a time. My grandpa told me that a good crop to a farmer is better than first love. Not being an expert on either subject I would shake my head in agreement, bringing smiles from my grandpa and a chuckle from Grandma.

On October first, the day before the World Series began. Hank walked down to the river while I was visiting.

"Well, Shorty, do you think the Braves are gonna beat those Yankees?"

"Heck yes," I said.

He then reached into his shirt pocket and pulled out a packet and handed it to me.

"I see the kids in town have these cards pinned to the spokes of their bikes and thought you might like a pack of em."

It was a package of Topp's baseball cards. I had started to buy a few packages of cards when I went to town and was trying to accumulate the entire Milwaukee baseball team.

"Thanks, Hank."

I opened the pack and put the stick of gum in my mouth and filed through the cards. There was a Lew Burdette card and I proudly waved it in the air to show Hank and Joan.

"Is he any good?" Hank asked.

"Next to Spahn he's the best."

"Do you think he can get those Yankee hitters out?"

As Hank was asking the question, Joan stood up and started her nightly walk to the river.

"Be careful, Joan. We'll see you in a bit," Hank said.

Hank watched his wife as she and the dogs made their way to the bridge. He didn't look happy and he didn't look sad, but he seemed to be content. I think he had accepted that this was what was meant to be, and he was going to hold onto it for however long he needed to.

"Your Uncle Joe and I are planning to start picking corn in a couple of weeks. I have a field about two miles up river and we'll be able to get most with the picker, but there are about ten rows on the edge that have a lot of wash outs. I'm not gonna risk Joe taking his picker through and getting it tore up. I told your dad that if he wanted the corn he could have it, but it would mean hand picking. And you know what that probably means?"

"Yes I do, but that'll be okay. I'll be able to take my rod and reel with and I'll pick some and then fish some. Thanks again for the baseball cards."

"You're welcome, Shorty. You know some fishing mixed in with the corn picking sounds kind of relaxing," Hank said as I was leaving.

That Saturday, Dad and I went to Uncle Joe's to help him get ready for corn harvest. Dad was replacing boards on the corncrib and Uncle Joe was getting his corn-picker ready. I was given the task of cleaning the calf pens. Not one of my favorite jobs and both my dad and Uncle Joe knew it. To make the job more appealing, Uncle Joe would give me a couple of dollars for cleaning the pens.

"Since you get the worst job, you should get paid the most," Uncle Joe said.

Two dollars always came in handy, but I was still dragging my feet some on the way to the barn and Dad noticed my faltering ambition.

"Shorty, I got a little extra incentive for you today. When you get done cleaning the pens, we're going to go and watch the game at Mirror Lake. Maybe we can even talk Joe into coming with. Their going to be back in Milwaukee for game three and we got to help Buhl get the victory."

"Don't know if they'll let me in the place. Think I'll just watch it here," Uncle Joe said.

"You haven't been down there since Roy and Ruth bought the place, and I'm sure they'd be glad to have you," Dad said.

"We'll see," Uncle Joe said.

Dad's added incentive worked very well and I had the pens cleaned before noon. As I was walking from the barn to the house I saw Dad and Uncle Joe walking in from the cornfield that was next to the house.

"Shorty, your mother put some clean clothes for you in a bag in the back seat. Get cleaned up and changed or they won't let you in," Dad said.

Dad was right. The odor I picked up while cleaning the pens was not very pleasant. I quickly washed up, changed clothes and ran outside. Uncle Joe and Dad were standing beside the car and Uncle Joe handed me two dollars.

"Now don't spend it all in one place and don't let your old man talk you into betting it on the Yankees."

"Thanks, but aren't you coming with?" I said.

"I might see you later, but if I don't see you today I'll definitely be over to your place tomorrow. Your mother is making furgeons and your grandma says she'll have all the lefsa we can eat"

As we were leaving I saw Uncle Joe driving his tractor towards the fields in back of the barn. When we reached the road Dad turned in the opposite direction from what he normally took to get to Mirror Lake.

"We got a good hour before the game starts and Tommy will save us a stool. That red dog of Joe's has run off and I want to see if we can find him, so keep your eyes peeled. He'll blend in real good with these fall colors."

"Heck, I didn't know that. How long has Red been gone?"

"I know what you mean. I didn't even realize he was missing until Joe told me while you were cleaning pens. Joe said he hasn't seen him since last night after milking. We checked the fields around the house and Joe's going to check the fields behind the barn again. I sure hope he didn't get hit by a car. That would break Joe's heart."

"Shouldn't we stop at the neighbors and ask if they have seen Red?"

"Joe's already called everyone. He told me that Red ran off last year for a couple of days, so maybe whatever caused him to take a small vacation last year has done the same thing this year."

We slowly drove along the dirt roads searching for the big red dog. Dad stopped the car at the top of each hill, because they provided a good location to search from. We thought we spotted him once running through the brush, but it turned out to be a red fox. When we reached the top of the last hill we could see the waters of Mirror Lake through the autumn colors.

"Well, Shorty, we didn't find the big red beast, but I bet he'll be back before long. He's probably visiting some lady friend and is too embarrassed to let Joe know about her. Now we got one more job to do and that's to cheer those Braves onto victory."

The parking lot was full when we arrived at Mirror Lake and as promised Tommy had a stool saved for my dad. Ruth, Roy and Tommy Frost were being kept very busy tending bar and preparing snacks for the capacity crowd. It definitely was a party atmosphere. The Milwaukee Braves in the World Series against the legendary New York Yankees. They had split the first two games in New York and now were back in Milwaukee for three games.

The television reception wasn't very good. More often than not it was so blurry that you couldn't make out the players. At times they appeared to be playing in a fog, and it was hard to pick up the ball against the gray background of the television screen. However, that didn't deter the people in the bar from getting excited and caught up in this historical moment.

Uncle Joe arrived at the tavern during the fifth inning. The Braves were already behind seven to one. Dad saw Uncle Joe and immediately stood up to greet his brother as he walked across the bar room floor.

"Here we go, Joe will bring some luck and the Braves can still pull this thing out. Ain't that right, Joe?" Dad said.

I could tell that Dad was happy to have his brother present, and the look on Uncle Joe's face showed that the feeling was mutual. Uncle Joe walked with his brother across the floor and took a position at the bar between my dad and the Wright brothers.

"They got an uphill battle, but they're not going to quit. You can bet on that," Uncle Joe said.

Joe no sooner sat down when Hank Aaron hit the ball over the fence to make the score seven to three. The bar erupted in cheers of excitement. My initial thought was the Braves would make a come back, but that hope quickly turned sour when the Yankees scored five runs in the seventh inning to take a twelve to three lead. The mood became somber and the excitement was replaced with wishful anticipation. The thrashing the Braves took wasn't what I expected, but the opportunity of being able to watch it was still very gratifying. When the game was over Uncle Joe bought me a pizza and brought it to where I was sitting.

"Sunday's another day, Shorty. We don't have to worry until there isn't another day," Uncle Joe said.

I finished eating a few slices of pizza and leaned back in my chair. I was starting to doze off when Dad came over and sat down next to me.

"Joes got an hour before he has to get home for milking, so we're going to play a few games of smear, then we'll head home. There's a blanket and a pillow in the back of the Pontiac. Why don't you go out and take a short nap. We'll be out in a few minutes.

That sounded like an excellent idea to me. The Braves had lost the game, but that wasn't going to stop my dad from enjoying the day with his brother. As I walked out the door I overheard a statement from my dad that emphasized that point.

"Now, Tommy, me and Joe are going to teach you guys how to play this game. Joe taught me and whoever invented the game taught Joe, so I think you should feel that the money you're about to lose is not going to be a gambling loss, but rather a educational cost, which will only benefit you in the future."

Dad was in the zone. The Braves may have got clobbered, but Dad reminded everyone that tomorrow was another day, and Spahn wasn't going to lose two in a row. The day was getting cool, and it felt good to climb in the backseat and rest under a warm blanket. I was drifting off to sleep when I heard a car door slam. At first I thought nothing of it, but then I heard voices.

"Bring that case of beer and set it over here," a man said.

I recognized the voice and slowly sat up to see what was going on. It was Jewel sitting at a picnic table that was on the lawn in front of where my dad had parked. Max Strum was carrying the case of beer and he sat it next to Jewel on the picnic table. I quickly ducked down before being noticed. I heard them open a couple of bottles, and then Jewel spoke.

"Here's to you, Max. We did good in Hillside. That damn killer Rott didn't even break a sweat. We got a damn winner. I'm telling you we can go on the circuit and make some big bucks."

"He did good, didn't he? I told you we didn't need that damn Slim anymore. I can train that dog and all the others we bring on," Max said.

"Maybe you can, buddy, but Slim could train five at one time," Jewel said.

"I know…I know…but I worked with him on most of the training, and have picked up all his techniques. Besides, wasn't it my idea to bring in other dogs for bait, and not just rely on them stupid rodents?"

"You did do that. The Rott sure likes to tear into another dog instead of getting rewarded with some worn out cat or rabbit," Jewel said.

"Damn right he does, and that's another thing we shouldn't of let happen. That black dog I got was perfect, a good scrapper. I still say Slim let the bitch go. If I would have done that the boss would have been all over me, but since it was Slim he let it slide. I think the boss is afraid of Slim," Max said.

"I don't know about that, but Slim is a person you gotta watch out for. He may be old, but he has that edge because he doesn't give a damn. Don't ever underestimate him. Give me another beer will ya? Jewel said.

"I ain't afraid of that old bastard. He may have been tough in his day, but his day is long gone. What you going to do about him not showing up for the meeting?" Max asked.

"The boss says to let it slide, because there's more money for us if we split three ways instead of four. And he says one thing's for sure, Slim will never talk," Jewel said.

Max started to laugh.

"What you laughing about?" Jewel asked.

"About that fight in Hillside and how Edgars was bragging up his Doberman. What it take? Twenty minutes and the Rott had it by the throat and there was a kill in less than forty minutes. Beats the hell out of any World Series, don't ya think?"

"It was a good fight for the Rott, and put some good money in our pocket. Do you have any more bait lined up? I figure a couple more weeks to get warmed up for that Chicago fight, and if the Rott proves himself there we can hit the circuit. I got a place south of Chicago lined up for training and there's room to hold all six of our dogs. You gonna come with?"

"Damn right, I'm in on both counts. I got some bait lined up, and I've had it with this hick farming backwoods stuff. My old man says he'll buy my share of the place if I stop farming. I figure I can make more money, and have more fun fighting these dogs, then I can ever make chasing cows into a truck. So whenever you're ready to leave, so am I.

"What's your brother say about it? Does he know you're into this?

"He knows I'm fed up with it around here and he expects me to move on any day now."

"You didn't answer my question. Does he know what you're into?" Jewel asked.

"No, he doesn't. He thinks I plan on going into the buying and selling business with you. Martin's alright, but he doesn't have the nerve to go into our line of work. He's better off staying with the old man. He likes to think he's a big business man, but really all he is, is another farmer," Max said.

"Well as far as I'm concerned you're in and old Slim is out, and if the boss doesn't like it, I'm about ready to skip out on him too. When we get to Chicago, we're on my kind of turf and we don't need the likes of him to plan ways to keep our operation quiet. You train 'em and I'll set up the matches. What do you think about that?" Jewel asked.

"Sounds like a winner to me and the sooner we do it the better. Only wish you could set a match up between the Rott and that Crazy Ladies dog. That's the last dog Slim trained by himself and I'd sure like to show him up," Max said.

"Forget about both those bitches, we got no time for it. Besides, it's been over five years and that dog is too old to put up any type of good fight. The boss is right about one thing though. Having that crazy woman roaming around the river has taken attention away from what we're doing. There's no doubt about it, so let her wander along the river with her dogs like the nut case she is. We gotta look to bigger and better things and forget about the small stuff. Besides…"

Suddenly Jewel stopped because someone was coming out of Mirror Lake Tavern. I heard the sound of people approaching and it didn't take long to figure out who they were.

"Hey boys you cost us two-hundred dollars up in Hillside. I was sure that Edgar's dog was quicker than that."

It was Toad.

"Sorry about that, Toad. Here have a beer on us," Jewel said.

"I never turn down a free one. Say, where in the hell was Slim? It's not like him to not be around when one of his dogs are fightin'," Toad said.

Before Toad completed the sentence, Max jumped off the picnic table and slammed Toad against our car.

"That wasn't Slim's dog; that was my dog, you drunken old bastard."

The impact of Toad hitting the car caused me to move, and when Jewel walked over to pull Max off of Toad he saw me lying in the back seat.

"Now shame on you boys, you woke up Mike's kid," Jewel said.

Jewel tried to open the car door, but it was locked.

"Sorry we woke you up, kid," Jewel said.

"That's okay," I said.

While Jewel remained standing on the driver's side of the car I slid over to the other side and opened the door. Just as I was stepping to the ground, my dad and Uncle Joe came out of the bar.

"Hey, what's all the excitement about?" Dad asked.

"Oh nothing, Mike, Max and Toad had a little misunderstanding is all and the noise woke up your kid," Jewel said.

"You okay, Shorty?" Uncle Joe asked.

"What about you, Toad? You look a little shook up."

"I'm fine," I said.

"Toad's okay. Kind of drunk is all. I'll get him home," Sam said.

Sam grabbed Toad by the arm and escorted him to the car. Without letting go of Toad's arm he opened the passenger side door and gave Toad a helpful shove to hurry his entrance. Toad had a bewildered expression on his face, but still managed to smile and wave as Sam drove off.

"Max, you got to learn to calm down. Toad couldn't hurt a fly," Uncle Joe said.

Max was in no mood to calm down. The small altercation with Toad had only gotten his blood to boil, and he was looking for a way to vent his anger.

Unfortunately he turned that anger toward Uncle Joe.

"That's right you should know all about that drunken stuff being one yourself. How did you get in Mirror Lake anyway? I thought they kicked your sorry ass out because of your war stories or should I say war lies," Max said as he faced Uncle Joe.

"Hey guys, that's enough, no one's been hurt here. Let's just call it a day and all go home," Dad said. "Come on, Joe, let's go."

"You're right, Mike. I'll see you tomorrow," Uncle Joe said.

He started to walk to his truck, but Max took a few quick steps and lunged into Uncle Joe from behind. Uncle Joe went sprawling onto the gravel and Max was on top of him. Dad started to run to Uncle Joe's aid, but Jewel grabbed my dad by the shoulder.

"Let 'em go," Jewel said.

"Go to hell, Jewel," Dad said.

Dad pushed Jewel's arm off his shoulder, but Jewel didn't like that and took a swing at my dad. To my amazement Dad was quick enough to duck under the blow. The force of Jewel's errant swing threw him off balance. As he was stumbling forward, Dad tackled him to the ground. When they landed, Jewel ended up on top of my dad with his back on Dad's chest. Dad wrapped his arms around Jewel and was holding on for dear life. There was no way my dad was going to let Jewel get up while his arms were still attached to his body.

Max was starting to throw punches at Uncle Joe and for whatever reason I tried to come to Uncle Joe's aide. I jumped on Max's back and locked my arms around his neck. My attack surprised Max, he quickly stood up, but I continued to hang on. He pulled my arms free from his neck and before I knew it I was flying through the air. I scrambled to my feet as soon as I hit the ground, not knowing what was going to happen next.

"You shouldn't be picking on kids, especially my partner."

It was Dale Wright.

Max turned to face the intruder and received a healthy fist against the side of his head. The force of the blow spun Max around and Dale hit him again. Max staggered backwards a few steps then lowered his head and attacked Dale. Max was seeing red and even though Dale landed another blow, it wasn't enough to stop the charging Max. Max slammed into Dale and the impact sent both men to the ground.

In the meantime Bruce Wright was pulling Jewel off my dad. Jewel started to brush himself off, but instead he pulled a switchblade from his pocket.

"I think this will even up the odds some," Jewel said.

Jewel assumed a threatening position and was slowly waving the knife back-and-forth in front of his body while he faced Bruce. Bruce stepped back, making sure he was out of reach from any attempted lunge by Jewel. Jewel's action immediately caught the attention of everyone.

Uncle Joe had wedged himself between Max and Dale trying to stop the fight, and now all three stopped to look at Jewel. Max was breathing like a raging bull preparing to attack. Blood was running down the side of his face, but when his eyes focused on Jewel's knife a small grin formed.

"You got the power now, Jewel. Look at 'em back away. Stick one of 'em and they'll all run," Max said.

Max was enjoying this and continued to egg Jewel on. He was caught up in this moment of violence, and liked his role of being considered tough and mean. Dad was still sitting on the ground and slowly stood up.

"Jewel, don't listen to Max. You've been around here long enough to know that if you try to cut anyone with that thing the rest of us are going to take you down. Whatever caused this here fight is not important enough to put someone in the hospital and someone else in jail."

"He's chicken, Jewel," Max said.

Jewel looked at Max and then back at Bruce.

"Shut up, Max. I know he's chicken. Hell they're all chicken, but I'm not going to jail for cutten some yokel. There's a better time and place for doing that," Jewel said.

Jewel flicked his wrist and the blade retracted into the knife housing. While he was putting the switchblade in his pocket, Sheriff Mead drove into the parking lot. He stopped the car so that the headlights were shinning on us. Everyone watched the sheriff get out of his car. He stood for a moment looking the situation over, then walked up and stood next to my dad.

"What seems to be the problem here, Mike? I didn't think you liked this rough and tumble stuff. I thought Maddie taught you better."

"You're right about that, Sheriff. We had a small disagreement, but it's over with now."

I don't know if everyone respected the sheriff's authority or not, but everyone stood quietly while the sheriff finished his visual examination.

"I don't know what happened here, but I can tell it was no church social. I suggest that unless someone wants to make a statement and file charges or something, you all go home and cool down."

"I think that's a very good suggestion, Sheriff. Come on, Shorty, let's go home. Joe, we'll see you tomorrow," Dad said.

I was in the car before dad opened his door. Uncle Joe looked at Max when he walked by him, but didn't say anything. The stare from Max showed nothing but hate. Before Uncle Joe reached his pick-up, he stopped to talk to the Wright brothers.

"Thanks boys. Be sure to let me know if you see that red dog of mine, and tell your mother I said hi."

While watching the game Uncle Joe made a point to ask all present to let him know if they saw his dog.

"Will do, Joe," Dale said.

As we drove out I looked though the back window and saw the Wright brothers walking back to the tavern and Jewel and Max were walking towards Jewel's car. The sheriff hadn't moved and was watching both pairs as they walked away in opposite directions. I turned around to face the front and Dad looked at me.

Shorty, you okay?"

"I think so, but my knees are still shaking."

"Mine are too. Toad really got Max riled up. Do you know what caused it?"

"I think they were arguing about something to do with dogs fighting. Max and Jewel are involved in fighting dogs. I didn't think the Strums had dogs," I said.

Dad thought for a moment, and when I saw him adjusting his cap I knew he was ready.

"I've been hearing some talk about that stuff starting up again around here. It don't surprise me none that Jewel could be involved in something like that, and the way Max acted today, well...I can see him buying into that back alley business too. Do you think they know you heard them?"

"I don't know...I don't think so."

I saw dogs fight before, and I knew they could get pretty serious. However, the fights I saw usually stopped as quickly as they started with one of the dogs running off or lying down in submission. It was like they were saying "okay, you're the king of the hill, if that's what makes you happy, it's fine with me." But that wasn't the type of dog fighting that Jewel and Max were talking about tonight.

"What kind of dog fighting do you think they were talking about?" I asked.

"The worse kind, Shorty, the worse kind there is. These dogs are trained to kill, and when they're put in a ring they'll do whatever it takes to kill the other dog. It gets vicious, and the people who are involved in it can be just as vicious. Hell...They can be meaner than the dogs."

Dad paused for a while then continued.

"I don't know what the law says about dogfighting. I thought it was gone from these parts, but looks like it's raised its ugly head again. I'm going to stop in and talk to Sheriff Mead about it one day next week before I go to work."

It was difficult to get out, but I had to ask.

"Did you ever go to, or I mean...see one of these dog fights?"

"No, Shorty, I've never went to one and never will, but when I was a kid I remember my dad, your grandpa talking to my mother about it one night."

The memory wasn't something that my dad wanted to talk about, so he quickly changed the subject.

"Shorty, you were a trooper back there. If the Braves can muster up that kind of courage they can put this lopsided loss behind them and still beat the Yankees, don't you think?"

"I sure hope so. I mean...I know they can," I said.

"You bet they can," Dad said.

We were just about home, and I knew if I didn't ask now I probably never would.

"What did Grandpa say?"

Dad grinned and shook his head slowly from side to side.

"You're picking up that Sherlock Holmes attitude from your mother more every day. I never talked about it with your grandpa or grandma, so you got to promise that you won't bring it up with them. Your grandpa wasn't very proud about it. As a matter of fact he was sick about it."

"I promise," I said.

"Some friends had apparently talked your grandpa into going to the fight. He must have looked bad when he came home, because as soon as he came through the front door Ma asked him what was wrong. I remember there was silence for a while and then your grandpa said. "*Rose, I seen the devil tonight. I went to a damn dogfight. It's the worse thing I ever seen. The fighting was bad enough, but the people were cheering and poking at the dogs with sticks to make them attack. And the blood, damn there was blood everywhere. I puked my guts out before I left and no one even noticed.*"

We pulled into our driveway. Dad stopped the car and turned off the ignition.

"Your grandma tried to calm Pa down. She put a kettle on to make some tea, and I'm sure she must have put a shot of whiskey in it. Your grandpa had to get it out and Ma was there for him. He always relied on her to help him through the bad times. I could hear Ma pouring the tea and then she pulled out a chair to sit down. I can't remember her saying anything, but I'll never forget what your grandpa said. 'Rose,' he said, '*Rose, I saw the devil or I saw the devil in a man. He was the owner of one of the dogs, and the look he had on his face was meaner than the dog he was commanding to attack. But the worst part was that he had his kid standing beside him, and tears were running down her face, but he wouldn't let her leave.*'"

"Did Grandpa know the person?

"He didn't know him personally, but he knew of him. It was Jason Abner."

Chapter Twenty-Five
World Series Ends and Corn Picking Begins

The Sunday World Series game provided enough excitement to last me for the entire year. Our house was packed, and there was as much to eat as on Thanksgiving Day. The previous night's activity was not brought up. Dad felt that my mother had enough on her plate, and there was no reason to get her all worked up. Besides, he didn't want to put an addition on Mom's list of reasons why he shouldn't go to Mirror Lake Tavern.

When the game went into extra innings you could feel the tension in the house, even Grandma was listening intently. When the Yankees went ahead, Grandma yelled "Damn."

That one word outburst brought a chorus of knee slapping laughter from her sons, which I'm sure she knew she would have to pay for later.

In the bottom of the tenth when Nippy Jones proved to the umpire that he had been hit on the foot by a pitch, by showing the umpire the shoe polish on the ball, Ronnie was quick to add his own commentary.

"Well I'll be damned, right, Ma."

Grandma remained calm and simply said.

"Be quiet now, so we can hear."

The Braves tied the game and when Eddie Matthew's homered for the win; our house erupted as if we were sitting in the right field seats. I thought nothing would be able to top the feelings of joy that ran through my body when the Braves won the World Series in game seven at New York, but I was wrong.

The Saturday following the World Series, I was helping Dad patch the roof on the hog shed, when over the noise of the pounding we heard my mother whoop at the top of her lungs.

"Yes! Yes!"...she was screaming in delight.

We sat on the roof and watched Mom run toward us from the end of the driveway, waving a piece of paper over her head. The only thing that topped the passion behind her cheers was the smile that crossed her face. We jumped off the roof and watched her run up the driveway.

"Maddie must have got some good news," Dad said.

By the look on my mother's face and the enthusiasm she was showing, I would say that was a major understatement. There was no need for us to go and meet her, Mom had it in high gear, and she was standing next to us before we knew it.

"What is it, Maddie? Did you finally win one of those crossword puzzle contests?"

"No...No...It's much bigger, much, much bigger. It's an answer to my prayers. We gotta go tell Hank. We got to go now."

Her excitement was unrestrained; to this day I've never seen her more openly excited.

"Slow down, Maddie, and let me and Shorty in on this big event," Dad said.

Mom took a deep breath.

"You know I've been corresponding with that psychiatrist in Minneapolis about Hank's idea. Well...Well here it is. Doctor Jonathan S. Frederick is going to come out and visit, if Hank agrees. He says that he has scheduled a meeting with Doctor Thompson in the last week of October and following that meeting he'd like to visit with Hank and Joan. He wants me to check with Hank to be sure that Hank is still agreeable to such a meeting. So let's go talk to Hank."

"Okay let's go, but how are you going to tell Hank? You've never met this doctor; you don't know what he's like. Doc Thompson isn't going to be too happy that you went over his head and he may still try to block it or something," Dad said.

"I don't think so; listen to what Doctor Frederick has written to Hank."

Mom then read to us what was on a separate sheet of paper.

"Dear Mr. Raycart. My name is Doctor Jonathan S. Frederick. I am a doctor of psychiatry and have been so for thirty years. I can identify with you and your wife's love for farming and the land. I also have a deep devotion to my profession, the field

of Psychiatry, and truly believe that it can be used to help people such as your wife to recover from what life has unjustly placed upon her. I do not want to give you any false sense that all will be well, but I would like very much for you to allow me the opportunity to at least visit. Normally I like my patients to visit me, but your good friend Maddie, has convinced me that your situation warrants a different approach. I look forward to meeting both you and your wife Joan. Respectfully Yours, Dr. Jonathan S Frederick."

Mom then neatly folded the paper and returned it to the envelope.

"What do you think?" Mom asked.

"I think we should go and talk to Hank. I don't know why we're standing around here waiting. Do you, Shorty?" Dad said.

"No I don't."

Mom was heading for the car and was calling for my brother and sister as she hurried along. My brother and sister knew by the tone of her voice that they better get moving, and they were in the back seat before we reached the car. In no time we were on our way and Mom's excitement had become contagious. I didn't think we could get there fast enough. This October was turning out to be a very good month.

When we arrived at the Raycarts, Joan was on the porch swing and Hank was sitting on the porch steps sharpening a scythe. He immediately stood and walked to greet us when Dad stopped the car. Mom had opened the car door and was getting out before my dad came to a complete stop. She walked around the car with a movement as brisk as the fall air. She couldn't wait to deliver a message that she was extremely happy about. Hank detected my mother's mood and smiled in anticipation.

"Maddie, you're grinning like that fox that got one of my chickens last night. What's making you so happy?" Hank asked.

Mom slowed her pace and tried her best to temper the joy she felt inside, but it was beyond control. She stopped in front of Hank and took the envelope from her front pocket.

"Hank, remember that idea you had about having a doctor come out here to visit with Joan?"

"Yes I do, but I thought Doctor Thompson said that wasn't the right thing to do."

"I know, but I've been in contact with a doctor in Minneapolis and...and...listen to this."

She calmly read the letter and when she finished, she handed it to Hank. Hank took the letter from my mother's hand and sat on the porch steps. He read the letter again to himself, while we all quietly stood by. When he finished he turned to look at Joan sitting on the porch swing and then at the shotgun leaning against the house next to the steps. He looked at the letter again and then turned to face my mother.

"We were going to name John, Jonathan, but decided against it because we thought we'd be calling him John all the time anyways."

He smiled at his recollection and turned to look at his wife. While he watched his wife swinging slowly back and forth he spoke to my mother, but continued to watch his wife.

"I think I'd very much like to have this doctor come for a visit. I feel I can trust him. Do you feel that way, Maddie?"

"Yes I do, Hank. This is the forth letter that I've received from him and he's always given me the impression that the patient and the patient's family are his first concern."

"If you don't mind waiting a few minutes, I'd like to write a short note to the doctor."

Hank didn't wait for an answer, but instead walked into the house. Mom followed and as she passed the dogs she reached down and patted Three Eye on the head.

"Good old Three Eye. We're going to bring someone else to help Joan. Is that okay with you?"

Mom then went into the porch and sat in a chair next to Joan. She placed her hand on Joan's arm, gave a light squeeze and smiled. Hank returned after a short time and handed my mother a piece of paper. Mom read what Hank had written while Hank sat beside his wife on the porch swing.

"I think this is very nice, Hank. I'll put it in the mail on Monday. No better yet...I'll have Mike drop it off at the Post Office in Sunset on Monday morning."

Before we left, Hank told us that he and Uncle Joe were going to start picking corn next week. They were going to start with the field next to the river, so I could start hand picking the corn they wouldn't be able to get with the corn picker by the end of next week. The corn picking was very important to Hank, but Mom's message was more important and Hank wanted to share his feelings with my mother.

"Thanks again for all the help, Maddie. I'll never be able to repay you for what you've done."

He glanced at the letter from the psychiatrist which he was still holding.

"I got a good feeling about this."

"It was nothing, Hank. I agree, I have a good feeling about it too," Mom said.

"Shorty, let me know when you get the corn picked. I'll bring a wagon down and we'll load it up and haul it to your place before the coon walk away with it," Hank said.

"I plan on starting next Saturday and should get most of it done," I said.

"Unless the fish are biting," Dad was quick to add.

Hank laughed and nodded in agreement to my dad's statement.

While we were driving home Mom began to tap her finger on the dashboard to the beat of a Tennessee Ernie Ford song that was playing on the radio. She was still enjoying what the day had brought, and I don't think anyone or anything could dampen her spirits.

"Maddie, you did a damn good thing here, and no matter how it turns out we're very proud of you. Isn't that right kids?"

"You bet we are," I said.

"Well I thank you all very much. It does make me feel good, but we have to remember it wasn't my idea. It was Hanks. I just kind of...well you know, pinch hit for him."

"That you did. What did Hank's letter to the doctor say?" Dad asked.

Mom took the letter out of her pocket and read it to us

"Dear Dr. Frederick: Thank you very much for taking the time to come and visit. I know we need help. I don't want to be a burden to my neighbors and I look forward to meeting you. Sincerely; Hank and Joan Raycart. p.s. I might not be able to settle up on the day you come, but we'll be able to pay for your time."

When Mom finished I leaned my head back and thought how wonderful it would be if the doctor could help Joan. If she did recover, I wondered if she would know me. Was I being selfish? I know this wasn't the time to be thinking about myself, but I still thought it would be nice if she remembered me a little.

The next week went by quickly. I saw Jewel and Max twice during the week. On both occasions I was able to hide in the ditch when they drove by. Dad thought it best that I avoid them as much as possible, and believe me he didn't have to worry about that. It bothered my dad that after the fight at Mirror Lake there was no shaking of hands or agreement between combatants to at least attempt to put the altercation behind as just a misfortunate turn of events. Dad was sure that both Max and Jewel left that evening with a bitter taste in their mouth, and thought time would be the best healer.

On Friday night Mom received a long distance phone call from Doctor Frederick. He had received Hank's letter and had scheduled a meeting with

Doctor Thompson on the following Wednesday. He would like to meet with Hank and Joan on Thursday and asked Mom if she could schedule the meeting with the Raycarts for sometime in the early afternoon, so he could have some time to visit with me and Mom in the morning. Mom told the doctor that wouldn't be a problem and was looking forward to meeting him.

I was in my bedroom reading a chapter from my history book when Mom came in to tell me about the phone conversation with Doctor Frederick. What she worked so hard to accomplish was actually going to happen, and it made her very nervous. She paced back and forth across the floor while relaying the conversation. When she finished she stopped and looked out the window at the river.

"That river keeps on running, seasons come and go, people come and go, but it keeps on running. Life is kind of like that. It changes some when good thing happens and it changes some when bad things happen, but it keeps on going. There's no guarantee that life will always be good, but it sure as heck doesn't have to always be bad," she said.

She seemed to be talking to herself in the window, and I got the impression that she was thinking out loud. She stood silently for a moment looking into the darkness of the swamp and then let go of the curtains and turned to look at me.

"Have you seen or heard anything strange along the river lately?"

"No I haven't. Whatever it was, must be gone," I said.

I was about to ask her why she asked, but she answered before I got the words out.

"Just the other day I was thinking about how your fishing rod appeared. No animal could have placed that on the bank, do you think?"

"Kind of shoots Dad's cougar theory in the foot doesn't it?"

"Yes, it does. Maybe it'll be one of those things that we never find a reason for."

"I guess," I said.

I hadn't given much thought to the river incidents lately, but Moms query brought them to the surface. Mom realized what she had done, and I think she wanted me to remember.

"Sorry about that. Maybe I shouldn't have brought it up, but it never hurts to remind a person to be cautious. You're getting to know that river like the back of your hand, but don't ever take it for granted. It's earned our respect. Don't you agree?"

"Yes it has."

She bent over and kissed me on the forehead and walked to the door.

"You better get some sleep. Sounds like you got a big day planned tomorrow with the corn picking and all."

I read a couple of more paragraphs then got up to turn off the light. I walked to the window and looked out at the river. Mom was right; I was getting to know that river like the back of my hand. Then I remembered the first words Joan had spoke to me: "*Watch that river.*" Joan definitely knew the river. I think she was telling me to be careful of not only the river, but also of what walked along its banks. There was definitely something watching what went on along the river. The more I thought about what I had seen or not seen, the more I began to believe that whatever it was meant me no harm. I think Joan knows who it is, but for some reason both her and her dogs want to keep it away.

Chapter Twenty-Six
Following the Geese

The next morning I woke fresh and was raring to go. While I was getting dressed I remembered parts of a dream that I had during the night. In the dream I was fishing and Joan and Hank were sitting on the bank beside me. Joan was talking and laughing. Both she and Hank were enjoying the day. At one point in the dream Joan stood, and for some reason dove into the river. The water was clear and I watched her swim below the surface with all the grace of a river otter. That was all I could remember, but it caused me to smile. I knew it was just a dream, but never-the-less thinking about it brightened my morning.

As usual Mom was already up and working in the kitchen. She was humming a song and greeted me with a big smile when I walked in.

"You look bright and chipper this morning. You must have slept well," she said.

"Yes I did, as a matter of fact I had a great dream."

"Isn't that a coincidence, so did I. Maybe it was the same dream," she said.

"I don't think it's possible to have the same dream," I said.

"Maybe not, but they had to be similar because they apparently made us both happy. From what I can remember the river was good in my dream. What was yours about?"

She was adding more wood to the stove. She poked at the red embers and when she was satisfied that the new pieces of wood were catching on fire she placed the lid back on the stove.

"It's definitely getting cooler. I'll make some bacon and eggs, so you can at least start the day with a warm belly."

Mom was going in ten different directions at the same time, but it was easy to see that she was having pleasant thoughts. I was going to tell her about my dream in more detail, but decided just to touch on it.

"My dream had the river in it too, but it wasn't the same dream."

"You're probably right. I'll have breakfast ready when you get back in."

The weather was definitely turning cooler. Frost covered the grass and sparkled as the morning sun reflected off it. It was the end of October and a lot of leaves had already fallen from the trees. It was fun to kick through the leaves as I walked along. Each fall breeze caused more to come loose and slowly drift to the ground. When I returned to the house after finishing chores, Dad was sitting in the kitchen having coffee with Mom. He was going to work the Saturday afternoon shift, and greeted me as I came in the door.

"Morning, Shorty."

"Morning, Dad."

"Don't work yourself to hard today. I'll be able to help you finish up tomorrow afternoon when you get back from church. Joe and Hank plan on finishing picking corn at Hanks sometime this morning and then start at Joes after dinner. If the weather holds I think they got a good shot at being completely done by the second week of November."

"I won't, when it starts getting dark I'll quit. I plan on stopping to see if Hank needs any help with chores. If I start again early Sunday morning I think I'll have all the corn picked by noon and then all we'll have to do is haul it back home," I said.

"Nice try, buddy, but like your dad said, you and he can finish picking the corn Sunday when we get back from church," Mom said, placing the emphasis on we and church.

Dad laughed and gave me a wink.

"Your mother's right, the corn will stand a few more days with no problem, but it would be nice of you to see if Hank needs any help tonight unloading wagons or getting ready for tomorrow. That'll be okay won't it, Maddie?"

"I think that would be just fine. I'll keep some soup on the stove to warm you up when you get home," Mom said.

After breakfast Mom fixed me a lunch and I started to get ready to leave.

"You're getting a pretty early start. Think you'll be able to get some fishing in?" Dad asked.

"Thought I might give it a try around noon," I said.

"That sounds like a good way to spend your lunch break," Mom said.

"Sometimes it's hard to come back from a good lunch break, especially if the fish are biting. So if the fish are biting, well like I said, the corn will still be standing tomorrow," Dad said.

"See you tonight, Mom," I said as I walked out the door.

I put my fishing equipment in a pail along with my lunch, and hung it from my handle bars and started out. Blackie was lying on the ground watching me leave, but sprang to her feet when I called her name. This was a treat for her, because usually when I left early in the morning it was to go to school and she wasn't allowed to come. It didn't take her long to catch up and her facial expression resembled a smile of satisfaction as she ran past me. The cool weather seemed to give her energy, and her short stubby tail wagged in delight as she ran ahead of me. She was having a good time running through the grass, but always made sure to stop every so often, and look back to make sure I was still following.

The field was about two miles up river from the Raycarts. All the corn had been picked except for the rows they couldn't get to because of the ruts caused from the rain water running down the side of the hill. I was able to bike quite a way into the field before having to get off and walk. I put my bike by the fence when I reached the middle of the field and hung my pail from a fence post. I was able to see the river through the trees that stood between the field and the river. It looked tempting, but I knew that if I started to fish now, there was a good chance that the corn picking would become secondary.

The field was made up of rolling hills and I couldn't see either end from where I was standing. Most of the corn stalks had fallen over and some of the ears were lying on the ground. I decided that the most efficient method would be to follow a row to the end and then come back on the next row. That way I wouldn't miss any stalks and could strategically place a corn pile about every twenty feet.

The leaves of the dry corn made a rustling sound as the cool fall breeze made its way through the field. It was a clear day and the sun felt warm on my face as I worked. By the time I made it to the south end of the first row I was getting pretty good at peeling back the husk and breaking the corn cob free. The yellow of the corn lying on the ground was easy to spot against the autumn brown of the corn stalks. Picking the corn and tossing the cobs so that they rested in the same piles became a game.

Except for the sound of the wind rustling the corn stalks, it was a quiet pleasant fall day. When I finished my first round I walked to where I had hung the pail to get a drink of water, and decided to snack on an apple before continuing. I leaned against the fence and looked in the direction of the river. Fishing this part of the river was going to be exciting, because I had never been this far up stream before.

As I looked at the river through the trees my thoughts turned to Joan Raycart. Mom gave every indication that she had confidence in this Doctor Frederick. I pictured him as a short thin man, with graying hair and a small thin mustache with a short goatee. He would be dressed in an expensive black suit with a bow tie. He would probably have a German accent, and be able to probe into Joan's mind by the use of hypnosis. I wondered what kind of questions he would ask me when he came to our house. What if he found out that when Joan spoke to me it actually did more harm than good? Or worse yet, what if he found that there was no cure possible for Joan, and she would have to be placed in a special hospital for the rest of her life? I began to recall the times Joan had spoke to me, so I could properly relay what was said to the doctor. I needed to be accurate, especially if it would help the doctor find a cure for Joan. I was making a list in my mind based on the times they occurred when a woodchuck came out from behind a fallen tree and brought me out of my daydream. I whistled at the woodchuck and he stood on his hind legs to try and figure out where the sound was coming from. However, he was more interested in getting into his den for the winter and quickly disappeared under the tree.

The sun was now midway in the morning sky, so I figured it was about ten in the morning. I decided to make one more round to the north end of the field and when I got back to the center location I'd have a sandwich and try fishing this new part of the river.

I finished my apple and tossed the core toward the river as far as my strength would allow. It landed in the trees and I thought to myself that it was a pretty good throw. I walked back into the field and continued to pick the corn. I was in the lowest point between two hills when a sound from overhead startled me.

H-ronk...H-ronk...The sound was coming from behind me. I knelt on my knees between the rows of corn and looked up. A flock of Canadian Geese was passing over my head. They flapped their long wings and musically chanted their calls as they flew over. I stood up and watched as they disappeared over the hill. I had seen geese before, but they were usually so high in the sky that they were hard to make out. They must have landed in the corn field to take a lunch break or had spent the night feeding on the corn to build up energy for their flight south.

"Let's go see if they landed on the other side of the hill, Blackie."

I took off on a run with Blackie at my heels. When we neared the top of the hill we slowed down and I got on my hands and knees and crawled to the peak. There must have been thirty geese walking around at the end of the corn field. They sensed that Blackie and I were present and started to run along the ground, flapping their wings and became airborne.

I watched as they flew toward the river. They delicately maneuvered between the trees and then started to land again, but this time they were landing on the ponds that were situated along the river. The ponds were a good distance away, but I could still see they were covered with the Canadian Geese. Wait until I tell my parents about this I thought as I started to run toward the ponds. I never made it to the ponds for fishing as I had planned, but I thought this would be just as good.

I was caught up in the excitement of seeing something new and made my way down the slopes toward the ponds. I ran between the trees and slowed my pace as I got closer to where they landed. I couldn't believe the numbers. There had to be over a hundred.

We snuck up on the geese by using the tall marsh grass for cover and watched as some more came in for a landing. Just before they touched the water they would extend their legs forward and lean back. When they came in touch with the water they made less of a splash than a mallard duck. We watched and enjoyed the moment; even Blackie seemed content with the view as she sat beside me. Then as quick as they had landed, they must have decided it was time to leave. When they started to rise from the ponds you could see the wing tips of some of the geese lightly touch the surface of the water as they became airborne. It wasn't long before they were high in the sky forming their familiar V-shaped flying formations.

As I watched them fly toward the horizon I felt drops of water landing on my head. At first I thought it was water dripping from the geese as they took off, but that wasn't the case. A late autumn storm had moved in. As the rain fell it was taking the form of sleet. I ran back into the trees to try and find some shelter from the oncoming storm.

The wind began to pick up and the sleet became heavier. Most of the leaves were gone from the trees and I wasn't able to find enough cover to stay dry. When I was running from the field to the ponds I had passed some pine trees and thought they were my best bet for shelter. At least they would provide a place to keep somewhat dry until the sleet stopped.

When we got to the pine trees we made our way to the center of the stand. On the other side of the pine grove I saw a building. I walked to the edge of the grove in order to get a better look. The building looked in pretty good shape. It was located in the middle of a field that was overgrown with brush. At one end of the field was a hill covered with trees and it bordered the river. At the other end of the building was a dirt road, so I figured the building must be used for some type of storage.

The sleet storm was getting worse and the temperature was continuing to drop. No one seemed to be around and I doubted that whoever owned it would mind if we took shelter in their storage building to wait out the storm.

The shutters over the windows were all closed, but a sliding door at one end of the building was open. It apparently had come unlatched and the wind was causing it to blow back and forth against the building. As the door bounced off the building it looked like there was enough room for me and Blackie to squeeze through and get inside. I started to run from the pine trees to the building and called for Blackie. When I reached the edge of the building I looked at the pine grove and saw that Blackie had decided not to follow. Apparently the pines provided enough shelter for her, but I was getting wet, so I squeezed through the opening. Once inside I felt relieved to be out of the storm.

I stood up, brushed myself off and looked around. There was no machinery, but there were pens along one side, so I figured it was a building used to house cattle or hogs. However, as I looked around I realized this was no ordinary storage building. In the center of the building there was a pole with two wire cables hanging from the top. On the floor, fifteen feet in front of the pole was a tire filled with concrete. In the center of the concrete was a steel rod with a log chain attached to it. All through the interior of the building similar chains were attached to most of the poles.

I walked to the pole that was in the center of the building and took hold of one of the cables. The cable was attached to a swivel at the top of the pole that allowed it to move freely around the pole. At the other end of the cable a loop was formed.

I started to feel uncomfortable and let the cable loose from my hand. I didn't know what this building had been used for, but I didn't like it. I decided I'd be better off to wait the storm out under the pine trees with Blackie. I walked to the sliding door and started to crawl out when a truck pulled into the driveway.

I quickly returned to the inside and found a crack in the sliding door to look through. The pick-up truck drove into the dirt area in front of the building and turned so that the rear end was facing the sliding door. A few seconds later I heard another vehicle driving in. It was Jewel driving his Thunderbird. He pulled up and stopped next to the truck. The sleet was falling at a heavier rate and white patches had started to form on the ground. Jewel rolled down his window to talk to the driver of the truck.

"I'll open the doors so you can back in, and then we'll unload," Jewel said.

He then parked his car off to the side and opened his car door. When I saw him getting out of the car I turned and ran for the door at the other end of the building. I pushed on the door, but it was braced shut from the outside. I couldn't get it to budge. I looked around the building to see if there was another way out. The windows were all closed and had shutters on the outside, but I thought if I could get a window open I'd be able to unhook the shutter. I ran to a window that was in the corner of the building on the opposite end from the sliding door. The bottom ledge of the window was about five feet off the floor. I unlatched the window and began to push it up. When the window was open about two inches, I placed my thumbs under the window and pushed up. However, as the window started to move up I heard the sliding door start to open.

"Okay, back it in," Jewel said.

While the truck was backing in I managed to open the window about twelve inches, which was more than enough room for me to squeeze through. I pulled myself up and was able to slide one hand down between the outside of the building and the window shutter. I could feel the hook, but couldn't get it to unlatch. Then a burst of wind blew the shutter tight against my hand, and in so doing put some slack in the hook that allowed me to unhook the shutter. Just as I unhooked the shutter I heard the truck stop in the center of the building and the door open.

"You want to get your T-Bird in out of this damn ice storm?"

It was Max Strum.

"Good idea, Max," Jewel said.

I looked over my shoulder and saw Max walking toward the sliding door. I pulled myself up and put my head against the shutter and started to push it open. However, the strong winds blew the shutter against me. I didn't have the strength in my neck to force the shudder open against the wind, so I started to lower myself to the shed floor. When I reached the floor, the wind caused the shudder to slam against the wall. At first I thought Max heard the shudder slam shut, but the noise from Jewel pulling his car in was enough to drown out the sound.

I thought I still had one last chance to get out before being noticed. I pulled myself up and swung my right leg through the window opening, so that my foot was pushing against the shudder. I pushed as hard as I could and began to force the shudder open, but when the shudder moved I lost my grip and fell to the floor. This time Max heard the shudder slam shut.

"Damn wind is starting to cause problems with this old barn. I'll go check it out."

"Help me shut this damn door first," Jewel said.

While Max was helping Jewel shut the sliding door I looked for a place to hide. There were some wood planks leaning against the wall at the end of the building. It looked like there was room for me to get between the planks and the wall. I got on my hands and knees and started to crawl toward the wall when I remembered that the window was still open. If they found the window open they would know someone was in the barn, because the window latched from the inside. I crawled back to the window and stood up and pulled the window down. As I was latching the window closed I heard Jewel and Max walking toward the center of the building. I immediately dropped to the floor and started to crawl toward the wooden planks, but before I got there the wind caused the unhooked shudder to bang against the side of the building.

"That's going to drive me nuts," Max said.

I heard the gate to the pen open just as I reached my hiding spot. When I crawled behind the wooden planks I heard Max open the window, I tried to lie as still as possible.

"Shudder came loose in the wind," Max said.

Max opened the window and hooked the shudder shut and returned to the center of the building.

"There, now let's get the beast out," Max said.

Jewel opened the truck tail gate then unlocked the door of a large crate that they were hauling.

"Come on, you killing machine," Jewel said.

"We better put a chain on him or he might decide to run right through these wood walls," Max said.

With all the commotion being caused by Jewel and Max at the back of the truck, I was able to crawl on my belly to the center of my hiding spot. There was a gap between the planks, and I could see the truck and the area from the truck to my hiding spot. I watched as Jewel took the chain off the concrete tire and dragged it back toward the truck. I heard the tail gate of the truck bounce when something jumped from it and then I saw Jewel pulling a dog from the truck to the center of the building. The dog was all black and was larger than any dog I had ever seen. Its head looked larger than Blackie's entire body, and Jewel used all his strength to pull the dog forward. The dog pulled against the chain and then suddenly lunged forward and grabbed onto the chain with his teeth. With the chain clenched tightly in its jaws the dog began to shake his head back-and-forth with so much strength that it was causing Jewels arms to swing uncontrollably from side to side.

"Give me a hand with this beast will ya, Max," Jewel said.

Max was carrying a long stick. Before he took hold of the chain to help Jewel, he swung the stick so that it hit the side of the dogs head.

"Calm down, Killer, or I'll give you something to be pissed about," Max said.

The dog seemed to succumb to the command along with being hit by the stick and let loose of the chain. Max and Jewel pulled the dog to the center of the floor then hooked the chain back onto the concrete tire. The dog was in no mood to be tied up and it immediately started to pull the weighted tire toward the truck. Its lips were folded back and the growl's that came through the exposed teeth were terrifying.

"I think Killer wants to play," Max said.

"I think you're right. We got a few minutes before the boss gets here. I'll get us a couple of beers and we'll let him have a good workout with the pole," Jewel said.

Jewel walked to the truck and opened the passenger side door. When he returned to the back of the truck he was carrying a cage in one hand and a bag in the other. He set both on the tail gate of the truck. He took a couple of beers out of the bag and handed one to Max. I could see something moving in the cage, but couldn't make out what it was because Max was blocking my view. Max then put on a pair of gloves.

"Before I hook 'em up, you want a make a small bet? I got five bucks that says Killer catches this mangy cat in less than three minutes," Max said.

"Make it two minutes and you got a bet," Jewel said.

The dog was going crazy. The muscles in his front shoulders were bulging out so tightly that they looked like they were going to break through his skin. His growls turned into snarls of anger as he continued to pull the concrete weight closer to the truck.

"You're on," Max said.

He then pulled a cat from the cage and held it up in the air to taunt the dog. The dog started to leap into the air, trying with all it's might to get at the cat. The weight of the chain around his neck and it being attached to the concrete filled tire was the only thing that prevented this from happening. Each time the dog left his feet the concrete anchor caused him to fall back to the ground, but the dog kept on trying. The cat that Max was holding was a large gray cat and it was clawing at the air trying to get free.

Max carried the cat to the pole that I had seen when I first came into the barn. The truck bed blocked my view and all I could see was the upper half of the pole. Max bent over and when he stood up he no longer had the cat. One of the cables hanging from the top of the pole started to move around the pole. Max had attached the cat to one of the cables.

"Got her hooked up, now let's hook up Killer," Max said.

"You hold onto Killer while I hook him up. You know he's rarin' to go," Jewel replied.

Max hit the dog with the stick again and then grabbed the dog by the collar. Jewel attached a short chain to the big dog's collar then unhooked the chain that was attached to the concrete weight. Max grabbed onto the chain with Jewel and they both held the dog back as it savagely clawed at the ground trying to get to the cat. They allowed the dog to move to the far side of the truck and then Jewel reached out for the other cable hanging from the pole. Jewel brought the end of the cable to where the dog was being held and bent down to attach the cable to the short chain that was attached to the dog's collar. The truck bed blocked my view, but I knew what was going on, and it made me want to scream out.

I could hear the cat scream and the snarls from the dog became intense and sent a chill deep into my bones. The cables hooked to the top of the pole began to spin around with the speed of a tornado. The cat stopped screaming. It was running for its life. The dog's snarls and growls echoed off the building walls as it chased the cat around the pole. Both men were now leaning against the side of the truck and laughing as they watched. They had their backs to me and I thought about trying to run past them to the sliding doors, but the distance was to great and I knew I would probably get caught.

It seemed like it would never stop and I began to feel sick to my stomach. I thought they might stop it when the time went over two minutes, but I knew that was an unrealistic wish. I put my hands over my ears to try and shut out the noise, but the growling from the dog mixed in with the whirling sound of the cables couldn't be blocked out. Suddenly the cables stopped revolving around the pole, and the dogs growls turned into a deep muffled guttural sound. The cables were now twisted together and vibrating back and forth in a whip like motion.

I shook my head in disbelief and felt guilty because I didn't try to stop them. It was a terrible feeling. I couldn't even begin to imagine the fear that must have been in the cat when it found out it was able to run, but couldn't run to escape.

"Damn, just a little over two minutes," Max said.

He reached into his back pocket to take out his billfold and handed a five dollar bill to Jewel. Jewel laughed and put the bill in his jacket pocket.

"Let's chain Killer back up before he gets bored and pulls that damn pole out of the ground," Jewel said.

Then both Max and Jewel went to the pole and when they came back into sight they were pulling the dog behind them. They reattached the dog to the heavy chain that was connected to the concreted tire then walked to the truck and opened another beer. The dog was still growling, but instead of pulling on the chain he began to pace in circles around the tire.

"Wish we had another dog for Killer to practice on before we leave," Max said.

"No, the hell with that...we leave for Chicago tomorrow, so we can get ready for the big fight next Friday. We got the rest of the dogs already down there, but Killer here is the one we have to take care of. He's going to make us some big bucks," Jewel said.

Then I heard the sound of another car approaching.

"Let's open up the doors so the boss can park out of the weather," Jewel said.

When they walked to the other end of the building I glanced at the dog. It had stopped making circles and was now looking in my direction. I stared at the dog and the dog stared directly back at me. It knew I was there and I knew I had to find a way out before I was discovered.

The sound of another car driving in distracted the dog and he looked toward the sliding barn doors. I started to back out of my hiding place when I heard the third man speak.

"Well boys, you ready for the big show?"

It was Sheriff Mead.

The three men walked to the back of the truck.

"Hell yes we're ready and what's more important Killer is more than ready," Jewel said.

"Are you going to come with Frank?" Max said.

"I sure plan on it. Don't want you boys to think you can make this a two-person operation," the sheriff said.

"We wouldn't do that, would we, Max? But me and Max figure it would be best not to come back to this part of the country. There's going to be a lot more money to make fightin' in the city and the travel back and forth takes too much time. I already got a training site set up and the other dogs are already there. All we have left is to transport Killer," Jewel said.

"I get your drift, boys, but remember I'm the one that started this little operation and I'm the one that can end it," the sheriff said.

"If we vote on that, Frank, I think it'll be two to one. And in my book that means the one with two votes can end it whenever they want," Jewel said.

The tension between the three was starting to mount. It was turning out to be more of a confrontation than a discussion, and the sheriff realized that he was holding the short straw.

"How much is in it for me if I decide to let you guys go off on your own?"

"Me and Max figure five hundred dollars is fair," Jewel said.

The sheriff looked at Max and then back to Jewel and laughed.

"Hell you'll make twenty times that on Killer alone next week in Chicago," he said while pointing at the big black dog.

The dog had started to growl again and was pulling the concrete tire across the floor. There was no doubt that he knew I was behind the boards and was coming directly toward me.

"Looks like Killer must have got the scent of another challenge. I'll let him loose from the tire, but we better keep the chain on him or he might chase whatever it is right through the wall," Max said.

"Hey, Frank, we'll let you watch Killer in action one more time and when he's caught whatever it is you can give us your decision," Jewel said.

Max then unhooked the chain from the tire and the dog sprang forward. Free from the weight of the tire the dog charged across the floor, dragging the chain behind him and pounced onto the planks. The boards began to fall to the floor from the impact and I started to crawl to the opposite end.

As the planks fell to the floor the dog backed away for a moment and then ran to the end I was crawling out of. I knew I didn't stand a chance if that dog got hold of me, so I tried to get into a position where some of the planks were between me and the charging dog. I grabbed a plank and was holding it like a shield in front of me when I heard the sound of another dog barking. It was Blackie. She had crawled through the opening in the sliding door and was running as fast as she could toward the big black dog. The big black beast took after Blackie, but Blackie was too quick and ran under the railings of the pen.

As Killer ran after Blackie, Max grabbed onto the chain and quickly wrapped it around one of the building poles. The dog came off its feet when it came to the end of the chain, but continued to pull with all its might trying to get to Blackie. Blackie must have determined his pursuer was restrained, because she stopped at the far end of the building and was watching the big black dog.

"Make sure that sliding door is shut tight and then I'll let Killer finish his business," Max said.

While Max was speaking I pushed the boards away and started to run along the wall in the direction of the sliding door. Jewel had an angle on me and grabbed me before I reached the middle of the building.

"Look, I caught me a rodent. Should we let Killer see if he can catch him playing on the maypole?" Jewel said.

Jewel spun me around and slammed me against the side wall.

"This is the third time I caught you spying on me, kid, and this is going to be the last time," he said.

"Hold on there, Jewel, we haven't done anything illegal yet, so don't do something stupid now," Sheriff Mead said.

"You know if we let him loose he's going to let everyone know," Jewel said.

Jewel was holding me against the wall and a weird grin came over his face as he pulled me towards him. He backed up a few steps and then violently pushed so hard that I slammed against the wall and fell to the ground.

"Damn kid," Jewel said.

Killer was still trying to break free to get Blackie, but Blackie ran to my side and started to growl at Jewel. Jewel picked up the stick they had used against Killer and swung it at Blackie. Blackie let out a sharp cry of pain when the stick hit her on the side of the head and she collapsed to the ground.

I jumped to my feet and grabbed for the stick. Jewel held onto the stick with one hand and back handed me across the face with the other. The force of the blow knocked me to the ground, but Jewel wasn't done. He was in an uncontrollable rage. He hit Blackie again with the stick and then turned toward me. As Jewel approached I could see the hate in his eyes and it was now directed at me. I knew I had to escape, but I was still stunned from the blow and wasn't able to run.

I managed to get on my hands and knees as Jewel walked closer. Suddenly a loud crash came from the end of the building. The door that was braced shut from the outside had the brace kicked away and door flew open. The door slammed against the inside wall, but no one entered. It was getting dark outside and all you could see through the door opening was a curtain of falling ice and snow. The sleet was coming down in torrents and the swirling wind was causing it to blow in every direction. Then the view of the outside was shut off as a figure emerged from the sleet and stepped into the building.

Chapter Twenty-Seven
Violence in the Night

Everyone watched and waited to see who was coming through the door. Whoever it was had a parka on with the hood covering the person's head to provide shelter from the storm. The parka was unbuttoned and the person had on pair of bib overalls, but wasn't wearing a shirt.

It was Jason Abner.

He stepped into the room and was soaking wet from the sleet storm. He was carrying a pail in one hand and a shotgun in the other. As he took a few steps inside the parka fell back from covering his head. He stood motionless for a few seconds and then he set the pail on the floor. I watched as he placed the pail on the floor, and recognized it as the ice fishing pail he had setting on his lean-to work bench. His piercing green eyes were focused on the sheriff.

"What's up, Frank, I didn't know you allowed your help to beat up on kids," Jason said.

"I don't, Jason. The boys here got a little carried away when they found Shorty spying on them. But it'll be okay now and I'll give Shorty a ride home," Sheriff Mead said.

"Is that true, Jewel, were you getting carried away?"

Jason said as he slowly took his gaze off Sheriff Mead and directed it toward Jewel.

Jewel had calmed down somewhat and took a couple of steps towards Jason.

"Ya, I think that's about right. The sheriff can take the kid home and me and Max are going to load up and get the hell out of here for good," Jewel said.

"I don't know if I can trust you to take care of the kid, Frank," Jason said.

"What do you mean by that?" Sheriff Mead asked.

"I mean just what I said. I don't trust you or your two helpers," Jason said.

"We're not his helpers anymore. We've bought Frank out and are going to take this show on the road and make some real money. Ain't that right, Frank?" Jewel said.

Sheriff Mead looked at Jewel, but didn't reply. At the moment he was more concerned with Jason than with either Jewel or Max. He looked at the rusty pail Jason had set on the floor.

"I can understand the shotgun, but what you doing toting a pail around with ice fishing gear in it?" Sheriff Mead asked.

"Interesting you brought that up, Frank. I found it this last May. It was setten in some brush by a tree on top of the hill out back. Do you recognize it?" Jason said.

"Nope, can't say that I do. It just looks like a ice fishing pail that someone must have decided to leave behind," Sheriff Mead said.

"What about you two boys, you recognize it?" Jason said as he glanced at Max then turned his head to look at Jewel.

"No, why in the hell would we?" Jewel asked.

Jason knelt on the floor with one knee resting next to the pail. He then reached over with one hand and tipped the pail on its side.

"Looks like whoever owned it carved their initials in the side. I don't think you would carve your initials in the side of your ice fishing bucket and then just leave it behind after a day of fishing. Do you?"

Jason set the pail back on its bottom and started to stand, while continuing to look directly at Jewel. Blackie who had been knocked unconscious from the blows she took from Jewel started to stir. She was still stunned from the beating and it took her a few seconds to steady herself. She saw me sitting along the wall and walked over and sat beside me. I was also still a little woozy and was trying to clear my head.

Jason looked at me and grinned.

"That dog's a tough one," he said.

"Maybe we should see how tough she is going up against Killer here. We were supposed to do that once already, but you let her go," Max said.

Jason cocked his head to one side as he looked at Max. He seemed surprised that Max spoke.

"Maybe you're the one I should be talking to, Max. Do you recognize the pail?"

"Can't say I do, what are the initials?" Max asked.

"Good question, Max. The initials are J.R. Now you boys know I can't read, but I know letters. Who do you think they might stand for?" Jason asked while still looking at Max.

It came to me right away. The initials were John Raycarts. Max must have felt uneasy with Jason's stare because he looked away, first at Sheriff Mead then at Jewel. I could tell by the look on Sheriff Mead's face that he knew something. He hadn't taken his eyes off the pail since Jason had told them what the initials were.

"I don't give a damn who or what the initials stand for. It looks like an old worn out rusty pail. Worn out like the person that brought it in here. Here's five bucks go buy a new one."

Jewel said as he reached into his jacket and threw the five dollar bill he had won from Max toward the pail.

The bill floated through the air and drifted toward the pail. Jason watched the bill as it came to rest in the bottom of the pail.

"I'm going to let you know who the initials stand for. They stand for John Raycart. He was my grandson, and I'm going to tell you that I got a notion what happened. I think he came onto you guys, and you didn't know how to handle the situation, so you chased him to the river. John must have put the pail by the tree, so it didn't hold him back none. But you caught him anyway and threw him in the icy water of Fox River and left him to drown," Jason said.

When Jason finished his account of what he thought happened, Sheriff Mead immediately took a couple of quick steps toward Jewel. He was red with anger and a frown of discontent formed a shadow across his face.

"You two bastards told me you lost the boy in the snowstorm. I didn't want to hurt the kid," the sheriff said as he returned his look to Jason.

"Jason, I just wanted to talk with him and let him know that we were training the dogs for sport. It was snowing so hard, by the time Jewel and Max got back there was no way we could find him in that blizzard."

The sheriff let out a sigh as if he was glad to have finally told someone about that night.

"With God as my witness I never harmed that boy," the sheriff said.

The sheriff was now standing within an arms length of Jewel and his breathing was becoming deep. There was a pause between each breath as it escaped between his slightly parted lips. Jewel was surprised by the sheriff's quick movement and turned to face him.

"We never threw that punk in the river. He got scared and fell through the ice. He must have got tired and couldn't get out. It was his own damn fault," Jewel said.

"And you...and both you bastards, you...you didn't try to save him. I knew I should have never went in with you, Jewel. You both love to watch the bait get killed more than anything else," the sheriff said.

The sheriff's anger continued to build.

"I'm going to place both you and Max under arrest and we'll all accept the consequences," he said.

The sheriff started to pull his pistol from the holster, but before he managed to get it clear Jewel lunged at him. Jewel grabbed the sheriff's arm and whirled him around. Their legs got tangled and they both fell to the floor. When they hit the floor a shot rang out.

Jason started to run toward them, but Max attacked Jason from behind. Max let go of the chain that he was holding Killer with and pulled a switch blade from his front pocket. As he ran toward Jason I saw the reflection of the blade when it was released from its housing.

"Watch out," I cried.

Jason turned and started to bring his shotgun up, but at the same instant Max thrust the knife into Jason's mid section. The shotgun fell to the floor. Jason took a few steps forward and collapsed. A puddle of blood formed on the floor beneath Jason's motionless body.

After the attack Max stumbled off to the side and was holding the knife in his right hand. A wicked smile formed on his face as he wiped the blood from the blade onto his pant leg. He looked at Jewel and Sheriff Mead lying on the ground and started to walk toward them.

As Max approached the two men, Sheriff Mead started to rise as if he was going to stand up. The sheriff's chest was blood soaked and his eyes were wide open. Jewel had hold of the sheriff with both hands and pushed him off to the side. Jewel then sat up and looked at Max.

"Give me a hand will ya?" Jewel said.

Max extended his arm and Jewel grabbed it to pull himself to a standing position. As this was occurring I slowly made my way along the side of the building. By the time Jewel and Max remembered that I was still a part of this violent night, I was out the door and running up the hill toward the river.

It was now completely dark and the sleet had turned to a wet snow. The ground was slick, and I loss my footing a couple of times as I ran up the hill.

When I got to the top of the hill I sat in the wet snow trying to catch my breath and looked back. Jewel and Max were both outside searching the immediate area around the building. Max stopped and pointed in my direction. Jewel looked to where Max was pointing and then went back inside. I knew they had spotted me and realized if they caught me I would more than likely meet the same fate John Raycart had. When Jewel returned he had a flashlight in one hand and tossed it to Max. With the other hand he pulled Killer from the building.

The sight of the big black dog sent chills down my spine. I thought I could out run Max and Jewel, but that dog was another matter. I pushed myself off from the wet ground and started to run for the river. I was not familiar with this part of the river, but I knew my best chance for escape was to follow it to the Raycarts. It was my only chance.

There was no moonlight and the falling snow was making it difficult to see. I started to run down the hill, but tripped and fell forward. I landed on a pile of leaves and while I was pushing myself up I felt something hidden under them. I brushed the leaves away and my hands started to tremble when I realized I was uncovering Red, Uncle Joe's dog. His body was torn apart, there were cuts everywhere.

"Those rotten bastards," I whispered to myself.

I knelt in the snow for a moment, wishing I had the strength to charge all three, so I could make them pay. When I got to my feet I watched Red's body being covered with the falling snow for a few seconds and then I ran down the hill into the trees that lined the river.

I made my way through the trees and stopped when I reached the river. The air was turning colder and the warmer river water was causing a fog to rise from the water. My first thought was to get into the river and let the current carry me down stream. However, the fog made it difficult to see, and there was a good chance that I would get caught up in the branches of the trees that had fallen into the river. I watched the fog lifting from the river and saw Blackie standing on the bank down river waiting for me. I ran along the river after her, but was constantly tripping over fallen trees and branches that cluttered the bank. Whenever I did fall I scrambled to my feet as fast as I could, and each time I saw Blackie waiting on the bank ahead of me.

The storm was getting worse and the wind made a howling sound as it forced itself through the tree tops. I was making my way through some brush that bordered the river when I thought I heard something running on the bank behind me. I looked over my shoulder to see what it was and tripped over a fallen branch. I stumbled forward, but couldn't maintain my balance and fell. The snow and sleet that covered the ground made it very slippery, and I slid along the bank toward the river. I grabbed onto some long grass at the edge of the bank, but it slipped through my fingers. The next thing I knew I was under the water. When I came to the surface I saw a tree root sticking out of the bank and managed to grab onto it. The water was cold and the current was swift, but I thought I could use the root to climb out.

I held on to the tree root and was trying to catch my breath when I heard barking. I looked up and saw Blackie standing on the edge of the bank looking anxiously down at me. I was five feet below the bank and started to pull myself onto the root when I heard sounds coming from up river. Sounds float on the wind along the river and it didn't take long for me to figure out that the sounds were the voices of Jewel and Max. They were getting closer. I could hear the cracking of branches as they ran along the bank in my direction. Then I saw a flicker of light through the fog that was covering the river and knew it was from their flashlight.

I looked up at Blackie and motioned her to leave, but there was no way she was going to leave without me. They were getting closer and I realized I had no choice, so I let go of the root and floated out into the current. The current took hold and carried me along as if I was a branch that had just fallen from a tree. As I was being swept along I looked at the bank and saw that Blackie was running along with me.

I was in the water for less than a minute when the current forced me against a tree that had fallen across the river. I grabbed onto a branch that was under the water and pulled myself below the surface. I used the branch to make my way under the trunk of the tree. When I emerged I was on the downriver side of the fallen tree. I looked over the trunk and could make out Jewel, Max and Killer standing on the edge of the bank where I had fallen in. Max shinned the light in my direction, but I ducked behind the tree trunk as the beam passed by. I watched the beam of light move through the fog. When it disappeared I let myself go.

I was getting colder, but I realized that being in the river was now my only chance of survival. They had caught up to me by following my tracks through the snow, but the river left no tracks. They would still be following the bank, but the current was moving fast, so I knew I was increasing my lead. They were not going to give up, but I knew if I reached the Raycart farm I would be safe. I was using a short log for support and I searched the riverbank for familiar landmarks as I floated down river. Then the current slowed and I felt my feet drag along the bottom.

The river had widened and branched into two different directions. I stood in the current and tried to figure out which way to go. I knew one way would take me to the main channel and the other would probably end in some backwater swampy area. To get to the Raycarts I had to stay in the main channel of the river. If I ended up in some backwaters I wouldn't have to worry about Jewel or Max, because the cold would eventually get me.

As I looked through the fog, trying to determine the best way to go, I saw a light on the bank of the left fork. My first thought was that Jewel and Max had managed to get in front of me, but I also knew I had to get out of the river soon or I would be overcome by the cold. I rubbed my eyes and looked in the direction where I thought I saw the light.

The trees formed dark statue like silhouettes along the bank. I slowly looked from one dark form to the next and then I saw the light shinning through the fog. The beam the light cast was not from a single flashlight. It was larger and reminded me of the glow my yard light made at home.

Then it struck me. It wasn't a flashlight, it was a lantern. It was one of Joan Raycart's lanterns. I didn't hesitate and waded as fast as I could into the left fork of the river. The river began to get deep again and it wasn't long before the water was over my head. The light from the lantern was getting stronger, and I was just about to it when one of my pant legs got hooked by a submerged branch. I reached under the water to pull at my pant leg, and the log I was using for support got away from me. The current was swift and the branch was holding me so that the water was splashing against my face. I knew I had to get loose or the river would eventually win out. I ducked under the water to try and free my leg from the branch. I worked with both hands trying to untangle the pant leg from the branch, but had to give up because I couldn't hold my breath any longer. When I returned to the surface I kicked at the branch with my other leg trying to break it from the tree. I was running out of energy and it was getting harder to tread water in the cold current. I knew I didn't have much time before the river would win, so I took a deep breath and went under again. Just as I submerged, I felt a large splash hit the water beside me. Damn, they caught me.

Chapter Twenty-Eight
The River Is in Control

I instinctively returned to the surface, expecting to see one of my pursuers swimming toward me to finish the job the river had started, but I didn't see anyone. Then I felt something pulling at my pant leg. In a few seconds whatever had hold of my pant leg freed me from the branch and I quickly floated away. I was floating in the river directly across from where the lantern was hanging, when I felt something brush against me as it swam past, under the surface. I looked into the water and put my hand down to see if I could touch whatever was swimming by.

It was to dark to see anything below the surface and all I felt was the cold water running between my fingers. Suddenly something broke the surface directly in front of me, and the current pushed me against it.

Immediately upon impact I felt an arm wrap firmly around my chest and turn me around in the water. I was being pulled toward the river bank, but I couldn't turn my head enough to see who it was. The river made a bend at this point and the water next to the bank was calm. When we reached the edge of the bank, the person who had hold of me helped me to my feet. I turned to see who my rescuer was. It was Joan Raycart.

She looked into my eyes for a moment and then looked at the river bank. A tree had fallen over the bank into the water, but its roots had not yet let go. Mrs. Raycart took my hand and pulled me to the tree. She then helped me get on the tree trunk and I climbed to the top of the bank. Blackie was on the bank waiting for me, and behind her stood Joan's three dogs. The sight of the dogs brought a feeling of security.

I was shivering uncontrollably and the sounds my teeth made as they chattered against each other echoed in my ears. Joan followed me to the top of the bank then walked to the lantern to pick up a blanket that was lying on the ground. It was the blanket Hank put around her to keep her warm when she was sitting by the river. She wrapped the blanket around me, took my hand and began to walk me back-and-forth along the bank. I couldn't stop shivering, but the blanket along with the walking was helping to bring some warmth back into my body.

As we paced back and forth she put her arm around my shoulders. I looked at her and she turned to look at me. There was a different look coming from her green eyes. It wasn't the usual blank stare that I had become accustomed to, but rather a look of concern.

After a couple of minutes of pacing I realized that we had to get moving. I knew that Jewel and Max were not far behind, and they wouldn't hesitate to finish this night of violence.

I stopped and looked directly into Joan's eyes.

"We gotta go and get back to the farm before they catch us," I said.

I took her hand from my shoulder and started to lead her down river along the bank. It wasn't long before we reached a part of the river that I was familiar with. We were getting close to the place where I had slipped on the rock and cut my rear end. The riverbank narrowed at this point and was bordered by a hillside densely covered with trees and brush. The bank was held in place by a cliff of limestone and the top of the bank was fifteen feet above the river. The river narrowed as it flowed through this area of steep hillsides and the water was deep.

The snow was continuing to fall and it was becoming more and more difficult to see for any distance. As we walked along the bank I saw the light from another lantern shinning through the fog and snow. It was hanging on a tree directly across from the rock that I had slipped on. We would have to descend a short hill to get to where the lantern was hanging; Blackie was already standing below the lantern. Without the light from the lantern it would be easy to take a wrong step and slide down the bank into the river. I started to walk down the hill toward the lantern when a thought entered my mind.

Could it be that Joan some how knew where to position the lanterns so they would provide guidance through this night. The thought caused me to turn and look at Joan.

The width of the river bank going down the hill was so narrow that we had to walk in single file. When I turned to look at Joan I found that she was no longer walking behind me. She had stopped at the top of the hill and was staring into the darkness that we had just walked out of. Her dogs had also stopped. Wrench was up river about fifteen feet, and Three Eye and Peg were positioned directly in front of Joan.

As I started to walk back towards Joan I heard the dogs begin to growl as they stared into the darkness. When I reached for Joan's hand I looked at Wrench and saw the flickering from the beam of a flashlight bouncing in the darkness. Then I heard the sound of branches snapping and I knew Jewel and Max were approaching. I grabbed Joan's hand and in that same instant the silhouettes of Jewel and Max took form in the darkness.

Joan pulled her hand from mine and extended both her arms from her side to shield me. The dogs had taken a position to protect Joan, and Joan had taken a position to protect me.

Jewel stepped out of the brush first. He was now carrying the flashlight with Max walking behind him holding on to Killer with the chain. When Killer saw the other three dogs he went wild and pulled savagely against his restraint. The fierce sounds Killer made pierced the night and echoed above the howling of the wind.

"Before we let Killer make mince meat out of that crazy bitche's pets, I'm going to even up the odds," Jewel said.

When Jewel ended his sentence he pulled the sheriff's revolver from his jacket pocket and started to raise his arm. In that same instant Wrench sprang forward and Jewel pointed the pistol in the direction of the oncoming dog. Wrench leaped at Jewel and a shot rang out. The impact of Wrench's attack caused Jewel's arm to swing toward the river and knocked the pistol out of his hand. I watched as the pistol and the body of Wrench fell through the night snow toward the river. The sound of the splash made me shudder.

Joan and her other two dogs maintained their position. The growls from Three Eye and Peg had become powerful and the hair between their shoulder blades was standing on end. The dogs were going to make a stand to protect us, and Joan faced Jewel with that same determination. I don't know what I felt at that moment, but it probably was a mixture of courage and fear. Jewel stepped towards us, but neither Joan nor her two remaining dogs moved.

"Too bad you were at the wrong place at the wrong time, kid, but now it's time to finish this. Max, let Killer go," Jewel said.

Max instantly let loose of the chain. The big dog stood for a moment staring in our direction and then Max gave the command.

"Attack," Max shouted.

The big black dog dug his front paws into the earth and charged. Max had forgotten to unhook the chain from the collar, but that didn't deter the violence of the charge. The dog was trained to kill and that was his intent.

When Killer charged forward Peg met him head on. The impact of the dogs colliding against each other spun both animals around. Killer's rear end was now facing us and he was forcing his head under Peg's front shoulder. He ripped a gash in Peg's shoulder and was about to sink his teeth into Peg's lower throat when Three Eye attacked.

Three Eye slammed into Killer's side with such a force that it sent all three dogs rolling over the bank. As the dogs rolled off the bank into mid air the chain attached to Killer's collar slid along the ground and wedged itself under a log. The big black dog never reached the water. The chain held tight and the momentum of the fall and the sudden impact that was caused when the chain became taut broke the big dog's neck.

The fight was over in an instant. When Jewel and Max saw what happened to Killer, they went into a rage. Max pulled the switchblade from his pocket and both men ran at us.

"You're going to pay," Max growled as he followed Jewel across the bank.

I didn't know what to do. Both men were so close that I could see the lines of hate and determination on their face. They were about ten feet in front of us, when Joan turned around and grabbed me by the arm. She pulled me to the edge of the bank and before I knew it I was in mid air.

When I came to the surface I looked up and saw that Joan was still on the bank. Jewel had grabbed Joan before she could jump and had both her arms pinned to her back so she couldn't move. I swam to the other bank and crawled out of the water. Joan looked down at me and smiled.

"Run, John, Run," she cried into the night.

"I didn't think you could talk, you crazy bitch," Jewel said.

He then threw Joan to the ground.

"You better come back up here or I'm going to slit this lady's throat right in front of you," Jewel said.

I stood up at the edge of the river and Three Eye and Peg were on the bank behind me. They were looking up and growling at Jewel and Max. There was no way we could cross the river and climb the steep bank, but Jewel didn't care. He wanted vengeance and blood. He and Max had become more violent than the dogs they trained.

I thought if I showed I was going to surrender myself to them it might open an opportunity for Joan to get free. I started to walk into the river, but stopped when I heard the sound of brush moving on the hillside above where Jewel and Max were standing.

I wasn't the only one who noticed the sound. Joan was sitting on the ground staring toward the hill side where the noise was coming from. Jewel looked at Joan and then turned his head to follow her gaze into the darkness.

The wind was still howling through the trees, but the wind wasn't making this sound. Something was coming down the hill through the brush. Could it be that the mysterious being that I had detected along the river this past summer was here again?

The sound of the brush cracking was getting louder. Whatever or whoever was coming down the hill was getting closer. I could now see the brush move as the visitor approached. As Max stared into the darkness toward the direction of the sound a shadow of fear formed on his face and he walked over and stood behind Jewel.

"What do you think it is?" Max whispered.

Jewel looked over his shoulder at Max but didn't say a word. He turned and stared back at the hillside where the sound was coming from. Then the noise stopped and all you could hear was the sound of the wind blowing through the trees. Then from behind a tree that was growing where the rive bank meets the side of the hill a figure appeared. It was as if one of the shadows in the trees had come to life. The figure moved slowly and deliberately from the shadows and stepped onto the river bank. The figure was a person. The person took a few steps forward and then stopped and stood motionless about five feet in front of Jewel and Max.

It was Jason Abner. His parka was off and the white of his upper body behind his bib overall front must have been warm because the snow melted as it landed on him.

"I thought you were dead, you old bastard," Jewel said.

"Maybe I am, but I don't think it's right for me to go to hell unless I can take someone with," Jason said.

Jewel and Max now stood side by side facing Jason.

"Looks like we have to finish this," Jewel said.

Jason looked at his daughter sitting on the ground.

"I've been watching you and I think you can hear me. Please believe me, I didn't have anything to do with your son's death and I'm sorry that I shot your dog."

He then turned back to face Jewel and Max. The blood had stained the front of Jason's overalls and it was dripping from his side and falling to the snow covered ground.

Max stared at Jason's wound and watched the blood drip to the ground. Even though the night was cold, sweat began to form on Max's forehead and run down the side of his face. He appeared desperate and wanted to run, but couldn't.

"Let's get him, Max," Jewel said and started to walk slowly toward Jason.

Max, however, didn't move. But Jason quickly moved forward. Jason side-stepped the slow moving Jewel and before Max could react, Jason thrust his arms forward against Max's chest. The sudden impact sent Max stumbling backwards, his arms spun in windmill fashion as he tried to regain his footing, but he couldn't, and he fell from the bank to the river.

As soon as Jason's hands left Max's chest he quickly turned and stepped behind Jewel. He wrapped his arms around Jewel's chest and locked his right hand over his left wrist, so Jewel couldn't break free. Jason slowly backed to the edge of the bank. Jewel was struggling with all his might to break the hold. Fear came into Jewel's eyes as he struggled against Jason's death grip.

"Now let's see how long you can hold your breath, Jewel," Jason said before he leaned back and fell over the bank.

Even with the impact of hitting the water Jason never let go of Jewel. The force of the bodies hitting the water sent small waves towards the shore. I stared into the river as the waves splashed against my legs. Max lost his knife when he hit the water and was now standing in water that came up to his waist. Both he and I watched for Jason and Jewel to surface, but the river flowed on and Jason and Jewel were carried along with it.

Max regained some sense of composure and decided his best course of action was to get out of the river. When he got about ten feet from me, he stopped. His eyes fixed on Three Eye and Peg who were now standing beside me, giving every indication that if Max tried anything he would have to deal with them first. Max thought better of it and started to walk along the shore, but the dogs followed. Every time Max tried to get to the bank the growls of defiance through exposed teeth kept Max in the water.

I sat down on the edge of the bank, exhausted both physically and mentally. I watched Joan as she stood up and walked down the bank to the lantern. When she got to the lantern she stepped into the river and slowly went under the water coming to the surface just off the bank from where I was sitting. She stood waist deep in the water and turned to look down river.

I could hear someone running along the bank on the other side. My heart started to pump against my chest. What if it was Jewel?

As the person running got closer I saw that it was Hank and Blackie was running beside him. Close behind Hank was my Mom and Dad. The relief I felt when I saw the three of them cannot be put into words, but I'm sure it was similar to the relief Mom and Dad felt when they found me.

Dad had returned home from work early and he and my mother had driven to Hanks in order to give me a ride home. When they found that I wasn't there, they were going to check the corn field, but Blackie came running into the yard. It didn't take long for them to understand that Blackie wanted them to follow her. The lanterns Joan had placed in the trees along the way served as a guide for them to maneuver through the darkness and the obstacles of the terrain. Mom called it a God send.

They used the large rock and the fallen tree to cross the river and ran to us. Dad saw Max standing in the river and walked to the edge and stood beside the dogs.

"Max, I don't know what your part in this is, but by the way the dogs are acting, I think we better hold onto you for the sheriff to talk to," Dad said.

Mom took off her coat and wrapped it around me and Hank took his coat off and put it over Joan's shoulders.

"We got to get you both home and warmed up. Then you can fill us in," Mom said.

Dad looked behind Max and saw the big black dog swinging in the air.

"What in the hell," he said.

Mom and Hank hearing my dad's comment turned their attention to the black dog and momentarily stared at it. Hank then noticed that Joan was walking to the brush. We watched as she walked into the brush a short way and then knelt in the snow. Hank immediately followed and knelt beside her when he saw his wife stroking the side of Wrench. The bullet had passed through Wrench's body between his shoulder and back. Wrench had managed to get out of the river and find a place to lie under some brush that provided shelter from the storm. Joan took Hank's coat from her shoulders and placed it over the dog.

"I'll come back and get Wrench in the morning and bring him home for a proper burial," Hank told his wife as he placed his arm around her shoulders.

He then took his wife by the hand and helped her to her feet. Joan continued to look at her protector lying on the ground and my mother walked over and stood beside them.

"Joan, we have to get you and Shorty home. You walk with Maddie and I'll help Mike," Hank said.

Mom then placed her arm so that it wrapped around Joan's and held it close to her body. Joan looked at my mother for a moment and then together they started to walk along the bank. Mom didn't say anything, but the smile she gave to me when she approached said that everything was going to be alright. Hank was now standing on the bank beside my dad, and they were both looking at Max standing waist deep in the river.

"Come on out, Max," Dad said.

Max seemed to be in a daze and offered no resistance. He crawled up the bank and staggered to his feet. The dogs stopped growling, but maintained their guard and didn't take their eyes off Max. Max walked silently behind my dad, with Hank and the dogs following behind. Max never spoke again that night and only stared at the ground as he walked along. The events of the night had brought an end to what he and Jewel had started, he was a defeated man.

When we reached the bend of the river where Joan went to meditate, Joan stopped. She turned and looked into the river and started to cry. Mom put her arms around Joan's shoulders and cried right along with her. Hank walked to his wife's side and placed his large hand on her shoulder. Joan looked up at Hank and put her arms around him and used his chest to cry into. We stood in silence respecting the tears that had been held back too long.

When we reached the farm, Hank and Dad gave Max some blankets and locked him in the smokehouse behind the house. Mom hurried me into John's bedroom and I took off all my wet clothes. She wrapped a blanket around me and we started to leave when the door opened. Joan came into the room and walked by us to the dresser. She looked at the mirror for a moment then opened a dresser drawer. When she turned around she was holding some of her son's clothes and she handed them to my mother. As soon as my mother accepted the clothes, Joan turned to leave the room. Hank was standing in the door way watching and smiled as he stepped to the side to allow his wife to pass by.

I put the clothes on and it definitely felt good to be dry again. When we walked into the kitchen, Mom sat me in a chair beside the pot belly stove. I wasn't sitting there long before Hank and Joan walked into the kitchen. Joan had changed into dry clothes and had a shawl draped over her shoulders. Hank placed a kitchen chair next to me and helped Joan sit down.

While I recounted everything that happened that day Hank warmed some soup and my mother prepared some hot tea. When I finished my soup I looked at Joan sitting quietly beside me sipping the tea and I wanted to say something to her, but I didn't know how to say it. I knew I owed her my life, but she had lost her father and a best friend today, so I decided to wait.

It was midnight by the time the State Patrol left. The sergeant was very understanding and told my parents to take me home and he would return tomorrow to finish collecting the information he needed.

They found Jason Abner and Jewel's body caught up in some branches about one hundred yards down stream from where they entered the water. Jason's arms were still tightly wrapped around Jewel's chest.

When the police left, Mom wrapped a blanket around me and we started to leave. Joan was still sitting by the stove. I walked over and stood beside her.

"Thank you, Joan…I'm so sorry about Wrench," I said.

I started to turn away, but she reached out and took my hand. When our eyes met, I felt more warmth than any soup or tea could ever provide.

"My dogs like you," she said.

Then she paused and looked at the door that led to John's room then looked back at me.

"Goodbye," she said.

Chapter Twenty-Nine
He's Watching Us

I looked up at the sky and watched the large white clouds drift silently by. It was a warm day and a small breeze was blowing gently through the Fox River valley. It was the second week of June in 1958. The Milwaukee Braves were expected to make another run at winning the National league pennant and defend their World Series championship. Sycamore Country School closed in May when we finished classes. Next year I will be attending the public school in Sun Set. I was working regularly for Uncle Joe and haying season had started. However, none of this was on my mind.

It was going on noon and I was lying on the bank next to the bend in the river where Joan went to meditate. As I watched the clouds drift overhead I remembered all the times that I tried to associate the cloud formations with things they resembled on earth or in my imagination. A large cloud was floating over that resembled a castle. It was starting to break apart and soon new shapes would emerge to those who were patient enough to watch them form.

As I watched the clouds, I saw a hawk riding the air currents. I wondered if it could see me lying on the bank. From the height it was at, it probably could see everything that happened along this river. I'll never forget what happened along this river, but the lady who was a part of it had to go away. I could picture Joan saying goodbye to me and I began to recall all that happened since she left last November.

Max was found guilty of assault with intentions to kill and was sent to the penitentiary for five to ten years. Uncle Joe thought the sentence was too lenient and sincerely hopes that their paths will never cross again. Max's mother goes to visit him once a week, but his father hardly ever goes. After the trial Mrs. Strum came to visit us. She drove over by herself. It was a cold winter day and my mother invited her inside for coffee. I remember her sitting at the table and earnestly relaying the reason for her visit.

"Unlike you, Maddie, I'm not one who can put into words what I feel in my heart. But I'm here to try. I apologize to you and Shorty for what Max did. I can't take any of it back and he'll be judged for what he did when he leaves this earth. I'm afraid that the violent acts he was part of have become rooted inside him. I pray that while he serves his sentence he'll be able to come to grips with himself and get his life back on course. In the meantime, we'll continue to work the farm and I want to continue to be a neighbor that you can trust. Harold is having a hard time with it and I feel that part of him has gone to prison with Max. We both feel responsible and we'll have to bare that cross for the rest of our life. I want to ask for your forgiveness and for you to truly believe that if there was any way that we could change things that happened, we would. Remember that day, Maddie, when you stood up for Joan Raycart in church. I hope that in time, you'll be able to stand up for us in the same way."

Mom was quick to respond. "Margaret, I've learned that I definitely was not put on this earth to judge other people. But I do believe that you and I are similar in that we both feel that we are just people, and have to continue to try and do our best. I know that we can't make it without being good neighbors. I can't speak for Shorty, but I feel that you are a good neighbor. A neighbor, who I'd gladly pick choke cherries with any day."

Mom continues to speak on a regular basis with Mrs. Strum after church. Harold Strum resigned from the church board and at times Mrs. Strum attends Sunday services without him. Their son, Martin, has taken over most of the business side of the farm, and Harold can be seen running the farm machinery and helping his wife with the chores.

I can still picture that night when Max climbed from the river to the bank. He had turned to look at his big dog hanging lifeless from the river bank and shook his head. He didn't have a look of remorse; it was more a look of contempt. He had trained that dog to be a killer and the events of that day stunned him, because it took from him the power he felt when he directed his dog to attack. Through his trial he gave no testimony that he was sorry for his actions, if anything, his body language and facial expressions became more defiant. The death of his dog was just that, the death of a dog, no more, no less. The dog had provided a way for him to feel powerful.

The day after the incident my dad, Uncle Joe and Hank went back to the river with Joan and her two remaining sentries following. She took the coat that was covering Wrench and placed it on the side of the hill that was out of reach from spring floods. They buried Wrench where she placed the coat and piled some stones over the grave. Joan then sat on the ground next to the burial site and gave a silent eulogy. Three Eye and Peg watched while lying on the other side of the grave site.

Joan then got on her hands and knees and used her hands to clear an area next to the grave site. When she finished she stood up and looked at the dog hanging from the bank. Hank didn't hesitate; he immediately understood his wife's wishes and went to the other side of the river. Uncle Joe and my dad followed, and together they took the big muscular black dog down and buried him in a grave next to Wrench. I knew that dog could have ripped me apart, but I wondered what he would have been like if he wasn't trained to kill.

When they finished they watched as Joan walked up river on the opposite bank. Dad had told Uncle Joe about his dog Red, and they knew that's where Joan was going next.

It was difficult for Uncle Joe. I don't know exactly why people become so attached to their pets, but I do know that a bond of loyalty forms between them that is as great as any formed between men. Uncle Joe says they can fill a void, and they don't require much in return for their companionship, only to be treated well. Uncle Joe buried Red next to the tree where he found him.

The dogfighting will always be hard for me to understand. We talked about it some and my mother told me something that will remain with me always.

"Shorty, I see dogfighting as a way for people to take advantage of a dog's unyielding devotion to please its master. Unfortunately, some men use that devotion to promote their greed for power. These people don't respect each other, nor do they respect life. For whatever reason, we as people walk the earth and can control what happens to other living things. When we take advantage of that control and use it to abuse other living creatures we are performing a sin against humanity."

After Red was buried, the three men walked down the hillside to the building used for dog fight training and burned it to the ground. The only thing that they bothered to salvage was an old ice fishing pail with the initials J.R. carved in the side.

I decided to change my position and sat up on the bank. I took my shoes off and waded into the river and crossed to the other side. I sat on the edge of the bank and put my legs into the cool water.

It had been eight months since I last saw Mrs. Raycart. That night when she said goodbye to me, I thought it was just for the night. However, she must have known that it was going to be for a much longer time, maybe even forever.

Doctor Frederick came to our house before visiting Hank and Joan. He wanted to talk to my mother and me first. The way I had pictured him was completely off-base. He looked more like a retired football player than a psychiatrist. He was a large man with gray hair. Wrinkles that come with age crossed his face, but his blue eyes still had a youthful brilliance. He didn't wear a suit, but instead wore jeans and a short sleeved bright red shirt. His voice matched his stature and was calming to listen too. Unlike some people who reach a certain position in life and feel they are a step above those around them, Doctor Frederick conveyed that he truly respected the person he was speaking with.

Doctor Thompson accompanied him, but he looked out of place wearing a suit and tie. He must have also pictured Doctor Frederick somewhat differently. They stayed at our house for over two hours. At times Doctor Thompson would interject what he thought was relevant, but Doctor Frederick was more interested in what my mother and I had to say.

I didn't go with when they went to visit Joan and Hank. When the doctor left our house he thanked me for being such a good friend to Hank and Joan.

"*Shorty, I only hope that my therapy can pick up where you laid the foundation to start. I want to let you know that I agree with your mother. Mrs. Raycart may have withdrawn into herself because she may believe that if she returns to her normal life, she will find out that she is the cause for all the tragedies that have fallen upon her family and may cause more to occur. But she found a way to speak to you, and because she can speak to you I truly believe that she has the strength and fortitude to regain a sound condition. Like you told me, she has the physical strength to match anyone, now we have to help her recapture that same mental strength.*"

That evening when Mom returned from the meeting between Doctor Frederick and the Raycarts she was very upbeat. She knew that I was very eager to hear what happened, but at the same time she felt obligated to be honest with me.

"*Shorty, we talked about this once before, and I want to be sure you understand that no matter how good something seems, there is always the chance that it may not turn out as good as expected.*"

I remembered our conversation vividly, but had not given it much thought since. I knew where my mother was coming from and I told her that I understood.

She then went on and recounted the meeting in detail. She was greatly impressed with the doctor and felt that Hank had similar feelings of confidence in him. Joan didn't speak during the meeting, but my mother said she seemed to be paying attention to the doctor as he spoke. Mom's biggest feeling of success came when Joan actually took my mother's hand and held it firmly throughout the meeting.

It was decided, and all agreed, that for Joan to have the best chance of returning to some type of normalcy psychiatric treatment was necessary. Unfortunately, because the distance between the farm and the doctor's office made it impractical for Hank to travel back and forth on a bi-weekly basis, Joan would have to be placed in psychiatric care close to Doctor Frederick's office. However, Hank would be able to visit her anytime and could take Joan out into the country. Mom said that it was easy to detect the hurt on Hank's face and Doctor Frederick addressed it immediately.

The Doctor suggested that Hank spend the first two weeks in Minneapolis, so that he could be with his wife on a daily basis. If Hank found that he didn't like the way Joan was being treated, the doctor would allow Joan to return with Hank to the farm. Hank drove Joan to Doctor Fredrick's office the following Monday.

That Sunday after church as we walked past the cemetery on our way to Mirror Lake, Mom stopped and pointed to the grave yard. On each of the graves of the three Raycart children an evergreen wreath with a red bow had been placed. A light covering of snow revealed the imprints of two adults and off to the side were dog tracks. We never said a word. The green of the wreaths against the white of the snow, said it all.

Hank agreed with what he observed during those first two weeks and returned to the farm without his wife. He would visit Joan every two weeks and usually stay a couple of days. Dad, I and Uncle Joe took care of their farm while he was away. When he returned from a visit, he made a point to come over to our place and talk to my mother about how Joan was doing.

Out of the corner of my eye a swirl in the water directly below the surface caught my attention. I bent over to get a better look and spotted a large black bass twisting in the current. I wonder if he knows it's me sitting here on this bank.

As I watched the bass disappear into the river bottom, I heard the sound of people walking in my direction. A large knot that comes from nervous anticipation began to form in my stomach, but I made every effort to appear calm.

Hank was bringing Joan home today and had asked me to meet them by the river. I looked down the bank and saw Hank. He was holding Joan's hand and they were walking side by side. Three Eye and Peg were loping along side, and walking close behind was Doctor Frederick and my mother. Hank waved to me as they approached.

"Hi, Shorty, got someone here that would like to meet you again, but first I guess I'm going to take a swim," Hank said.

Hank turned and looked at Doctor Frederick.

"You got a nice day for it, Hank," the doctor said.

Hank and Joan were across the bank from me. Hank sat down on the edge of the bank and took his work boots and socks off. Joan remained standing and was watching me. I smiled, but couldn't find any words to say.

Joan continued to look at me as she sat on the bank next to Hank, and a slight smile began to take form across her face. It reminded me of a rainbow that appears at the end of a rain storm.

She sat beside Hank for a few moments, then took hold of his hand and stood. She walked toward the center of the river, leading her husband by the hand. We all watched as they walked deeper into the water. When the water level reached Joan's neck, Hank squatted down so he was at the same height as his wife. They then disappeared under the water. I looked at my mother and saw that her eyes were focused on the location where Hank and Joan submerged. The current flowed slowly over where they went under and nothing was left behind to even suggest that the river had been disturbed. I watched a red wing black bird land on a reed at the rivers edge and noticed that both Mom and Doctor Frederick were walking up the bank. By the look on their faces I could tell that they were both becoming somewhat concerned.

The dogs continued to lie on the bank, relaxing in the shade from an oak tree.

"Shorty, can you see them?" Mom asked.

"Not yet, but don't worry," I said.

Doctor Frederick stepped into the river, but stopped when he saw the current in the center of the river begin to separate. The river was making room for Joan and Hank. Joan emerged first and directly behind her came Hank. Joan was still holding her husband's hand. When they appeared an expression of enlightenment brightened Hank's face. Joan let loose of her husband's hand and he walked over and sat on the bank resting his face in his hands. The doctor sat beside him and put a hand on Hank's shoulder.

"What did you feel, Hank?" the doctor asked.

"I don't know if it was the river or holding onto Joan's hand, but I felt the presence of my children," Hank said.

Joan stood knee deep in the river watching her husband for a few moments, then turned and began to walk toward me. I watched as she approached and wondered if she knew me. Her smile broadened as she waded closer and I saw that the blank stare from her eyes had been replaced by a look of calmness. She sat next to me for a moment, then turned her head and looked directly at me.

"John and Hank Jr. would have liked you, Shorty," she said.

The emotions that a person encounters in their lifetime are unpredictable, but the one I experienced at that moment will be everlasting.

"I'm sure I would have liked them too," I said.

We sat quietly watching the water, enjoying the moment and what the calm afternoon had brought to us. I looked at my mother and saw the dogs had moved and were now standing on the edge of the bank beside her. They stood quietly looking across the river at the side hill in back of where Joan and I were sitting.

I heard a rustle in the bushes on the hill behind us and turned to look. I looked in the direction that the dogs were staring and saw the brush about half way up the hill move as though it was caught by a sudden burst of wind. Joan was watching too.

She watched for a few moments then turned to me, smiled and said, "My dad loves me."

Printed in the United States
97676LV00004B/121-123/A

9 781424 135547